Blood on Their Hands

Phil Davies

Published in the United Kingdom by
21:Twenty-one Publishing in 2009

© Copyright Intellectual Property Rights Office,
No. 258970985

ISBN 978-0-9562673-0-6

Phil Davies has asserted his rights under the Copyright, Designs and Patents Act 1988 to be identified as the author of this work

Blood on Their Hands is a work of fiction. Names, characters, places, and incidents are either the product of the author's imagination or are used fictitiously. Any resemblances to actual persons, living or dead, events or locations are entirely coincidental

This book is sold subject to the condition that it shall not, by way of trade or otherwise, be lent, resold, hired out, or otherwise circulated without the publisher's prior consent in any form of binding, cover other than that in which it is published and without a similar condition, including this condition, being imposed on the subsequent purchaser

First published in the United Kingdom
in 2009 by 21:Twenty-one Publishing

Addresses and contact details for the various divisions within the group can be found at: www.21twentyone.net

Printed in the UK by
Mackays of Chatham part of the CPI Group
Front cover by Dan Harris Design

"The heart of man is wicked and deceitful above all things"

DEDICATION

All of us are products of our past; formed before we even know it, influenced by factors often beyond our control. But while we are products of our past we do not have to be slaves to it. A new beginning point is always only a moment away. This book is dedicated to the process of finding the new beginning point; drawing a new line, reaching the place where the past doesn't have to determine our future. Once we reach the age of reason, these things like most things in our life, become a choice. Me? By the grace of God, I've made *my* choice.

CONTENTS

The Prologue

* * * * *

Introduction: Nothing Is What It Seems

* * * * *

PART ONE: The Crime Scene

* * * * *

PART TWO: Twenty-five Years Later

* * * * *

PART THREE: Vengeance and Justice

* * * * *

The Epilogue

THE PROLOGUE

As dates go, June 17th 1972 is more significant than most.

At 2:54 AM Eastern Time, a group of five men broke into the offices of the Democratic National Committee in the Watergate building, Washington, D.C. The events that followed led all the way to the White House and to the downfall of a U.S. President and his entire administration. It shocked a nation, changing attitudes, outlook and politics forever.

But unbeknown to all but God himself, a few hours later that same June day deep in the jungles of Southeast Asia, another significant event would take place.

Like the break-in, it was supposed to be a closely guarded secret but three decades of stored-up malevolent energy would eventually spew it out into the public domain.

America looked on spellbound and helpless, the horror mixed with an almost naïve bewilderment. But it was much more than just a national phenomenon. It was global, people from every corner of the planet shaking their heads in stunned disbelief.

INTRODUCTION

NOTHING IS WHAT IT SEEMS

USA, Super Bowl weekend 2004

CHAPTER ONE:

His smile lit up the room. It was a confident successful smile that gave the impression he could achieve anything he wanted. He could.

Rudi Kingsbridge was Chairman and CEO of KBI, the Kingsbridge Bank of Illinois. It was January 30th 2004 and twenty-four hours earlier, he'd closed a takeover deal, swallowing up one of the bank's more serious competitors.

The directors and largest shareholders had gathered at KBI's plush headquarters on Chicago's South Michigan Avenue. They were in celebratory mood. The bank had leapt into America's top ten largest financial institutions and while each had started the week seriously rich, they were all ending it seriously richer.

But it was neither a gathering of peers nor of equals. Rudi wasn't the kind of man who had peers or equals. His was a life pre-ordained; a king on his throne, born to rule.

His manner, like beauty, was in the eye of the beholder. To some he appeared overbearingly arrogant, to others downright charming. But however you saw him, physically, Rudi cut an impressive figure; his obvious athleticism enhanced by a lavish taste in clothes. At fifty-four, but looking more than ten years younger, he had a full head of black hair and a dark complexion that set off the outrageously handsome features he'd inherited from his film star mother. In many ways, he was the kind of person the media describe as having got-it-all. He did. And now, as America's newest multi-billionaire, he had even more.

Though he was married to ex-supermodel Kay Ferrano and father to their two children, Rudi was a sexual predator with a voracious appetite for women. At thirty-nine, he'd come to marriage late but even before the wedding, he'd drawn up a list of twelve women he called the *lucky dozen*. Though the make-up of the twelve had changed over the years, no-one had ever declined the chance of being part of his secret harem, every last one keen to be part of his life even if it was for just a sweaty hour or two's sex.

At fourteen million dollars-a-year, the arrangement didn't come cheap but in every way, he considered it money well spent.

Conscience was never a problem to Rudi Kingsbridge; he didn't have one.

Celebrations, any celebrations, meant sex was a must, a pre-requisite. So without fanfare, he excused himself from the party and took the senior management lift to the 37th floor where he waltzed into the office of KBI's community affairs executive Maria Vander, the only one of the lucky dozen who worked for him full-time.

Twenty-seven year old Maria knew she was being used but she couldn't help herself. He was the richest, best looking man she'd ever seen and the most exciting bed partner she'd ever had. He also happened to be the boss, a boss who paid three hundred thousand dollars-a-year more than the going rate for the job. How could she say no?

Rudi was always direct. He wasn't interested in kissing her but it didn't stop her trying. Just as her lips closed in on his, he grabbed her hair and turned her round until they were both facing the window and Lake Michigan beyond. As he nudged her forward, her thighs came into contact with the desk forcing her to bend forward from the waist. Ten minutes later it was over. There was no dignity in it for Maria. But that wasn't something her boss would've considered for a moment and, as for Maria, well, in a battle between her self-respect and her bank balance there was only ever going to be one winner.

When Rudi re-entered the Jordan Kingsbridge Board-room Suite, named after the father he despised, it was Bill Mitchellson who was first to notice. Aside from Rudi, he was KBI's largest individual share-holder, owning almost thirteen per cent of the company. At six-two he was as tall as Rudi but at twelve billion he was richer, almost three times richer. His wealth gave him the confidence to be more direct than the others. He knew where the chairman of the board had been. He didn't approve and wanted to make a point.

As Rudi poured himself a Jack Daniels from the bar, he sensed Mitchellson loom up behind him. In a previous life, when some knew him as *Hollywood*, he wouldn't have waited to ask questions; his knife would've done the talking for him. But that was then and this was now. Even so he couldn't prevent his mind exploding into flashback, the graphic violence in stark contrast to the civility of the sumptuous boardroom.

"Hey Mr Chairman," Mitchellson said, bringing Rudi crashing back from the darkness of his past. "What is it with you? You got a fantastic business, everything you could ever want, and what's more, you got that fabulous looking woman waiting for you at home. Why on Earth would you want to keep playing the field?"

It was a question that invaded his thinking throughout the forty-five minute journey home.

Kay was everything a man could want: great in bed, devoted, loyal, a good wife and mother, and even at forty-two so stunningly beautiful she was still averaging twenty or more cover shots a month.

"We're here boss," the chauffeur said interrupting his thoughts as the car sped down the long drive towards Chateau Chantalle. Built by his great-grandfather and named after his great-grandmother, the two hundred acre estate had been home to the Kingsbridge dynasty since the mid 1880's. Kay, ten year old Becky and her brother Andy, who'd be fifteen the following month, were in the sitting room waiting for him. After greeting the kids, he looked at his wife admiringly before pecking her gently on the cheek. She was stunning he thought; the most beautiful thing he'd ever seen. But she wasn't.

The thought inadvertently pulled the trigger to another bout of flashbacks. But unlike in the bank, this time, it came with a soundtrack.

"No she's not!" hissed a poisonous audible voice in his head, "She's the *second* most beautiful thing you've ever seen!"

The thought, or the voice, or whatever it was, disorientated him so much he found it difficult to breathe.

"Are you OK honey?" Kay said with concern.

"Uhhh, yeah, I'm fine. I think I'll pour myself a Jack and go through into the conservatory."

Rudi was a man who always got what he wanted and the million-dollar conservatory he'd had built two years earlier, was no exception. It was his favourite room. Kay had been the inspiration behind the homely interior and, aside from the planning stage and paying for it all, Rudi's only hands-on contribution was hanging a few pictures, his old war photos from his time in Vietnam. Both his mother and wife had voiced their disapproval but Rudi was having none of it. He loved his time in the military, well, most of it, and he loved the way he looked in the photos: young, fit and handsome, the world his oyster.

"There, Becky's asleep and Andy's on his PlayStation," Kay said, returning to find him staring at one of the photos. "You were one fine looking man Mr Kingsbridge!" she added peeping over his shoulder, her eyes fixed on a picture where he was wearing nothing above the waist except black ties round both upper arms.

"What you mean *were*?" he said, feigning indignation.

"OK, *are*!" she replied, nestling in beside him, her hand fumbling with his shirt buttons. Rudi smiled as he realised it'd been just four hours since his liaison with Maria Vander. Did he have the energy to respond, he wondered?

According to the magazines, at fifty-four he was way past his peak. But the glossies referred to the average man and there was nothing average about Rudi Kingsbridge.

He looked into Kay's big blue eyes knowing he was minutes away from being where virtually every other man on the planet would like to be: in bed with Kay Kingsbridge, formerly, Kay Ferrano supermodel.

It would be a climactic end to a stupendous day.

As he and Kay stood gazing out over Chateau Chantalle's manicured floodlit gardens and the Lake Michigan shoreline, he really did think he had it all, absolutely everything.

But his life hadn't always been like this.

CHAPTER TWO:

There were a couple of dollar bills, a quarter, two dimes and a penny in the glass cookie jar.

It was the last day of January 2004 and the hobo was sat on a bench in Obregon Park, Los Angeles, thankful the earlier part of the day had been more fruitful. Twenty-five bucks all-in, meant it'd been a good day. He smiled. But he certainly didn't look a picture. He had a big bulbous scar under his bottom lip and when his lips parted, two of his bottom teeth were missing. His hair was filthy and he had six days of grey whiskers, his callow sharp features making him look old, haggard and malnourished.

But by his standards, Frankie Fernando was feeling good.

His routine had been the same for more than seven years, ever since he'd first arrived in LA from the Hemet Valley, two hours or so to the east. Back then in the summer of 1996, Frankie wasn't sure what he would do. For more than twenty years his life had been on a downward spiral, consumed by guilt he couldn't shake off. He wanted to hide and dropping-out of society seemed his only choice. Anonymity wasn't an option in Hemet, so home became the cardboard city under the place where the 60 crosses the 710. It was where he'd lived ever since.

As his shift ended, Frankie found himself staring zombie-like at his glass cookie jar.

The Park wasn't safe after dark so in winter, Frankie made a point of leaving for home by four o'clock. His route back to his cardboard box took him past a 7/11 store where, top of his shopping list was Sierra Valley Red Zinfandel, his favourite wine.

It helped make his guilt more manageable, helped him forget his weakness.

Though two bottles had been enough for his first six years in LA, he'd needed three-a-night for more than eighteen months. At just over five dollars-a-bottle, the few occasions he failed to make his sixteen bucks-a-day target were among the most depressing days of his life. And it'd been a depressing life. But his twenty-five dollar take, meant he could eat as well: a meat pie, a hot dog, two bags of potato chips and a packet of cookies all following the wine into his shopping basket.

Frankie was off to his very own special party, a party where he was the only guest. It was also a party he didn't really want to be at; he didn't like the guest list.

He got back just as the last of twilight disappeared. Some of his co-dwellers had lit fires, their flames sending shadows dancing all over the concrete walls and ceilings of the overpass. It was a surreal world. He grunted as someone greeted him. It was the best he could do. As unlikely as it may have seemed, Frankie was once a respected leader of men but now, he couldn't even say "Howdy" let alone hold a conversation.

Frankie's corner had always been a no-go area for the rest of Cardboard City. They knew he was different and no-one challenged him, their instincts confirmed early one evening during his second summer in LA.

The arrival of three local hoodlums sent the hobos scurrying away to their darkest hiding places but one resident, too slow on his feet, was caught and beaten mercilessly.

Frankie slept through the entire incident. Though they couldn't see him, the gang heard him, his loud snoring pointing the way as effectively as any signpost.

As the young Hispanic gang leader stood over him, he smirked at his two compatriots.

"Wake up you worthless piece of filth," he screamed before kicking Frankie hard in the chest.

He came to in an instant and without thinking, switched on the auto-pilot.

"Woaah there guys," he said, "I got some money. Lemme be and I'll let you have it."

It was an utterance that achieved its objective.

"Get up, you stinking piece of dog crap," the gang leader growled, anxious to explore what might be a money-making opportunity, even if it was likely to be only a few bucks.

Frankie rose to his feet looking old and feeble as he did so. It was a façade.

"Gimme what you got old man and if you're lucky, we might let you live," the gang leader screamed, hissing and cursing.

Luck would have nothing to do with it.

With his hands raised like the baddie in a movie, Frankie said, "I don't want any trouble," and by the time the word *trouble* began to leave his lips, he'd already turned his raised right hand into an iron fist. He'd also pulled his arm slightly backwards into the cocked position. Without having the slightest idea of the preparations he was laying, his assailants continued to assume they were the predators dictating proceedings, their victim cornered, totally submissive in the hands-up position.

It was pure illusion.

Without warning, Frankie's fist shot forward, slamming the gang leader full in the throat. He collapsed to his knees, hands clutching at his neck as Frankie turned towards the other two gang members. He may have been just a month short of his fifty-second birthday but Frankie wasn't shuffling about like some old man struggling to preserve his life. He knew exactly what he was doing. Crouching low but all the time closing in on the bigger of the two men, he exploded upwards with a vicious right hand to the groin. As his torso buckled under the impact, Frankie's elbow caught him hard above the right eye, splitting the eyebrow like an over-ripe tomato.

He collapsed to the floor, blood everywhere.

Frankie locked a cold stare on number three who wasn't looking overly enthusiastic. But there was nowhere to go, nowhere to hide. He knew there was something happening he didn't understand. The evidence was all around him, his two friends crumpled on the ground, one in agony gasping for breath, the other on his knees covered in blood. In a flash, Frankie lunged at him, two lightening fast blows sending him crashing to the floor. But it wasn't over. Frankie dived on him, slamming blow after blow into his kidneys the same time he sank his rotten teeth deep into his left cheek. It may have looked bizarre but coming from the world he did, it wasn't a position that was new to the man some knew as *Frankie F*.

As he stood to his feet readying to walk away, he spat out the contents of his mouth all over his prone, unmoving victim. By any rules of warfare, the fight was over. But the trio's pain was only just beginning. Hobos who'd been avidly watching the fight, suddenly descended on the three men like a hungry wolf-pack beating them with sticks and slabs of concrete before dragging them a quarter mile and dropping them over the railway embankment. No-one knew if they were alive or dead. No-one cared. They'd messed with Frankie F and paid the price.

From that day on, the hobos gave Frankie even more space than previous. It was their way of affording him the respect he'd both earned and deserved.

And so it was seven years later, when Frankie arrived back at his corner at the end of another dayshift. After putting down his 7/11 bags, he carefully removed the glass cookie jar, the tools of his trade, and hid it inside the cracked concrete in the very corner of his corner. And then he began. After wolfing the food, he reached for the wine.

He knew it was killing him. But it made no difference.

Next morning when he awoke, all he had in the world was twenty-seven cents and the filthy clothes on his back. Despite the fact he had the respect of the unrespectable, he hated himself, hated his weakness; loathed his guilt.

As he saw it, his life was worthless, convinced he had absolutely nothing.

But his life hadn't always been like this.

CHAPTER THREE:

"C'mon! One more, one more! You can do it."

A four hundred and forty pound bench press is an impossible dream to most but the ability to perform four sets of five or six with such a load elevates the lifter into the superman category. This would be true of any gym anywhere in the world. But Gold's Gym on Fort Worth's Sierra Pines wasn't any old gym and the man doing the lifting wasn't any old superman.

It was Sunday, 1st February 2004 and remarkably, Eugene Sanders was just days away from his fifty-third birthday. He may've been in phenomenal shape but he was also drug-free, the steroids as absent as the narcissistic pride so prevalent in many serious gym-goers. The raw power of his persona converged seamlessly with an affable gentleness that made him appear laid back, in control, like nothing ever fazed him. But there was a time when he was different, when his mood swings raged from the downright angry to the volcanically dangerous. This period of his life lasted fifteen years and ended with a four-year prison term after it took an entire SWAT squad to quell his fury following a disturbance at one of Fort Worth's newer Chinese restaurants.

Jail held few surprises for Eugene; he knew what to expect. As a teenager, he'd spent three years at a Young Offenders Institution for manslaughter before finding salvation from the most unlikely source, the Vietnam War. He was a young man then, not so angry; not so much experience of life. It was in stark contrast to what was to come later.

Within hours of starting his second stretch, Eugene had worked out that *the Mamas*, a gang of blacks mostly from Alabama and South Carolina, ruled the prison with an iron fist.

He saw it as a test and thought he'd go to the Mamas before they came to him.

Their leader was an ugly mother called Lucas Riley who liked to demonstrate his kingship by eating alone. The unwritten rule was that anyone who walked within twenty feet of him at meal times was likely to end up getting hurt. The guards didn't interfere. They saw it as the natural order of things, survival of the fittest and all that. But the huge dining room made for a bizarre sight: over eight hundred men packed together on tables sitting thirty-a-side and there in the middle, one man eating alone, surrounded by nothing but space.

For two days, Eugene watched and evaluated. There was no fear, just preparation.

The dining hall was a noisy place but when he stepped inside the twenty foot circle an instant deathly hush descended all over the massive room. Riley seemed unperturbed, slowly lifting his hand to restrain his minders. The gang leader wanted to see what the big black brother was after. Was he looking to enlist or was he throwing down a challenge?

Lucas Riley was about to find out.

Eugene stopped eight feet inside the unmarked circle and lowered his head. Riley interpreted it as respect and felt confident, beckoning him forward.

It was a huge mistake that in different circumstances would've been fatal.

With just three feet between them and Riley still turning as he sat, in the weakest of positions, Eugene sensed the kill and couldn't help think it was a no-contest. He bowed exaggeratedly, the overt display of reverence further disarming the Mamas leader. Eugene saw the confusion flash across his face and knew he was right; it was no-contest.

He lunged at Riley stunning him with a powerful open-handed blow high to the sternum. As the heel of his hand landed, Eugene was in behind the Mamas leader in a flash, his left hand reaching round to the far side of Riley's prison all-in-ones. With his free right hand Eugene pulled a shank out of his pocket, a spoon with a handle sharpened into a point. It may have been crude but it was also effective. He plunged it with frightening force into the fleshy part of Riley's upper cheek, about an inch under his left eye, withdrew it, before slamming into his right ear.

Eugene knew exactly what he was doing. He thought the Mamas complacent and unlikely to be carrying weapons. He was right. After letting Riley slump to the floor, he turned his attention to the minders as eight hundred pairs of eyes looked on. It was mayhem, blood everywhere, but not even one drop Eugene's. Seconds later, he was spirited away by the guards for a three-week spell in the cooler. There wasn't a mark on him.

On his release from solitary, Eugene escaped further charges, the guards report claiming the Mamas leader had started the fight and pulled the shank. Riley was transferred to the Florida State Prison where he spent six months in a hospital bed. Though his face eventually healed, he never heard another thing through his right ear. With two other gang members also having long spells in the hospital and another three given transfers, no-one ever mentioned the "Mamas" again. It was as if they'd never been.

Eugene's anger eased after the Mamas incident and the remainder of his time in the slammer was the stuff penal reformers dream about. Early in 1990, after serving just over four years of a six-year sentence, he was out on parole, resolute he'd never return.

He'd been introduced to body-building as a teenager during his first jail term. His early years shifting iron were one of the few parts of his past he didn't mind remembering. His childhood had been tough by any standards but it was a joy-ride compared to what came later, when life in the military took him to the other side of the world, to Southeast Asia. For more than four years he'd lived life on the edge, wondering if he'd live long enough to see the next day. It didn't frighten him. In fact, he fed off the adrenaline rush it gave him. But the man a select few knew as *Kong* had seen things he wished he hadn't seen and worst of all, he'd done things he wished he hadn't done.

Nightmares and flashbacks were part of his life. It may've been a while since the last one but he knew they'd be back. They always came back.

He'd met his girlfriend Marlena a few months before he'd gone down a second time. Though thirteen years his junior, she'd brought stability to his life, stood by him faithfully throughout his time inside and was waiting the day he reclaimed his liberty. They'd been inseparable ever since, though it wasn't till the fall of 1999 that she finally became Mrs Eugene Sanders.

There were no children. Eugene had no desire to pass on his violent genes to a son or to see a daughter become the object of some man's lust or perhaps another rape victim. Someone's daughter, someone's grand-daughter, they always are; but not his. And Marlena didn't desire children enough to risk losing the most important thing in her life, her husband.

Though he spent lots of his free time at the gym and Marlena often saw body-building as her rival, the other woman, he always came home. But there was an up-side. She lusted after his muscular body and she loved the overflow of testosterone that meant he came running whenever she whistled.

When she heard the car pull into their drive, she ran for the door.

"C'mon baby," she said with a smirk, "Get your black ass up those stairs!"

In the bedroom, Eugene stripped off and started running through his body-building poses.

"What you think, baby?" he teased.

Marlena pretended to sulk but her hungry eyes never left him. Though she'd never admit it, she enjoyed his showing off and especially loved it when he flexed his buttocks making the unusual star-shaped birthmark on his right bum cheek dance up and down.

"Will you get in this bed lover? You keep me waiting and I'll bite that birthmark clean off your butt!"

But he was only half-listening. In his mind's eye, he was lifting the Senior Mr Universe title. His body-building not only kept him fit, it also allowed him to dream and looking forward was so much better than looking back. There was less regret, less guilt.

"Eugene . . . now!" his wife screeched, jolting him from his thoughts.

"You got it baby; here I come!"

With testosterone surging through his veins, Eugene Sanders was feeling as content as he'd felt in a long time.

But his life hadn't always been like this.

CHAPTER FOUR:

The room was buzzing, the excitement almost tangible.

It was 1st February 2004, Super Bowl night, and everyone was looking forward to watching the New England Patriots take on the Carolina Panthers at Houston's Reliant Stadium.

With roots reaching all the way back to southwest Ireland, the McBride's were a proud and close-knit Irish American family. Their two senior generations, sixteen people in all, had gathered to enjoy a special night in the relaxed company of family and to pay their respects to a man who'd done so much to enrich their lives; Michael McBride, the revered head of the dynasty and CEO of Cork Construction, the family business.

But the McBride's weren't in Texas; they were in their hospitality suite at the Patriots stadium in Foxboro Massachusetts. They used it for company meetings as well as the more obvious sporting events. And whatever the occasion it was luxury all the way: expensive furnishings, two massive Plasma screens, superb catering and of course, the huge glass wall that looked out over the Gillette Stadium's playing surface.

Fifty-four year old Michael McBride was an intensely private man, very different from your average corporate chief executive. A church-going, committed Christian and a true family man in every sense, his integrity and character shone through in everything he did and was. It was what made him so loved and so likeable.

As he gazed out over the deserted floodlit stadium, his thoughts turned to the real king of the clan, his grandfather, Fergus McBride. Michael was still in his mother's womb when his father died in a work-related accident so it was Granddad Fergus who became his father figure. Michael missed him deeply. He may not have been there in body but he was present in spirit, his fingerprints everywhere. His was an all-pervasive, seemingly eternal presence, able to touch his world even from beyond the grave. Every one of the sixteen people present carried his hallmark, eight privileged to inherit his genes, the other eight, blessed that their spouse was part of his bloodline. All were better people for the connection.

Michael had been closer to the mighty Fergus than anyone else. It was why he was the undisputed leader of the clan, carefully groomed for the role even as a boy sat on his Granddad's knee. Fergus was the reason he was who he was and thirty-five years after his passing, he could see it was the way it was always meant to be.

Fergus was also the reason that, save the odd glass of wine, there was no alcohol being consumed in the Cork Construction Suite. "It affects yer judgment," he used to say "And a man without sound and accurate judgment won't be his own man for long 'coz sure as eggs is eggs someone's gonna come along, impose his will on yer and make the decision for yer."

It was a life-lesson that made Michael want to curl up and die. He'd done some terrible things in the ten-year period following his Granddad's death but however much he may have wished it, Michael knew that there could be no turning the clock back. He'd let himself down and worse, he'd failed the memory of the man who'd filled so many roles in his life: grandfather, father, best friend, fishing and ball-game buddy, comforter, mentor and life role model.

How he wished he could have lived up to Fergus' standards. But he hadn't and he didn't.

"It's starting! Go Pats, go!" yelled his seventy-eight year old Uncle Declan, cutting across his thoughts. Michael smiled contentedly as he watched fifteen pairs of excited eyes fix on the Plasma screens.

Fergus had been a baseball man through and through but four years after his death in 1968, the family moved from Boston to Foxboro, home of the New England Patriots. It meant that when Michael returned to the family fold, it was inevitable he'd become an avid Patriots fan.

He'd grown to love the Pats but most of all, he loved his family: Maddie his wife of twenty years and their three lovely children, Joseph, sixteen, Ryan, fourteen, and the youngest, little Charlotte, the apple of his eye, just a few months off her thirteenth birthday.

He was head-over-heels in love with his wife but had he looked for it, he would've had ample opportunity to play the field. He was ruggedly handsome, in great shape and exuded a confidence most women found enormously attractive. But Michael wasn't interested.

His life had changed immeasurably over the years and on the odd occasions he found himself thinking about the dark days of his past, he'd experience a voyeuristic sensation, like as if he was looking in on someone else. As he saw it, he'd been given a second chance; and he knew it was down to the grace of God and to the memory of Fergus McBride.

When Fergus had been there to guide him, his potential seemed unlimited but after he died, Michael's life didn't so much as go off the rails as crash into a brick wall.

In his early days in the wilderness he'd become a trained killer prepared to do whatever he was ordered by his superiors, without a trace of emotion. It was a time when the lines between right and wrong became blurred, a time when the man nicknamed *Irish* didn't care whether he lived or died.

In the spring of 1978 he finally came to his senses and went home. Though his uncles welcomed him back like a returning prodigal, there was no favour or special treatment. It was the way he wanted it. He worked diligently, treated everyone with respect and was always first on site and last to leave. But there was a hard edge to him too. Six months after his return, one of the plasterers called him a *privileged little rich boy* once too often. It was a grave error of judgment. The plasterer had a tough-guy reputation and fancied his chances but Michael smashed him to a pulp in front of forty or fifty of his co-workers. The legendary Fergus had once been the bare-knuckle champion of all-Ireland. He'd passed on his pugilistic skill to his grandson and most important of all, inside both men beat the never-say-die heart of the prize-fighter.

The fight was a major talking point with the men for months but Michael never bragged about it, never even mentioned it. Despite the brutality, because of it maybe, he leapt even further in the men's estimation and the more perceptive among them, especially those old enough to remember Fergus, could see that Michael was a prince waiting to be king, the natural heir to the throne at Cork Construction.

When he became CEO in 1985, he'd experienced every level of the business from the bottom to the top. The staff and workers had immense respect for him and those who'd worked under Fergus would often say that "Mikey" was the image of the old man; how he looked, what he said, what he did and how he commanded respect. Michael heard the talk but unlike everyone else, he knew it wasn't true. Fergus would never have done what he'd done.

With the game in full flow and the Pats trailing by a point, Michael was surprised at how reflective he was feeling. Before he could ask himself why, the Pats scored and everyone leapt to their feet yelling and celebrating wildly. But Michael's excitement disappeared in the blink of eye.

"What's wrong Mikey? You look as if you've seen a ghost," his seventy-four year old Aunt Shauna said, much closer to the truth than she could've ever imagined.

"Nothing, uh nothing," Michael replied unconvincingly.

But something was wrong.

Just after the touchdown the TV camera swung to the Patriots cheerleaders and to a close-up on one girl in particular, a startlingly attractive Asian girl with dark shoulder length hair, gleaming white teeth and big, beautiful brown eyes. Aware the camera was on her, she flashed a sparkling smile that lit up every corner of the two giant Plasma screens.

In an instant, Michael had been transported half-way around the world and back through the years as if in a time machine, until he was face-to-face with his moment of weakness, the moment of his greatest shame.

Though he tried to hide it, not even Adam Vinatieri's field goal to seal the Pats narrow victory could rekindle his interest in the game. Truth was he just wanted to go home.

Two hours later, he had his wish.

"You were great tonight, darling," Maddie said sincerely. "I love you so much. We're all so proud of you; the family really appreciates you and they appreciate what you've done for the company too".

As she chattered away, she didn't seem to notice that he wasn't listening, that his mind was elsewhere. Though blissfully happy and confident in the present, Michael McBride was haunted by a past he'd hoped had gone away. It hadn't. And it wouldn't.

The beautiful Asian cheerleader had resurrected memories he'd tried to lock away; he'd suddenly become a deeply disturbed man.

But his life hadn't always been like this.

PART ONE

THE CRIME SCENE

Southeast Asia, early 1970's

CHAPTER FIVE:

Bleeding Dog Company was the brainchild of Lieutenant Colonel William T. O'Donnell.

A war hero in his own right, O'Donnell was a Medal of Honor winner in Korea. But it was in Vietnam that he really discovered his niche, in the most special of Special Operations. In nine years in 'Nam, he'd become something of a legendary figure, the Mr Fixit of Southeast Asia's black ops community. Based at Command Control Central in Kontum, O'Donnell reported directly to Washington, to the slightly sinister General Matthew Kedenberg.

"Come in," he barked in response to the knock on his door.

It was Master Sergeant Doug Miller, his confidante and right-arm man. Official records had him listed as Master Sergeant U.S. Special Forces, "K.I.A., Quang Tri Province, Vietnam, October 1967."

Despite being killed in action, Miller was very much alive.

"What's up Sir," he said, noticing the papers on the desk.

"We got a green light Doug."

"For the All-Star team Sir?"

"Yep; the General's finally taken our advice. Bleeding Dog Company is live and active."

"That's great Sir; what's the deal?"

O'Donnell pushed the papers across the desk, Miller's eyes hungrily scanning the pages.

"Hell Sir, he's really going for it!" he exclaimed, "And we even get to select the players!"

From the mid-Sixties, U.S. Special Operations was outworked through MACV-SOG, Military Assistance Command Vietnam – Studies and Observation Group. Teams were used on a wide variety of missions, the menu including assassinations, strategic recon, psy-ops, intelligence gathering and the carrying out of SLAM (seek-locate-annihilate-monitor) missions. The units usually comprised six to twelve men with between two, three or four being U.S. personnel and the rest made up of indigenous locals. It was rare for teams to be formed outside this remit.

"Look Doug, he wants a four-man, all-American team and by having us report to him alone, he's taken us off the conventional radar by putting us outside the MACV-SOG umbrella. He's got something in mind and my guess is we'll be working the wrong side of the fence."

"Laos and Cambodia, Sir?"

"I reckon that's why he repeatedly stresses the secrecy element?"

Laos and Cambodia was as off-limits as it got, because Richard Nixon had given personal assurances to Congress there'd be no ground troops in either country from the spring of '71.

"We'll be so undercover Sir, we'll be invisible!"

O'Donnell smiled. "OK Doug, now you know it's on, you think it through and we'll reconvene 15:00 hours to talk detail."

"Yes Sir, look forward to it Sir," Miller replied, standing to his feet, thinking the thought he'd never meant anything so much in his life.

* * * * *

One minute after three, the two men were down to business.

"Before we look at people Doug, what's your thoughts on training venues?"

"The secrecy element's a big one Sir. There's so many disenchanted troopers in 'Nam I think we should go right off-site; to Thailand maybe."

If O'Donnell was surprised, he didn't show it. "What exactly are you after?"

"I'm thinking Air Force base Sir, and Ubon's my favourite. Those fly-boys are so far up their own butts they won't be interested in what we're doing."

"And the time-line Doug?"

"The General wants the team ready to roll 1st December Sir, so that gives us less than seven weeks. We assemble fifteenth; one week at Ubon followed by four in the mountains."

"And then?"

"Back to 'Nam, Sir, somewhere nice and quiet, not Kontum. Not too far from the border either. Somewhere like Black Lady Mountain?"

"Good Doug. What you need from me?"

Miller leaned back so he could remove a piece of paper from his pocket before reading out a long list of requirements.

"Is that *all* Master Sergeant?" O'Donnell said with a smile.

"Yes Sir. We sure gonna have some fun Sir!"

Ignoring the quip, O'Donnell leapt into his next question. "So, what's your thoughts regarding personnel, Doug? Who's our leader? Fernando?"

"Yes Sir. He's first pick!"

"But doesn't he suffer from migraines and depression?"

"Yes Sir, but with respect Sir, if the Lieutenant Colonel had been as close to as much gunfire as Fernando, you'd have a bitch of a headache too Sir!"

"What about the depression?" O'Donnell added, his deadpan expression not cracking in the slightest.

"Sir, that boy's seen things no-one should see. It would be a friggin' miracle if he woke each morning with a grin on his face and joy in his heart Sir!"

"You sure he's right for this one?"

"Sir, Fernando's your man. He was first up the beach at Da Nang and hasn't wanted to go home since! I mean cut him in half and I bet he's got 'Viet-friggin'-nam' running round his inside like a stick of rock candy! He's won the Silver Star and the Medal of Honor and fought undercover in Cambodia, Laos and up north. Hell Sir, he's been such a boil on Charlie's butt, a hundred thousand Gooks know him by name! You want me to go on, Sir?"

"No, Master Sergeant. I get your drift! Where is he now?"

"Chau Doc Province Sir working with a Special Forces unit under Colonel Hagen Zabitosky."

"When's the last time you spoke to him Master Sergeant?" O'Donnell said suspiciously.

"Sir: about an hour ago Sir!!"

"And what condition is he in?"

"Sir, he tells me he's in need of a new challenge!"

"I'll pretend I didn't notice you jump the gun Master Sergeant . . . in the interest of team!"

"Thank you Sir, appreciate it Sir!"

"I'll call the Colonel and see if we can't get our boy a Thai vacation!"

"Yes Sir!!"

"And what about the other three slots?" O'Donnell said, anxious to move on.

"Like Fernando Sir, they all done time with MACV-SOG. Sir, for two, I'd go for Mike McBride, the Irish kid, and Eugene Sanders, the big black mother we had do explosives instruction down near Cu Chi in April. They're top-of-the-tree Sir. McBride's hard as nails and a crack shot marksman, among the top three or four shooters in the Marine Corps. Sanders is a Green Beret and one of the best explosives men I've worked with. They're two of angriest sons of bitches I ever come across and my gut feeling is working together, they'll be pure TNT!"

"What they angry about Doug?"

"It seems McBride was real close to his grandpa and been off the rails ever since the old fella died a couple of years back. He's a tough one Sir, a real street fighter; caused hell at Boot Camp but his Gunnie knew a good Marine when he saw one."

"And Sanders?"

"He's the business Sir, a real scary son-of-a-bitch; I mean he's so scary you have to be eighteen just to look at him!"

"I think you're exaggerating Master Sergeant."

"No Sir, its true Sir; the Bogeyman checks his closet at night just to make sure Sanders isn't hiding in there!!" O'Donnell smiled as Miller continued. "When he was sixteen he caught a white guy stealing his brother's car; ended up killing him and serving time. At his first attempt at parole he went before the Young Offenders Restitution Board told them he wanted to serve his country and incredibly, they let him sign up! He was at Fort Benning six days past his nineteenth birthday!"

"He sounds crazy! You sure he's our man?"

"Sir, what I didn't say and what the Judge didn't want to hear was that Sanders caught the guy hotwiring the car. The guy pulls a gun. Sanders grabs his hand, slips his finger in behind the thief's, turns the gun and pulls the trigger! When the police show up, they can't understand why his fingerprints aren't on the gun. He explained but no-one was listening. In his words Sir, he'd have got a fairer hearing at a Ku Klux Klan convention!"

"Hell Doug, no wonder the boy's upset! OK, who gets the last spot?"

"Rudi Kingsbridge Sir: 101st Airborne; our radioman."

"I've not heard you mention him before Doug?"

"No Sir, that's because I haven't Sir. He's a talented son-of-a-bitch for sure, and I'm told that if it wasn't for his arrogance he'd have got himself a Medal of Honor at

Hamburger Hill. He's confident and clever Sir, Harvard Business School clever! His father's a hotshot Chicago businessman and his mother's a friggin' movie star!! He might be a pretty boy Sir but he's a tough son-of-a-bitch who also happens to be the best radioman in 'Nam; he'll get you a signal in the middle of a thermo-nuclear winter!"

"You sure he's right for Bleeding Dog Company Doug?"

"I am Sir," Miller said, sounding more convinced than he actually felt.

* * * * *

Four days later, Miller set eyes on Frankie for the first time in over a year, Miller thinking he looked more thirty-six than twenty-six.

The two shook hands vigorously. It was as warm as tactile communication between two war heroes got. Minutes later, they were reminiscing, lost in a sea of memories.

"Let's take a walk," Miller said, indicating it was time for business.

Frankie got straight to the point. His way was strictly Route1.

"A four man team sounds like a death squad to me Doug."

"Yeah: me too. I reckon DC's called time on Southeast Asia and my feeling is Uncle Sam's concerned with what'll happen when we gone. I reckon they want us to take out a few more bad guys before we leave."

Whatever Frankie was thinking didn't show on his face. He was a professional soldier who took orders; emotion didn't enter into it.

"So who've you got in mind for the team?"

"Their files are in my office. Let's go get us a coffee."

Ten minutes later, Frankie immersed himself in the personnel files of Eugene Sanders, Michael McBride and Rudi Kingsbridge.

"You pick 'em Doug?"

"Yep, that's what the chief pays me for!" Miller said before briefing Frankie in much the same way he'd briefed O'Donnell.

As he was talking about McBride, a bell rang in Frankie's head. "I've heard of this guy," he said. "He put six Navy SEALs in a Saigon hospital this time last year; they even thought one of them wasn't gonna make it."

"That's my boy," Miller chirped, like a proud father told of his offspring's good and noble deed.

"What's his story?" Frankie asked.

"His grandpa was a bare-knuckle prize-fighter back in the old days in Ireland and clearly, our boy's inherited his fight skills. I understand the old fella died a couple of years back and the kid misses him like hell. 'Nam was his way of dealing with it and he's kicked the hell out of lots of Gooks and more than a few Americans ever since!"

"What about Sanders and Kingsbridge?"

"They're the type you want standing by your side when the battle's at its rawest. The black fella, Sanders, is up for the fight and won't back down no matter what. His fitness tests are unbelievable."

"And Kingsbridge?"

"Kingsbridge performed with distinction at Hamburger Hill and is the best radioman there is. He's a talented son-of-a-bitch who can do just about anything, at least, anything he pleases."

The emphasis Miller put on his last three words had Frankie's antennae twitching.

"What you mean Doug? Is there something you aren't telling me?"

"Well, he's a bit of a loner and . . . there were some rumours," said Miller realising he was about to trust Frankie with something he felt unable to share with O'Donnell.

"Rumours? What rumours?"

"His unit hit a village in the Central Highlands; some women and children got hurt."

"How hurt?"

"Two dead, a woman and a kid, and er . . ."

"What?"

"Some old woman claimed she'd been raped!"

"You what?"

"But the deaths were never proved. The old bird was like a hundred and twenty with a face like untreated leather. Kingsbridge is a good looking boy and it got put down to wishful thinking on her part!"

Frankie paused for a few seconds. "So why you telling me, or perhaps I should re-phrase that Doug, why you warning me 'bout this?"

"Because I think this guy has a cruel streak that goes beyond the normal meanness and violence you expect in soldiers of this quality. If it wasn't you leading Bleeding Dog Company I'd probably pass him by. OK, that'll do for now; get some shut-eye. We meet the Chief at 21:00 hours. Just shake his hand, say hello and don't forget, no mention of Kingsbridge's darker side."

And that was that; the conversation was over.

Frankie returned to his quarters intending to read the three files thoroughly. He'd read somewhere that knowledge gave you the edge and he suspected that as team leader, he'd need all the edge he could get.

* * * * *

Lieutenant Colonel William T. O'Donnell didn't look up once through his entire dinner.

He too, was totally engrossed in a personnel file; Frankie's, the newly appointed leader of Bleeding Dog Company. Unlike Miller, he wasn't quite so sure about Fernando. Something didn't sitting right. It was almost as if just picking up his file was enough to arrive at the obvious conclusion: Fernando was an outstanding soldier, the son of a war hero who'd become a war hero himself. But there was an undercurrent that nagged at O'Donnell. The file notes and citations made frequent reference, albeit impliedly, to his moroseness and emotional detachment. It seemed to indicate that at one level, the Corporal was a joyless son-of-a-bitch, but at another, it had alarm bells ringing. Why did he not want to go home? Why was he so morose and what was the root cause of his depression? Was it Vietnam or did it go deeper? Was he about to have a breakdown or was he already in the middle of one?

The unanswered questions concerned him but the U.S. military machine needed one more job out of the top-notch Corporal and O'Donnell guessed all it would take was three or four months, five at the most. If he'd known the unit would be together for nine months he may've thought the risk too big to take. But without a crystal ball, he did the only thing he could; he pored over the file of a real life war hero.

"Hell, this guy makes John Wayne look like a pussy!" he exclaimed, as he read Frankie's Medal of Honor citation for the third time in under an hour.

He'd just reached the end when there was a sharp rap on the door. Miller was first to enter.

"Good evening Sir. Let me introduce Corporal Frank Fernando, U.S. Marine Corps, lately seconded to U.S. Special Forces, now Sir, team leader Bleeding Dog Company."

"Welcome to Kontum Corporal, though the Master Sergeant tells me you won't be staying long?"

Frankie saluted before offering O'Donnell his right hand and grunting.

Miller interjected, feeling the need to cut short what was the first of several slightly awkward silences. "Yes Sir, we fly to Thailand tomorrow," he said.

Fifteen minutes later the meeting was over, O'Donnell no closer to answering the unasked questions but convinced Frankie was a man with a past. He was. Like all who walk the planet, Frankie was a product of his experience and environment. Who he was and what he'd become was as much formed in the cradle, in grade school and through his teenage years as it was on the battlefields of Vietnam. He'd found a niche for himself in Southeast Asia, warfare giving him an enemy he could fight; one he could seek out, identify and destroy. But the battle inside his head didn't conform to the black and white criteria of war; there he fought the indefinable enemy within, the demons running amok amidst a family background melancholic in the extreme.

Frankie's early years saw none of the love that should be mandatory in every childhood. The war with the Japanese had turned his father into a pale shadow of himself, his dark moods dominating the poverty-strapped family home. His mother, consumed with disappointment and deprived of love, had given up on life, accepting a lack of fulfilment as her destiny. Frankie would've loved to have dreamed big dreams but no-one ever took the trouble to show him how. It made for a mundane, loveless existence. But as bad as it was, it got worse. One day when he was sixteen, he got home from school an hour early to find his mother in bed with the insurance salesman. In a frenzied attack, he beat the man to a pulp. His father arrived the same time as the police. When he realised what'd happened, he threw his wife out the house and Frankie hadn't seen his mother since. Two years after the incident, he found his father hanging from the punch-bag hook affixed to his bedroom ceiling. It sent him hurtling into his first nervous breakdown and dep-ression at one level or another, had been a virtual everyday companion ever since.

It was a context vital in any effort to understand Frankie but such intimate detail doesn't easily find its way into a personnel file.

Though both his commanding officers had reservations, O'Donnell more so than Miller, both men consoled themselves with the thought that even if the entire Bleeding Dog thing went pear-shaped, no-one would know any different. Theirs was a hush-hush world where, deep in the shadows, greatness and obscurity walk so close together as to be indistinguishable. If anything went wrong, it would never see the light of day.

It was O'Donnell's last conscious thought and satisfied him enough to allow him to nod off to sleep.

For Frankie though, restful sleep was an impossible dream. Stretched out on his bunk a hundred yards away as the crow flies, he was doing what he always did at night: fighting the enemy, the demons that made him what he was, a manic depressive.

CHAPTER SIX:

Frankie and Miller stood outside a dilapidated hut on the edge of Ubon Royal Thai Air Force Base, Southeast Thailand, watching the Jolly Green Giant lower towards the ground.

With the rotor still spinning, they moved forward as McBride set foot on Thai soil seconds before the massive Sanders. After the four had greeted one another, Miller barked. "Let's walk," and nodded towards the hut.

Sanders and McBride led the way, obviously carrying on where they'd left off on the flight from Da Nang.

"Looks like these two have connected," Miller said.

Frankie didn't reply. He was wondering how the newcomers would react to the less than luxurious accommodation. The hut was full of unused fence posts, barbed wire, rolls of fencing and other materials used to erect the airfield's perimeter fence.

As it was, neither man uttered a word of complaint.

"There must be a thousand shovels in here!" McBride said to Sanders.

"Yeah; just imagine being the poor mother to fence-in this base!"

"It must've felt like fencing in Oklahoma!!" McBride replied with a smile before turning to Frankie, "What time's Kingsbridge due in Corp?"

"An hour, maybe two; he's coming up from Saigon."

Two hours later, a jeep pulled up, its wheels locking as the driver brought it to a skidding halt. Four men watched Rudi Kingsbridge exit the passenger side. Stripped to the waist, he had black straps tied just above both elbows and a kitbag slung over his shoulder.

"Hell fire!" Miller exclaimed. "He really does look like a friggin' film star!!"

"Hey guys," Kingsbridge said through a big toothy grin. "I can tell my arrival's made you feel a little inadequate," he said winking at no-one in particular. "You're all pleased to see me but much as you try, you can't stop yourself wishing you were as good looking as me. Don't let it worry you; everyone I meet thinks the same thing!"

"Is he for real?" Sanders whispered to McBride.

McBride didn't respond; speech beyond him.

Miller had no such difficulty. "Now listen to me numbnuts," he screamed amid a torrent of profanity. "You'd better keep those precious cherry lips firmly shut otherwise you are gonna be eating crap instead'a talking it! You understand me son?"

"Yes Sir, Master Sergeant, Sir," Kingsbridge replied cool-as-ice.

"I hope you understand son. Now, park up your kit and get your pretty-boy ass back out here. We got work to do."

"Yes Sir, Master Sergeant, Sir."

"That was a neat entrance!" Sanders said offering his hand to Kingsbridge as they walked.

"I like to make a good impression!"

Their conversation was cut short as Miller halted alongside the gear dumped by the Jolly Green Giant. "I want this lot shifted over to the hut. You got an hour!"

"Begging your pardon Master Sergeant," Kingsbridge chirped, "But can't they find a truck that isn't being used on a base this big?"

"Now listen to me 'Ollywood," Miller snarled slowly, swearing every other word and stumbling on a nickname destined to stick. "If I hear another whining word emerge out them luscious lips, you got serious trouble headed your way."

"Yes Sir, Master Sergeant, Sir."

"I hope you got it son. Because believe you me, you do not want *me* as an enemy."

It was the ice-cold delivery that made it a conversation stopper, no-one speaking a word till the job was done. But Miller wasn't finished. "Next, we clean up the hut!"

The hut was the last resting place for all the things nobody else wanted or at least, thought they'd never need again.

Kingsbridge cut his hand on a roll of barbed wire. "Owwwwww!" he yelped.

"Keep it down man," McBride said, shooting a look in Miller's direction. "You already got the Master Sergeant spitting razor blades."

Kingsbridge's four-letter word reply couldn't have been curter.

"How is it girls?" Miller said, preventing McBride from responding. All he could do was bite his lip and bide his time.

As the clean-up was coming to an end, Sanders chirped, "I got the bedroom with a window!"

"Mine's the one with the view down to the river," McBride said before adding, "And faggot, you can sleep outside with the lizards. You'll feel at home out there."

The comment drew another sharp four-letter word response from Kingsbridge.

"Easy boys; it'll be time for bed shortly," said Sanders, spotting the warning signs.

But it wasn't bed that was next.

"Great job ladies, you'll all make someone a nice wife someday!" Miller blasted. "Get your kit on, we're going for a run. It's time to see how big a fence this really is."

Despite the fact all four Bleeding Dogs were elite soldiers; Miller felt the need to put them to the test. Twelve miles and seventy-five minutes later, it was Sanders who was first home. Seven minutes had elapsed when Miller, McBride and Fernando all arrived within a minute and two hundred and fifty yards of one another. It was another six minutes before the exhausted Kingsbridge plodded in.

With Miller and Frankie in conversation, McBride couldn't resist the opportunity. "It'll be no good you going to the bar to get ice," he said, "It'll have melted before you got back!"

"You pathetic Irish Mick; I'll smash your face in."

"I don't think so faggot."

"Easy boys," said Sanders, trying to take the heat out of the situation.

None of them knew if it would've gone further, the door opening behind them as Miller and Fernando re-entered the hut. Ten minutes later, all five men, still fully clothed, were fast asleep.

Unbeknown to the others, Corporal Frankie Fernando silently gave thanks for the all-consuming fatigue.

It meant even his demons were exhausted.

* * * * *

At precisely 05:30 Master Sergeant Doug Miller stood over the snoring soldiers.

"C'mon girls; beauty sleep's over! We got work to do; we're gonna take another look at your favourite fence! And proving I'm all heart, we'll run in the opposite direction, just for variety. I must be going all soft in my old age!" he said, shaking his head in disbelief.

But the difference between the previous night's run and what Miller had in mind second time round wasn't the daylight, or even the direction; it was the fact all five men would be carrying an M60, the machine gun popularly known as the Pig.

"OK, here's the low-down," Miller snapped, pleased there'd been no grumbles. "We run together as a team with each of us carrying a Pig for company. Now forty pounds, hand-held for twelve miles will be a challenge to body, soul and spirit, so, get your heads right. Corporal . . ."

"I can tell this is gonna be a bitch of a morning," Kingsbridge said forebodingly as Frankie and Miller separated themselves from the team.

"It'll be easy for us faggot," McBride chirped, "The way you canter about like a big girl, we'll be able to walk and still keep up!!"

He'd picked up that Kingsbridge didn't like the homosexual putdowns and resolved to press home his advantage. But Kingsbridge wasn't going to take it on the chin. "Hey Mick-thick, hole-digger, you heard of Harvard? I go to Harvard see, but you don't do you?" he snarled, every other word a swearword. "They don't take Micks at Harvard!

There's a sign on the door, 'No Micks allowed, too thick, get back to the building site!'"

"Let it go boys," Sanders said, sensing things shift to a new level just as Miller put his head round the door.

"You boys ready? OK, let's go," he said.

McBride had lost his chance. "Faggot," he mimed before sending it on its way to Kingsbridge behind a big kiss. It was the best he could do.

The awkwardness of the M60 forced the men to constantly shift it around, changing grip, slinging it over a shoulder, or carrying it across their backs. But whatever the position, it wasn't long before something ached so much it needed to be shifted again. The exception was Sanders, the M60 looking like a kid's toy gun nestled into his massive arms and shoulders. He seemed to keep it in the same position for ages before needing to shift it someplace else. Everyone noticed. In the pain and cussing, each man coped his own way. Sanders was the most positive. By the end he'd be fitter and stronger and they were two of his key goals in life. For Frankie the opposite was true. He ached so much he thought it might be the day he died. Kingsbridge tried to take his mind off it by dreaming of his inauguration, as President of the United States. And McBride dreamed too, of smashing Rudi Kingsbridge into bloody unconsciousness.

"Into the river," Miller blasted shaking each man from his thoughts.

For two miles they ran against the gently flowing waters of the Mae Nam Mun River. It was tough going but just as their time in the water was coming to an end, McBride's right boot jammed between two rocks hiding below the river's dark surface. He went down with a shriek of pain, his pride hurt as much as his knee. Imaging is all-important in the early days of any group of males getting together but in the jungles of Southeast Asia it was more important to people like Michael McBride than life and death itself.

Kingsbridge sensed his opportunity. "You are one awkward Mick!"

"That's enough Kingsbridge!" snapped Frankie.

"Sorry mate," Kingsbridge said loudly as he squatted down alongside McBride, adding, in a whisper, "You skiving, shamming Mick!"

"We need a plan," Frankie said oblivious to the comment. "Sanders, can you carry him?"

"Sure thing Corp."

"OK, Kingsbridge and I will each carry two M60's and we'll half trot it back to base."

Miller hadn't needed to say a word; Frankie had it all under control.

As Sanders lifted McBride fireman-style across his massive shoulders, Kingsbridge whispered another jibe at McBride. "I know your game, pussy, I got your Pig and there's dick wrong with you. I can see straight into your soul Mick. You're just another Irish skiver."

McBride had no choice but to take it. Outwardly, he looked calm but inside he was seething.

"That faggot!" he snarled as Sanders somehow managed to get up to a full-on run. "I'm gonna rip his eyes out first chance I get."

"Stay cool dude," Sanders said sensing his friend meant what he said.

"No way; I'm gonna have him."

There was no more talk and not once did anyone stop. It was an impressive effort that had Miller purring. With Frankie leading from the front and Sanders looking the ultimate team player, the potential was obvious. He knew there was some chemistry between McBride and Kingsbridge but he hoped their afternoon session might fix it.

"Great effort guys!" he said as all five men crossed the finishing line together.

His first priority was medical treatment for McBride's knee. They had no idea how he managed it but as they arrived back at the hut, there waiting for them, was an open-top jeep complete with driver from the base hospital. McBride climbed onto the stretcher fixed across the back seats and waved to the others as the driver revved the engine before pulling away.

Four pairs of eyes were on him. Three men looked genuinely concerned, the fourth mimed obscenities.

* * * * *

An hour-and-a-half later the jeep returned McBride to his colleagues.

"It's just minor ligament damage," he said, "It'll be fine in a few days, a week at the most."

"See, I told you he was shamming," Kingsbridge said snidely.

"Button it Kingsbridge," Frankie snapped before adding, "Let's get some chow."

As the men chatted over dinner things looked to be improving. But looks can be deceiving. As soon as Frankie and Miller separated themselves from the others, the simmering feud bubbled to the surface once again.

"This is good," McBride muttered approvingly.

"Yeah dude, I love my meat," Sanders agreed, "And there must be half a cow in here!"

"All that's missing is a bottle of Jack to wash it down," Kingsbridge said making what appeared a positive contribution. Sanders and McBride knew it couldn't last. It didn't. "That's bourbon Mick," he added poisonously, "A real American drink; not your Irish whiskey dishwater!"

"Listen in you faggot queer," McBride snarled, his ice-cold glare suddenly oozing menace. "You're quick with the words but light on the action. Me? I'm under starter's orders; so just in case you ain't hearing me right faggot, any time you want it, it's yours."

Just as McBride finished making his point, the group's two senior men emerged from the side of the hut. "Glad to see you boys getting along so well," Miller said, proving that even the most experienced leaders can sometimes get it totally wrong! After eating, he stood to his feet. "I know it's hard to believe but you mothers are the pick of the litter, Uncle Sam's finest. For the next few months you gonna be so far up one another's butts you deserve to know about the man stood next to you. To give a flavour, I've prepared a short résumé on each of you; so tune in."

The men listened in respectful silence till Miller, who'd left Frankie to last, was halfway through the Corporal's pen picture.

"Holy cow Corp, you make Audie Murphy look like a dress-wearing faggot!" McBride blurted, reducing the room to hysterics. Only Frankie wasn't laughing; laughing wasn't his style.

But the résumés made it clear: despite an average age of just twenty-two years and nine months, the four Bleeding Dogs were a hugely experienced quartet of combat veterans.

"OK girls," Miller chirped, ready to move on. "I'm terrible with names so every unit of mine has to have team names."

"How'd you mean, Master Sergeant?" Sanders asked, not understanding the point.

"A nickname: an official Bleeding Dog name."

Unsurprisingly, Kingsbridge was first to speak. "At Harvard I was *Mr Perfect* to the guys and *Mr Drop-Dead-Gorgeous* to the girls. Either's fine by me!"

McBride groaned the same time he made an obscene gesture with his hand.

"No cherry lips, that's not how it works," Miller said, shaking his head. "In my units I choose, and you're *'Ollywood*! McBride you're *Irish*. Sanders, you can be *Kong* and Corporal, you're team leader so I guess that gives you a voice."

"Most every Marine I know calls me *Frankie F*, or just plain *Frankie* will do for me!"

Kingsbridge couldn't resist it. "You are one boring son-of-a-bitch Corp! I bet you take the swing out the budgie's cage so he can't have any fun either!"

No-one laughed. He was trying to be funny, light, but all he'd done was show poor judgment.

"There we are guys, job done" Miller huffed, ending a short but uncomfortable silence. "The evening's yours. Get a good sleep 'coz trust me, you're gonna need it! Corporal, I need a word before I go."

With that he and Frankie left the hut.

As the door closed, *Irish* McBride immediately turned to Kingsbridge, sending a string of expletives flying off in his direction. "What is it with you faggots?" he snarled as the distance between the two narrowed to just a few feet. "After hearing the Corporal's history you could'a given him more respect."

It was a valid point which, given the recent history, couldn't stay just words.

Kingsbridge growled an expletive. A second later, McBride's head smashed into his face, the well-aimed butt landing with thundering force flush on the right eyebrow, immediately opening up a deep and bloody inch-long gash.

Irish McBride's head had been in many faces over the years and without fail, it always did damage. But there was more to follow as he landed several blows, rights and lefts, to Kingsbridge's face and body before aiming a kick with his damaged leg into the side of Kingsbridge's left knee, looking to collapse his weight in sideways. It hurt him more than it hurt Kingsbridge. He yelped with pain as the two men separated.

As the only other person in the room, Sanders knew the problem needed fixing. Though he said his usual, "Easy guys, easy," he did so knowing the stakes were high; after all, both men were trained killers, not two drunken bar room brawlers arguing over their beer.

"Leave it Eugene, the faggot's got it coming," Irish snapped, his eyes fixed on his rival.

Kingsbridge said nothing. Instead, he aimed an oriental type kick. But it was telegraphed and Irish, even on a bad knee, was able to sway out of its arc easily. As he did so, he re-balanced himself before catching Kingsbridge with a searing right hander that broke his nose with a sickening splat. But he didn't go down.

Clearly coming off second best, he thought he'd front it up and swing punches.

It was a grave mistake. Michael *Irish* McBride was of fighting stock. Toe to toe, he'd never come off worse against anyone, anywhere, and plenty had tried. His balance was near perfect, prize-fighter perfect. His clean hits went bang, bang, bang and over went Kingsbridge. Most would've been content the fight was won and over but Irish wanted more. In a second, he was on top of the prostrate Kingsbridge with his right thumb buried deep into his eye.

As Sanders tried to pull him off, McBride whispered into Kingsbridge's ear, "This ain't over faggot!"

"What the hell?" Frankie said as the door opened. "Oh my God, you ain't so pretty now Hollywood!"

He had a point. Kingsbridge's left eye was partially closed above an obscene swelling all through his upper cheek and his eyebrow was split and oozing blood. His nose was broken and bloody and a one-inch gash decorated a badly swollen bottom lip. In addition, he could hardly see out his right eye, the vision blurred and the eye watering.

With McBride unmarked, the conclusion was indisputable; the street-fighter had made his point.

Pugilistic skill mixed with the prize-fighter's heart and a will that didn't care if he lived or died meant McBride was a man who couldn't be beaten. If he didn't win and died, he still won. And then there was his motivation, what made him tick. In a word, it was anger; anger that the grandfather he idolized had been snatched from him. Someone had to pay. He didn't care who: him, Charlie, or Pretty Boy Hollywood.

Frankie knew the score. He'd been around. Put four men in a room in a place like Vietnam and trouble was about as sure to happen as night following day. Without a flicker of sympathy, he turned to Kingsbridge, "Son, you must'a been blind not to see that coming. You gotta give these boys more respect and show them your better side."

Good advice it may have been but it was wasted on Rudi Kingsbridge.

He didn't have a better side.

* * * * *

If it hadn't been for the moonlight outside it would've been pitch black in the hut and aside from Sanders light snoring, the room was still with silence.

But Rudi Kingsbridge was awake and on all fours. Making less noise than a shadow, he crawled the twenty feet to McBride and held a seven-inch knife to his rival's throat.

Irish woke instantly, his eye-lids the only part of his body to move.

"I'm gonna cut out your Adam's apple and feed it to the birds!" Kingsbridge whispered in his ear.

In no position to retaliate physically, Irish chose his words carefully.

"Like I care!" he said slowly, his voice loud enough to wake the others. "I don't give a crap. If I die I die. So come on faggot, do it; do it!"

No-one knew whether he would have, Frankie and Sanders pulling him off before he had a chance. Instead, Kingsbridge shuffled back to his sleeping bag; the fact he was two-nil down keeping him awake most the night.

By contrast, Irish was sound asleep a few minutes later, seemingly without a care in the world. He'd called his adversary's bluff and won the game for the second time in less than three hours.

Rudi Kingsbridge thought he could take him to the edge, to that line in every man's life he won't go beyond. What he didn't know was that Irish McBride didn't have such a line.

He was a man who had no fear of death let alone men.

But then again, what else would you expect from the grandson of a legend?

CHAPTER SEVEN:

Michael McBride was born on January 26th 1950, his birth threatening the lives of both mother and baby. If he'd not been a fighter he'd have died even before he left the womb, the doctors having to perform an emergency C-section to save him from the umbilical cord wound round his neck.

"Are you his father?" the nurse asked the man with his nose up tight to the glass, dotingly looking at the baby who, with tubes up his nose and drips in his arm, couldn't have looked more pathetic.

"No lass, I'm his Granddad but I already love him more than a son you understand," the man replied in a lilting Irish accent which was melodic and gentle, almost musical. "It saddens me to say, but his Dad, Conor was his name, died in a work accident five months ago."

"Oh, I'm so sorry."

"Me too lass. Conor was a special boy, the only one of my four to be born in the old country. The Germans tried to kill him for three years, yet he came home with a Medal of Honor round his neck. And then he goes and slips off a scaffolding platform in Beacon Hill!"

"That's so sad."

"Aye, it was sad alright but I praise God he was able to leave a little something of himself behind before he went."

"The baby you mean?" she said, checking.

"He's a miracle that boy. His mother was told she'd never have kids yet, here he is. And six hours ago doctors told me to expect the worst; one of them telling me within the last twenty minutes that he still wasn't in the clear. But don't you worry lass; this little fella's got friends in high places. Inside that tiny ribcage is the heart of a lion; and every drop of blood flowing through his little veins is full of the never-say-die spirit of the fighting man. Aye, he'll fight the good fight alright; it's in his blood see lass."

And it was. Michael McBride was from fighting stock. His grandfather was Fergus McBride, once the prize-fight champion of all Ireland.

"I think you're right; he is going to make it," the nurse said, as surprised at the tears on her cheek as she was by the goose-pimples on her shoulders and arms. Like most medical professionals, she'd built a wall of resistance over the years and few things penetrated to the point of tears. But there was something about the man that touched her deep down: his eyes, the look, the baby. It all went way beyond blood-lines or genetics and somehow, reached far into the spiritual, the unseen.

As baby became toddler, Fergus would tell him in a thousand different ways, "You're gonna make it lad. You got me, you got your uncles, you got the angels and you got the Lord Jesus himself all looking out for yer!" Sat on his Granddad's knee, little Mikey lapped it up.

"Show me your hands," Fergus would say as the boy offered out his open palms. "Tell me lad, what's special 'bout those hands?"

"They gonna prosper," Michael replied in a tone so cute it could melt ice.

"Aye, that's right lad. The Bible says whatever you turn your hands to will prosper so as you grow up son, whatever you decide to do you'll succeed at. You're gonna make it lad."

Mikey loved it and most of all he liked the stories about the "old country."

Fergus grew up in the city of Cork, close to the Emerald Isle's southernmost tip.

"I loved Ireland Mikey," he said, "But feeding your family is always a man's first priority and it was never easy. And then there were the Republicans, always pushing for independence. I'm all for dreams Mikey you understand, but war with the British was always going to be fought in streets and in back gardens all over Ireland. It was these things that started me t'inking 'bout coming to America, the land of opportunity."

The route was one trodden by millions of Irish folk: train to Dublin, boat to Liverpool, steamship to New York. But there was one hitch, money, and to pay his passage Fergus needed a miracle. His answer came in a dream, a dream that took him to fight promoter Patrick O'Malley's office in Dublin.

As a teenager, Fergus made a name for himself as a bare-knuckle boxer in the boxing booths and travelling fairs. It was a track record that left O'Malley distinctly unimpressed.

He gestured to two burly minders that it was time for Fergus to leave. But seconds later, both men were flat on their backs unconscious.

"I t'ink it's time we talked Munsterman," the fight promoter said drily, his words confirming his rapid re-evaluation.

Four weeks later, on April 29th 1915, the unknown Fergus fought all-Ireland heavyweight champion Kieran Barton, on a hillside to the northwest of Ballymena, Northern Ireland. It was Barton's back-yard. Nearly ten thousand people gathered for the illegal prize fight, all but a handful rooting for the odds-on champion. They were to be disappointed as underdog Fergus overcame a huge height and weight disadvantage to win in the twenty-fourth round in what was the greatest upset in Irish fight history. Neither man ever fought again: Barton because of the damage he sustained, Fergus because the fight was simply a means to an end. Even so, as the youngest, lightest man ever to hold the title of all-Irish, heavyweight bare-knuckle champion, his place in history was assured. It gave him his start-point and like it or not, seek it or not, Fergus McBride's destiny was forever linked to the term *legend*.

Like a shadow, it would follow him everywhere.

When they reached America, the McBride's travelled to Boston where they lived with Declan and Glenna O'Connell who'd left Ireland five years earlier. In Cork, Declan and Fergus had attended the same Presbyterian Church but Declan had rebelled in his teens, built himself a reputation as a bar-room brawler and left for America. His family were upset he went and even more upset that he'd turned his back on God. But a year after setting foot in the new world, he attended a revivalist meeting where he had a deeply spiritual experience that changed his life forever.

The two became close friends, Fergus instantly identifying Declan had something he didn't.

It both fascinated and troubled him and he didn't know why.

Declan persuaded his boss, another Irishman called Paddie McNiff who'd left southwest Ireland three decades earlier, to give Fergus a job. But Declan wasn't amused when Fergus got into a fight at work, laying out the bullying Mac Berryford, a travelling cement salesman.

"We need to talk Fergus," he'd said, as they walked home. "You having to use your fists all the time ain't right. You know the truth of Scripture, but it just ain't setting you free, is it?"

That night was a life-changer for Fergus as Declan explained what'd happened to him ten years earlier. He'd started the evening knowing Declan had something he didn't have; he finished it in tears, with Jesus making the leap from good teacher to Lord and Saviour.

When he told Shannon his wife, her first thought was he'd gone mad. But it quickly passed; his extra attentiveness, patience and softness winning her over almost immediately. They fell more in love than either thought possible. And it was the same at work. McNiff had expected Fergus to be just another Irish boy with a talent for the pick and shovel but his understated charisma made him a hero-figure with the men and a natural leader. Promotions came his way in rapid succession and when childless Paddie was looking to return to Ireland, it was Fergus he looked to as a potential successor. It looked impossible; yet the impossible happened. With the help of an English aristocrat he'd met on the journey across the Atlantic five years earlier, Fergus came into ownership of a business worth more than a quarter million dollars while Shannon got the home of her dreams complete with all new furnishings. Miraculously, it didn't cost Fergus one cent and yet there were no borrowings, no debt and no repayments.

It was a remarkable business deal, the stuff of legend; the legend of Fergus McBride.

The business was renamed Cork Construction and grew year-on-year, impervious to the ravages of the Great Depression. During the Thirties, the company played a significant role in the creation of the Quabbin Reservoir. Twenty years later, it was a place of stunning natural beauty, with dozens of islands and over sixty miles of shoreline. Like his Granddad, young Mikey loved fishing and in 1960, Fergus purchased two acres up near Quabbin's north-eastern corner. The following year he built a sensational fishing lodge complete with boathouse, veranda and their very own fishing jetty. It was Mikey's Disneyland: the tree-houses, the dens, canoeing, fishing, mastering the longbow and learning to rifle-shoot. He loved it all but most of all, he loved being with his Granddad. It was the way it was meant to be.

Then, one day when he was thirteen, Michael got into a fight at school and went home with a bloody nose. Fergus took one look at him, "OK boy, it's time to learn d'er noble art."

Every day after school for six months, Mikey followed his Granddad to the gym at the bottom of the garden. Stripped to the waist, Michael was hungry for everything his Granddad had for him, and it was plenty. Not once did he grumble; he knew it was for his own good. Fergus had said so and that was good enough for him. It was a crash course in the science of physical combat and by its end Michael was transformed.

The training deepened the special bond between them, Fergus dedicating himself to mentoring his grandson. He spent hours with him, his life lessons punctuated with a rhetoric that etched itself deep into Michael's soul. "Never let any man force his will on yer when you know that will to be wrong," he'd say. "Better to die trying to stop him than to live knowing you'll have to look yer weakness in the eye day after day."

As a teenager, Michael McBride had no way of knowing just how indelible an impact these words would have on his life. That would come later.

They were as close as close could be. They had the same genes, thought the same thoughts, felt the same feelings, liked the same things but most of all, they liked being each other's best friend. And then, in October 1968, the unthinkable happened. Fergus died.

The family was devastated. But most devastated was Michael who, at one stroke, had lost his grandfather, father, best friend, soul-mate, mentor and life role model.

Michael knew his grandfather was a great man but he didn't know how great until, in his deceased father's stead, he joined his uncles at O'Meara and Co. the family's lawyers, for the will reading. Three generations of O'Meara – Seamus, Walter and Robert – were waiting for them, old Seamus first to speak. "Fergus McBride was the greatest man I ever knew," he said, his Irish brogue, like Fergus, impervious to even five decades in a foreign land. "Aye, he loved to dream and he loved to teach others to dream too. I remember I was digging holes for Paddie McNiff when one day, Fergus looked me in the eye and said, 'What's yer dream Seamus O'Meara?' I told him I wanted to be a lawyer."

Michael's Uncle Declan couldn't help himself, "And your dream came true, Mr O'Meara?" he said gesturing at the obvious affluence all around them.

"Aye lad, it came true alright, but without your old man, it would have been just another dream doomed never to become reality."

"What you mean?" Declan asked, sounding confused.

"It was Fergus who arranged for me to go to law school, paid all my costs and even gave my wife and me enough money to live. Through four years of law school he did that and boys, the 1920's weren't the 1960's! Your father did this for me when the rest of America was starving in a depression like had never been seen before or seen since. And you know what? He didn't just do it for me; there were others too, lots of 'em!!" His eyes filled up as he was speaking and by the end, tears were streaming down his face as he fixed his gaze on Pat and Declan. "Aye," he said, "Yer father was the greatest man I ever knew."

Fergus and Seamus O'Meara had obviously met many times to discuss the will and funeral. Fergus had left specific instructions for the service; the hymns and choruses, the music as people arrived and left and he'd also given one other instruction: he wanted Michael to read his favourite Bible passage, *Love*, the thirteenth chapter from the first book of Corinthians.

In many ways, it felt like as if he'd out-thought even death itself.

The family was well looked after, Michael inheriting twenty-five per cent of Cork Construction and over a quarter million in cash. But it was no substitute; he wanted, he needed, his Granddad. But he was gone.

A few days after the funeral, Michael left for New York not knowing it would be ten years before he returned. His life became one long party but his partying always ended the same way, with him fighting, his festering anger taking him in search of desperate situations as if pursuing a death wish.

He used girl after girl to fulfil his physical needs but never let any of them get close. His male friends always thought he was great fun until the next desperate situation he got involved in, involved them. Everyone said the same thing: that Michael would either end up dead or in jail.

And then, a brawl in Queens put him in hospital, courtesy of a stab wound to his lower back. In the next bed was a Vietnam vet, a former Marine Sergeant who obviously missed army-life like hell. Three mornings later, Michael walked gingerly to the phone booth in the hospital foyer. In his head was the one thought that'd dominated his thinking ever since his first conversation with Sergeant Pete Shapiro.

"Marm, sorry I've not called. Yeah, I'm fine. Marm, shush for a second. I phoned to say I'm gonna Vietnam. I've enlisted in the Marine Corps."

Two days after his nineteenth birthday Michael McBride boarded the plane for Southeast Asia. He knew he was running away, from both the pain and his destiny. But walking in the footsteps of a legend would have to wait awhile. For now, he had business with Charlie.

CHAPTER EIGHT:

Three days after the fight between McBride and Kingsbridge, Bleeding Dog Company were in northwest Thailand aboard a Chinook flying over a thick quilt of early morning mist, the celestial brightness broken by rugged mountain peaks. It was an awesome scene but Mother Nature had still more to offer. As they neared the LZ, the cloud suddenly cleared, the mountains looking awesomely huge, a tapestry of dozens of different shades of green with gallons of water cascading over majestic waterfalls down into the valleys below.

Two hours after putting down, the men set up camp on the foothills of Doi Khun Bong.

"It looks like Irish and Hollywood are over their spat Corporal," Miller said after he and Frankie separated themselves from the others.

"I ain't so sure Doug."

"Why?"

"I just got a feeling Kingsbridge won't let it go."

"You don't think he's learned his lesson?"

"Nah, he ain't the type to learn lessons."

"You don't rate him?"

"I rate him plenty Doug, as a soldier. But for all his bravado and film star-isms there's something not right; like he's hiding something."

"And McBride?"

"He's different; I reckon what you see is what you get with Irish."

"You think we should drop Kingsbridge?"

"I think it's too early to call. Let's see how things go up here in the mountains."

"I hope he comes through; replacements ain't easy to find, especially experienced radiomen. I mean there's so few troopers left out here now, it's not like we got a big pool to pluck 'em from."

In the event, their four weeks in the Thai mountains passed without incident. Miller was delighted. It had been gruelling, non-stop, but all his objectives had been met and exceeded and by way of a bonus, there'd not been as much as a harsh word between his two warring sons. At a team meeting the night before they were due to be picked-up, he verbalized a thought he'd had a hundred times over the previous four weeks.

"You guys are the real deal," he said like a proud father.

Frankie was pleased too but he didn't do "happy," so he just grunted.

McBride still hated Kingsbridge but he'd learned to control it better and keep it hidden. The chemistry was always going to be there but the fight at Ubon had gotten some of the venom out of his system. The four weeks had been easier than he thought, the men so busy there'd been no time to think about anything other than the immediate task at hand. He wasn't sure it would last, but he loved being a Bleeding Dog more than he hated Kingsbridge and although it didn't exactly equate to forgiveness, he didn't intend doing anything to jeopardize his place in the team.

Kingsbridge wasn't in the business of forgiving and forgetting either but he too, had learned from the fight at Ubon. He didn't like coming second; losing wasn't something he was used to. So as he lay on his back looking up at the stars, he was doing what he'd done every night for four weeks: plotting revenge. Night after night he'd wondered what his strategy would be and three nights earlier he found the chink he was looking for, proof that good things surely do come to those who wait. He'd known from the beating he'd taken at Ubon that revenge wasn't going to be toe-to-toe in hand-to-hand combat, so overhearing McBride share his fear of rats with Kong brought a smile to his face. It was a nugget of information he knew he could use.

And when the time came he wouldn't hesitate. He just hoped it'd be soon.

* * * * *

Next morning, it was time to wave goodbye to the Thai mountains. The men thought they'd be returning to Ubon but Miller had a surprise in store.

"You guys have earned yourselves a break."

"R & R Master Sergeant?" Kingsbridge said, immediately catching his drift.

"You got it pretty boy."

"Yessss!" said Kong excitedly, "We're off to Saigon!"

"No, it's not Saigon son. You're going to Sydney."

Amidst yelps of delight, only Frankie was quiet.

"What's up Corp?" Irish asked, "You don't fancy Sydney?"

"I'm a professional soldier son; I don't need R & R. And anyway, being banged up in Sydney with you psychos isn't my idea of taking it easy!"

R & R, rest and recuperation, was built into the tour of duty in 'Nam. Usually five days, a GI's one-year tour would be broken up with a jaunt to Vung Tau or China Beach inside Vietnam or if he was really lucky, to the more exotic out-of-country locations like Bangkok, Hawaii, Hong Kong, Penang, Taipei, Kuala Lumpur or Sydney. Unfortunately for Sydney, *it* drew the short straw.

The men were booked into the Buckingham Hotel, a fleapit of a place in Kings Cross, Sydney's Red Light district. They were on the street within half-hour of checking-in.

"Read your palm, tell you fortune?" an old gypsy woman shouted from an alcove alongside the entrance to a department store. As she spoke, she looked directly at Irish.

"Go on, let her tell your fortune," Kong said egging him on.

Irish had been brought up to scoff at fortune-telling and the like. "It's crap man," he said.

"Go on; see what she's got to say. Bet I can guess your immediate future better than her," Kong said suggestively. "Drink – fight – sex: and in that order!!"

The men laughed but Irish found himself strangely drawn to the old woman.

"Come on darling. Tell your fortune," she persisted, sensing he was her next client.

"How much?"

"Three dollars."

"American or Aussie?"

"Aussie," the old woman said, as Irish handed over his three bucks. "Gimme your hands," she said beckoning him to sit down.

Irish held out his hands, resting his elbows on the small table.

"Oooh!" she said mysteriously, staring intently at his palms. "You have the hands of Jesus."

"What you mean the hands of Jesus? What you talking about?"

"Your life-line goes from one side of your palm to the other," she said. "I've heard of hands like this but yours are the first I've seen. The line is said to flow as if creased by the nails of the crucifixion. You're a special young man, chosen for a purpose; you can run from it, but one day, it will catch up with you."

"What'd she say?" Kong asked.

"Load'a trash!" Irish exclaimed before adding, "Let me see your hands."

"What?"

"Just let me look at your hands," Irish repeated as Kong held out his open palms that showed a lifeline that was two distinct lines, one starting on the right, the other on the left, the two never merging.

"What's up?" said Frankie.

"Irish fancies himself as a palm-reader!" Kong said, poking fun.

"Let me see your hands Corp," Irish said, "And yours too Hollywood."

Both men's hands were exactly like Kong's; split lifelines.

Irish wasn't sure what it meant but he couldn't help wondering if Fergus had the same hands, the same life-line.

Three hours and several bars later, hands had become a distant thought as the men arrived at a club called the Wild Cat. Irish immediately clocked the latent hostility, the ambience anything but friendly.

"You sense it?" Kong asked.

"Felt it soon as we walked in," Irish said, turning to wink at one of the bouncers.

"What you talking about?" Frankie said, confused. "Am I missing something?"

"You mean you can't feel it?"

"Son, I been fighting Gooks too long. The night-club scene is like a different planet to me. Now what the hell is the problem?"

"We getting eyes Corp; someone wants a pop at us!" Irish replied excitedly.

"Whoever they are son, they must be crazy to wanna fight you!"

In the end, it was a stripper who used flaming torches in her routine that lit the fire. Wandering through the audience, she flicked her torch at Frankie who instinctively pulled the guy on his right, one of the bouncers, in front of him as a kind of shield.

The angry bouncer hurled a stream of abuse at Frankie.

"Woaah there!" Frankie said his hands up as if to say he didn't want any trouble.

The bouncer misinterpreted it as weakness and didn't even see the vicious neck punch coming. He hit the floor as if he'd been shot.

Irish was ecstatic. He'd always had a problem with bouncers who he always thought, believed they could take him. Given half a chance he loved to prove they couldn't.

Within seconds the place was chaos, the lights on, music stopped, the act on the stage frozen to the spot; every eye transfixed by the brutality of the violence.

It didn't last long, six bouncers no match for four Bleeding Dogs.

"Come on Corp, let's get out'a here," Irish said, pulling at Frankie's T-shirt.

Frankie was facedown on top of a doorman, his teeth sunk deep into his cheek. He let go his bite and stood to his feet looking like something out of a Dracula movie, blood trickling down his chin from both corners of his mouth.

"Bleeding Dogs six, Australia nil!!" Irish shouted as they took the stairs two-at-a-time.

But the war wasn't over; not yet at least.

The way things worked in Kings Cross was when trouble kicked-off, a coded call went out on the short wave radio system to all the other bars and clubs. So, like frenzied hyenas sensing a kill, bouncers from all over Kings Cross descended on the Wild Cat.

First through the door, Irish took the brunt of the initial assault, a baseball bat to the forehead opening up a two-inch vertical cut. Bouncers swarmed round him as he watched blood squirt from the wound as if in slow motion, all over the side of a white boxvan. In fights like this, and Irish had been in plenty, there were only two rules: don't go down and put every man you can out of the game permanently.

The bouncers thought their numerical superiority meant certain victory but within a minute the tide turned, bouncers strewn unconscious all over the street, many of them victims of the mighty Kong.

Irish had fought his way across the street trying to get to Kong when a heavily built South Sea Islander type, obviously martial-art trained, snarled, "I'm gonna kill you mate!" in a heavy Aussie accent.

It was a bizarre sight, something of a *coup de grâce* for the hundreds of people gathered all the way across the wide street both sides of the Wild Cat. In one corner you had the karate kid, all twirls and high kicks, and in the other, the prize-fighting pugilist, hands held high, feet beautifully light and balanced.

"Yearghhhhh!" screeched the Aussie, pirouetting, his swinging right foot aimed at Irish's head. Cool as ice, Irish swayed back, let the man's foot pass his nose, and smashed a thundering punch into the middle of the South Sea Islander's forehead. He dropped like a stone, his head crashing into the corner of the sidewalk as he fell.

As he straightened up to see if there were any more takers, Irish felt a tap on his shoulder. It was a military policeman, gun in hand, blowing excitedly on his whistle.

The battle of the Wild Cat and the war for Kings Cross was over.

The Dogs were taken off to the Prince of Wales Hospital in Randwick in a security wagon.

"You sorted them vermin tonight boys!" one of the MP's said, an American. "People die out here and it's always the same MO: body in an alley beaten to hell. It's those short-wave radios, gives 'em numerical advantage every time. Didn't do them much good this time though did it?"

The men didn't comment.

"What unit you guys from?" the MP said, desperate to get a conversation going.

Again, there was no reply.

"Their injured are going to St. Vincent's," he said, seemingly unperturbed that he was the only one talking. "I just heard there's like twenty needing treatment and two or three are really smashed up. We hate 'em anyway, bleedin' piranhas."

At the hospital, the doctors had seen it all before.

"Thanks Doc; don't worry about a jab, just stitch it," Frankie said, grimacing in pain. Just below his bottom lip there was a gaping inch-and-a-half gash through which his bottom teeth were visible even without him opening his mouth.

Sixteen stitches later, eleven to Frankie, five to Irish, the men were ready to leave.

"Just a minute," one of the MP's said, moving towards the door, "One of the doormen looks like he won't make it. You have to stay in custody."

Frankie's ice cold stare threatened to drill a hole in the MP. "Son, you better call every pal you got 'coz believe you me, you gonna need all the support you can get. Now, if you don't mind, we're going back to our hotel."

The MP's Adam's apple danced a jig up and down his throat, his anxious glances at his colleagues confirming that if he wanted a set-to with these men-with-no-names, he was on his own. "OK," he said, defeated, "What hotel you staying at?"

"We're at the Buckingham but son, be careful how you knock the door."

Two hours later, the phone rang. It was Master Sergeant Doug Miller.

"What the hell's happening Corporal? I got O'Donnell spitting blood at me down the phone?" he said, every other word a swearword.

"Sorry Doug, we took some enemy fire."

"Any casualties?"

"Only on their side."

"Yeah, I heard; the boy's on life support. There'll be hell to pay if he doesn't make it."

"Will it hold us up Sir?"

"Just keep your head down till I call."

It was fifteen minutes before Miller called back.

"Good news Corporal. The boy's breathing again and I got you a lift home, tomorrow 15:00."

The news relieved the tension, Hollywood blurting, "We gotta get laid before we go back to 'Nam. I'll get us a girl or two."

Twenty minutes later he was back with two girls, one a stunning blonde the other dark-skinned, dark haired.

"This is King Kong," he said suggestively as the door opened, "The one I told you about."

The girls giggled.

Two drinks later the blonde started to realise that four randy soldiers who hadn't seen a woman for months had serious potential to get out of hand.

"I'm going," she said to her friend.

"Get back on the bed you teasing bitch!" Hollywood snarled loudly, his sudden sharp tone frightening the girls and surprising the others.

"If the girl doesn't wanna stay, let her go," Irish snapped, beating Frankie to it by a millisecond.

"Go on off you go," he said holding the door open.

The other girl, the dark one, hesitated.

"You going?"

"No," she said quietly, "I'll stay."

"Whoopee!!" Hollywood exclaimed.

Though neither Irish nor Frankie thought they'd ever get involved in a group sex situation, their loins got the better of them. Kong had pulled the inter-connecting door off its hinges and the grunts drew them through the open doorway like bees to pollen.

Hollywood was insatiable. Three times the others were woken; forced to listen to his grunts, thrusts and climactic screams. Irish covered his head with a pillow. It blocked out much of what was coming at him from the outside but he could do nothing about his grandfather's voice on the inside.

"Why weren't yer listening lad? What did I tell yer? Didn't I say never open a door you'd rather stay shut?"

It started the second his lust broke and had been relentless ever since. He knew what he'd done. He'd participated in a gang bang, sharing a girl with a man he hated. By any stretch of the imagination it was a bad choice, even if the girl was up for it. And Hollywood's orgasmic groans made it worse, each "oooooh" and "aarrrrrrrr" drifting through the open doorway, carrying with it an unmissable note of triumph, victory even.

During the taxi ride to the airport, Irish gazed uneasily out the window knowing he was carrying more baggage than just his kitbag. He might not have understood the full implications but something deep inside him told him that he, Frankie and Kong had somehow, become victims of Rudi Kingsbridge.

He was right; they had. And what's more, a precedent had been set.

CHAPTER NINE:

Only Frankie had been to Tay Ninh before.

As he glimpsed the mystical Nui Ba Den through the open door of the Huey, he nodded, "Black Lady Mountain: our home for the next few months." Despite the chopper still being more than fifteen miles away, the mountain dominated the landscape, overlooking the province like a pointed hat rising out the flat characterless plains all round it.

Just ten miles from the Cambodian border, the three-and-a-half thousand feet high mountain also doubled as a military base.

Two days after settling into their billet, Miller called Frankie to his office.

"The Chief's sent through orders for our first mission."

"What we got Doug?"

Twelve days later, on December 1st 1971, the four-word question had led to the assassination of Ky Dinh Nhu, a blood-thirsty rising star within the Khmer Rouge, as well as the death of sixty-five militia and the destruction of a massive KR munitions dump. And all despite Nixon's assurances to Congress that no American soldier would set foot in either Cambodia or Laos after the spring of '71!!

It was why the Dogs had to be the best of the best; invisible enforcers who left the enemy chasing nothing but shadows.

"Great job Corporal; the country's proud of you," Miller said when debrief was over.

Frankie doubted it; he'd seen the TV coverage. But he didn't care anyway. He needed some shut-eye and hoped his demons would let him sleep.

MACV-SOG was unlike any other element of the military. Although missions were always hazardous, they were usually of short duration, three to five days, with each team conducting only one mission a month. This afforded units more time to mentally and physically prepare and ensured they'd be fresh, highly trained, and most of all, deadly.

It meant the Bleeding Dogs were looking at five days down-time.

Frankie thought it was too long but it was Miller's call.

Aside from throwing a football around, one of their favourite ways of passing time was poker.

Irish insisted on playing wearing his M-1 helmet. By the start of the third or fourth session, he'd initiated a kind of ritual, dramatically taking the helmet off the shelf above his bed, the others banging the tables and chanting as he did so.

At the start of the evening session on the third day, Irish reached for his helmet, his fingers curling under the rim, sinking into something soft and moist. He knew something was wrong and slowly lifted the helmet to see what it was. Someone had dumped on a piece of card, put it on the shelf and carefully placed the helmet over the top.

Irish checked the webbing, saw it was clean, put the helmet on and sat down.

"No problem," he said as he looked down at his fingers smeared with excrement. With Kingsbridge ready to deal the cards, he leaned forward and rubbed his open hand all over his cheek.

"Are we playing tonight or what?" Kingsbridge said his reaction as cool as McBride's.

But everyone knew it wasn't over.

In both the morning and afternoon sessions the following day, Irish had been more careful as he'd reached for his helmet. But there'd been no repeat.

Forty bucks up on the day, he was keen to get the evening session underway. Just as he reached his helmet, Frankie declared, "I'm out. I'm sick of poker." It distracted Irish, his eyes on Frankie as his fingers curled under the rim of the M1. Instantly, he knew he'd been caught out a second time.

But when his eyes returned to the helmet, he had the shock of his life; looking straight at him was a huge brown rat.

Flinching backwards, he screamed as the rat reared up onto its back legs before leaping down onto the bed and heading off towards the room's darkest corner. He didn't make it. Irish blasted him with six or seven deafening rounds from his CAR-15, the air immediately thick and misty with a mix of rat blood and gunpowder.

"This time you die faggot!" he screamed before tossing the gun onto his bed and flinging himself across the room. Hollywood stepped inside the lunge and caught him with a heavy right hander that sent him crashing into the hut wall. But he didn't follow-up. Instead, he pulled his knife. Instinctively, up went Irish's hands: the bare-knuckle prize-fighter face-to-face with his knife-wielding enemy.

Hollywood shimmied forward whispering, "I'm gonna cut your heart out Mick."

But Irish didn't do intimidation. "It ain't over till it's over, faggot," he growled before dummying with his left and catching his rival with a right cross that broke his nose for the second time in two short months. But Kingsbridge didn't go down. Instead he lashed out with the knife, catching McBride on his lower left triceps, his long-sleeved T-shirt immediately awash with blood.

"Drop the blade film star!!" boomed the unmistakable voice of Master Sergeant Doug Miller who, like the rest of the camp, had been alerted by the gunfire.

"McBride, hospital, Kingsbridge, go for a walk; Corporal, my office, five minutes!"

Though all three men said, "Yes Sir, Master Sergeant, Sir," it was with less conviction than ever before.

* * * * *

"What the hell was that all about?" Miller said to Frankie, his tone more accusative than he'd intended. "Why didn't you take the action I did?"

"I didn't see it as my problem Master Sergeant."

"So, whose problem is it? Snow White's?"

"Don't know no Snow White."

"Corporal, do I detect an issue between us?"

"Yes Sir, Master Sergeant, Sir."

"So let me ask you again, whose problem is it?"

"Yours."

"Mine? Why is it my problem?"

"Either you command Bleeding Dog Company or I do. As we just seen, it ain't working as it is. I told you five days on our butts was too long; trouble as certain as the next friggin' downpour in this bitch country. You over-ruled me and we're picking up the pieces because of it. So yes Master Sergeant, it's your problem. You made it; you fix it."

"Watch your tone, Corporal, or we really will have a problem."

"Yes Sir, Master Sergeant, Sir."

"So where does this leave us Corporal?"

"Sir, if things stay as they are, I don't give a crap. If you want me to lead these boys you gonna have to get out the way!"

"Corporal, watch your tone!!"

But despite the warning signs, Frankie wasn't going to back off. "It's decision time Doug. If you wanna pull rank on me, that's fine, but you'll have to lead these misfits yourself."

Miller was amazed how badly he'd misjudged the situation. Unlike Frankie, he was aware the orders for their next mission had arrived from Kontum that morning; Christmas may have been approaching but there was no festive spirit, just a sense that Bleeding Dog Company was staring into the abyss, on the edge of disintegration.

"OK Corporal, let's sleep on it and see how we feel in the morning."

It was a long night, only two-fifths of Bleeding Dog Company sleeping well.

Frankie had what he thought was his best night's sleep in six long years in Vietnam, while Kong slept as he always slept, without a care in the world.

For the others though, it was a different story.

Kingsbridge spent the night outside under the stars thinking his hatred for McBride had probably cost him his place in the team and nothing could be worth giving up his Bleeding Dog status. Or could it? As the droning ache in his nose exported pain to all parts of his face he remembered McBride's terrified look as the rat winked at him from under his helmet. Then he remembered his rival bleeding and realised it had been worth it. If he was finished as a Bleeding Dog then at least he'd ended on a high.

As Irish thought it through in the hospital, he too reached the conclusion the Bleeding Dogs were probably over. He didn't think he'd be shown the door but he was pretty certain Miller and Frankie would send Hollywood packing. And that really would be a disaster, because he'd have to traipse all over Vietnam looking for Kingsbridge so they could finally resolve their conflict. It'd been a long time, but his "Lord, let me have him" was the closest he'd been to praying in the three years since his Granddad died.

Doug Miller had never considered himself a religious or praying man but like McBride, he knew he needed help. When O'Donnell gave orders they had to be carried out, always, or someone paid big-time. As he scanned the pages, he knew he was in trouble. "Target: High-ranking NVA Commander. Location: Southern Laos. Time-scale: 2/3 weeks." The worse bit was the heading, "Bleeding Dog Company – Next Assignment," because Miller doubted whether Bleeding Dog Company even existed anymore.

And how was he going to explain that to O'Donnell who in turn, would have to explain it on up the line to DC?

"I've thought about the leadership issue," he said next morning, hoping for a miracle, "And I'm prepared to step back and let you run the show."

"You sure?" Frankie asked, surprised.

"Yeah, I'm sure. You get final call on all operational matters with me acting as advisor, providing logistical back-up and liaising with O'Donnell and on to DC. How's that sound?"

"Sounds good Doug," Frankie replied, suddenly realising he was still leader of Bleeding Dog Company.

"OK," said Miller, "What we doing with Irish and Hollywood? We dropping 'em?"

"No Doug, no personnel changes; there isn't time," Frankie replied nodding at the orders. He'd seen the words, "Bleeding Dog Company – Next Assignment," and wondered if Miller intended briefing him. "We talking about that now?" he asked.

"No," Miller replied abruptly, "We'll do it after lunch."

He needed time to compose himself, time to get over his relief that Bleeding Dog Company was back from the dead.

CHAPTER TEN:

General Luong Thau had been fighting all his life.

Born in Ha Tinh Province, his earliest memory was sharpening stakes for the Viet Minh's booby traps against the Japanese occupiers of World War Two. By the time he was twelve he was a seasoned guerrilla fighter and at sixteen he helped rout the French at Dien Bien Phu in 1954. It brought him to the attention of General Giap, commander-in-chief of the People's Army of Vietnam. Three years later, Giap promoted him to Major and appointed him to Group

559, a transportation and logistical unit charged with creating the Ho Chi Minh Trail, a supply line from North Vietnam to Vietcong paramilitary units in the south of the country. Giap needed to find a way round the demilitarized zone, the DMZ, which was created by the Geneva Accords after the French left. The DMZ divided Vietnam into two, North and South, and Major Luong Thau was personally responsible for the section that passed through Southern Laos and north-eastern Cambodia.

Known to indigenous Laotians and Cambodians as the *Raging Bull*, the ruthlessly efficient young Major delivered a super-highway that ensured North Vietnamese sympathisers in the South wouldn't lack for food, training, weapons or encouragement. It earned him further promotions and Giap never forgot.

After the 1968 Tet Offensive, Giap reassigned him to Laos where he ran the south of the country like a medieval fiefdom. His power base was an NVA encampment three miles east of Ban Palong, close to the Ho Chi Minh Trail he helped create.

The General was a workaholic, sixteen hours-a-day, six days-a-week, his day off dedicated to his two vices, Sea Horse whiskey, famed for its aphrodisiac properties, and prostitutes.

For four hours every Tuesday afternoon, the brothel in Ban Palong was sealed off, General Luong Thau its only patron.

"How good's the Intel Master Sergeant," McBride asked as Miller briefed the team

"As good as it gets! We got two sources, one in Ban Palong, the other in the Camp, and neither knows the other exists. They both corroborate the General's movements, the timing and the fact he travels in a three vehicle convoy. He's definitely a man of routine."

"Yeah," said Kong, "And routine's what's gonna get him killed!"

Miller nodded. "OK guys, here's the deal. We go in Monday night. Early Tuesday, we select an ambush site between the camp and Ban Palong and we observe and confirm that he really is a man of routine, just like Intel says he is. Then – while he's surrounded by his geisha's – we get back on the bus and come home. This time-out is strictly recon only and it's vital that both insertion and extraction preserve maximum secrecy. The following Tuesday will be the real deal and we don't want anyone expecting us to ring the doorbell!"

The NVA had enjoyed several years of sanctuary in Cambodia and Laos. With the exception of the occasional threat from SOG teams and the one and only invasion into Cambodia in the spring of 1970, they'd had a free rein. The political fall-out from the invasion in the U.S. meant the NVA had virtually discounted a repeat as a non-option. So, free from the threat of attack by ground troops, they established major hospitals, training centres, and rest and recuperation areas all over Southern Laos, the entire operation under the command of General Luong Thau.

The NVA camp was situated twenty miles northeast of the Bolovens Plateau, close to where the Ho Chi Minh Trail not only moved southwards but also swept east into Vietnam.

Seven miles to the southeast, the Bleeding Dogs were on the ground, moving slowly but every step taking them closer to the target zone. Their timing was perfect, ghosting into position just as the first light of Tuesday morning began to extinguish the clinging claustrophobic darkness. As they edged nearer the lip of the mountain, the scope of their vision allowed them to see further and further down into the valley below.

"Wow, what a view!" Irish said, breaking a long silence.

"It's unbelievable man!" Kong replied, just as awestruck.

The mountain on the opposite side of the valley was five or six hundred feet lower, allowing them to take in the view to the north beyond. And what a view it was: thirty maybe forty miles of mountain-top after mountain-top all the way to the Laotian side of the Central Highlands. Like icing on a cake, patches of white-as-snow mist and puffy cloud clung to the breathtaking scenery, somehow adding a sense of mystique and aura to the amazing scene. And as every second passed, the sun claimed a bigger and bigger part in proceedings, its influence increasing as the light continuously transformed the dull deep greens to something several shades brighter.

All four men had their field glasses out but only Frankie was looking down into the valley.

"You boys make great tourists!" he snapped. "Look, there's the camp, cut into the mountain!"

"Yeah, and look at the caves," said Kong, the first to react. "It's no wonder the B52's haven't been able to take it out!"

But Frankie had already moved on. He was busy tracking the road to Ban Palong, looking for an ambush site. "That's where we'll try first, that ravine; see, the road's all windy and that'll mean they won't be going fast. The other good thing is it's nearer Ban Palong than it is the camp so, it'll give us a bit more time for the getaway."

Two hours later, the men were on the Ban Palong side of the ravine.

Frankie knew exactly what he was looking for. "Me and Kong will walk the road and pick us a site. McBride, you go high on the left side and select yourself a sniper position looking down at the target from the front. Kingsbridge, you go up the right side and find a site where you can observe the vehicles entering the ravine and fire down from their rear once they're in the zone."

The ravine was about thirty to forty yards wide and about a hundred and fifty feet high, the left side sheer, the right less so.

It took less than fifteen minutes for Frankie and Kong to select the kill zone.

"Here we are Corp; this is perfect," Kong said confidently. "The General always travels in the second car. We'll use a pressure device so that the first car activates the mines and the second detonates them. And just in case, we'll run a command wire!"

Kong was in his element. If explosives were his degree course, ambush was his favourite module. "When they hear the explosion, the first vehicle will screech to a halt, about there," he said pointing. "Corp, if you've got an M60 this side of the ravine, say, on that ledge by those rocks, my guess is they'll seek refuge in that ditch over there. So, we'll give 'em a nasty surprise, and claymore the whole nine yards! I'll wire them in series and use a thirty second timer, so that when one of the Gooks puts his foot in the wrong place, it'll trip the whole lot."

"Yeah," said Frankie, "And with McBride and Kingsbridge picking off the runners there'll be no escape. Talking of them two, I wonder if they're in position yet."

Irish was a hundred and fifty feet above Kong and Frankie and had been watching them recce the ambush site for a full five minutes when suddenly, a thought dropped into his mind.

"Where are you, faggot?" he said to himself quietly, searching the opposite side of the ravine through his telescopic sights.

On his third or fourth sweep, his eye caught something that made him go cold all over. As he doubled back to check-out what he thought he'd seen, his M14 came to a stop on the man they called "Hollywood." But he wasn't looking down into the ravine as he'd expected. Instead, he was in behind his CAR-15, eye to its telescopic lens, looking straight at him! It was a bizarre moment; both men gazing down their rifles able to reach into the very soul of the other, each knowing they had the power to end the other's life.

But Kingsbridge had beaten him to the position. "Bang, you're dead" he said, miming the words exaggeratedly so Irish would know exactly what he was saying. Then he smiled coldly, a look of unmistakable triumph flashing across his face. Irish was seething but he knew he'd come second and revenge would have to wait. The best he could do was mime a four-letter word response followed by the word "faggot."

Before he could do more, he heard Frankie whistle. The Corporal wanted him to move twenty yards down the ravine and Kingsbridge to shift fifty yards in the opposite direction. He also indicated that he wanted all four men to assemble at Hollywood's position so they could observe the General's convoy make its Tuesday afternoon pilgrimage to Ban Palong's house of ill repute.

"Here they come; right on cue," Frankie said as three vehicles, thirty yards apart, came into view on the windy road that led into the far end of the ravine. Front and back were two open jeeps with four soldiers in each, one manning a mounted machine gun, the other three hugging AK 47's. The middle vehicle was a staff car. Up front, an obviously armed soldier sat alongside the driver. Alone in the back seat was the target, General Luong Thau.

As the first jeep passed the rock Kong had taken as his marker, the big black man quietly said "Click." Two seconds later it was the staff car's turn to pass the marker. "Boom!" said Kong.

The General was as good as dead.

* * * * *

Seven days later, 21st December, the men were in position.

Everything had been planned meticulously, down to the minutest detail. They all knew their role in what was a team mission and all perversely, were looking forward to it.

Kingsbridge spotted the convoy first, gave the signal to McBride on the other side of the ravine who, in turn, signalled Kong and Frankie who were hiding at the side of the road on Kingsbridge's side of the ravine. Kong was down at road level while Frankie was in behind an M60 up on a rocky ledge, ten maybe twelve feet above the road.

Two or three minutes later, the first vehicle drove over the line of mines as Kong tensed at the audible "Click" and braced himself for the explosion. Boom!! Then it all went off. The two jeeps skidded to a halt as Frankie and Kingsbridge opened up with M60's. In an effort to escape Frankie's fire, the four soldiers in the first jeep dived into the far ditch, exactly as Kong had predicted. In case the explosion hadn't killed the General's driver and front seat passenger, McBride put several rounds into each man. At the same time, Kingsbridge sprayed the rear jeep with M60 fire, the height of the ravine wall too high to allow the machine gunner to even return fire. And then the claymores exploded with a deadly thud, bodies hurled into the air like rag dolls.

As suddenly as it started, it finished.

Kong appeared from behind the rock with pistol drawn. As his three colleagues scanned the dead soldiers for any sign of life, he carefully approached the staff car and opened the rear door. The General was barely conscious on the back seat, blood streaming from a head wound, his eyes the only part of him to move. He looked at Kong, knowing certain death was the only possible outcome.

"Merry Christmas," Kong said coldly, before putting three rounds into the side of his head. He then pulled a photograph from his thigh pocket, held it alongside the dead General and added, "It's him," before doing a thumbs-up to McBride who was crouching over the rim of the ravine.

It was job done.

Frankie was already on the road running towards Ban Palong, McBride doing likewise his side of the ravine. Kingsbridge was on the radio to Black Lady Mountain, making sure the choppers were in the air. It wasn't good news but he had no time to dwell on it; he had to get to the assembly point and there was no time to lose. The NVA camp was only two miles away and the Dogs estimated there'd be at least fifty troops constantly on alert, a kind of rapid response reaction unit. They were almost certainly already on their way.

By the time the team had reassembled, they could hear the trucks rumbling towards the ravine.

"The jeeps will hold them up. They'll be on foot like us so let's get going," Frankie snapped.

"Corp, there's a problem," Kingsbridge said vacantly, his eyes all spaced-out.

"What problem?"

"Black Lady's covered in fog so they're sending us a Huey from Kontum."

"Yeah? So?"

"The Huey's coming alone Corp; there's no Cobra escort available."

Frankie didn't answer. He knew there wasn't time. He also knew that while they had a mile-and-a-half start on the NVA, they'd pick-up their trail virtually immediately.

For fifteen minutes they ran flat-out towards the pick-up point which was close to the top of a mountain marked as *+1437* on their maps.

Half-way up, a gap opened up between Kong and the others. The black man thought he'd stop to see how they were coping with the gradient. As he turned, he suddenly went ice cold. Beyond the trio of Bleeding Dogs, a mile away in the distance, he could see a hundred or so NVA in hot pursuit.

As Irish, Frankie, and Hollywood reached him in turn, they too, turned to see what he'd seen.

"Get me Kontum on the blower," Frankie snapped at Kingsbridge.

When he was done, he addressed his team. "The chopper'll be here in ten minutes. By then, the NVA will be on top of us. Kingsbridge and I will go up another half-mile and put some smoke up for the chopper. You two stay here, wait for the Gooks to come in range, let rip with all you got then leg it to the chopper. We'll cover you from the Huey."

There was no dissent, not even a look that hinted there could be a problem. They all knew it was Frankie's call.

"OK, it's me and you white boy," Kong said with a smirk, firing his CAR-15 till the magazine emptied. "Bet I beat you to the chopper."

"In your dreams . . ." Irish said turning to make off up the mountain.

As the Huey's skids descended to within a foot or two of the ground, Frankie thought he'd die from the sense of relief and fatigue that threatened to overwhelm him.

"It's good to see you," he said to the door-gunner who didn't look old enough to shave.

The young private didn't reply. He was lost in his work, screaming and cursing above the loud rat-tat-tat of his M60.

Kingsbridge climbed in first, he and Frankie turning to see Kong and McBride running for their lives, the pack of chasing NVA no more than two or three hundred yards behind them.

"Are they gonna make it Corp?" Kingsbridge asked sounding all goofy, Frankie noting the crazed look in his eyes.

"They'll make it," he replied, feeling a lot less confident than he sounded. "They're so competitive I bet they're racing one another!"

They were.

Irish was doing everything he could to stay with his friend but the big powerful black man had eased fifteen yards in front. Behind them, the hundred or so NVA were running hard too, their pursuit interrupted only by occasional stops to aim some AK47 gunfire at their prey.

As Kong reached the chopper his first thought was that he'd won, the second, how much had he won by? Hearing Frankie scream "McBride's down," cut short his dreams of Olympic gold. He turned to see Irish back on his feet, hobbling, as the NVA closed in with every step. He reached into the Huey grabbed Frankie's CAR-15 and turned to go back for his friend.

Without a gun, Frankie could do nothing save sit back in his seat and watch the drama unfold. Kong was running back towards McBride, the door-gunner giving it everything he had and Kingsbridge blasting away too. But then something sinister happened, perhaps the most sinister thing he'd ever seen; he noticed Hollywood lower his CAR-15 down and slightly to the left before letting off a burst of ten maybe twelve rounds. It was a subtle adjustment but a definite adjustment nonetheless.

Instinctively, he barked "Hey Kingsbridge!!"

Hollywood turned towards his Corporal, his face vacant, like as if there was no-one at home.

"Sit down! Gimme your weapon!!"

Frankie half expected to see McBride dead on the ground with Sanders kneeling over him. But the mighty Kong had Irish over his shoulders, just like at Ubon, making good pace towards the Huey.

The pilot gunned the engine ready for the getaway.

Kong tossed Irish in through the Huey's open door, the door-gunner screaming, "Go! Go!"

With his engines roaring, the pilot spun the chopper to the right away from the chasing pack and suddenly they were thirty, forty feet in the air, the NVA – still firing their AK47's – getting smaller and less threatening by the second.

The corporate feeling was one of relief but Frankie felt as if he'd crashed into a brick wall, more there in body than mind. Already hurtling into his latest bout of dark depression, he was fighting a war in his head. Had he seen what he thought he'd seen? Or was he just so tired he'd misinterpreted something amid the pandemonium and adrenalin?

As he looked across the Huey at Kingsbridge, he could see there'd been no mistake.

The eyes said it all: told him he'd called it right. Kingsbridge looked a man capable of anything, even shooting a fellow team member trying to escape the enemy.

Had Frankie been aware of Rudi Kingsbridge's roots, he would've known such a scenario wasn't just feasible, it was more than probable.

Why? Because he couldn't help himself; it was in his genes.

CHAPTER ELEVEN:

To truly understand a man, you have to understand his past, understand what and who has gone before him.

When Rudi Kingsbridge entered the world on March 13th 1949 his mother, Hollywood actress Marlene Moorer, was face up on the bed screaming in agony. His father, high-flying banker Jordan Kingsbridge, was face up on the bed too, the bed of Sarah Hooper, the prostitute he'd secretly shared with his own father for the previous fifteen years.

It wasn't exactly happy families but the Kingsbridge dynasty was rotten to the core: built on murder, corruption, deceit, adultery, bribery, extortion and extreme violence.

It all began when Rudi's great-great-grandfather Jacob Schmidt, founder of the dynasty, arrived from Germany in the early 1850's. Jacob was full of hate. He hated his parents, hated the way his mother called him *Yackob*, hated that his father didn't talk at all. He hated the way they were always exhausted, hated Sundays. He hated the Lutheran church he was forced to attend morning and night, hated the unsmiling congregation and hated God who he held responsible for it all.

His parents never married and though it stayed hidden because no-one ever asked to see a license, it didn't change the fact their only child was what he was: illegitimate. Later in life, others would often use the "B" word to describe both the person and character of Jacob Schmidt. It was a description that followed him everywhere. It also happened to be accurate.

With a friend called William Bruckner, he started Michigan Trading, selling wares door-to-door throughout Chicago's South Side. It not only made money but also allowed handsome Jacob, a serial womanizer, to indulge himself with stay-at-home wives while their husbands were at work.

Business soared after meeting Hymie Goldstein, a wide-eyed Jew-boy with all the answers, his unimpressive five feet one belying the brutality of his ambition. Hymie was a thief and Michigan Trading became his key fencing operation. William wasn't so sure but Jacob didn't care. He was pursuing the American dream. It was what made him tick, his motivation from the age of nine.

For most, the 1871 Great Fire of Chicago was a disaster. For Jacob, it was a launch pad. He'd been with one of his regulars, an Irish woman, the night it started. The flames sparked a thought: "Where's William?" It wasn't that he cared; he'd just seen an opportunity.

As William left his house and headed east to the safety of the Lake Michigan shoreline, he heard a voice call out from the blackness between two houses close to his home.

"Help me, help me . . ."

It could've been his helpful nature or it could've been that he'd detected something familiar about the voice. Either way, it didn't matter. He took a thundering smash to the head so powerful it caved his skull in, death as instant as it was unexpected. The assailant was Jacob Schmidt, the opportunity to cease having to divide every net profit by two proving impossible to resist.

As Jacob walked away carrying William's leather bag, he couldn't help think how tragic that his friend and business partner should perish in Chicago's worst ever fire. In the event, over three hundred lost their lives and more than a hundred thousand lost their homes. Chicago was decimated but Jacob Schmidt felt lucky. He was. Miraculously, both his offices were untouched by the blaze and when he added the cash in William's holdall and the contents of both office safes to his own cash reserves, it totalled over twelve thousand dollars.

He also had an idea but first stop was lawyer, Jermaine Bayoux.

"You get stung in the fire Jacob?" the lawyer said, supping Jim Beam direct from the bottle.

"Stung? I lost everything! My offices were looted and worse still, my partner and best friend, William . . ."

"William's dead?!!"

"Yes, burnt to death in his home!" Jacob said lifting his hand to wipe away a tear.

Half-hour later, Jacob signed papers winding up Michigan Trading and incorporating Kingsbridge Trading – the name came from "the King's Bridge," where he'd rested up the night of the fire. He was the sole shareholder. When it was all done and he was back out on the street, he couldn't wait to congratulate himself. "If ever I couldn't make business work," he said smugly, "I could always get a job on the stage, in theatre. I'd be brilliant at that too!"

Michigan Trading's demise meant William's fifty per cent shareholding and more importantly, his family's rights to it, was now as groundless as it was worthless. Kingsbridge Trading had been born with a true working capital of twelve thousand dollars, more than half William's. But only Jacob knew. "Thanks William, I appreciate all you done for me," he said out loud before adding, "Loser!!" as a kind of one-word epitaph. He was smiling as he walked.

It was while sat under the Kings Bridge that Jacob got his idea. With thousands homeless, he reckoned on building cheap, quick-to-erect, prefabricated homes and thought the City's housing department would bite his hand off. After some astutely perceptive bribery, they did.

Twelve months and a hundred thousand homes later, Jacob was living his dream.

He passed his first million by 1876 and his second, four years later.

When he met William Le Baron Jenney he was intrigued, the architect convinced he could build buildings with more floors than ever before. Jacob sensed both a money-making opportunity and history unfolding. He wanted in. But he wasn't alone; he had competition.

For the first time in a decade, bribery got him nowhere; so he turned to Hymie Goldstein who'd become one of the most feared men in Chicago's north side.

Two professional hit-men visited the competition, their instructions to make it messy. They did.

There was no guilt or conscience; Jacob caring only that it was him who signed the contract not the competition. Three years later, he attended the lavish reception to officially open the world's first skyscraper. As he stepped from his carriage onto the sidewalk, he heard someone call his name. Chantalle D'Arcy looked stunning, Jacob imagining taking her right there, right then, the thought of the crowd gazing on open-mouthed just adding to the fantasy. A decade earlier, she was married to an Army Major but it didn't stop her throwing herself at Jacob throughout a five-year affair that ended when she wrote to say the Army was relocating her husband to St. Louis. Ten years later, she was ready to explain.

"I'm sorry if I hurt you Jacob, by leaving I mean."

She needn't have worried, but he was curious. "Well why did you leave so suddenly?"

"I was pregnant!"

"You have a child?"

"Yes, a son. His name's Joseph; he'll be ten next month."

Jacob didn't make the connection.

"He's *yours*, Jacob. Joseph is *your* son. You're his father!"

"How can you be sure? You've had loads of men. How'd you know he's not the Major's?"

"I've always known he's yours; he's the absolute image of you."

The boy's face said it all; the dark hair, dark brown eyes, the longish straight nose and feminine full-lipped mouth, all pointed the same way.

"He's so handsome," Jacob said, "He must be mine."

Six months later, Jacob and Chantalle wed; Joseph, their best man, delighted the marriage brought closure to his illegitimate status.

Jacob had a family home built in Lake Forest, on a two hundred acre plot that looked out over Lake Michigan. It was modelled on a French Chateau and to his wife's delight, he called it Chateau Chantalle.

Father and son became inseparable, Jacob allowing Joseph to have whatever he wanted as long as he could put up a lucid argument as to why he wanted it.

"Most people are born losers Joseph, but not you," father said to son. "When you see what you want, just go get it. Keep no conscience; conscience is for losers."

Born into a world created by Jacob Schmidt, Joseph, like the generations to follow, never had a chance.

Despite being turned down at interview, Joseph was the first of the family to go to Harvard, one call to Hymie Goldstein ensuring a hasty re-evaluation by the admissions department.

At Harvard, Joseph met Mary-Lou Pender, daughter to the Pender steel family from Detroit. He'd claimed her virginity just the second time they were together but what she didn't realise was that he was having similar encounters with a half-dozen other willing females and although they were all daughters of fat-cat daddies, none were heiresses to the kind of fortune Mary-Lou was. It was what won her the race.

As they stood at the altar, Mary-Lou was already five months pregnant.

Little Bobby Schmidt was six years old when the family decided to buy up hundreds of the city's liquor licenses. It was a time when the "Huns," German-Americans, were accused of driving the liquor trade. Joseph suggested a change of family name, to Kingsbridge, and oversaw a campaign to turn the family into philanthropists, though theirs was a brand of philanthropy that wasn't exactly noble, a means to an end more than anything else. But it gave them what they wanted. They were strictly non-stick; the all-American Kingsbridge family, numbered among Chicago's finest.

The liquor business brought the family into daily contact with the criminal classes and kick-started three decades involvement with the Chicago underworld. Kingsbridge clientele read like a *Who's Who?* of the Chicago crime scene: Big Jim Colossimo, Johnny Torio, Al Capone, Dion O'Banion, John Dillinger, Dutch Schultz, Bugsy Moran and Machine Gun Kelly. All became national icons, sharing two things in common: a thirst for violence and Kingsbridge finance.

Jacob would've been thrilled but he missed most of it. Within a year of Joseph assuming the reins in 1917, both his mother and father were dead. Chantalle passed away quietly but Jacob wasn't so lucky. Four months after being diagnosed with throat cancer, he died an agonizing death, a pitiful figure weighing less than sixty pounds. When the end came, father and son were alone, Joseph straining to hear his last words. "Remember, the world's full of bastards," he whispered, grimacing in pain as the words left his lips. "The trick is, be a bigger bastard than they are. Look after Bobby." It was Jacob Schmidt's legacy to his blood-line; being a bastard a matter of both birthright and destiny.

Teenage Bobby loved the gangster scene but most of all he loved the hookers. His favourite was Katie Spearman. She ended up bearing him a son, Jordan, and two years later, becoming his wife, albeit a wife he cheated on at least twice-a-week for the rest of his life.

Young Jordan Kingsbridge may have despised his father but on two things they were one and the same, their handsome, almost regal good looks and their love of prostitutes.

Jordan quickly worked out what his father was up to. He got off on it. One particular morning, he'd been with his father when he'd visited Sarah Hooper. Next day, he decided to visit her himself. He was fourteen, she was twenty-nine. He had no experience, she had plenty. For fifteen years it went on, father completely oblivious that he and his son were paying top dollar to share the same woman. Bobby may have been ignorant to what was going on but Jordan knew exactly what he was doing and never once felt guilty.

Deceit was part of the Kingsbridge culture and guilt wasn't.

Jordan saw himself as a hunter, sex, a game. His opening line to Marlene Moorer, one of Hollywood's most beautiful actresses, was to ask her to marry him. It took just twenty-four hours to persuade her to accept and only a few more minutes to get her into bed. Two months later she was pregnant, yet another Kingsbridge conceived illegitimately. Little Rudi's agonizing birth turned his mother off sex forever. Jordan didn't mind, he just went elsewhere. Though his wife knew, she never let on.

When his parents were killed in a plane crash, Jordan found himself in sole control of Kingsbridge Financial and sole residence at Chateau Chantalle. He may have been just twenty-five but he was also very shrewd. Bribery had always been a tool for Jacob, Joseph and Bobby but Jordan turned it into an art form; his personalised corruption more relationship-based than fear-inspired.

He first met Bob Casey, an ambitious Irish American, in the fall of '49. It was the relationship he'd been waiting for. Casey's running for Mayor was the first seven-figure campaign in American political history, most of the cost borne by Kingsbridge Financial.

But it was no gift; Jordan was simply investing in his family's future.

It took Casey just one four-year term to establish himself as all-powerful, his personal and political influence reaching into every area of Chicago life, touching everyone and everything. He became a six-term Mayor. It was an era where the company became the Kingsbridge Bank of Illinois and saw the family make the quantum leap from rich to seriously rich.

The Kingsbridge's had arrived and, save one exception, Jordan had never been more fulfilled.

The exception was his son, Rudi.

Rudi had always been difficult, always scheming and manipulative. At one level it was charming, funny even, but the longer it went on the more sinister it became. As a young boy, he drilled holes so he could watch staff members undressing or making love. Had something been done the few times he got caught, things could've turned out differently. But his mother kept it to herself and the seed of deviance took root and flourished, to a point where at fourteen he forced one of the younger maids to have sex with him. Though he denied it, the girl cried rape, and it cost Jordan fifteen thousand dollars to make the problem go away.

Then there were Rudi's troubles at school.

By far the most expensive school in the state, Warman's had a rich history and a student roster that included the offspring of the Midwest's most powerful and influential families.

All the girls had their eye on Rudi. When Chuck MacGuire, the school football star, found out his girl had been playing away, he challenged Rudi in front of the whole class. That evening, on the school football field, a large crowd watched Rudi kick Chuck into semi-unconsciousness.

"Your bitch is gonna have it and trust me, she'll love every minute," he whispered into Chuck's ear as he was carried to the waiting ambulance.

The fight cost him a six-week suspension from school.

"You're a joke!" he ranted at the headmaster amid a barrage of the foulest language the educationalist had ever heard. "He asked for the damn fight, not me. I just won it," he screamed, Jordan squirming with embarrassment by his side.

His first day back at school, leaflets were circulated inviting everyone to the *Big Event*, twelve-thirty, Warman's main courtyard. Come lunchtime the place was teeming with students, all wondering what the big event was all about.

As the big hand struck the six on the courtyard clock, Rudi suddenly appeared to the right of the impressive timepiece. "Ladies and gentlemen," he bellowed, waiting for the throng to stop talking and look up. When he was sure every eye was on him, he added, "My sincerest thanks to you all for attending today's big event." As the words left his lips, he dropped his pants, most of the boys cheering, the girls giggling, some pretending not to look.

The commotion saw Warman's headmaster storm into the courtyard. He was outraged at the exhibitionism but the show wasn't over; Rudi wasn't done. Totally naked from the waist down, he turned round so his rear-end faced his audience. As he bent forward from the waist it had the effect of sticking his backside out and over the edge of the building. They thought he was mooning but the cheering turned to stunned silence as he pushed back the boundaries.

Fifteen seconds later he was done.

After pulling up his trousers and descending the stairs, he stopped in front of the open-mouthed headmaster.

"See, you son-of-a-bitch, you and your school are full'a crap," he hissed before walking out the school gates and into a cab he'd ordered for twelve thirty-five.

His father went ballistic.

"Taking a dump off the school roof!!" he said incredulously, shaking his head in disbelief. "You've been expelled; just how in hell we gonna get you into Harvard now?"

"I didn't wanna go to Harvard anyway," Rudi replied defiantly,

He may not have wanted to go but he went anyway, mostly because it put a thousand miles between him and his father. He found Harvard tedious and set himself the goal of bedding every single female freshman in his year, uglies an' all. He was well on target by the end of his first term and looked odds-on to succeed in the fall.

But what he didn't know was that it would be four long years before he'd return.

Prior to Harvard he'd no interest in the Vietnam War save his father had pulled some strings to keep him out of it. But seeing the way his fellow students eagerly leapt on the anti-war bandwagon made him mad. He hated the demos; hated the media coverage and hated the way a photograph of a young girl stripped of skin by napalm or a Vietnamese police captain executing a Vietcong terrorist could stir up such moralistic indignation. His view was that conscience and morals didn't come into it; war was war and you did what you had to do to ensure you won.

Jordan had hoped to begin his son's integration into KBI but the only time all summer when Rudi got excited was when the Chicago riots kicked-off during the last week of August. But it wasn't the politics or the policing methods that enraged him, it was the anti-war protestors. If he'd had his way, the police and National Guard would have shot more than they did.

It all nonplussed his father who thought it was just part of his son's angry student years. But unbeknown to Jordan, Rudi had already made the decision he wasn't going back to Harvard. Partly convinced by the anti-war protests and partly because a thousand miles between him and his parents wasn't far enough, Rudi was going to Vietnam.

On the day his parents waved him off at Union Station, they thought for Harvard, he was actually headed for Fort Campbell in Kentucky, to one of the toughest boot camps of them all.

Fort Campbell was home to the 101st Airborne and Rudi Kingsbridge was joining the regiment they call the Screaming Eagles.

The last in a long line of bastards was off to fight for Uncle Sam.

CHAPTER TWELVE:

It was June 13th 1972 and the mission to assassinate the General seemed a lifetime away.

Lt. Col. William T. O'Donnell shielded his eyes as he watched the C-130 taxi into position. He was feeling edgy; General Matthew Kedenberg wouldn't have flown up in person unless he had an agenda.

"This bitch of a war has got so far up my butt it feels like I got something stuck in my throat!" he said sharply, his words liberally sprinkled with expletives. "Who would've believed it? Nixon's already met with Mao Tse Tung and just yesterday, he's sipping vodka with Brezhnev; that's one Russian son-of-a-bitch you wouldn't trust to mow your friggin' lawn!"

"Yes Sir," O'Donnell replied, feeling the need to show he was listening.

"Do you know we're fighting history's first television war? There's like fifty million Americans watching GI Joe take a dump live on the evening news! How ridiculous is that?"

"Yes Sir, couldn't agree with you more, Sir."

"And what about this Vietnamization crap?" he said as they reached O'Donnell's office. "I mean the very idea a South Vietnamese soldier can defend himself is a friggin' fairy tale! Mark my words, when Saigon falls, Cambodia and Laos will follow in weeks." His head dropped as he spoke. "Truth be told, Ho Chi Minh was right all along.

Despite our fire power, he knew we'd never sustain the political and national will victory required."

"Yes Sir; coffee Sir?"

"Black, and make it quick; I'm back in the air in an hour."

O'Donnell poured the oil-like liquid into two of his least-chipped coffee mugs.

"Right, let's get down to business."

"Yes Sir," O'Donnell replied a little nervously.

"Now, what's this crap about winding-up the Dogs? Why for heaven's sake?"

"They're past their best Sir. They were supposed to do four or five months and they've done nine. They're creaking big-time and we think they're ready to self-destruct."

"What's your evidence Lieutenant Colonel?"

"Sir there was an incident as far back as Christmas that we've still not got the full story on. To outsiders, they're a tight bunch but inside the group there's some real chemistry between McBride and Kingsbridge."

"Is that all Lieutenant Colonel?" said Kedenberg, deliberately sounding incredulous. "Either there's something you're not telling me or you're pulling my pecker!"

"Yes Sir, there is more. On the back of the Christmas incident, whatever that was, there's now a problem between Kingsbridge and Fernando, the team leader."

"What problem?"

"Last time out Sir, it seems Kingsbridge used unnecessary force during a village raid."

"What force?"

"Burning Sir; and shooting water buffalo, chickens, pigs and goats."

"You're kidding Lieutenant Colonel? We shoot a few friggin' chickens and you're calling it unnecessary force! What the hell's going on? This is the Vietnam War and we may be losing son, but it's still a war!"

"Sir, I know war better than most. Check my personnel file Sir. You'll see I ain't never been more than a rat's whisker from the front line, in Korea or 'Nam!"

With the conversation on the edge of disintegration, Kedenberg tried to bring it back.

"Look Lieutenant Colonel, I know you know war but we're about to turn the lights out on Southeast Asia and I gotta job for your boys. So if you don't think they're up to it, then firstly, I wanna know why, and secondly, I ain't sure of where I'll find someone else with the skills to get the job done. Now as you well know, not getting the job done is not an option."

"Thank you Sir, apology accepted."

"Oh c'mon Lieutenant Colonel . . . I gott'a plane to catch . . . let's move forward shall we?"

"Sir, I think Fernando's in some kind of depression."

"Depression?" said Kedenberg, the incredulous tone making an immediate comeback.

"Yes Sir. He could well be in need of psychiatric care. Miller and I think it was kick-started by the thing Christmas time, whatever it was, and been worsening ever since. And this incident with Kingsbridge last time out seems to have tipped him over the edge. He's hardly said a word Sir, in three weeks. Goes through training saying what has to be said and not a word more."

"Holy moley!" said Kedenberg scratching his head. "Anything else?"

"Yes Sir, on the village raid . . ."

"The one Kingsbridge used unnecessary force?"

"Yes Sir. Well, it seems Kingsbridge engaged the villagers and suddenly started shooting at everything, killing the animals and three locals."

"These things happen. You know the drill."

"Yes Sir, I know the drill Sir. But all three were old men. There wasn't a person in the village under sixty!" Kedenberg motioned to say something but O'Donnell cut him off. "The unit was on a search and destroy assignment Sir, looking for enemy agents. When the shooting started, they hit the ground firing at random. But there was nothing moving. Fernando heard grunting come from one of the huts and when he kicked the door in, Kingsbridge was on his knees stuck fast up a sixty year old Gook woman wailing like a banshee. It seems to have fried Fernando's brains. He's told Miller he wants out. He's on the edge Sir; another mission could be a step too far, the straw that breaks the camel's back."

"Cut the clichés Lieutenant Colonel. I hear you loud and clear. So, we got a team leader who's a candidate for the asylum and a player who's a pervert with a taste for older women! What about the other two? Anything amiss with them?"

"No Sir; Sanders and McBride are model soldiers Sir, though McBride has a weakness in the fact he hates Kingsbridge with a passion."

"Sounds to me like Kingsbridge is an easy fella to dislike!!"

"Yes Sir."

After his quip Kedenberg wandered over to the window. When he turned, he looked sombre and serious. "Lieutenant Colonel, we're about to experience the first ever defeat in our military history and close the door on a twenty year involvement in Southeast Asia. We owe it to our friends down here to do as much damage as we can before we disappear to our side of the world. That's what Bleeding Dog Company was always about; why I listened to your advice and why I gave you the green light."

"Yes Sir," said O'Donnell, once again feeling the need to show he was tuned in.

"Now, I have some specific Intel which will give us a chance to go out with a bang."

"What you saying Sir?" O'Donnell said, cutting to the chase.

"I want, I need, one more mission."

"Sir, I don't think it's a good idea. It's asking for trouble. If you're asking my advice General, I'd have to say no."

"Lieutenant Colonel, we've worked together for longer than either of us would probably care to remember. I respect your advice but circumstances dictate that this is a job that needs doing and there's no-one else left with the skills to get it done. So, I'm sorry, but this is an order. I want your boys on standby in three days awaiting final orders."

"Yes Sir. But can I respectfully ask that you record that my advice has been over-ruled?"

"What the hell? Just where do you think it's gonna be recorded? No-one even knows I'm here; the top brass think I'm in Paris smoking a peace pipe with them lying North Vietnamese negotiators. We're invisible Lieutenant Colonel. There's no paperwork trail to my office, your office, or to anyone else's office. Got it? We're invisible! But if it makes you feel better, your point's duly noted. Now, are you up to getting this job done Lieutenant Colonel?"

"Yes Sir," O'Donnell barked, silently resolving to journal the conversation. He wanted it on the record. He didn't care where. But how would he do it? A letter to his wife in Seattle maybe or perhaps he should write to his brother Gus of *Angus P. O'Donnell & Associates*, his lawyers?

Ever since Kedenberg had rung him to say he was coming in person, O'Donnell had known saying "no" to whatever it was he wanted was never a realistic option.

"Right Sir, now you've noted my objection what can you tell me about the mission?"

Kedenberg huffed before pulling a map out his attaché case. "There's a Pathet Lao camp two clicks north-east of the village of Ban Xakse," he said pointing to the area east of the Bolovens Plateau. "We want it destroyed and four key personnel terminated. There's a high level meeting taking place on Saturday the 17th with the Pathet Lao and Khmer Rouge due to agree some kind of mutual assistance pact. We understand that three of the Pathet Lao's top men, Sathea Thao, Chanta Xiong and Kasa Say Kao, will all be in attendance."

The Pathet Lao, the military arm of the Laotian Communist Party, had been fighting alongside the NVA for a decade. Though mostly based in north-eastern Laos, they'd established a camp near Ban Xakse in the extreme south of the country close to the Ho Chi Minh Trail where it passed to the east of the Bolovens Plateau.

"You said *four* key personnel Sir. Who's the fourth?"

"Ke Pauk . . ."

"Ke Pauk!!" O'Donnell exclaimed. "He's as close to the top of the Khmer Rouge as it gets."

"Yeah, it seems there's a bit of a power struggle between him and Solath Sar – the guy they call Pol Pot. Irrespective of who wins, the world will be a better place without Ke Pauk. But don't under-estimate the Pathet Lao trio; they are top dollar!!"

"Sir, so the order is to terminate four targets and wipe out the Pathet Lao base?"

"You got it; these guys have got to go!" Kedenberg replied, taking four photos from the file, each one inscribed with the subject's name.

"Have Intel looked at getting us in and out?" O'Donnell asked, his eyes scanning the photographs but his brain already having moved on.

"The best LZ looks to be up on the Bolovens Plateau, six maybe seven miles to the northwest of Attapeu. About here!" Kedenberg said, pointing at the map.

"What about the pickup Sir?"

"We're looking at a site three clicks southeast of Ban Hatsati, two clicks north of Saisettha, here and here. Its flat marshland so any chasing pack won't be able to hide from the Cobras."

"And the timing Sir?"

"The four targets are only expected to be in Ban Xakse long enough to hold their pow-wow. So we have a narrow window: we're looking at a drop-off Friday evening with an early morning trek to the target area and a bulls-eye sometime after mid-day on Saturday. Four or five hours later, your boys will be on their way home and that'll be that; the end of the Bleeding Dogs."

"Thank you, Sir. Will there be anything else Sir?"

"No Lieutenant Colonel; just get the job done."

"Yes Sir."

The meeting was over. General Matthew Kedenberg had got what he'd come for.

* * * * *

As he watched Kedenberg's plane leave the ground, O'Donnell wondered how Miller would take the news.

"How you doing Doug? How's the Dogs? All rested up?"

O'Donnell asked three questions but wasn't interested in having any of them answered. He knew it, Miller knew it.

"What's up Sir?"

"We got orders for another mission."

"But Sir, I thought we were done."

"The orders came to me in person Doug. Saying *no* was never an option."

"OK Sir; what's the mission?"

O'Donnell told him. Miller whistled appreciatively, "And the timing Sir?"

"Friday night."

"Mmmmm," Miller said thoughtfully, wondering how he should best use the few days to prepare.

"Right Doug," O'Donnell said, keen to bring the conversation to a close. "Expect my call early Friday."

"Yes Sir. Look forward to it Sir."

And that was that. The dice was thrown and there was no getting them back.

* * * * *

Three days later, the Bleeding Dogs were aboard a Huey flying due west, the silence moody and sullen.

Miller felt more exposed than he could ever remember and couldn't help thinking all four Bleeding Dogs would die on what he and O'Donnell felt was a mission too far. When they reached the LZ he shook each man's hand, grunting, "See you tomorrow," as hopefully as he could.

Seconds later, all four Bleeding Dogs were on the ground, running hard.

Thirty minutes march in the last light of day brought them to the edge of the Bolovens Plateau.

"That's it for tonight," Frankie barked. "Get some chow and bunk up."

It was the first time he'd spoken since leaving Kontum four hours earlier.

The other three all clocked it but said nothing; no-one wanting to risk an unwanted conversation.

The silence added to the sense of disharmony, the camaraderie noticeable only by its absence.

* * * * *

At the precise moment they began abseiling down off the Plateau, an old lady called Mai-Ly stirred in a hut at the southern end of the small village of Ban Hatsati.

As she stood by the side of her bed, she had no way of knowing the Bleeding Dogs were less than three miles away as the crow flies. And neither she nor any of the four, had any idea their destinies were about to converge.

A simple peasant woman who sowed her life into her rice fields, Mai-Ly was forty-nine years old though she looked at least ten years older. The dark brown deep-set eyes had seen lots of pain and she had so many lines on her weather-beaten face it was impossible to tell where one began and another ended. Every line had a story to tell and none had a happy ending. Yet she'd once been a beautiful woman, the object of many a young teenage villager's fancy.

Her father had died from a snake-bite when she was young and she grew up independent and stubborn, determined to cut her own groove. On the day of her sixteenth birthday, she left for Attapeu, the largest town in southeast Laos, hoping to make her dreams come true. By Laotian standards Attapeu was a busy town, leafy, attractive, with lots of wooden houses with verandas and large ornate buildings built by the French. The town was situated at the convergence of the Se Kong and Se Kaman rivers and had a thriving commercial sector.

To Mai-Ly, it was another world.

She quickly acquired a job as a domestic for the wife of one of Attapeu's half-dozen French officials. For a while life was good but then, one day, while she was in the laundry room, she heard the door open behind her. She turned expecting to see her employer Madam Monique Sharnouir. But it wasn't her; it was her husband.

Jean-Pierre Sharnouir was a tall handsome man with a leering look and lecherous smile. He'd arrived in Laos ten years earlier as a low-level government clerk but the absence of any real competition facilitated a social climb of cosmic proportions. As Attapeu's senior official, he had interests in the local coffee plantations and also moonlighted as a well-paid consultant for the Michelin Tyre Company who had several rubber plants in the area. The sudden impetus to his social standing had made him arrogant, believing he could do what he liked, when he liked and how he liked; as long as his wife didn't find out. And earlier that morning, he'd heard her say she was off to market. It was the opportunity he'd been waiting for.

Sharnouir was a serial adulterer with a taste for the indigenous female population whom he found attractive on the eye and submissive in bed.

He'd wanted Mai-Ly the minute he'd first set eyes on her.

As he stood in the doorway, he had no idea he was about to commit a brutal rape on an innocent sixteen year old virgin. In his mind, he thought he'd seduce her, his first instinct to smile his most alluring smile. It usually worked; but not this time, Mai-Ly refusing to engage in eye contact. But he persisted. "Come here, my little angel," he crooned in his native French, the same time he stretched out his long arms in an effort to entrap her.

"Non monsieur: Madam will be home soon," she said pleadingly.

"Now, now, you naughty girl; you know very well she's gone all morning."

"Non monsieur."

"She's gone; now come here!"

"Non monsieur, please monsieur."

She tried to pull away but he was too big, too strong. He forced her chin up, trying make he look up at him. She resisted. Infuriated, his patience snapped. He slapped her hard, forced her backwards until her backside came into contact with the big laundry table behind her. With nowhere to go, he pushed her down onto her back, hissing, "Look at me girl; look at me!"

But still she refused, her wriggling efforts to escape doomed to failure.

"I wanted this to be pleasurable for you too. But it's your choice," he growled knowing the last thing Mai-Ly had was choice.

He lifted her skirt, used his hip to prize her legs apart, and opened his trousers.

Pinned and helpless, the tears of injustice quickly turned to tears of pain as her innocence and purity disappeared with every thrust. Then he grunted and the power was gone.

He reeled backwards seeming to suddenly realise what he'd done. But there was no guilt, no fear of retribution; simply a concern his wife might find out.

"If my wife finds out," he snarled, both his words and delivery full of menace, "I'll kill you and every one of your family with my bare hands."

Mai-Ly was in shock, words beyond her. She nodded, eyes fixed defiantly downward as she gathered her long black skirt into her groin in an effort to ease the agonizing pain pulsating through her body.

It lasted no more than ten minutes, but it was ten minutes of injustice that never left Mai-Ly. She'd gone to Attapeu wide-eyed, young, beautiful and innocent. She returned to Ban Hatsati six months later, bitter, angry, and four months pregnant.

When she told Sharnouir, he made her leave Attapeu before his wife asked questions. In his one act of compassion, he gave her five hundred French francs before she left. She almost didn't take it but 1930's Laos was no place for a woman to bring up a child alone and she had no intention of having a man again, ever.

Mai-Ly never shared the truth of what'd happened with anyone.

Her daughter Minh-Ngoc was born in the spring of 1939, her big round eyes, narrow nose and light complexion all testimony to the European blood flowing through her veins. Mai-Ly used the francs to purchase land and by Minh's fifth birthday, her paddies enjoyed a reputation for producing the best rice for miles around.

Even more attractive than her mother, Minh became a beautiful young woman who didn't lack for male attention. In the end it was inevitable she'd succumb and it was handsome Xiantha Dyong who won her hand. Eighteen months later, they had a baby girl, Bian Nhu Dinh, and six years after that, a boy, Tong Tenh.

As Mai-Ly rose off her bed early Saturday morning June 17th 1972, she was as content as she'd ever been. She loved her family and especially treasured her relationship with granddaughter Bian who'd be sixteen the following month. She dreamed she could give her the best possible start in life. But by late afternoon the same day, Mai-Ly's dreams would be in tatters once again.

* * * * *

Saturday was laundry day.

At twelve noon, Mai-Ly bade farewell to son-in-law Xiantha and left him to work their rice paddy alone. Minh and Bian were waiting at the edge of the village, the three strolling the three-quarters of a mile to their washing place by the river with young Tong dragging his feet behind them.

Even though nearly thirty-five years separated the trio of women, they were firm and close friends, able to relax and talk freely in one another's company. By the time they reached the river they were in jovial mood: laughing, smiling, cracking jokes.

The river was a tributary that fed into the giant Se Kong and Mai-Ly had been washing clothes in the same spot for decades. The sun was high in the sky, the colours radiant; the verdant greenery perfectly complimenting the giant grey sun bleached rocks that rose out the silvery waters. Out of sight, eighty yards upstream, was a six foot high waterfall which helped ensure everything looked freshly washed and rinsed.

And the women too, even wrinkled Mai-Ly, looked a picture, all three dressed identically in long dark skirt, white blouse and pointed hats like big lampshades. Though thirty-three year old Minh was still a beautiful woman, daughter Bian was breath-taking.

She took her hat off to reveal long jet black hair into which she'd inserted two purple flowers, one above each ear. Her longish neck seemed to act as a pedestal to the most perfect face, her stunning features dominated by huge brown eyes so dark they were nearly black. Her eyes were wide with an innocent kind of beauty and reflected the sunlight dancing on the river's crystal clear waters. Atop her eyes were black as soot eyebrows that seemed to have no functionality at all, looking simply as if they'd been placed there purely as decoration. Her high cheekbones and perfectly crafted bone structure bore testimony to her Gallic European blood though her nose was more oriental, flat at the highest point between the eyes before splaying outwards into two dark flaring nostrils.

As the three began to unpack the washing, Minh said something funny and Bian, the woman-child, smiled the most perfect smile. If the eyes dominated normal facial expressions, it was the full-lipped mouth and wondrously perfect teeth that took over when she smiled. The smile was more than just an external thing; it came from deep within. Her joy, like the smile, said so much about the life she'd led. Bian was a girl who knew love and especially knew the love of her family. And as the three women busied themselves with the family's weekly washing, they were at peace, with each other and with the world.

But like the calm before the storm, the peace was more illusion than reality, the matriarchal Mai-Ly about to crash headlong into her worst nightmare.

CHAPTER THIRTEEN:

Four hours after beginning their descent off the Bolovens Plateau the men were on a hilltop overlooking the Pathet Lao camp that looked more like a small rural village.

As they scanned the camp through binoculars, it looked deserted, as did the entire area.

During their five-mile journey to the hilltop, the only human beings they'd seen were three village women washing clothes by the side of the river.

They'd been on the river's eastern bank, southeast of Ban Hatsati. The men had heard their laughter as they approached on the opposite riverbank. After stopping to observe through the bushes and quickly eliminating them as a potential enemy threat, they moved on, the women completely unaware of their presence.

Even though there'd been no conversation, not even the brooding silence could hide the fact all four had clocked the haunting beauty of the youngest of the three, the woman-child.

* * * * *

"It's been nearly two hours and we seen no sign of life." Frankie said looking at his watch.

"You gonna call in the planes Corp?"

"What: to bomb a deserted camp? Nah, we'll go down and check it out. Put your silencers on."

When they reached the edge of the camp, the four men separated and moved slowly forward.

Just as Frankie was starting to think it was totally deserted, he edged round a hut to find a uniformed soldier snoozing on the steps leading up to a kind of Great House, built on stilts, the sound of animated conversation coming from inside the building.

Frankie caught McBride's eye, communicating his instruction in sign language.

McBride drew his Bowie knife and approached from underneath the Great House, the voices above his head sounding impossibly loud as he closed in on his victim, death as instant as it was silent.

"We going in?" Kingsbridge whispered excitedly.

"Why don't we just nuke the place, Corp?" Irish said noticing Frankie's eyes had glazed over.

"Because we need to know if our four targets are in there," Frankie replied as he gently put his foot on the bottom step hoping it wouldn't creak. One-and-a-half seconds after kicking the door in, all four Bleeding Dogs were inside the Great House and two of the incumbents were dead.

"Sha kam! Sha kam!" Frankie screamed in Lao, meaning *lie down*.

Ten terrified men fell facedown on the floor, fingers intertwined behind their heads.

"Ke Pauk?" Frankie barked loudly, before naming the three Pathet Lao leaders also on their hit-list. He was the only one talking, only one moving, slowly walking up and down barking in Lao, the monosyllabic tonal sounds exiting his lips like staccato machine-gun fire.

There was no response. Frankie repeated himself and still no-one moved.

"Hollywood, pick me a Gook!"

"Corp?"

"Pick me a Gook!!"

"No problem Corp," Kingsbridge said reaching for the enemy soldier nearest him and pulling him so forcefully into the half-squat position he nearly choked.

"Take his revolver and put it in his mouth," Frankie snarled.

Kingsbridge smiled as he forced the muzzle between the man's teeth.

Again Frankie barked something in Lao and again, the other Bleeding Dogs heard the names on their four-man death list.

"Take it out his mouth," Frankie instructed before barking at the little man again.

He shook his head furiously indicating he either didn't understand what Frankie was saying or had no idea who or where Ke Pauk, Sathea Thao, Chanta Xiong, or Kasa Say Kao were.

"Put it back in his mouth."

"Corp?" Kingsbridge said, looking as surprised as the soldier looked frightened.

"Pull the trigger!!"

The ear-splitting crack assaulted all five senses at once as a fine red blood mist suddenly appeared from nowhere; the bright sunlight slanting in through the wooded slats of the Great House reflecting the sharp scarlet colour of death that hung in the air.

"Oh my God!!" Kingsbridge shrieked his excitement fever pitch. "You see that? You see his brains explode?"

"Pick me another one," Frankie said his tone even more authoritative.

"Holy cow, he's lost it," Kong said quietly to Irish stood alongside him.

Kingsbridge grabbed a uniformed soldier by the collar. Frankie barked at him in Lao. Though everyone assumed Lao to be the soldier's native tongue, nothing could be taken for granted in a country with so many dialects. But the soldier did understand and seeing his former colleague decorating the walls had loosened his tongue.

As he told Frankie all he knew and more, one of the men facedown barked what must've been a warning for him to shut-up. Frankie immediately swung his CAR-15 to the right and let rip with six or seven rounds. The man died instantly, one of the bullets hitting the hamstring area of the soldier next to him. He shrieked in pain, his screams so loud the glass would've shattered had the Great House had windows.

"You shot the son-of-a-bitch in the crapper!" Hollywood screeched excitedly. "Shut up you low-life!!" he growled before coldly blasting the wailing soldier in the back of the head.

Only a few minutes earlier, twelve men had been holding a meeting inside the Great House.

Seconds after being introduced to Bleeding Dog Company, five were dead.

The terrified soldier stood alongside Hollywood was repeatedly bowing, submissively rocking back and fore, sweat dripping off his nose down onto the wooden planks beneath his feet. The scope of his eye-line took in the men on the floor. He gestured towards the nearer of the two last to die, blurting, "Kasa Say Kao, Kasa Say Kao!"

"One down," said Frankie, before barking, "Ke Pauk? Sathea Thao? Chanta Xiong?"

The level of tension had reached breaking point.

"How's this gonna end?" Kong said quietly to Irish.

"They're all good as dead."

"I reckon."

Though there was no way he could have overheard the conversation, the uniformed soldier facedown, second from the left, was thinking exactly the same. He carefully shifted his weight off his right side before moving his hand slowly downwards towards his revolver. He knew he'd die but he thought it better to die resisting than be shot in the head, facedown on the floor. He turned as quickly as he could, managing to get off one ill-directed round before Irish and Kong splayed him with fire from their CAR-15's.

But the sudden sense of movement was a catalyst to all hell breaking loose, four men spewing death and destruction, the bodies of their helpless victims leaping about like macabre puppets, the bullets pulling their invisible strings.

Then, the mayhem stopped as suddenly as it started, the silence every bit as deathly as the dull thuds of the muzzled CAR-15's. It was carnage: the sun's hazy rays slanting in through the gaps in the slatted walls, thick cordite smoke hanging in the air like death itself and the fine red blood mist all combining to create a cocktail that was potently atmospheric, almost surreal.

"That was friggin' awesome!!" Hollywood screeched, a manic spaced-out grin decorating his face, his brain teetering on the edge of adrenalin overload.

Frankie too, looked spaced-out, his haunted eyes staring but not seeing. It took him several seconds to come back from wherever he'd been. "OK; 'Ollywood radio in and let the Phantoms bomb the crap out this place. Then Sanders, you and Hollywood go secure the LZ. If we lucky no-one even knows we're here so we'll have a stress-free getaway."

"What you gonna do Corp?" Sanders asked.

"Me and Irish will pick through this lot for Intel and see if we can identify the subjects," he said, pulling the photos Miller had given him from his thigh pocket.

Twenty-five minutes later, three low-flying F-4 Phantoms flew directly over McBride and Frankie before dropping their bombs on the Pathet Lao village and sending huge plumes of smoke into the afternoon sky.

"We got the Pathet Lao trio Corp but what about Ke Pauk? What you think happened to him?" McBride asked.

"The grass told me he left with sixty soldiers first light this morning. He was recruiting Pathet Lao support to reinforce the KR attack on Pnomh Penh."

"So that's why the place was deserted!"

"I guess. Now, no more talking; I ain't in the mood for talking."

* * * * *

The Phantoms also flew directly over three village women washing clothes by the side of the river.

Bian, the youngest of the three, looked nervous as bombs exploded in the distance.

"It's OK," Minh said. "It's a long way off and we're nearly finished. Where's Tong?" she added, suddenly realising they hadn't seen him for what felt like ages. "Tong?" she called.

As Mai-Ly noticed the grey smoke high in the sky in the distance, she realised she didn't feel as confident as her daughter.

Something didn't feeling right but she didn't know what.

Her trepidation was well-founded; her darkest hour imminent.

* * * * *

Kong and Kingsbridge evacuated the Pathet Lao camp at a half-trot.

"Slow down Kong, you're killing me! There's no-one on our tail – no-one even knows we here. We got plenty of time."

"There's no way I'm missing the bus for you film star!" Kong replied as the low-flying Phantoms screamed past over their heads.

Ten minutes later, it was Kong who saw the three women first, seeing them before they saw him. Instinctively he slowed. He'd seen too many die at the hands of helpless looking women to be anything but careful. There was nothing weak about the weaker sex in Southeast Asia.

They were forty yards away when the women spotted them. They froze, transfixed, like rabbits caught in the headlights of a car.

Kong passed first, then Hollywood, the air thick with tension, the women lowering their eyes to avoid eye contact. But the men kept walking and disappeared round the rocky promontory that protruded out into the river. The women heaved a huge sigh of relief not knowing that out of sight the other side of the promontory, Hollywood had come to a sudden halt.

"I'm gonna have me the Gook bitch!" he exclaimed.

By the time Kong realised what was happening, Kingsbridge was already out of sight.

It was Minh who saw him first. He oozed danger, the crazed look in his blazing eyes confirming what she already knew: he was after her daughter. She tried to head him off, at first submissively bowing the same time she chattered away in pleading tones. But then, as he neared, her tone changed, barking at him staccato-fashion, cursing him with every swearword she knew.

But he wasn't listening. "Shut up you bitch!" he screamed, as the unforgiving butt of his CAR-15 caught her a crunching blow just above the hairline, opening a huge bloody gash before sending her reeling backwards over the riverbank, her small frame lacking the bodyweight to even partly absorb the impact.

Though frozen with fear, Mai-Ly knew it was her turn to try to stop him. But it was futile. He caught her with a glancing blow to the temple; it wasn't fatal but it still sent her tumbling into unconsciousness. Like Minh, she never had a chance. In Rudi Kingsbridge's world, it was everyday normal to eliminate anything stood between him and that which he desired.

With mother and daughter out the picture, he moved for the grand-daughter.

Kong appeared from behind the promontory just as Minh disappeared from sight. From thirty or forty yards away he watched Kingsbridge smash the old crone to the floor before turning his attention towards the young girl cowering down on the ground.

What should he do? Where were Irish and Frankie?

A glance over the riverbank confirmed his worst fears. It was a gory sight, the woman face-up, eyes open but obviously dead, a pool of thick black-red blood filling the dip in the rock beneath her head. Kong felt numb. It was like someone had pushed the slow motion button, the commotion and screams muffled and distant, as if coming in from afar rather than from just a few feet behind him. The loudest noise he could hear was the bump, bump, bump of his blood negotiating a pulse point somewhere in his head and all through, he couldn't take his eyes off the motionless woman, her stare somehow more than matching his. He was sure he could see the hate frozen into her eyes as they stared what would've been their last living look before taking centre stage in her death mask. The longer he stared, the more oblivious he became to what was going on behind him. And then he noticed the pool of blood suddenly overflow out the dip before trickling down the rock and dropping into the water at the river's edge. It diluted on impact but was still potent enough to discolour and darken the water.

The horror show had anaesthetised Kong's sense of time and he didn't know if he'd watched two, twenty or fifty drops of blood find its way into the river. But Hollywood's scream suddenly brought him crashing back to reality. Mai-Ly had come to, stood shakily to her feet and slammed a rock into the back of his head hoping it would kill him. It didn't.

Kong turned to see the girl on her knees, her white shirt ripped and torn and her black skirt halfway up her back. Her head was down and though he couldn't see her face, she was obviously crying, her body trembling and convulsing.

"You Gook bitch, I'm gonna kill you!" Hollywood screamed at Mai-Ly as he straightened up. He smashed her to the ground, his size twelve boot shattering her left shoulder with a sickening crack of splintering bone. The pain sent Mai-Ly sailing into her second bout of unconsciousness, unaware he wasn't finished. As he lifted his foot ready to bring it down on her unprotected head, Kong barked, "That's enough!!"

Swearing and cursing, Kingsbridge turned back to the girl, opening his trousers.

Bian didn't need English lessons to understand his instructions. She was as sure she was about to die as she was certain her mother and grandmother were already dead. Mercifully, the more he brutalized her, the more she felt it was happening to someone else, her mind floating away to the wonderful memories of childhood.

"Where's Tong?" she thought to herself as she endured the increasingly powerful thrusts before hearing the soldier let out a triumphant grunt and pull away.

Unbeknown to Bian, her brother was no more than forty feet away, terrified, hiding in the rocks; the pool of urine beneath him evidence he'd seen everything. He'd seen his mother brutally smashed in the head and disappear out of sight. He'd seen his grandmother kicked about like a rag doll until she'd stopped moving. And he'd seen his beloved sister stripped and abused.

But it wasn't all he'd see; there was more.

As Kong watched Hollywood take the girl, he was surprised and slightly ashamed to find he was getting aroused himself. When Kingsbridge pulled away, the girl lifted and slightly turned her head. Despite her humiliation and pain, her stunning beauty defiantly shone through.

It was the moment Kong knew he couldn't resist it.

"Get in her you black stud!" Hollywood said, "The bitch just told me she's always wanted a bit of black."

"Just get out'a my way you greasy son-of-a-bitch."

Again, Bian managed to lose herself in her thoughts and again, it was Tong who dropped into her mind. "Please let him be safe," she said to herself over and over, imagining that bored with watching the women do the laundry, he'd returned to Ban Hatsati.

But Tong had done no such thing. He was a few yards away, forced to watch the sister he adored violated in ultra close-up, his eyes fixed on the star-shaped birthmark flexing and unflexing on the black man's backside as he thrust his hips forward and back, forward and back.

And then, Frankie and Irish, on their way to the LZ, arrived in the clearing.

"What the . . ." Frankie said as he caught his first glimpse of Kong taking the girl.

"C'mon Corp, shouldn't we put a stop to this?" Irish said desperately.

"Can you hear her screaming?" Frankie replied callously, his eyes vacant and glazed over.

"Join the queue Corp, its reservations only!" Kingsbridge said grinning.

Kong was oblivious to what was going on around him. His body jerked, his head came back and he let out a roar.

As he withdrew Hollywood exclaimed, "Hey look, you got blood all over you!"

Kong instinctively wiped himself and then wiped his blood covered hands under his arms.

Frankie fell to his knees behind the girl, his hands bloodied by the discharge, her virginal innocence reduced to nothing more than a distant memory.

Less than a minute later, he was done.

Hollywood cackled with mocking laughter. "That has to be the fastest jump in history Corp!"

Frankie ignored him and just wiped his hands.

"And what about you Mick?" Hollywood said turning towards Irish. "You gonna do something with that boner or you gonna jerk off later?"

"Shut your faggot mouth or I'll rip your face off."

"Easy Mick! All I was doing was giving you the opportunity to share my girl. But if you're not man enough that's fine by me. I *am* a tough act to follow!" he said, the mocking tone making a swift return.

"I swear I'll . . ."

"We all know you can fight Mick but what we're wondering is, can you get it up for the ladies? Or perhaps, it's *you* that's the faggot! C'mon, the bitch is waiting."

"Back off him man: if he don't want it, let him be," Kong said.

It was Irish's chance, the moment he could've walked. But he blew it. Later, searching himself, he wondered if it was his weakness or the fact that to his shame, he'd felt a stirring down below. Or was it because of the adrenalin that always came in the immediate aftermath of combat?

Whether it was one, two, or all three, it didn't matter.

"I'll have her," he said shifting into position. He'd slightly hurt his knee in the shoot-out at the Great House and he winced as it came into contact with the rocky ground. Without thinking, he put his hand out, straight into the girl's blood.

The second his lust broke, he pulled away, wiping his hand in his T-shirt, his mind instantly consumed with guilt.

Kingsbridge basked in his victory. "Nice one Mick," he smirked, "You had her panting for more. So I'm gonna have her again. Watch closely and you'll learn how to *really* satisfy the ladies."

Seconds later, Bian was on auto-pilot, her mind telling her body it felt nothing. But Kingsbridge hadn't plumbed the full extent of his depravity. As he grunted a second time, he viciously yanked her long black hair pulling her head back towards him. As her body arched, he sank his teeth into her right shoulder. The pain was excruciating, its suddenness causing her to shriek in agony. As she lurched instinctively forward, a bite sized chunk of flesh separated itself from her body.

"Yahhhhh!" he screamed, his eyes blazing demonically as he took the flesh from his mouth, held it in his blood covered hands and bizarrely tried to squeeze it back into the bloody hole it had come from. But much to his obvious confusion, he couldn't get it to fit.

Bian's agonized scream snapped Irish out of a clinging fog of self-pity. He jumped to his feet kicked Hollywood hard to the side of the head and sent him crashing down onto the floor.

"That's enough!" Frankie screamed the same time he splayed a dozen rounds from his CAR-15. "It's over; it's time to get the hell out'a here!"

Frankie was wrong. It was far from over.

* * * * *

The men departed the scene of their crime in total silence.

Michael McBride wanted to die. He knew that just like in Australia, he'd taken part in something he should not only have steered clear of, he should've stopped altogether. The incident in Sydney opened the door, set a precedent. But this was different; the girl in Australia had a choice, a luxury never afforded the girl on the riverbank. He knew he'd be haunted forever.

The last of four to reach the promontory, he shot a furtive glance backwards. The girl seemed to be looking straight at him, her big dark brown eyes teary with pain and betrayal.

As the guilt hit him like a wave, he couldn't help think she was the most beautiful girl he'd ever seen.

And then he remembered something he'd once heard in boot camp.

"Beauty is the first casualty of war," he said quietly, wishing he could undo what had been done.

* * * * *

But it hadn't just been Bian's eyes that watched the men disappear out of sight.

Her brother, nine year old Tong Tenh, had watched their every move too. Hid behind a rock, he'd been a helpless fourth victim, forced to witness the destruction of his family.

Oblivious to his presence, the men were unaware that as soon as they'd left, he'd run crying to his big sister curled up on the ground. They were unaware of his efforts to gently rearrange her clothing, unaware of him hugging her tightly in the kind of embrace that only comes from surviving trauma together.

In torrential rain and total silence, the men ploughed forward, every step putting distance between them and the scene of their crime.

But the facts remained unchanged. While some were more guilty than others; all four had blood on their hands.

CHAPTER FOURTEEN:

The heavens opened the moment they rounded the promontory, the rain and gloom fitting accompaniments to the brooding silence, each man all alone with his thoughts.

For Irish, there was no escape. Hounded by voices, the loudest belonged to Fergus, his grandfather. "What did I tell yer lad? Why weren't yer listening? Didn't I say never let any man force his will on yer when you know that will to be wrong? Didn't I say it'd be better to die trying to stop 'im than having to look yer weakness in the eye day after day? And you're gonna lie about it too, ain't yer lad? Lies are malignant boy; they contaminate yer soul."

It was relentless, the image of the girl repeatedly flashing in his mind's eye. He wasn't alone. Though none of the Bleeding Dogs knew her name, the face of Bian Nhu Dinh had been forever burned into each man's soul. Where they differed was in the amount of guilt they felt. Irish wanted to die he felt so guilty. Frankie was so deep into his latest bout of depression, he felt sorrier for himself than he did for her. Kong was sorry someone had to suffer but his dog-eat-dog philosophy reasoned that in a war without rules, people got hurt. Kingsbridge felt no remorse at all, wishing simply he'd taken her three times instead of twice.

The men kept walking and the rain kept falling.

They were over three miles southeast of Ban Hatsati when Frankie called a halt.

"OK, this is the LZ," he said, checking his compass, his eyes scanning the open marshland that gently sloped towards two heavily leafed trees that looked out of place in the marshy wilderness. "Let's get over to those trees and we'll check-in to see where the Huey is."

Ten minutes later, Kingsbridge crouched over the radio. "Alpha One this is Bleeding Dog. Come in Alpha One, do you read me?" At the third time of asking, the radio crackled.

"We read you Bleeding Dog. We're in the air but the weather's against us; ETA 17:20. Over."

Their ride home was running twenty minutes late but no-one said anything. Conversation, like camaraderie and banter, had disappeared long ago. In the moments where he actually cared, Frankie had thought about it many times. Things had never been the same ever since the Huey pick-up the previous Christmas. Though Kingsbridge had denied it, Frankie was convinced he'd shot at Irish as he and Kong ran towards the chopper with the NVA in hot pursuit. It may have been just their second mission but the camaraderie evaporated from that moment on.

In its absence, silence had become the Bleeding Dog way.

And on June 17th 1972, the mood was charged with emotion; something had to give.

* * * * *

"Well if no-one else is gonna say something, I'll volunteer," Kong said, relieved to have broken the heavy silence.

"Say something about what?" said Hollywood.

"About the girl: stupid."

"What about the bitch?" Hollywood said with a smirk. "I'm gonna have her over and over; every time I go to bed!"

"You're the pits faggot," Irish snarled.

"No worse than you Mick. You had her too; once you could get it up."

"You son-of-a-bitch; I swear I'll rip your eyes out."

"What's up Mick? Truth hurt?"

Both men were on their feet eye-balling each other, twelve feet separating them.

"This is it faggot," Irish growled threateningly. "This time we go all the way."

As the rain lashed in, three pairs of eyes locked on Kingsbridge.

"I'm up for it," he said the same time he pulled his knife from the sheath strapped to his right calf.

Irish did likewise and the two men eye-balled each other across an imaginary five foot diameter circle, their feet dancing slowly round its circumference, rain lashing into their faces.

All four men sensed the same thing; whatever the history, this time it was different.

"You gonna do something Corp?" Kong said anxiously.

But Frankie'd lost interest. "I've had it man. It's time this was resolved; time for a winner."

"Corp, this ain't the bleedin' Olympics! One of them's gonna die if we don't do something."

"Who gives a crap?" Frankie replied.

Rudi Kingsbridge couldn't have looked more confident. He knew he had the edge on his rival when it came to a blade but under-estimating McBride was for fools.

As battle-hardened warriors, both men knew that in any fight patience is priceless. The two circled each other for what seemed an age, neither feeling confident enough to make the first move. Then, just as it started to look as if it could go on forever, Irish's slight slip on the saturated ground gave Hollywood his chance. He lunged forward. Irish saw it coming and thinking at lightning speed, threw himself forward at Hollywood's shins hoping his adversary's reactions wouldn't be quick enough to adjust the upward arc of the knife thrust. His dive took him under the lunge but the knife caught the flesh at the back of his right shoulder, sending a chunk of his trapezius muscle up into the air. It hurt but it was far from fatal. Irish's downward momentum slammed his left shoulder into Hollywood's knees with all the force of an NFL line-backer, sending him onto his backside and into six inches of marsh water, the water exploding outwards in all directions.

If the situation hadn't been so deadly serious, it would've been comical.

Though still holding the knife, Kingsbridge was in the weakest of positions. Irish, in like a flash, thrust his blade forward. Hollywood tried to evade it and for a second, looked as if he had, shifting enough for it to miss his heart, miss his ribcage, and miss his torso. But that was where his luck ran out. It slammed in under his left arm, four inches of knife immediately appearing out the top of his shoulder.

He screamed in agony; but his pain had only just begun.

The lunge with the knife meant that Irish's bodyweight was committed to following in behind the thrust. He slammed a head-butt into his arch enemy's face at precisely the same moment he blocked off Kingsbridge's right hand and the knife he held in it.

In thought and deed, Irish McBride was two steps ahead.

With his right hand firmly turning the knife that'd gone clean through the shoulder, Irish, after smashing another head-butt into his unprotected face, turned towards Kingsbridge's right arm and sank his teeth into his biceps. As he bit as hard as he could, Hollywood had no choice. He dropped the knife.

In excruciating agony both sides of his body, he knew he'd lost, beaten once again by his arch nemesis. But Irish wasn't finished. This time he was going for the kill.

With his teeth firmly embedded in his biceps and his right hand turning the knife in his shoulder, his left hand searched the marshy water for Hollywood's knife.

As warm blood washed over his fingers, Kingsbridge wailed in agony before drifting off into semi-unconsciousness. When he came to, his vision blurred from the beating and from the rain that lashed vertically into his face, he looked up to see McBride's contorted face, eyes blazing. It was the face of death. He'd found the knife and it was already on its way into Kingsbridge's neck. But with the tip of the blade three or four inches from its intended target,

Kong's two hundred and sixty pounds slammed into his side, sending McBride sprawling into the marsh water.

"That's it; that's as far as it goes," Kong screamed as Irish scrambled to his feet.

"You said you wanted a winner!" he hissed, eyes blazing with adrenalin.

"That weren't me, that was the Corporal and he don't know what day it is! This fight's over. You got the gold medal man. Now sit down, cool off; it's time to go home."

Irish didn't argue. He slumped against one of the trees and watched Kingsbridge pull the knife from his armpit. He was wrecked: his left shoulder in bits, his right arm screaming with pain from the bite wound two inches above the trademark black tie he'd wound around his elbow. Facially he was a mess too; his once handsome features swollen like a giant red melon. His left eye was closed and his bloody nose had broken again, the third time in nine months; each painful break down to the man he hated more than any other. But he had to give it to McBride; he could fight like no-one he'd ever met. He thought he could take him with a knife. He'd been wrong, again. Next time, he knew it would have to be a bullet. And then he remembered the time the previous Christmas when they'd confronted each other across the ravine on the mission to assassinate General Luong Thau. They'd trained rifles on one another, looking eyeball-to-eyeball through their telescopic sights. How he wished he'd pulled the trigger. But he didn't, so he shuffled to the two trees, their leaves taking the sting out of the torrential rain.

Kong opened the first aid kit and took out the biggest dressing.

Hollywood winced as he wound it under and over his left shoulder, blood quickly turning its soft gauze material a rich dark scarlet.

Watching but not seeing, Frankie looked haunted, like a man staring into the abyss. He had a glazed vacant expression and his face looked long and drawn, the scar under his lip somehow appearing even more bulbous than normal.

Only Kong looked fully in control. Though he'd never considered himself a leader, he knew it had to be him who spoke first. But the radio beat him to it.

"Bleeding Dog this is Alpha One, come in Bleeding Dog."

Kong reached for the radio-phone. "We read you Alpha One."

"Hey Bleeding Dog; our ETA is fifteen minutes. See you shortly. Over."

"We're looking forward to your arrival Alpha One."

His confidence boosted by the sound of his own voice, he turned to the others.

"What we gonna do when we get back to base? What's our story?"

"What you talking about man?" Hollywood said, wincing in pain.

"Well we can't just walk in and say nothing happened can we? Look at the state of you! And what about the girl?"

"What about the bitch?"

"What's our story?"

"There's no need for a story," Frankie said, surprising the others by the suddenness and lucidity of his unexpected contribution. "It never happened. I'm the only one Miller questions at de-brief. I'll tell him Irish and Hollywood had a squabble before we got to the Pathet Lao camp and I'll explain away the knife damage by blaming it on a Gook bayonet."

"What if he wants more?"

"He can take it or leave it. I don't give a damn."

"So that's that then. We say nothing, they know nothing," chirped Hollywood.

"Yeah," said Kong. "We're the only ones who know anything anyhow, so as long as we don't talk about it, nobody's gonna know a thing. That OK with you Corp?"

Frankie nodded.

"And what about you Irish, where are you with this?"

"I'm not sure what you mean," Irish said, his voice little more than a whisper.

"That's typical of you Mick," Hollywood snarled, his aggression and brashness bizarrely paradoxical to his battered appearance.

"Shut your face Kingsbridge!" Kong barked before Irish could respond. Then he turned back to his friend, his tone calmer, friendlier. "What I'm saying I guess is that we need to leave what happened with the girl in our past, go home, and get on with our lives."

"Yeah, we all enjoyed the bitch," Hollywood said, keen to remind everyone of their part.

"An oath of allegiance!" Frankie said suddenly, taking the others by surprise once again.

"A what Corp?" Kong asked, just as the faint hum of the helicopters came into earshot.

"We swear an oath of allegiance," Frankie said. "Pledging to never again speak of what happened, either to each other or to anyone else."

"That's a great idea Corp. You up for that Irish?"

It was Michael McBride's turn to have three pairs of eyes bear down on him.

The drone of the helicopter's engines had deepened as they emerged out the low cloud cover about a mile to the south.

"I love you Irish," Kong said, "But we need an answer man. Shall we put this thing behind us?"

Had it been Frankie or Kingsbridge who'd posed the question Irish would almost certainly have rebelled. But it wasn't them; it was Kong, his great friend and he'd backed him into a corner.

"Yeah, I'm in," he said reluctantly with head bowed low, missing the triumphant smirk on Rudi Kingsbridge's battered face.

His three-word sentence sealed his shame and guilt.

It also sealed the unholy alliance between the four men of Bleeding Dog Company.

* * * * *

After a change of chopper at Kontum, the men arrived at Black Lady Mountain three hours later.

"Welcome home," Doug Miller shouted above the thunderous noise of the Chinook. "The chef's done you a T-bone," he said to Frankie.

The canteen was empty save the chef and two or three kitchen staff. Seniority took Miller and Frankie to the front of the queue. They took their food and sat down, Miller keen to begin debrief.

"So, how'd it go?"

"Three out of four but we missed Ke Pauk. He was at the camp earlier today; left with sixty Pathet Lao militia. We found only skeleton cover, thirteen in all. All thirteen were terminated, including the three Pathet Lao targets."

"Shame about Ke Pauk but great work Corporal . . ." Miller said his thoughts interrupted after spotting Hollywood. "Holy cow; what the hell happened to cherry lips?"

"Today wasn't his day," Frankie said dryly.

"That sounds like the mother of under-statements! What happened?"

"We had some hand-to-hand stuff in the camp; he took a knife to the shoulder."

"And how'd his face end up looking like that? Him and Irish have another spat? From what I can see, the only thing missing is McBride's signature!"

"Who gives a crap?" Frankie said glibly, taking Miller by surprise.

"I do Corporal. I give a crap. Now, what happened?"

Frankie sighed. "Yeah, they had a go, but frankly, I'm past caring. I've had enough. It's time to go home, wherever the hell that is."

"OK, that'll do for now Corporal," Miller said knowing he wasn't getting the full story. "Bleeding Dog Company's over; in fact, it never was. Rest-up and we'll chat through where we go from here over the next few days."

Within ten minutes he was on the telephone to O'Donnell.

"What we got Doug?"

"We missed Ke Pauk Sir; but the other three targets and ten others were terminated," Miller said, quickly getting to the military equivalent of the bottom-line.

"How'd they let Ke Pauk slip through their fingers?"

"It was another Intel screw-up Sir. Ke Pauk had gone by the time we arrived."

"Your encouraging words about Army Intel are duly noted Master Sergeant! Anything else?"

"Yes Sir, it seems that there was another spat between McBride and Kingsbridge Sir, and that both of them were injured in the attack on the Pathet Lao camp."

O'Donnell sensed Miller's hesitancy. "You don't sound convinced Master Sergeant."

"No Sir; feels like I'm only getting half-a-story."

"What you think happened?"

"It's hard to tell Sir, but something's amiss."

"Well, whatever it is, we'll bury it with the Bleeding Dogs. It's time to draw a line and move on."

"Yes Sir, they never existed; the end of an era, Sir."

"What will they do Doug?"

"Kingsbridge's war's over Sir; he'll be on the next plane home. Fernando's on the edge and he needs to go home too I reckon. As for McBride and Sanders, my guess is they'll probably want to stay but McBride's looking a bit spaced-out too."

"It's been a tough nine months Doug but there you are, it's over now. Thanks for the update."

"No problem Sir."

"And Doug?"

"Yes Sir?"

"Thanks."

"Thank *you* Sir. It's pleasure to serve you Sir, and Uncle Sam."

O'Donnell didn't reply; the conversation was over.

With Miller still holding the receiver, the phone clicked and the line went dead.

* * * * *

Lieutenant Colonel William T. O'Donnell lay restlessly on his bunk, his thoughts dominated by the fact he'd not done what he said he'd do and written to his brother in the aftermath of Kedenberg's visit a few days earlier.

He knew he wouldn't sleep till it was done. So after a few minutes deliberation, he began.

"My dearest Gus . . ."

An hour later he was finished.

He inserted the letter into a standard army issue envelope, sealed it and scribbled on the front. "To be opened in the event of my death or before on my specific instructions – Lt. Col. William T. O'Donnell, U.S. Army, 17th June 1972," saying it out loud as he wrote.

He then scrawled a brief note. "Dear Gus . . . Please put this somewhere for safe keeping. Thanks . . . William."

After scribbling his brother's address on the front, he tossed the envelope into his mail tray.

Less than a minute later, his index finger dialled Washington; it was his turn to brief his boss.

"Ke Pauk is one lucky son-of-a-bitch but all-in-all, another successful mission Lieutenant Colonel. It beats me why we've got to wind these boys up. It seems like a helluva waste of resources to me. But there we are; it was fun while it lasted!"

"Yes Sir."

The briefings were over but restful sleep didn't come easy to two-thirds of the chain of command above Bleeding Dog Company.

Experience told both O'Donnell and Miller that something was amiss. Their one saving thought was that whatever it was, it would never see the light of day.

But you don't get more wrong than a hundred per cent wrong.

CHAPTER FIFTEEN:

Bian Nhu Dinh, though still six weeks away from her sixteenth birthday, was on new ground. But her grandmother wasn't so lucky. She was on a return ticket; she'd been to hell before.

More than three decades after being raped by Jean-Pierre Sharnouir, she emerged from unconsciousness into a nightmare so horrific it was beyond imagination.

With rain lashing into her face, she winced at the pain in her left shoulder. She heard her grand-children crying. It seemed far off, hazy, but she knew it wasn't. Neither grandchild saw her move, Bian facing the other way all curled up in a ball, Tong cuddled into her back holding her tight like as if he was afraid she'd leave him. She shuffled to the river bank, dreading what she'd see. She was no stranger to pain but the agony of seeing her daughter dead and broken made her wail with misery. Tong ran to her and the two shuffled over to Bian so the three could hug one another tightly.

Mai-Ly knew they needed help and sent Tong to fetch his father. After he'd left, she took clothing from the washing basket, soaked it in the river and tended to her granddaughter, all the time whispering soothing words of comfort. She was a highly qualified nurse who loved her patient and had the personal experience of having endured similar trauma.

Xiantha arrived at the riverbank to find Bian facedown on the floor and Mai-Ly hunched over her. His eyes locked with Mai-Ly's. She nodded towards the riverbank and instantly, he knew his wife was dead. When he saw her he fell to his knees, face in hands, yelping like a whipped dog. Then he looked at Bian, her scratches, tear-strewn face, ripped clothes, unkempt hair and had his moment of realization: his daughter had been violated by the same man or men who killed his wife. He turned his head and threw up all over the floor.

For Xiantha Dyong, hell had come to Earth.

Then four or five other villagers appeared on the scene, the men retrieving Minh's body while the women helped Bian to her feet.

As broken Mai-Ly looked on, she was gripped with undiluted agony. Though she cried, there was no noise; the inner torture matched only by her frustration at not being able to let it escape. Her wrinkled face was contorted with pain but unable to scream it out, she was forced to suffer as if in a silent, almost theatrical mime. It was a pitiful sight. Every one of them innocent victims of lust; lust so fleeting it was satisfied in minutes but so potent it could sustain a lifetime's agony.

* * * * *

The only thing that makes agony manageable is time; it really is the healer everyone says it is.

1st August was Bian's sixteenth birthday.

She looked more beautiful than ever, blossoming as childhood gave way to the alluring maturity of womanhood. But robbed of her wide-eyed innocence and virginal purity, those who knew her best could see the eyes were different.

In the absence of the mother she missed desperately, she'd become maternally protective of Tong Tenh and drawn even closer to her grandmother. But her father had become distant, cuddling her less and seeming to have little to say in her company. What she didn't know was Xiantha was at war with his own mind, unable to erase the image of the soldiers brutalizing his little girl. From the snippets of information he'd been fed, he'd worked out that though his wife had been killed by one man, his daughter had been raped by four.

It meant normality was gone forever.

Tong never spoke of what he saw and no-one, not even Bian, knew he'd seen so much, seen it all. When darkness came, Tong's fears multiplied. In tight to his sister, he'd drift off to sleep, forced to watch over and over again, the murder, the abuse and the rape of the three women he loved most in the entire world. It made him a bed-wetter, the point of no return reached the same time each night: when his eyes fixed on the star-shaped birthmark on the black man's backside.

Mai-Ly was exhausted: her mind numb, her heart ripped out and her body broken. Though the pain in her shattered shoulder had eased, her left hand was near useless. The soft tissue damage to her face had healed but the facial injuries included a fractured cheekbone which made eating difficult.

Her weight, and there wasn't much of it, fell like leaves off a tree in the fall.

Both Mai-Ly and Bian needed hospital treatment but none were available in 1970's Laos, at least, not in Attapeu Province.

And then, the family made a discovery destined to blow them still further apart; Bian Nhu Dinh found she was pregnant.

* * * * *

It was Mai-Ly who saw the signs first; the appetite and mood changes, tiredness and vomiting, all pointing to the inevitable.

By the end of September Mai-Ly knew she had to tell Xiantha. It was a thought that made her sick; she knew he'd be heartbroken all over again.

She told him when the two were alone in the rice paddy. He fell to his knees, his face contorted by the unseen agony from within as tears streamed down both their faces, the never-ending nightmare moving effortlessly into its next chapter.

Mai-Ly never imagined her son-in-law could be so broken. But she'd only seen the pregnancy as a tragic consequence of the original tragedy. Xiantha saw it differently, immediately realising he'd lose both Bian and Mai-Ly because once the baby was born, the family would be in mortal danger. Ban Hatsati was just a few miles southwest of Ban Xakse and the Pathet Lao camp. Soldiers and militia often came to the village for supplies and once they heard about the baby, mother and child would be executed on the spot. They wouldn't ask questions. The facts would speak for themselves. Whether boy or girl, it wouldn't matter. The baby would be white or black but certainly not Laotian, Bian seen as having had an affair with an American GI, committing the unforgivable sin in the process: collaboration with the enemy.

As Mai-Ly and her son-in-law consoled each other, Xiantha knew the roles had reversed; now it was his turn to dread telling Mai-Ly what *he* knew. He needed help. Though he'd uttered many prayers over the preceding four months, every one had been said without any real faith they'd be answered but then, one day late in 1972, the help he'd prayed for arrived.

It came from an unexpected source.

* * * * *

Father Francoise Mesnel was a French Roman Catholic missionary who'd been in Laos since the early Sixties and in late 1972 he found himself visiting Ban Hatsati.

Xiantha was out on his porch when Father Mesnel walked into the small courtyard surrounded by huts. With the December sun low in the sky behind him he appeared to radiate goodness, a kind of celestial aura both all around him and seeming to emanate out of him.

As soon as their eyes met, Xiantha knew he was the answer to his prayer: the sent one he could bear his soul too.

The Catholic priest wept when he heard of the events the previous June. He was stunned when he saw the beautiful Bian, her glowing youthful features in stark conflict with the invasive unwanted bump in her belly. He ached for the resources to give Mai-Ly's broken body the surgical help she needed and sobbed uncontrollably for Tong when he heard of his fear of the night.

Father Mesnel was a deeply compassionate man who felt called to serve the people of Laos as a small schoolboy after reading about the country in a history book. Xiantha was greatly impressed with his integrity and with the Christian love that oozed from him. They quickly became friends, the priest becoming Xiantha's closest confidante.

But even with wise counsel, it was weeks before Xiantha could bring himself to tell Mai-Ly that she and Bian would have to leave Ban Hatsati.

This time it was Mai-Ly who was broken; news of the family's forced separation hacking her heart in two. Two weeks later, Bian had her baby. It was March 1st 1973.

Nguyen Thimay was a healthy baby boy, his pale skin, round eyes and western features testimony to the fact his father was neither black nor Laotian. But though born in Ban Hatsati, he'd spend no more than a few days in his native village, the village that had been his family's home for as long as anyone could remember.

Xiantha was terrified every time Pathet Lao militia were seen in the village, sure one of them would demand to see the baby before bayoneting him and turning the blade on Bian and the rest of the family. Twenty times-a-day, he'd prepare Mai-Ly for the monumental task in front of her, repeating his mantra: keep the baby hidden, trust no-one.

Vong Tho was a former North Vietnamese soldier who'd fought against the French before crossing into Laos and making the two-year, five hundred mile trek to Ban Hatsati. He explained that Mai-Ly, Bian and the baby had as much to fear from the Vietcong as they did from the forces of North Vietnam. Like the Pathet Lao, the common denominator was always a hatred of the Americans.

Xiantha was terror-stricken, devastated; the cancer of injustice sucking the marrow from his bones.

* * * * *

In late March, Father Francoise Mesnel brought news the war was over.

"Xiantha," he said, "In the great city of Paris, the capital city of my country, the Americans and North Vietnamese have signed a ceasefire treaty that became effective on January 29th. The Americans will withdraw by the end of this month. This is good news Xiantha; perhaps Mai-Ly, Bian and the baby will not have to go after all."

Xiantha hoped the impossible hope; but it only lasted till his next conversation with Vong Tho.

"Whatever's been said to get this treaty signed means nothing Xiantha; the brothers won't stop till Vietnam is one." But seeing that his friend didn't want to believe him, he added, "Go to Pa'am and see if the people on the Ho Chi Minh Trail walk north or south. If they walk south it is to reinforce the effort to conquer South Vietnam. Trust me Xiantha: the war will not be over till Saigon falls and Vietnam is one."

Xiantha had taken Vong Tho's advice as a challenge and, the next day, walked the ten miles east to Pa'am, a village directly on one of the most secret paths of the Ho Chi Minh Trail, the umbilical cord linking North Vietnam to the South.

Vong Tho had been right, the Trail a hive of activity; and all roads led south.

* * * * *

Xiantha knew he had to make preparations if his loved ones were to survive.

He sought advice on routes, directions, landmarks, villages and towns and sought counsel from Father Mesnel who consulted maps for guidance. He spoke to Vong Tho and to those he knew had experience of travel beyond Attapeu. And when the information gathering was over, he spent hours briefing Mai-Ly.

Then, the fateful day of separation arrived. He and Tong Tenh accompanied Bian, Mai-Ly and the baby, walking the first few miles together as a family united for the very last time. There was no jollity, no gaiety, no high spirits; it wasn't that kind of family occasion.

They headed southeast out the village but detoured around the riverbank where the incident had taken place ten months earlier. None of them had been there since and they had no intention of doing so during their last moments together. They walked across the wide flat marshland along the track to Saisettha. Along the way they passed the two big leafy trees that looked so out of place amid the flatness of the wetlands, ignorant to the fact the four men responsible for their pain had rested under the same trees after doing their dirty deed almost a year earlier.

The family smelt Saisettha long before they saw it, the pungent aromas of market drifting into their senses on the late March breeze.

Father Mesnel was waiting for them at the intersection where the road led east to Vietnam. He walked them to the edge of town, tears running down his face as he tried to minister comfort in what was an impossible situation. He prayed for them all in turn, asking for God's protection, for travelling mercies and for them to be reunited some point soon. Though everyone was in tears, the prayers especially resonated with Bian who sensed that whatever the future held, they were going to make it. But for poor Xiantha, the priest's words couldn't dent the agony, the clock ticking irresistibly towards the final goodbye. They all knew it was coming but it didn't cushion the jolt. It was heart-breaking for them all but for Xiantha it was unbearable.

It felt so unfair, so unjust, his family ravaged through no fault of their own. He knew his life would never be the same. He knew he'd never recover and despite the words of comfort, he knew he'd never see them again.

He was right on all counts.

* * * * *

Xiantha and Tong walked in silence back towards Ban Hatsati, through Saisettha, across the wetlands, passed the two trees that looked as if they had no right being there and all the way back to their soulless empty hut.

The heavy silence clung to them like a death sentence.

Tong had been confused all day, never really understanding what was unfolding in front of him. His moment of understanding would come four hours later, when, terrified, he'd wake after watching the black man with the star-shaped birthmark violate his sister. She was no longer there to comfort him through the dark hours, no longer there to clean the urine that seeped from his body as he endured the unasked for, unwanted replay of his family's darkest hour.

Tong Tenh was all alone: just him and his urine.

The family's first night apart was an experience none wanted and none enjoyed.

Twelve miles away as the crow flies, Bian, Mai-Ly and Nguyen Thimay tried to sleep at the side of the road that led east to Vietnam.

Xiantha lay awake for hours, only a thin curtain separating him from his sobbing son. He wished he could give him the love he needed but his reservoirs had been bled dry. Then he remembered something Father Mesnel said about the war being over.

"The war might be over," he said out loud, "But it'll always be with me."

* * * * *

Four days later Mai-Ly, Bian and the baby were ten miles inside Vietnam.

The journey had passed without major incident, only crossing the Ho Chi Minh Trail south of Pa'am causing them to miss a heartbeat or two. They'd heard it before they saw it – troops, people, trucks, wagons – a unique kind of wave, part human, part machine, its progress ever-rolling, unstoppable: everyone and everything headed south.

Both understood the danger as they crossed what was more track than super-highway. In the end, they needn't have worried. Aside from Bian attracting admiring glances from a group of grinning North Vietnamese infantrymen, to whom she smiled coyly and lowered her head, nobody seemed interested.

By the time they reached Plei Can, fourteen miles inside Vietnam, they made for a sorry pair. The wound to Bian's shoulder which had refused to heal properly ever since the incident, had flared up angrily while tiny Mai-Ly was totally incapacitated down her left side. Both were totally exhausted.

Vo Thi Dinh was even more wrinkled than Mai-Ly, both old women sharing a look that suggested they'd seen things no-one should see. When Vo saw Mai-Ly and Bian stagger towards her, she offered them the chance to drink from a large water pitcher and beckoned them to rest-up inside her tiny hut. The connection was immediate.

Three days they stayed, Vo feeding them and tending their injuries as best she could.

When it was time to leave, Mai-Ly and Vo cried in one another's arms looking more like sisters forced to endure a separation than two people of different nationalities who'd met just a few days earlier. As Bian watched the touching scene in tears herself, she prayed that the favour and blessing would stay with them throughout the next stage of their journey: a sixty-mile trek through the mountains to Chu Pah.

Five days later, with both women once again on the point of collapse, her prayers were answered.

In nearly fifty miles they'd seen no more than a handful of people, all at a distance. Then, on the slopes of Cu Di Coi, a five-and-a-half thousand foot high mountain, they walked into a remote village and more than three dozen people.

As with Vo Thi Dinh, the hospitality was beyond their wildest imagination. Though the welcome party was mostly male, it wasn't the beautiful Bian who stole the show, it was Mai-Ly!

Mountain tribes like the Ede, the Jarai and the Bahnar peoples are an eclectic mix: peace-loving, agrarian, friendly and very insular, many never having been outside of the immediate vicinity of their village. But something else they had in common was that they were all matriarchal and the older and more wrinkled the woman, the more wise she had to be and the more reverence she was due. So wrinkled old Mai-Ly, not yet fifty but looking more than sixty, became the belle of the ball!

A party was thrown in their honour and two hours after their arrival, two women appeared with vividly coloured hand-woven sarong-type dresses; Bian's dark blue and purple with white pattern and streaks, while Mai-Ly's was a rich burgundy. The colour transformed both women: Bian, the princess, looking radiant and statuesque, her grandmother, the queen, looking positively regal.

As darkness descended, ushers led them up the stairs of the long-house at the centre of the village. At the top was a pair of wood-carved breasts meant to symbolize the power of women. The nipples were enormous.

"Look Mama," Bian said laughing, "Someone's been watching you at bath-time!"

The party lasted two days. Bian and Mai-Ly loved it; it was a welcome respite from the trauma of their immediate past. Their departure was another tearful separation but with two tribesmen as their guides, they were shown a short-cut to their destination.

"Chu Pah," the guides said in harmony, pointing to the town in the distance.

After bowing to both women in turn, they set off back towards the village, Bian and Mai-Ly sad to see them go. They'd both enjoyed being queen and princess, even if it was for just a day or two.

* * * * *

Bian and Mai-Ly were surprised by Chu Pah's busy, earthy atmosphere. It was a thriving commercial town where every day is market day, the air thick with smells: sometimes perfumed like flowers, sometimes sharp and acrid, always heavily tinged with body odour.

They knew it was no more than a staging post on the road to Pleiku and ultimately, to Saigon, but neither woman had any idea how they'd proceed.

Then they came upon a roaring argument between two men, one stood in front of a small truck piled high with produce and the other stood behind his market stall.

It wasn't what they saw that grabbed their attention; it was what they heard.

The man with the truck was very angry and the more annoyed he got the more he ranted and when he ranted, he did so in Lao. He must've been from one of the villages in Southern Laos because his dialect for shouting and cursing was the same as that spoken in Ban Hatsati.

Four years earlier, Phan Van Mui had left the village of Ban Sok, ten miles north of Ban Hatsati, to visit his older brother who'd moved to Ban Me Thout in Vietnam. By the time he reached the city he found that his brother had been killed by the Vietcong. On the way home, Phan had been struck with Chu Pah, everything looking a million miles from war. It was why he decided to make it his home.

But this particular late April morning of 1973, Phan Van Mui was waging a war of his own. He'd been offered one price the previous day only to find that after running round the villages buying up all the produce he could, the trader had halved his promised price. Phan was furious, hurling a tirade of stinging insults in the man's direction, every word measured and carrying a curse.

"You putrid lump of cow dung; I will sell it in Pleiku myself," he spat in his native Lao, adding, "I hope you urinate blood every day for a year and that your slut mother is raped by a herd of water buffalo," his words peppered with every swearword he knew.

As he turned angrily away he found himself looking straight at Bian. She was the most beautiful girl he'd ever seen. She was smiling the most impossibly attractive smile, and what's more, she was smiling at him.

"Could we come to Pleiku with you?" the angel said, in the softest voice.

Lost in her beauty, Phan took a second or two to digest what she'd said.

"My God, a vision of heaven!" he said quietly to himself.

Then the thought struck him that she'd asked her question in his native tongue, quickly deducing she'd understood his cursing at the market trader.

"I'm so sorry," he spluttered, consumed with embarrassment. "I didn't think anyone could understand what I was saying."

"That's OK," Bian said quietly before repeating her request. "Could we come to Pleiku with you? Are you leaving now, this minute?"

Phan was never going to say no. After re-arranging his produce, he and the angel climbed into the van's cab with Mai-Ly sat between them.

To call the twenty mile route from Chu Pah to Pleiku a road or highway does the English language a grave disservice. But Phan couldn't have cared less; his mind was on Bian. Every once in a while, he'd take his eyes off the road to glance across at her and on one occasion, he saw the baby let go her engorged nipple and it popped into view. He pulled so hard on the steering wheel they nearly ended up in a rice paddy!

"The baby's got to feed you stupid fool; keep your eyes on the road!" Mai-Ly snapped.

"Sorry Mama," he said respectfully, risking another peek at the giggling Bian.

An hour into the journey, they stopped for a break, the women disappearing into the bushes while Phan prepared some fruit by way of some lunch. When Bian sat down against a tree ready to eat a slice of melon, she winced with pain as the wound to her rear shoulder brushed the rough tree bark.

"What's wrong . . . Mary Mother of God!" Phan said incredulously as Bian leaned forward. "How did you do that?"

Bian didn't answer.

"You need hospital treatment. There's one in Pleiku. We'll sell my fruit and go straight there. It's run by nuns from the Catholic seminary in Kontum."

"Do you think they'll be able to fix Mama too?"

"What's wrong with Mama?"

"She has a bad shoulder."

"Yes, I'm sure the doctors will fix it."

Phan Van Mui was having a good day. A recent convert to Roman Catholicism, he was convinced his God was smiling down at him. Not only had he spent several hours with the most wondrously beautiful girl he'd ever seen but he now had the opportunity to introduce her to his brothers and sisters-in-the-faith who would give her the medical treatment she desperately needed. Add in the fact he got nearly three times for his produce as he'd paid and all in all, he knew he was halfway through a day he'd remember for the rest of his life.

CHAPTER SIXTEEN:

Troy P. Templeman was also destined for a trip to the hospital in Pleiku.

A Diplomatic Attaché at the U.S. Embassy in Saigon, he was sat aboard an AC-47 on route to the Laotian capital Vientiane where he was due to meet the U.S. Ambassador to Laos, McMurtrie Godley. The plane had a crew of six and a passenger list of one, Troy.

U.S. forces had been in a progressive state of de-commission for more than three years and the last American troops had left Vietnam a month earlier, on March 29th 1973. It meant the plane had no escort, no weaponry and no way of defending AA fire or missile attack. But it was neither the NVA nor the Vietcong that brought the plane down; it was plain simple engine failure.

An hour out of Saigon's Tan Son Hhut Airport, the plane's fuselage shuddered so violently, all seven people aboard instantly knew their flight was over. Cool as a cucumber, navigator Buster Hartmann plotted a course for the former U.S. airstrip at Camp Holloway, a mile to the east of Pleiku and a half-mile north of Highway 19. But it was forty miles north of their position and the plane was losing height at an alarming rate. At one point it didn't look as if they'd make it. Then suddenly Buster screamed, "There she is; there she is!" pointing to the grey concrete airstrip in the distance, heat waves pulsing off its shimmering surface in the blazing afternoon sun.

The landing was safe but bumpy, Troy the only casualty: his head rocking forward and catching the lip of the window, opening a nasty two-inch gash over a left eye that closed virtually instantly.

Camp Holloway was a ghost town, soulless and empty. It took just one minute to realise that the help they needed would have to be flown in and just ten minutes more for chief engineer "Pinky" Sherbourne to identify the source of their trouble.

"A split hydraulic hose!" he pronounced. "I'll radio the quartermaster at Tan Son Hhut but I'm not holding my breath!"

For almost two years, the supply chain from the U.S. had been squeezed. It meant when something was needed it usually was cannibalised from somewhere else or sometimes, it even got flown in from Thailand or the Philippines at a cost of thousands of dollars to the U.S. tax-payer. Just as Pinky expected, the news was mixed: Tan Son Hhut had the ten gallon drum of hydraulic fluid but there was no hose.

"Sit tight Pinky," the quartermaster barked, "I'll get you a hose from somewhere even if I have to fly it in from LA!!"

An hour later, Troy was still bleeding.

"We need to get you to a hospital and get that wound stitched," Buster Hartmann said with obvious concern.

"Great idea Buster, but I can't see a road-sign saying 'Hospital' anywhere!"

"Ah, now, that's where you're wrong. I reckon it's only a mile or two to the 71st Evacuation Hospital which, if my Intel's correct, is still operational."

"You sure?"

"Yep; I heard someone say the American and French Red Cross are running it."

"But I thought the American Red Cross had all pulled out?"

"Yeah? But that still leaves the French don't it?"

Fifteen minutes later, the two set off north, Troy holding a bandage to his forehead. He'd lost a lot of blood and the thought crossed Buster's mind the walk could be too much for him.

As they climbed over the perimeter fence, out onto a dusty track, they heard the put-put-put of a small motor-cycle driving towards them. Buster flagged it down and to both men's surprise the driver stopped. He was a tiny, heavily wrinkled Vietnamese man who Buster guessed couldn't have been a day less than a hundred and thirty-five! He bowed and chattered relentlessly, smiling a gummy, toothless smile.

Buster somehow managed to convey that he wanted to buy the motor-cycle.

Five minutes later, with three ten dollar bills safely tucked away in his scruffy trousers, the still chattering man bade them farewell and walked off back in the direction from which he'd come.

"Not quite a Harley is it!" Buster quipped.

"More like a friggin' lawn mower with wheels!"

"But it will be better than walking Troy, I promise!"

With Troy sat on the cargo stand hanging on for dear life, the two miles to the 71st Evacuation Hospital took more than twenty-five minutes, partly due to the lack of power between their legs and partly due to taking a wrong turning or four or five! When they finally arrived, they were met by a nun who'd been alerted by the put-put-put of the machine's tiny engine.

"Mon Dieu!" she cried when she saw Troy's face.

The American and French Red Cross made the joint decision to keep the 71st Evac open after it had been deactivated at the end of 1970 and when the last American troops withdrew from the area two years later, the American Red Cross left with them. To help alleviate the staff shortage, the French sought help from the Catholic seminary in Kontum, the nuns more-than-happy to relocate to the dome-shaped tents and tin buildings of the 71st Evac.

The nun sat Troy down just as the door burst open.

"Hey man, it's so good to see another American!" declared the white-coated doctor in a booming West Coast accent.

Mike Lelonde was a big man in every sense of the word. Six-two, two hundred and thirty pounds with a voice to match, there was plenty to catch the attention. But even more than his size or volume, the thing that stood out most was his hair. Thick and curly, it was as near blood red as Troy had ever seen atop anyone's head. Together with his pale white skin, he looked as if he'd never seen the sun let alone sat in it.

"Where yer from and what's up with your head?"

"Florida," Troy said before adding, "We had to putdown at Camp Holloway."

"Mike Lelonde, Phoenix Arizona," he boomed, extending his hand in greeting.

He talked non-stop as he stitched the wound with surprisingly soft and gentle hands.

By the time he'd finished he'd unloaded his life story.

He arrived as Chief of Surgery at the 71st Evac in May '68, six months before receiving a letter from his mother telling him his wife had moved in with another man.

"I couldn't face going home, so I stayed," he said. "With the hospital closing, I took a jeep, loaded it up with six crates of Jim Beam and disappeared. It was the middle of February before I came round! And if I'd not run out'a Jim I'd still be out there somewhere!" he added with a mischievous smile. "Uncle Sam left everything behind, tens of thousands of dollars worth of equipment! So I decided to become a proper doctor again and started delivering babies and the like, doing things doctors are supposed to do instead of just sowing brains back together and amputating arms and legs."

In the two-and-a-half years since, Mike Lelonde had looked after the locals. He'd never been more fulfilled.

"There you go Troy, good as new!"

"Thanks Doc. OK to go now?"

"You said your plane was grounded till tomorrow so, just in case, I think you should stay in overnight for observation," the doctor said, his diagnoses only slightly affected by the fact he hadn't seen an American for more than three months. "Shall I tell your partner or will you?"

"You tell him Doc; I need to sleep."

"No problem," he replied, turning to go look for Buster Hartmann.

* * * * *

The road was so bad, Phan Van Mui wondered if his truck would shake to bits.

The tension in the cab was unbearable and surprisingly, it was a road-sign that provided the release. The sign said *Highway 14* and below an arrow pointing right, *Ban Me Thout 194* and *Saigon 537*. The numbers signified distances in kilometres and for Mai-Ly, the sign was a big deal; Xiantha having told her a million times that *Highway 14* was the key to heading south.

But just a mile-and-a-half down Vietnam's major inland artery, Phan threw a left and once again, the truck was on yet another bumpy and dusty trail.

"That's the old U.S. Army base," he said pointing to his left towards the deserted camp, once MACV headquarters.

Five minutes later, he was acting as mediator between Mai-Ly and Bian, and Mike Lelonde.

The big doctor clocked Bian the moment he walked in the room.

"Wow!!" he said to himself quietly, pursing his lips and gently blowing outwards as if to whistle.

When he saw the festering shoulder wound, he whistled again. It was weeping badly, the edges red-raw and bleeding. "Oh my God," he whispered, knowing none of them would understand. "This is one ugly bitch of an ulcer for a peach of a sister like you."

After conducting the initial examination on Bian, he turned to Mai-Ly, his trained eye immediately noting the left arm hanging limp at her side. With Phan interpreting, he explained that both women needed operations. They looked terrified, as if they were ready to run for it.

"No, no," Phan said, "The doctor is great and mighty surgeon; he fix you good!"

Given that Phan Van Mui had never before met or even heard of Mike Lelonde it was an amazing endorsement; a statement of faith even. But it worked: Bian and Mai-Ly stayed put.

* * * * *

Troy woke from a deep sleep to find the hospital had other guests.

The double doors to the dorm had been wedged open and he could hear a Vietnamese man conversing with two women who had their backs to him. He had no idea what they were saying but the man saw Troy sit up in bed and raised his index finger to his lips, nodding so the women became aware they may be disturbing him. Instinctively they both turned, Troy suddenly finding it so difficult to breathe he thought he'd die. As Bian smiled coyly, he felt himself flush over. Though their eyes met for just a few seconds, her face left a photographic image imprinted on his soul, her huge dark brown eyes, statuesque bone structure, full lips, wondrous teeth and jet black hair all equating to breath-taking perfection.

She was the most beautiful girl he'd ever laid eyes on.

Later the same day, Mike Lelonde called in to check on his progress.

"How you feeling Mr Ambassador?" he said, indicating he'd found out that Troy worked at the Embassy.

"I'm OK Doc; had a bit of a headache but then I saw this amazing girl and it went!"

"Oriental chick? Black hair? Biggest brown eyes you ever seen?"

"Yeah, she was amazing. Who is she?"

"Damned if I know! But we do have our first date in twenty minutes!!"

"You what?"

"Steady! You two ain't married are you?"

"I wish! But what'd you mean you got a date in twenty minutes?"

"A date; at my place!" the doctor replied, enjoying the wind-up.

"Your place?"

"Yeah, my place: the operating room!"

"Why? What's up with her?" Troy asked.

"Well it ain't plastic surgery!"

"Doc . . . I swear I'll wet this poxy bed."

"She's got some kind of infected ulcer behind her right shoulder," he said, finally putting Troy out of his misery. "It sure looks out of place; something that ugly has no right attaching itself to something so beautiful! But I don't mind telling you, this is one op I'm gonna enjoy!" he added, his face cracking into a big toothy grin.

Troy couldn't get her out of his mind but something had made him angry and it wasn't the carrot-haired surgeon playing games. He was angry with himself; he hadn't asked Mike Lelonde her name.

* * * * *

Troy slept badly, his thoughts invaded by the wondrously beautiful girl-with-no-name.

At first light, he went outside into the garden where a loud rasping snore alerted him to the fact he wasn't alone. Stretched out on a bench, he found the man he'd seen talking to the two women the previous evening. He coughed and spluttered loudly, hoping he'd wake. He did. Phan sat up, rubbed his eyes and nodded a greeting. Troy adroitly steered the conversation round to the two women and quickly learned they were grandmother and granddaughter from Attapeu Province in Southern Laos travelling to Saigon and that their names were Mai-Ly and Bian.

"Not bad for a chance chat with someone who can't speak English!" he said to himself as he wandered back through the hospital hoping to glimpse Bian's tantalizing beauty.

Instead, he bumped into Mike Lelonde.

"How'd the op go with the girl?" he asked, adding her name, "With Bian I mean?"

"You tell me how you know her name and I'll tell you how the op went," the doctor replied, immediately picking up as he'd left off the night before, in full wind-up mode.

"I spoke with their driver this morning in the garden. Now tell me, how'd the op go?"

"It went really well. It was nasty man but I grafted some skin from the prettiest, pertest bum cheek I ever seen and shut off the crater. There'll be a scar but it'll fade in time."

"Is she conscious?"

"Yeah, course: it was only a twenty minute op. Nothing like what it'll be like for grandma. If I'm lucky, I'll be out by sunset!"

"Really?" said Troy, "Why so long?"

"It's a full shoulder reconstruction, takes ages!"

Troy shrugged, his thoughts quickly refocusing on Bian.

"How long will they be here Doc?"

"Well, the girl will be fine in a week, but it'll be months before the old woman's fit enough to leave." The doctor could see Troy thinking. "Why'd you ask?"

"The Vietnamese guy told me they were trying to get to Saigon. I think I can help."

"And why would you want to do that I wonder?!"

Troy ignored both the question and innuendo. "Mike," he said, suddenly looking serious. "Make me a promise will you?"

"For you pal anything! What you want? What you need?"

"Don't let them leave before I come back."

"Are you serious?"

"Mike, I've never been more serious; it's like my whole life's led up to this moment."

"Wow! You really been bitten man!"

"I'll be back in two weeks, and between now and then, I'll work out how I'm going to get them to Saigon."

"You are one crazy mother Troy, but I've grown very fond of you man!!"

Troy knew she'd changed something inside him. He was more focused than ever before and planned doing all he could to help his damsel-in-distress. It didn't matter that he'd never even talked to her. He was sold; and if necessary, he was ready to dedicate his life to pursuing her.

Troy Templeman was on a mission. It's codename?

"Bian!!"

* * * * *

Buster Hartmann was a born negotiator who seemed to know everyone and what's more, they all appeared to owe him a favour.

Sat on the back of the bike, clinging to Buster's rib-cage for dear life, Troy popped the question. "Hey Buster, if I needed to get back up here, how would I do it?"

"What?" Buster shouted above the put-put-put of the machine's straining engine.

"How would I get a return ticket to Camp Holloway and a jeep to take me back and fore the hospital?"

"It's doable," Buster blared confidently.

"Yeah?" said Troy, "How?"

"Just get me on the case!"

"I was hoping you'd say that," Troy said smiling, as they pulled up alongside the plane.

An F-4 Phantom had flown up two five gallon drums of hydraulic fluid from Saigon while a chopper had dropped in from Dalat with the all important hose; nobody seeming to mind that the government of the United States was thousands of dollars poorer as a result.

Two hours later, Troy and Buster were on the tarmac at Tan Son Hhut, Troy taking the opportunity to make sure Buster understood what he wanted of him.

"Don't worry Troy, relax; I won't let you down," he said reassuringly.

Night and day Bian dominated his thoughts, Troy not needing anyone to tell him he was head-over-heels in love. But what would he say to her when they finally met? How would he make the offer of a lift back to Saigon? Would her grandmother want to accompany her? What would he do with her, or them, once they were in Saigon? Where would they stay? Could he get them a job? What about the baby?

Some of the questions were answered quicker than others. He knew a half-Vietnamese, half-Indian woman called Mrs Jayanda who owned the Rivers Edge Hotel. She agreed to give Bian and her grandmother jobs and even better, she said both could live in.

"Good start," he said to himself, his planning interrupted by the phone.

"Troy, its Buster."

"Hey Buster, what's up?"

"You know you wanted a return ticket to Pleiku? How does this weekend sound?"

"It sounds great!" Troy said excitedly.

"Just get yourself over to Tan Son Hhut for 09:00 Sunday and tell the guard you're flying with Eagle One."

At the gate, Troy was amazed when the guard pointed him towards a massive C130 Hercules.

"Troy; it's good to see you man!" Buster shouted from the top of the ramp that led into the plane's cavernous interior. He was stood alongside a shiny brand new jeep, grinning.

"What the hell?" Troy exclaimed.

"I thought we'd give it to the Doc as a kind'a loyalty bonus! What do you think?"

Troy smiled, his mind caught between imagining the delight on Mike Lelonde's face and thinking what a great guy Buster Hartmann was. He was privileged to call both men "friend."

But Buster wasn't finished. "What about this?" he said.

"What is it?"

"A friggin' dentists chair of course! The nuns told me the Doc has to fix teeth off a trolley so I thought we could be their answer to prayer!"

"That's amazing; how'd you get it?"

"I'm like best pals with a purchasing guy at the Defense Attaché's office. He owes me one! Actually, he owes me nine or ten!!"

A truck screeched to a halt at the bottom of the ramp.

"What's this?" Troy asked.

"It's fuel for the Doc's jeep."

"Holy cow, he'll be able to drive half-way round the world on that!"

"Don't exaggerate man; it's only forty ten gallon drums!"

And still it didn't stop. Another truck pulled up, and then another one, and then another one. The final inventory read, one mint condition jeep, one unused dentists chair, forty ten-gallon drums of fuel, one thousand assorted bandages, ten thousand wound dressings, a box of plasters and mixed tapes, one hundred vials of morphine, a hundred kilos of anti-biotic powder, twenty mattresses, six boxes of surgeons gloves, countless boxes of cleaning fluids, twenty packets of bed-sheets and pillow cases, four heavy duty laundry irons and last but not least, three cases of Jim Beam.

"Buster, you're like Father Christmas!"

"Yeah and here's the crew," Buster chirped, pointing.

It was only when the massive plane was airborne that Troy, the only passenger aboard, realised Buster had worked an even bigger miracle than was first apparent. It wasn't just the cargo; it was the crew, all more-than-willing to be part of a very private mercy mission.

"It's a miracle!" Troy said to himself quietly, happy that every minute of flight closed the distance between him and the woman of his dreams.

* * * * *

By the time they pulled up outside the hospital, Troy was more nervous than excited.

"Hey boys; it's great to see you again! What's all this?" Mike Lelonde boomed.

"We thought we'd bring you some prezzies!" Buster exclaimed. "The jeep is Uncle Sam's thank you for your outstanding service."

The carrot-haired surgeon looked stunned, his eyes suddenly becoming all glassy.

"Are you serious?"

"Yeah Doc, it's yours."

"I love you guys," he blubbered.

Everyone laughed, even the nuns.

"Is *she* still here?" Troy said, once he and the doctor were alone.

"Is *who* still here?" Mike said pretending he didn't understand; Troy's annoyed look persuading him to cut short his wind-up. "Yeah, she's here, looking more beautiful than ever. She's also picked up loads of English; she's a clever cookie as well as a looker."

"How is she? Physically I mean?"

"She's good. The wound's healed."

"Can I see her?"

"Sure, they're in hut number four."

Troy hesitated, swallowed hard and opened the door.

In a mix of spoken English, sign language and mimed gestures Troy made his offer, both women's smiles confirming he'd been understood.

"Hey Mike, how long before they're ready to leave?" he said when they were outside.

But the doctor was busy ogling the growing pile of goodies arriving from the Hercules.

"Yessss!" he exclaimed when he saw the dentist's chair. But the biggest cheer was reserved for the Jim Beam. "I am gonna get so blasted!" he said shaking his head in disbelief

"Mike; how long before they can travel?"

"Oh, sorry man, this is like the best day of my life! I really love you guys."

"No problem Mike. But tell me man, how long?"

"Six weeks, maybe seven."

It was 13th May as they spoke.

"OK, I'll be up for them July 1st," Troy said pausing before adding, "And if you're lucky, I'll get Buster to bring some more goodies."

Troy knew he was being manipulative. It was something he was often accused of.

But for Bian, he was happy for the end to justify the means.

CHAPTER SEVENTEEN:

At heart, Troy was a really nice guy but like lots of people, he'd had some bad experiences.

The son of Randy and Jeanette Templeman, Troy was born on Independence Day 1951, in New Port Richey, on Florida's Gulf Coast. His Dad was a supervisor at Pepsi Cola's bottling facility in Tarpon Springs, working six days-a-week to provide for his wife and three children, two girls and Troy, the youngest. With his older sisters just as ready to spoil him as their mother, Troy was molly-coddled as an infant and never one for sports or for rough and tumble. Together with his academic prowess, it made him a target for the bullies and all in all, High School wasn't a good experience. At fourteen, he even contemplated suicide but by the time he was sixteen, he coped with life a little easier. After finally standing up for himself, and taking a bit of a beating in the process, he put up a good enough show to persuade the school bully to move on in search of a new victim. He'd also discovered he was clever and could influence those around him with persuasive words. Though it made him manipulative, he'd been marked down as a high-achiever, teachers keen to give him all the encourage-ment he needed.

By the late-Sixties, the family had moved five miles down the coast to Tarpon Springs. Their lifestyle had improved and Randy and Jeanette dreamt that Troy would be the first of the family to go off to university. Though they'd eventually get their wish, Troy decided to first enlist in the

U.S. Diplomatic Corps after attending a State Department careers fair in the spring of '69. Six months into his training, he moved sideways into the U.S. Foreign Service. He did so well he was one of only three from seventy students to be offered a sponsored place to study international law at Jacksonville University.

Though he was a clean cut, quite good looking boy, his self-esteem had been battered by the bullies and his lack of confidence did him no favours with the girls. Half-way through his first year at Jacksonville and still aching for romance, he was offered a post as Diplomatic Attaché at the U.S. Embassy, Saigon.

The job started January 1973 and Troy knew it would change his life forever.

Over Christmas turkey, his parents tried to counsel him to say no but he'd already made up his mind; he was off to Vietnam.

* * * * *

Saigon was a culture shock for twenty-one year old Troy.

It was a potpourri of a place; multi-cultural in the broadest sense, yet brash and manic, its sidewalks swarming with commerce. Street sellers were everywhere selling cigarettes, candy, chewing gum, satay sticks, rice, noodles, anything.

Traffic was unruly and chaotic, the noise on the streets so loud it was deafening. Cars, scooters, motor-bikes, taxis of all descriptions, bicycles, horse drawn carriages, jeeps, three-wheeled charabancs, glorified lawnmowers, the variety endless: every last one driven recklessly in whatever direction the driver pleased, oblivious to other drivers and to highway rules. What Troy didn't realise was that Saigon didn't have highway rules!

But the city in early '73 was an exciting place. There was no over-crowding, no panic; no fear. They'd all come later.

As he started his new job all wide-eyed, the first thing he noticed was the corruption and the "black market" thinking and culture. Everything had always been for sale in Saigon, theft and corruption almost routine. Everybody was in on it, the entrepreneurial spirit operating with chaotic abandon. Troy was also amazed by the lack of objectivity, disease a perfect example. A proper plumbing and sewage system would've done more for the people of Saigon than a thousand top neurosurgeons. Disease was everywhere: cholera, plague, small pox, TB, typhoid, dysentery, every conceivable disease known to man, all part of a recipe more deadly than even the VC.

America's crusade to improve Saigon's lot hadn't been universally appreciated. While Americans saw the Vietnamese as inscrutable, corrupt and lazy, the Vietnamese thought Americans loud, brash and aggressive, each learning a few words in the other's language but having no desire to understand one another's culture or psyche.

It was the ongoing paradox; America seen as both rescuer and abuser.

Though the War ended in March '73, the uneasy peace did little to hide the fact that a state of war still existed between the NVA and the ARVN, the Army of the Republic of Vietnam. Saigon however, seemed ignorant to the dangers, the city spoiled by an absence of any real fighting since the Tet Offensive way back in January 1968. From the extreme south of the country, the threat of the North seemed remote. But ignoring the threat didn't make it go away.

War was on its way to the city whether its population liked it or not.

It was to such a Saigon that Troy received his Laotian Princess.

* * * * *

Buster Hartmann came through big-time.

Everything he promised he delivered: plane, crew, goodies for Mike Lelonde, and most important of all, three first class tickets for his guests.

Troy was thrilled, excited, nervous, unsure, all at the same time!

For Bian and Mai-Ly too, it was an emotional period. They may have reached their destination but there was no sense of fulfilment, both still aching for the family and life they'd left behind.

When Troy took them to Mrs Jayanda at the River's Edge Hotel, she took one look at Bian and said, "I know you said she was beautiful Troy but I couldn't have imagined how beautiful!" before showing them to their room in the basement.

As they lay on the bare mattresses that first evening, the women had no way of knowing that the tiny basement would be "home" for the next twenty-two months.

Bian minded Thimay through the day while Mai-Ly worked as a chambermaid. Then, later in the day, they'd swop roles for Bian to wait tables in the restaurant. It was an arrangement that worked well, Mrs Jayanda especially delighted that Bian's presence in the restaurant saw a rise in clientele, especially male. She wasn't surprised. She joked with Troy, though he didn't share her hilarity, that Bian had a look that could straighten the most bent homosexual! Impartial observers had to agree. She was breathtaking, gorgeous and sexy without having the slightest understanding of what sexy was or what it meant. This was part of her allure but when men came on to her, she'd recoil like snapped elastic, bubbly and buoyant one minute, withdrawn and sullen the next.

Mrs Jayanda sensed something wasn't right with the over-reaction.

"What's the story with the baby?" she asked Troy during one of his frequent visits.

"I don't know! I guess she had an affair with a GI but I've never asked and she's never talked about it!"

"You have pokey-pokey with her?" Mrs Jayanda asked straight and to-the-point.

"No, I'm not having pokey-pokey with her; we're just friends."

"Oh yeah Troy, and I'm Ho Chi Minh's love-child!"

Troy pushed his chair back as if to leave.

"You touchy boy Troy: you in love with her! I know you long time now. Six months long time in Vietnam. I feel like your Mama, so I can tell you things I can't tell others. You be careful Mr Troy. Our girl has tragedy inside her and she gonna take much loving to come through. Trust me, Shande Jayanda knows these things."

All night the words buzzed round his head. Had he sensed the tragedy too? Was that why he hadn't made a pass at her? Why he hadn't even given her a farewell peck on the cheek?

As usual, there were no answers but Mrs Jayanda had made him think. But it was still several months before he finally summoned the courage to ask Bian about Thimay's father.

The question turned her ice-cold. For three days she blanked him. Troy was devastated. On the fourth day, much to his relief, she was waiting in the park near the River's Edge Hotel. Wearing a black pointed hat held in place by a purple ribbon, she looked staggeringly beautiful. When she removed the hat, Troy was awestruck. She'd inserted a purple lotus flower into her jet black hair above her left ear. The flower, like her, was perfection.

He knew he was besotted with her, head-over-heels in love.

"I am so sorry Bian. Please forgive me," he said, unable to stop himself half-hoping the apology would see her share the truth about Thimay. But it didn't happen.

"It's OK, it's over now," she said, the big bonus of which was that she reached for his hand.

Troy thought he should apologise again.

"Bian, I'm sorry. I'll never ask again, about Thimay I mean. I'll wait till you want to tell me."

What he didn't know was that that she no intention of telling him; ever.

* * * * *

As 1974 started, Saigon became a different place.

South Vietnam's President Thieu repeatedly proclaimed that the North was bent on unifying the country and that war had resumed. The Communists, he said, had been violating the cease-fire ever since the treaty was signed in Paris on March 2nd 1973. Sixty thousand people dying while the cease-fire was in force suggested he had a point!

The mood of the city had changed dramatically, people suddenly fearing for the future. The population had swollen with thousands of people arriving daily. Slum areas burgeoned, shacks and shanties springing up everywhere, all in streets with no names. Begging became a boom industry with thousands of kids chanting "Give me money," "Give me candy," before singing, all smiley and big-eyed. But when the last light of day disappeared, Saigon became a different world, disconcerting and threatening.

The VC terror campaign inside the city escalated with devastating effect signalling that the war had finally reached Saigon. A day couldn't pass without an explosion or two sending people running everywhere like ants, the war raging on Saigon's streets every bit as confusing as the war in the countryside.

Fear was everywhere and the changed environment had everyone thinking about their tomorrow, or whether there would even be a tomorrow. Troy tried several times to get Bian to talk about her future which he hoped would be entwined with his.

"I'll be able to get you out," he said, alluding to an inevitable NVA victory. But the one he tried often was, "You can come live with me in America," which he'd said in about a hundred different ways.

Though he'd seen the signs and was very worried, like everyone at the Embassy, he couldn't believe the country he was so proud to serve would stand by and do nothing, or even worse, walk away. He wasn't certain how it would end, but he was sure America would call the shots and dictate the terms.

1975 would show him how wrong he was.

* * * * *

South Vietnam's fate was sealed, and Saigon doomed, when the NVA violations of the Paris peace agreement evoked no retaliation from the Americans save a few empty words of protest.

NVA commanders saw it as an open door to march south.

Their victory at Ban Me Thout on 5th March prompted South Vietnam's President Thieu to evacuate six provinces in the Central Highlands in an effort to gather all his forces in and around Saigon. It would prove a fatal mistake, a gambler's desperate last throw of the dice.

NVA commanders rubbed their hands, readying themselves for the battle of Saigon.

They thought it would take two years. It took just fifty-five days.

For the Americans, Thieu's decision confirmed that Congress had been right to resist Ambassador Graham

Martin's frequent lobbying trips to Washington. The cause had become hopeless, Thieu and his army unworthy of support.

Giving up the Central Highlands had other effects too. It clogged the country's highways with people. It lessened the ARVN's already dubious ability to resist. And at the U.S. Embassy, it birthed a siege mentality whereby Ambassador Martin gave the impression it was Washington who were the enemy rather than the North Vietnamese.

Troy's position at the Embassy gave him the inside track. South Vietnam was in meltdown with millions of refugees milling everywhere, massive food shortages, ARVN troops defecting in droves and rumours everywhere that the advancing NVA were committing atrocities: murdering, raping, torturing. It was chaos, anarchy, as fear turned to blind panic.

"It's confusing but it looks over to me," Troy said to Bian one afternoon. "As hard as it is to say, I can't see the U.S. helping now."

"But it's not your fault Troy. You've tried so hard. Will the war come to the city?"

"Yes, it's coming to Saigon," he said reluctantly, his eyes focused on two year old Thimay. He'd been there when he sat up for the first time, crawled for the first time, walked for the first time. He felt like his father, wished he was his father.

"Troy, what will happen?"

"I don't know," he replied, meaning it.

"I was talking to an old woman Troy, from Ban Me Thout, who told me the NVA will kill me because of my American baby. Is it true?"

Troy knew it was but he saw a chance to be gentler and to offer her, once again, a way out.

"All I know Bian is that the Embassy staff will be evacuated and that we'll be able to get some people out with us. Will you come with me Bian?"

"What about Mama and Thimay?"

"We'll make arrangements for them to come too of course."

"OK Troy," she said slowly, "We'll come to America with you."

Troy was ecstatic, determined that whatever the future held, he'd be ready.

* * * * *

The bigger picture deteriorated with alarming rapidity.

Sensing the kill, the NVA captured Hue, Vietnam's third largest city, and found themselves in control of twelve provinces and the destinies of more than eight million people. Then, on April 20th, they took Xuan Loc. It put enemy troops thirty-eight miles from Saigon with just space between them and the big prize. Inside the city, the VC stepped up their terror campaign still further: explosions, fires and sirens becoming hourly occurrences. Everything pointed the same way: Saigon's biggest industry, war, had made the long journey home.

In imminent danger of collapsing in on itself, Saigon became the most crowded, panic-stricken and chaotic city in the world. Everything had changed. Troy could see it in the peoples' faces. The women looked desperate, less beautiful, while the men looked haunted, devoid of aspiration, wanting to survive but not sure why.

With the NVA paused outside the city limits awaiting orders and re-supply, President Thieu gave up the ghost and fled to the U.S.

The NVA commanders had achieved their goal: they'd beaten the rainy season to Saigon.

Fear and panic was everywhere, Saigon a seething cauldron of anarchic chaos.

Americans departed in droves, workers and secretaries reaching their place of work only to find the boss gone, without a word. It kick-started a sense of betrayal and despair that was very personal.

Troy was besieged everywhere he went, people pleading, grovelling, thinking that as an American he could wave a magic wand and everything would be alright. It made him feel inadequate and frustrated and then he'd feel guilty, selfish, as his thoughts invariably turned to Bian and to how he'd get her out the city.

Washington confirmed the NVA were executing those who'd collaborated with the Americans and though Bian was Laotian rather than Vietnamese, Troy knew she was in grave danger: Thimay's obvious Western features condemning mother and baby to certain death.

Like millions around him, Troy was in danger of being overwhelmed by fear.

* * * * *

The confusion and chaos saw ARVN troops ignore the age-old maxim *women and children first*, army officers and their men first to run.

There were two hundred and fifty thousand South Vietnamese soldiers inside Saigon in late April 1975 but none were interested in fighting. Like everyone else, they wanted out but aside from the Americans, all routes out the city were barred.

Teetering on a knife-edge, Saigon stared into the abyss.

With the rich and wealthy bribing anyone who'd take their money, an American identity card became more valuable than gold, its holder able to by-pass the queues at Tan Son Hhut on the basis they'd assisted the Americans and were therefore, in imminent danger. Planes came and went and commercial airlines risked being shot down during mercy flights that saw thousands evacuated to safety. But then, the NVA bombed the airport. It was the beginning of the end as people lost the ability to influence their own destiny, their lives overtaken by a tsunami of fear, panic and history.

Troy spent most of 28th April shredding papers. Like the rest of the Embassy staff, he was confined to the compound and hadn't seen Bian since the previous day. He was at his wits end. Telephone lines were down all over the city and he couldn't call the hotel. Was she waiting for him? Would she realise she should come to the Embassy? Was she still at the River's Edge Hotel? Would she be safe walking the mile or so to the Embassy?

He was upset with himself. He thought he'd prepared well but his predicament proved he hadn't. And worse, what would he do if he were ordered onto a helicopter?

Troy wished he'd had the courage to ask her to marry him even if he couldn't envision her saying yes. It would have made things so much easier because all over the city, last minute shotgun-type weddings were taking place in an effort to get a loved one a guaranteed ticket out of Saigon. In lots of cases the loved one was just someone who'd paid a bribe but people were past caring; there wasn't time.

It was a bizarre situation, so many hating the Americans for betraying them but prepared to do anything to get their ticket to America.

* * * * *

The order to begin Operation Frequent Wind was given 11:08 AM local time, 29th April.

When Troy knocked Deputy Ambassador Walter Lieberhouse's door, he could hear the first wave of helicopters hovering over the Embassy.

"What is it?" his boss snapped irritably, the stress obvious on his heavily lined face.

"Sorry to disturb you Sir but now the evacuation's underway, can I request permission to fly out some friends of mine?"

"Who?"

"A Laotian girl: and her mother and child."

"You want to take an entire Gook family out, and they're not even Vietnamese! No chance!!"

The expletive-ridden answer and lack of respect had Troy's spirits plummeting new depths.

"But Sir, she has a Caucasian child! She and the baby are at-risk targets for the NVA."

"Where is she?"

"The River's Edge Hotel Sir."

"Now listen to me Templeman. There's nearly a thousand American citizens still out there somewhere, unaccounted for. Add in the fact there's Vietnamese loyal to our cause sat at bus stops all over the city waiting for buses that aren't going to arrive. You know what that is son?" The Deputy Ambassador answered his own question, his phraseology once again peppered with swearwords. "I'll tell you what it is. It's the worse bitch situation I've ever known! And you know what, there's nothing you, me or anybody else, can do about it. Now get the hell out'a here; I'm having the worse day of my life dammit!"

All afternoon Troy sat dejectedly looking out over the main gates from one of the Embassy's vacated offices. Word was out that Americans and Vietnamese-at-risk could get a helicopter ride to safety. Wave after wave of people showed up in a last-ditch effort to exit the city. The Marine Security Guard battled to keep order and to let those who qualified, through the gates and into the compound. The U.S. Embassy wasn't designed as a landing zone and the chopper pilots had to land and lift off in very confined areas, the smaller CH46 choppers landing on the roof while the bigger, heavier CH47's used the parking lot after the Marines felled a few trees. As the crowd peered upwards at the choppers, Troy scanned the faces hoping to glimpse Bian in the sea of faces and all the time he could hear the Deputy Ambassador's words echoing inside his head.

He felt bullied, just like in High School, and then, something broke.

"I am not going home without her!!" he screamed. He knew how serious it was to disobey a direct order. He knew the risk. But in a battle between his mind and his heart there could be only one winner. Her name was Bian Nhu Dinh.

* * * * *

At the gates the air was thick with tension and despair.

It sounded like there were a thousand babies all crying the same time, people shouting, pushing, every eye gazing upwards as the helicopters ferried others to safety. The Marine guards looked weary, drained, many wearing sun glasses and those that didn't avoiding eye contact as people chanted, mantra-like, "Let me in, let me in; please let me in."

Troy recognised a big black Marine Sergeant.

"Hey Sarge, this looks volatile as hell!"

"Yes Sir. I'll be glad when we're all on our way home!"

"Sarge, I gotta go fetch someone," Troy said, hoping his honesty wouldn't backfire.

"I thought you guys were grounded?"

"We are Sarge but this is one girl I gotta take with me."

"Wow! She's a doll!" exclaimed the Sergeant as Troy handed him a photo.

"Look Sarge, I'd really appreciate your help with this."

Just as he was about to get his answer, Troy heard a shrill but instantly recognizable voice over the crowd. It made him want to weep.

"Troy, Troy, over here, over here!"

Tight to the fence thirty yards to the right of where he was stood, his eyes locked on Bian and he couldn't help marvel that even in such a distressed condition she still looked stunning.

"Sarge, she's here. Look, over there!"

"I see her Sir, but how the hell we gonna get her in through the gates?"

Bian was face up to the railings, Mai-Ly immediately behind her holding Nguyen Thimay. The crush factor and the sheer people numbers meant it was impossible for them to move in any direction. But as Troy ran to the fence, he already had an idea.

"Bian, I was just coming for you," he said, the tears running down his cheeks.

She was crying too. "Troy; help us!"

"OK. I'll be back in a minute," he said, already turning towards the big black Sergeant who'd moved back to the main gates. "Sarge, can I borrow two of your men?"

"What you got in mind, Sir?"

"I'm thinking we can lift her straight up from where she's standing, up and over the top to this side of the fence. Look, there's no barbed wire where she is. She's no more than a hundred and ten pounds Sarge. It'll be a piece of cake for two U.S. Marines!"

"But Sir, I don't mean to be a party-pooper but this fence is over nine-and-a-half feet high!"

"I'll get something for us to stand on," said Troy before disappearing into the Embassy. He knew exactly what he was looking for. He took the stairs to the third floor library two-at-a-time, ran passed an aisle or two and there it was:

the triangular steps the librarians use to reach the highest shelves. The top step was four feet off the floor and the unit had wheels that could be locked in place so that whoever stood on them could shift their body-weight or stretch a little in complete safety. "Perfect!" he said out loud.

When he emerged out the Embassy entrance the Sergeant smiled and winked.

"Mendez, Williamson, go help our friend get his girl!"

"Thanks Sarge!"

The men helped push the steps into position directly in front of Bian before taking up their positions: Mendez on the top step, Troy one side, Williamson the other.

All three were tight to the fence, Troy's lips close to Bian's ear, explaining his plan. She nodded when Troy asked if she understood, but it wasn't like she had a menu of choices.

As Williamson and Troy reached through the bars, they put one hand under her arm and the other behind her knee and lifted. Everything looked to be going according to plan when a man suddenly barked something in Vietnamese and reached over Mail-Ly and grabbed Bian's right foot, pulling at her leg.

It took the black Sergeant to restore the situation. Appearing at Troy's side, he pointed his M16 through the railings and barked something sharply in Vietnamese. The man let Bian's foot go.

"What'd you say to him?" Troy asked as Mendez helped Bian down onto the top stair.

"I told him he could either let her go or he could die where he stood."

"Would you have done it? Shot him I mean?"

"Yes Sir, stone dead, Sir."

With Bian safely over, Troy's attention moved to Thimay. Mai-Ly had moved forward into the space Bian had left. Troy put both his hands through the railings and under the toddler's armpits. He lifted him as high as he could, passed him to Mendez who in turn, a few seconds later, reunited him with his mother who was crying tears of joy.

"Right," said Troy, "Come on Mama, your turn."

"Sorry Sir," said the Marine Sergeant unexpectedly from behind him. "The old woman can't come. The crowd's agitated enough as it is. We'll have ourselves a riot if we're not careful. And Sir, orders are orders."

The conversation took place a yard from where Mai-Ly stood. Although she didn't understand all that was said, she knew it wasn't good news.

"Please no Sarge; don't split them up," Troy begged, his eyes filling up instantly.

"Sir, please don't put me in this position. We know why the girl qualifies for a ticket, because of the kid. But there's no reason to let the old lady through. She's not at-risk so let it go Sir . . . please!"

Troy knew he was right but it didn't help. Thirty feet back from the fence, Bian had been slow to realise there was a problem. Then she saw Mai-Ly's face, their tear-filled eyes fixing on one another. "Noooooooo!" she wailed, as she ran towards the fence.

Seconds later, granddaughter and grandmother were face-to-face, one the right side of the nine-and-a-half foot high fence, the other the wrong side. It was proof that even in its dying embers, the Vietnam War still had the potency to break hearts, end relationships; inflict misery. Troy cried aloud as Bian fell to her knees in front of Mai-Ly, both sobbing heartbroken tears.

As always, the two conversed in Lao.

"Mama, Mama, I stay; look after Mama."

Mai-Ly gently rubbed her granddaughter's head, reaching as she always did for her ear lobes, squeezing, stroking. It was an intimacy the two had shared since Bian was a baby.

"No child," she said, "You take Thimay to America, make new life with Troy."

But all Bian could think about was the pain. Having endured the horror of the rape, the murder of her mother and the enforced separation with her father and brother, she now had to leave her beloved grandmother behind, the woman who filled so many roles in her life. It was unbearable, the tears of joy a few minutes earlier, turned in an instant, to tears of despair, tears of horror.

"No Mama, no!" she said again and again, "We stay with you Mama."

"Shush child," Mai-Ly said through her own tears, not wanting the separation but knowing it was inevitable.

It could've gone on and on but the Sergeant who looked broken himself, turned to Troy.

"Come on Sir, we need to end this now," he said, the desperation betraying itself in his tone.

Williamson and Mendez had trained their M16's on the crowd as the Sergeant walked back and fore showing-off Thimay, hoping his white American features would quell any feelings of unfairness and help explain the girl's preferential treatment.

"Bian, Mama, we have to go," Troy said reluctantly, the same time he put his hand on Bian's shoulder. "I'm sorry Mama," he said, wiping the tears from his cheeks.

Defiantly, grandmother and granddaughter looked at each other through the fence, the palms of their hands touching, each knowing they were sharing their final moments together.

"You fly like eagle Bian Nhu Dinh," Mai-Ly said, "The gods look down on you with great favour."

"Mama, Mama!" Bian screamed as she was led away, tears rolling down her contorted face, her body bent double by the agony that came both from without and within. As Troy opened the big door into the Embassy, Bian pulled away and turned back towards the fence looking as if she'd broken free.

"Mama!!" she shrieked loudly before being ushered inside the Embassy building.

It was the last time Bian saw her grandmother.

* * * * *

The tearful scene was watched by thousands: every face confused, mystified, their features bearing testimony to numb and scrambled emotions.

What they'd witnessed wasn't normal but it wasn't a normal day.

Mai-Ly was deep in shock, feeling as if some invisible force had sucked the lifeblood straight from her veins. She knew Troy had done his best but she felt betrayed, abandoned, and worse, like the darkness, she knew the NVA were coming.

She headed for the River's Edge Hotel. It was the only place she knew. Lawlessness and anarchy was everywhere, ARVN soldiers, MP's and police all doing the same as everyone else: looting. People hauled away anything they could carry: furniture, filing cabinets, mattresses, cushions, dishes, pots and pans all suddenly growing arms and legs. It was a free-for-all and for the looters, their bounty was the fulfilment of their aspirations, proof that they too had been robbed: robbed of their dreams.

Mai-Ly hurried along, jumping at bursts of gunfire or explosions, watching the fires that littered her route, the flickering flames adding to the confusion and malevolent sense of danger. Some buildings were aflame but mostly the fires were lit to get rid of designer clothing and the like, anything that could constitute a perceived link to the Americans.

She reached the hotel just as a twenty dollar bill blew into her face. She had no way of knowing that all over the city, millions of dollars were fluttering about in the evening breeze.

They were worthless; money couldn't help anyone now.

She thought it was a sign she'd escape and perhaps, even become prosperous.

It wasn't and she wouldn't.

As she reached the hotel, she noticed Mrs Jayanda in the restaurant, propped up on a stool by the bar, whisky glass in hand.

"American swine!" she mumbled, her eyes glazed over with hate. "They took what they want and now they've gone; left my business; left me; left my country to die!"

Similar words were being uttered all over the city and all over the world too.

Mai-Ly spent the night in the small room she and Bian and Thimay had shared together for nearly two years but aside from the familiarity of the surroundings, she was on new ground.

She was all alone.

* * * * *

All day and all night the helicopters came and went.

The courage and commitment of the helicopter crews was amazing, history eventually recording that Operation Frequent Wind air-lifted to safety over seven thousand Americans, Vietnamese and third country nationals.

It was gone midnight when Troy and Bian emerged onto the roof as the weather closed-in. The queue snaked its way forward up a metal staircase to the highest point and helipad, the roof of the building that housed the Embassy's air conditioning and lift systems.

Three choppers came and went and then, it was their turn.

As Troy looked out the Chinook's porthole window at fires burning all over the city, he wondered what the future held, wondered where Mai-Ly was, wondered what Bian was thinking, and wondered if he'd ever see Vietnam again.

The last week apart, Troy had loved Vietnam. It had given him Bian, even if she was Laotian, and he'd grown to love the people of the tiny but torn country.

"Troy, where are we?" Bian said, surprising him with her first words in over two hours.

"We're on our way to America Bian."

"Will we be able to go back for Mama?" she said, asking the dreaded question.

"Yes, when everything settles down," he said lying.

In the bigger picture, the early hours of April 30th saw Ambassador Graham Martin receive the order direct from the White House, to personally evacuate the Embassy. He was told there'd be just nineteen more chopper sorties and that he was to be on the nineteenth. At 04:58 AM, with smoke billowing from a fire somewhere deep inside the Embassy and dollar bills fluttering on the breeze, Ambassador Martin reluctantly climbed aboard carrying the Embassy's carefully folded American flag.

Behind him, the situation was deteriorating quickly. With thousands congregating outside the gates, Major James Kean, officer-in-charge of the Marine Security Guard, made the decision to pull back inside the Embassy. They barricaded the doors and moved up to the top floor where they had easy access to the roof. When the people realised what was happening, they stormed the gates, smashed in the front door and swarmed through the offices on the lower floors, lighting fires and throwing anything they could pick up out the windows for looters below to carry off into the darkness. It was raw anarchy, humankind out of control.

A few hours later, in the first light of early morning, the Marines got their ride home. They were the last of more than seven thousand to leave.

It was an inglorious end to an inglorious chapter in American history.

Later that same morning, NVA tanks entered the city from six different directions. They came expecting a battle but not one shot was fired in anger.

In what was a day of complete victory for Vietnam, the war was over.

Oblivious to what was going on behind him, Troy P. Templeman was overwhelmed by a sense of relief. Finally, he, the woman he loved and the child he saw as his own were on their way. The feelings of indignity, betrayal and humiliation would come later.

America was calling and the Promised Land beckoned.

CHAPTER EIGHTEEN:

The *USS Hancock* was swarming with frenetic activity.

As Troy looked out the Chinook's window, he could see dozens of servicemen working frantically to clear space for the chopper to land. With everything lit up by the ship's powerful searchlights, the hyper-sense of movement was accentuated by the long dark shadows that followed everyone everywhere. It looked surreal, like something out of a bizarre nightmare.

But it wasn't; it was all real.

As the chopper doors opened they were blasted by a wall of deafening noise: roaring engines, swooshing rotor blades, babies crying, women wailing, men shouting. The picture of chaotic mayhem increased further as U.S. naval personnel pushed helicopters over the edge of the ship into the South China Sea below. What Troy and the chopper's other passengers didn't know was that in the chaos, South Vietnamese air force pilots were landing ARVN helicopters without permission or even, when access was blocked, just ditching in the seas around the armada of ships: desperate times calling for desperate measures.

All over the massive deck, people spewed out the choppers into the claustrophobic atmosphere: the black sky, deafening noise, artificial light and extreme humidity. Some spewed literally, one woman's hand too slow to prevent a stream of vomit leaving her lips.

It was utter pandemonium, the *Hancock* overnight, becoming *home* to three thousand men, women and children. People of every age, colour and description, all wearing the same haunted look, all led below deck into an underworld city made up of hundreds of canvas booths.

Within minutes of settling into their own eighty square feet of space, Bian and Thimay were out cold, exhausted, so Troy went back up to the deck where he bumped into a young Major called Dwight Reimer.

"What's up Major?" he said, watching him drag heavily on his cigarette.

"Just reflecting Sir. I been back and fore Southeast Asia since '64 and I can't help but feel a sense of personal guilt."

"I know what you mean Major. I worked at the Embassy and we made so many empty promises; it's hard to believe we could behave in such a way."

They'd been chatting for over two hours when the conversation turned to the immediate future.

"Do you have any idea where we headed Major?"

"The Philippines Sir: Cubi Point Naval Station, Subic Bay."

"How long will it take?"

"Day after tomorrow."

"What then?"

"There's a camp been set up on Grande Island. I bet you'd rather give it a miss and get yourself back to the States soon as?"

"You bet!"

"I know someone at Cubi Point," said the Major hopefully. "Perhaps he can help you get a ride to LA without having to queue."

"That would be great!" Troy replied, silently resolving to hold Major Reimer to his pledge.

Forty-eight hours later, the *Hancock* sailed into Subic Bay, Troy and Bian just two of over a thousand people on deck.

"There he is! Major! Major!" Troy cried.

Reimer looked over, made the OK sign and pointed down to a quayside processing point.

"Meet you there," he mimed.

From thirty yards away, Troy watched Dwight Reimer whisper into the ear of a Marine Sergeant and point, the Sergeant's eyes immediately fixing on Troy and Bian. Troy thought he smiled slightly as his look lingered on Bian for several seconds longer than they did on him. It was a phenomenon he'd seen many times before and one that often made him angry. This time though, he could live with it. If the Sergeant could fast-track them to the States, a little disrespect seemed a small price to pay.

Four hours later they were in the skies above the Pacific, headed for Camp Pendleton, the Marine Corps base in southern California, which had been set-up as one of four U.S. processing centres for refugees and evacuees. Though packed with people, there was little conversation and no merriment. Troy was glad; he wasn't in the mood to talk. He felt defeated, only the thought of seeing Bian set foot on United States soil for the first time keeping him from sinking into serious depression.

What he didn't know was that already there, albeit in different corners of the vast country, were the four men whose destinies were inextricably entwined with his.

* * * * *

Forty-five miles north of Camp Pendleton, a man sat in a small rowing boat a hundred yards out from shore. Though still three months short of his thirtieth birthday, he looked older, his hawkish features lifeless as he hunched over his fishing line.

It was a serene scene, the smooth-as-glass waters reflecting the browns and greens of the surrounding hills in the warm, early May sunshine. California's Great Hemet Dam looked a picture but the man cut a lonely, isolated figure.

Though his limbs were on auto-pilot, gently jerking the line, Frankie Fernando's haunted mind was miles away.

A winner of the Medal of Honor and Silver Star, no-one served longer on the front-line in Vietnam than the man known as Frankie F. His long service earned him an honourable discharge in the summer of '72 and, after a three month stay at the Silas B. Hayes Army Hospital in Monterey, he went home to Hemet. But despite what the U.S. Military said, and despite what people may have thought, he knew he was no hero. In fact, it was worse than that; he was a man without honour.

But it wasn't the ferocity of the conflict in Southeast Asia that scarred him; his scars came from being out in front. He'd once been a leader of men and how he wished he'd led differently. But he hadn't. He and his men crossed a line and innocent civilians became victims of his weakness. He knew he'd pay a heavy price and in three years, it had got worse not better. He knew he was on a slippery slope and he knew his failure would always be part of him.

Frankie Fernando wasn't a man who frightened easily but something from deep within was making him more scared than he'd ever been.

He could feel himself turning into his father, suicide waiting at his door.

* * * * *

Attracted to his rugged good looks and hard athletic physique, twenty year old Rachel Harden had only met him two nights before. She thought they'd connected but she had no idea what she was letting herself in for when she invited him to a concert at New York's Iona State where she was studying international history.

With the music blasting, the New Rochelle Campus throbbed with youthful vitality and the general opinion seemed to be that the band was fantastic.

But Michael McBride wasn't interested. He was busy proving a point.

Anastasia were a band on the up. They saw themselves as New York's answer to Led Zeppelin and liked to take their own security men to gigs. Lording it over drunken college kids had their minders thinking they were a bit special but the man some knew as *Irish* was taking great pleasure in proving they weren't. Stripped to the waist covered in blood, he looked every inch the warrior. The music had stopped, the lights were on and the college kids had all turned to watch him bounce the bouncers.

As the police and ambulance sirens neared, Rachel Harden whisked her bloodied warrior out through a back entrance and off to her small apartment on Lincoln Avenue. After he emerged from the bathroom rubbing his hair, she was amazed to see there wasn't a mark on him and that all the blood had belonged to his victims. It made her even hotter.

Forty-five minutes later, seconds after his climax, McBride was in the place he despised above all others: the place of his greatest weakness. Like his fighting, the sex was nothing more than a temporary reprieve, a few fleeting moments to try to forget the unforgettable.

But he knew it wouldn't last long, it never did; the demons in his head, the unmistakable voice of his dead grandfather and the flashbacks to the riverbank in Southern Laos all combining to block his escape route from his past.

Michael McBride was consumed with hate. He hated himself for not being what he should have been and what his grandfather would've wanted him to be. He hated God and the world for taking his grandfather. But most of all, he hated Rudi Kingsbridge, the man he saw as the catalyst to his committing the unforgivable sin.

In the absence of getting his hands on Kingsbridge and ripping his heart out, the world, for now at least, was going to have to pay.

* * * * *

The atmosphere was electric, the crowd on their feet punching the air, whooping and shouting. It was pose-down time at the 1975 Mr U.S.A. body-building competition and Danny Padilla, barely five foot four of perfectly balanced, solid muscle was holding off the competition from his much bigger rivals, Roger Callard and Mike Mentzer.

Whatever the result, it was going to be tight.

But for the huge black man sat in the fifth row of the Dallas Embassy Auditorium, there was an almost overwhelming sense of dissatisfaction. Eugene Sanders had been looking forward to the May 4th event ever since he and his brother had purchased tickets a month earlier.

Somehow though, it didn't scratch his itch.

Fact was, he was bored, had been ever since his five year spell in the military came to an end the previous January.

The man his fellow soldiers called *Kong* loved every minute of army life, the adrenalin rush of combat and constant threat of danger like a drug to his system. It was the reason he and his great friend *Irish* McBride elected to stay on in Vietnam after the Special Ops unit they were part of was decommissioned in June '72. The pair spent the next two-and-a-half years advising the forces of South Vietnam and the Cambodians and when their services were no longer required in Southeast Asia they still managed to avoid coming home, preferring instead to stop off in darkest Africa.

Irish said Kong was just going back to his roots but the truth was both men liked the fight too much to stay away. The African sortie was an assignment so secret that neither man ever really understood who exactly it was they were working for. But a covert operation deep in the jungle, training opposition forces to Zaire's Dictator Joseph Mobuto, was right up their street. They spent eight months on African location and so cut-off were they, it wasn't till they arrived back in the States that they realised Muhammad Ali and George Foreman had fought their legendary *Rumble in the Jungle* just a hundred and fifty miles from their base camp.

Big Eugene missed everything about military life. There were a few things he'd change if he had his time over, one or two people he'd treat differently if he could, especially that little oriental chick they'd run into in Laos after taking out the Pathet Lao big-wigs.

But life's a bitch and then you die. It was Eugene's motto for a dog-eat-dog world.

* * * * *

It wasn't often he slept alone. But this wasn't enforced isolation; it was isolation by choice.

When you're as handsome, fit and rich as Rudi Kingsbridge, prospective bed partners are everywhere. But to the twenty-five year old heir to the Kingsbridge millions, having someone share his bed was more about convenience than a desire for relationship or a quest for love. He wasn't a people person or someone needing the company of another. He just needed sex. He saw it as pure entertainment, a game of pursuit that also happened to be his favourite way of fuelling his inflated self-image.

In many ways, he was a serial sex addict, hooked long before he lost his virginity at fourteen after forcing one of the house maids at the family home on the shores of Lake Michigan to have sex with him.

As the early morning light flooded his bedroom, he smiled as he realised something was stirring down below. Minutes later, his body and mind were in perfect harmony, his thoughts flicking the pages of mental imagery he'd filed away in his library of sexual history. Then he turned to the page that always tipped him over the edge. He'd taken her twice, brutally and callously, but since that June day of '72 he'd had her in his mind a million times.

Ten seconds later, it was a million and one.

As he rose from the bed still smiling, his eye caught a twenty by sixteen framed photo hanging over the marble fireplace in the corner of the plush master bedroom suite. There were nine or ten soldiers of the 101st Airborne stood side-by-side behind a hand drawn banner that declared *Screaming Eagles – Charlie's worst nightmare!* They looked relaxed and were obviously enjoying some downtime. Rudi smiled again, his eyes fixing on himself, second from the left. Six years younger, he looked more youthful, a little fitter and seven or eight pounds lighter, the black ties round his elbows accentuating the muscularity of his upper arms and shoulders.

"You handsome son-of-a-bitch!" he said out loud before heading off to the bathroom mirror, keen to resume his love affair with himself.

After taking the private penthouse lift to the ground floor, he set a gentle pace for the half-mile stroll to the pillared entrance to Harvard Business School. New England in the springtime is a sight to behold but Rudi didn't even notice. May 4th 1975 was the start-point of two weeks of exams – the culmination of his first year studies – and he intended doing well. It wasn't his first go at Harvard and he was taking life at the esteemed establishment much more seriously second time round.

It was the reason he'd made the sacrifice to sleep alone.

As he walked up the steps towards the entrance, two girls looked his way, whispered to one another, then giggled.

"You handsome son-of-a-bitch!" he said to himself once again, the arrogance oozing out his every pore.

* * * * *

Like Subic Bay in the Philippines, Camp Pendleton was just a staging post.

Eighteen hours after arriving at the Californian home of the U.S. Marines, Troy and Bian were winging it across the southern States together with sixty or so other passengers being repatriated to Florida and the southeast.

Troy enjoyed the thought that when they landed at Eglin Air Force Base in northwest Florida, they'd be less than four hundred miles from their ultimate destination, the home of his parents, Randy and Jeanette Templeman.

Along with Camp Pendleton, Eglin was one of four Refugee Processing Centres set up to deal with the "Southeast Asia problem." By the time Troy, Bian and

Thimay arrived; there were more than eight thousand refugees at the Air Force Base's Tent City.

"Troyyyy!" Jeanette Templeman shrieked seconds after picking up the phone. "Randy, it's Troy! Where are you Troy? Are you OK? You coming home? You hurt?" she added in quick succession, passing the receiver to her husband before giving her son the chance to answer.

"Where are you son?" Randy said, more composed than his wife but nonetheless repeating one of her questions. "We were worried son."

"I'm OK Pop. It's been crazy but guess what? We're only up in Eglin: a hundred miles west of Tallahassee."

"Tallahassee? Tallahassee, Florida?" his father said incredulously, seeming not to notice that Troy had said "*We're* up in Eglin" not "*I'm* up in Eglin."

"Yeah, we're just three hundred and fifty miles away I guess!"

"And your mother and I thought you were on board a ship bobbing round the Pacific!"

With his wife tugging his arm, Randy Templeman handed her the phone. Ten minutes later, she passed it back to her husband.

"Son, you said we're up in Eglin. What you mean *we*?"

Despite his father's directness, it was the opportunity Troy had hoped for.

"I haven't come back from Vietnam alone, Pop."

"What you mean? You haven't gone and done something stupid . . .?"

"No Pop, I've not gotten married! But I have brought someone with me; a Laotian girl," he said, pausing before adding, "And her little boy."

"You've what? Is the boy yours?"

"Pop, will you relax? I'm in love with this girl. Her name's Bian by the way, and I intend caring for her best I can. So Pop, get used to the idea. If you don't want us to come home, just say, and I'll make alternative plans."

It was Troy's turn to be direct.

"Don't be so soft son. You come on home and bring Bian and the boy with you. What's his name?"

"His name's Thimay," said Troy doing well to hide his surprise at how quickly his father softened and how easily he remembered Bian's name.

"Yes Troy, you come on home as soon as you can. You understand?"

"Yeah: I understand Pop. And Pop?"

"Yes son?"

"Thanks; I really appreciate it."

"We've missed you son."

"I missed you Pop and Marm too. I love you both," Troy said wiping a tear off his cheek.

"We love you too son; you keep in touch now."

As the conversation came to an end, father, mother and son were in tears, Randy and Jeanette relieved their son was safe, Troy relieved he'd told his parents about Bian and Thimay.

But it would be another six weeks before everyone would meet up face-to-face, Bian's non-American status requiring her to go through a sponsorship process.

"My parents are really looking forward to meeting you Bian," Troy said confidently, pleased he was able to mean it.

"I'm grateful Troy but I want my family back," she said, her eyes filling to overflow.

Every time it happened, it had the same effect: she withdrew, Troy lied, and conversation dried up for hours, sometimes days. What neither Troy nor Bian had any way of knowing was that one part of the Mai-Ly, Xiantha and Tong Tenh trinity was already dead: Mai-Ly's tiny right foot big enough to tread in the wrong place, her frail seventy-five pound body heavy enough to trigger the mine's detonator of death.

Lost in the loneliness of her isolation, the old woman was just fifteen miles out of Saigon when she took her fatal last step; the suddenness of the explosion allowing her death, unlike her life, to come pain-free. She was dead even before the *USS Hancock* pulled into Subic Bay.

* * * * *

Randy and Jeanette Templeman stood in station six as the Greyhound pulled in.

"Troy, Troy, over here," mother excitedly shouted to her only son.

It was an emotionally charged few minutes.

"Marm, Pop: this is Bian and Thimay," he said proudly.

"Oh Troy!" his mother cooed, "Bian, you're just lovely, so beautiful. Isn't she dear?" she said turning to her husband.

"Yes dear," Randy replied, dutifully agreeing but not needing anyone to point out something so obvious. His eyes caught Troy's and father winked to son, pursing his lips and raising his eyebrows as if to say, "Wow!!"

Worried there'd be too many awkward silences, Troy had been dreading the moment they would all meet up. He knew he'd got it wrong when he turned to see Bian and his mother walking to the car arm-in-arm, Bian smiling, his mother chattering away.

It looked good and it looked right. Troy relaxed.

The Templeman household was a semi-detached one-storey property at North Orange Drive, just over a half-mile to the west of Highway 19.

As the Pontiac pulled into the drive Troy was surprised how glad he was to be home.

After a week where the sense of *family* was everywhere, father and son found themselves together on the porch.

"What you planning on doing with yourself son?"

"I'm resigning from the Diplomatic Corps."

"Isn't that a little drastic?"

"If you'd seen what I seen Pop, you'd know why I could never work for the government again."

"Tell me about it son, sounds like you need to get it off your chest."

"It was betrayal Pop; betrayal of the worst kind," Troy replied, lowering his eyes. "Hundreds of our friends were left behind to face certain death. Congress betrayed a trust we'd given South Vietnam and being as I was a representative of the government, I feel as if I was betrayed too. I'd made promises that we'd honour our agreements but all we did was cut and run. It hurts me to say so but it made me wish I wasn't American."

Knowing his father was a fierce patriot, Troy half-expected an argument. But Randy's response surprised him. "Things are never what they should be son. You know what it was like; you were there. Whatever you want to do is fine by me Troy. I never wanted you to go to Vietnam in the first place. So tell me son, what you thinking of doing?"

"I'm gonna be a lawyer Pop."

"A lawyer?"

"Yeah, I'm gonna see if I can get myself into Stetson University College of Law."

"That's a great Law School son. Only this week, I heard someone refer to it as the Harvard Law School of the South."

"Yeah: I heard that too Pop. I got a meeting with their admissions department this coming Thursday. You like to come along Pop?"

"I'd love to son!" his father replied glowing with pride.

Eight days later, Randy and Troy were cruising down Highway 19.

Named after the millionaire hat-maker from Philadelphia, Stetson University College of Law had an interesting history. Officially part of Deland University in central Florida, Stetson's problems after World War Two prompted the unprecedented step of canvassing Florida's major cities about hosting a possible relocation. Jacksonville, Tampa and Orlando all showed interest but in 1954, against the odds, it was Gulfport that won the race.

On highly favourable terms, the University purchased the former Hotel Rolyat and landed a ready-made, architecturally distinct campus styled after a medieval Spanish village, complete with towers, arches, fountains and walled enclosures. The relocation proved an unmitigated success and Stetson's reputation had grown year-on-year ever since.

"Wow!" said Randy in genuine admiration as they walked through a huge arch into the Plaza.

"Isn't it fantastic Pop?"

"I'd say! If they turn out lawyers half as sharp as their buildings, you'll be able to carve the Thanksgiving turkey with your tongue!"

"Troy Templeman from Tarpon Springs for an 11:30 with Admissions," Troy said confidently before turning back to his father. "See you in a minute Pop."

"Good luck," said Randy, knowing whoever his son was sat in front of couldn't help but be impressed. He was right. They were.

"Pop, they've offered me a place for the coming term!"

"That's great news Troy," said Randy positively glowing with pride.

"Hey Pop, isn't it incredible that Stetson's no longer in Deland?" Troy said excitedly when they were back in the car. "It's only twenty-six miles door-to-door so I'll be able to commute daily. If it were still in Deland the four hundred and fifty mile round trip would make that impossible."

"See son, it's like your grand-pappy used to say, the sun shines on the righteous!"

"Now don't you go getting all religious on me now Pop," said Troy mischievously.

It was one of many cracks that passed between them on the forty-five minute journey, father and son enjoying one another's company as never before.

"Meet our very own Perry Mason!" Randy triumphed as he opened the front door to find Jeanette, Bian and Thimay waiting expectantly. "Troy starts at Stetson in six weeks!"

"Oooh Troy!" Jeanette purred.

"Troy, I'm so proud of you," Bian chirped excitedly before kissing him on the cheek. "I thought today was just an interview!!"

"I did too. But they were so impressed they rolled out the red carpet!!"

As his parents chuckled, Bian kissed him again.

It was Troy's turn to glow with pride.

* * * * *

If Troy was enjoying himself, so was Bian.

She'd been made to feel very welcome and felt especially close to Troy's mother Jeanette.

It had helped her relax and settle into life in a foreign land. Then, one night, she had a dream where she was walking through lush green fields alongside Father Mesnel who was praying out loud, just as he had in Saisettha, the last time she'd seen him face-to-face. As she woke, she sensed something had changed, broken. It was a tranquil moment where she sensed a providential hand working in her life.

Life afterwards was different. She thought less about Laos, less about the rape and less about the family she'd left behind. She made a conscious effort to appreciate what she had rather than dwell on any perceived loss. Her speech became more positive as she realised her words could and would, frame her world. She focused forwards and resolved to not let her past deter-mine her future, or more imp-ortantly, her son's future.

"Things are good and they're going to get even better!" she'd say to herself over and over.

It became a self-fulfilling prophecy.

The job offer she'd been waiting and praying for, from the Kentucky Fried Chicken chain of restaurants, came through the same morning Troy received his pay-off from the Diplomatic Corps, Troy waving a two thousand dollar check as Bian shrieked "Yes! Yes! Yes!"

Two weeks later, the new Tarpons Springs KFC opened on the intersection of Benita Drive and Highway 19. It was a day of firsts: the restaurant's first day trading, Bian's first day in her first job, all coinciding with her nineteenth birthday, on 1st August.

It took just a week for the restaurant's franchisee to identify the beautiful oriental girl as one of his key assets, only marginally behind the bearded Colonel Sanders' secret recipe!

She'd originally been offered five lunchtime afternoon shifts. But seeing the effect she had on the male population of Tarpon Springs, her boss quickly persuaded her to move to four evening shifts.

Bian couldn't believe her luck; only three weeks into a new job and she'd somehow secured a sixty per cent pay increase in return for a twenty per cent reduction in working hours! Bian was thrilled, her boss ecstatic and Jeanette more than happy to take on the lion's share of baby-sitting little Thimay.

They were all delighted; everyone except Troy.

When he'd visited the restaurant, he couldn't believe how many people could cram into such a small space. Just four weeks after opening, Tarpon Springs became the only KFC in history to take table bookings. Those who took the chance on a table without making a reservation, invariably ended up disappointed, forced to make do with a takeaway. And if you were male, the last thing you wanted was to eat out, a takeaway only allowing a fleeting few minutes to gaze at the most amazingly beautiful girl ever seen behind a fast-food serving counter, anywhere, anytime.

For many, the food was incidental and to some, it was funny to watch.

But Troy wasn't amused.

When he broached the subject one evening, she reacted sharply. "Troy I'm not interested in anyone, not now, not ever," she said, not fully realising what she was saying.

"So where does that leave *me*?" he said, the hurt obvious.

"I didn't mean it like that," she spluttered, her eyes glassing over.

"Well how did you mean it? And while we're on the subject where exactly *are* we going?"

"Oh Troy: why does it always have to be like this? You put me under such pressure. I can't help the way I look and if men like to look at me what can I do to stop them? You've seen me. I don't dress provocatively. I don't flirt. I don't respond when someone comes on to me. Troy, I'm not interested."

"So where does that leave *me*?" Troy repeated.

"Troy, I love you more than a brother; I've never loved anyone like I love you."

"But I don't want to be your brother Bian; I want to be your man, your husband. Though the way you treat me, I can't imagine why."

"There's no need to be horrible Troy. I'm only just gone nineteen so if you can't wait, then I'm sorry." She was surprisingly forceful and wasn't finished. "And Troy," she added, "I can't live life with you getting jealous every time a man looks at me. It's horrible and if we're not careful, you'll be telling me what I can do, where I can go, and who I can speak to. I won't live like that Troy."

"But Bian," Troy said, feeling as if he'd overstepped the mark. "I love you so much. I'd cope easier if I knew where I stood. But sometimes I forget how old you are, you're so mature and so beautiful. I'm sorry I put you under pressure. I don't mean to. I can wait Bian. I love you Bian."

It was his turn to go all glassy-eyed even if she suspected it was more contrived than real.

"Troy, I know you love me and I know I love you but it can't go any further," she said sounding sad and hesitating a little before leaving the door slightly ajar, "For now at least."

She hated the fact she couldn't be truthful and despised the way something that'd taken place over three years earlier, something she had no control over, could so totally envelop her with fear; the never-ending pain able to reach from the nightmare in her past right into the present as easily as walking across the street. It was poison, pure poison.

And for Troy who was unaware of the bigger picture, it was pain time, again.

He ached he loved Bian so much, but seeing her go off to work knowing every male in town would be ogling her, lusting after her, insidiously undermined him. Thought after thought washed through his mind and none were positive. His manhood, his self-esteem was on trial and he was haunted by the fact that baby Thimay was evidence that Bian had obviously had her first sexual experience. But for him, there'd been no hugs, no kisses, and no sex.

Lost in his thoughts lying on his bed, Troy felt physically sick. It was entirely psychosomatic; his sub-conscious interpreting the signs and transmitting them to his body.

The message?

The future was coming . . . and life wasn't going to be easy.

PART TWO

TWENTY-FIVE YEARS LATER

New Year's Eve, December 31st 1999

CHAPTER NINETEEN:

10, 9, 8, 7 . . . it was countdown time.

Counting down the last seconds as one year ends and another begins is a big deal in most parts of the world, but on December 31st 1999 it wasn't just big, it was huge. Ushering in the new millennium, the last day of '99 brought with it a prevailing sense of optimism as people celebrated the dawning of what they hoped was a new age, a new era where dreams really could come true.

But under the overpass where the 60 crosses the 710 in LA's Central City East, there was neither a sense of celebration nor anticipation. Unbeknown to the thousands that drove across the intersection, a few feet below them was a community without hope, a community on the periphery of mainstream society, on the margins of life itself. In Cardboard City there were no dreams just existence, the primary goal of life to make it through to tomorrow. It was a place where nothing really mattered and a Millennium New Year's Eve was no big deal.

In the surreal light of a half-dozen fires, their flickering flames sending shadows dancing up and down the concrete walls and pillars, Frankie Fernando cut a lonely forlorn figure, even for a hobo. Dates meant nothing to him. He wasn't interested. Squeezed into one of the lowest corners of the overpass, he was three-quarters the way into his second bottle of wine. It was a nightly routine: a well walked road to his favourite destination, oblivion.

While he looked just like any aging hobo – unshaven, stinking and dressed in rags – the man once known as *Frankie F* was no ordinary hobo. He was a hobo with a past. Once a leader of men, Frankie was a real-life war hero; a veteran of the Vietnam War and a winner of the Medal of Honor and Silver Star. It wasn't something he talked about. In fact, he didn't talk.

Frankie didn't like people but most of all he didn't like himself.

On his return to the U.S. after serving seven years in Vietnam, he spent three months in the mental health facility at the Silas B. Hayes Army Hospital in Monterey, a hundred miles south of San Francisco. Fancy name or not, Frankie knew he was in the Looney Bin.

Within days of arriving, he was diagnosed as a manic depressive with suicidal tendencies. But however skilled the doctors were at eking information from their patients, they soon realised they were on a loser when it came to Corporal Franklyn Fernando, U.S. Marine. Frankie was amongst the most unresponsive and uncommunicative patients they'd ever had and whatever tipped him over the edge was going to remain a mystery, doctors forced to watch him go through the full spectrum of rebellion: violence, abuse, self harm, withdrawal, and finally, silence. In the end, they gave up, signed the papers and watched their patient head off home, to Hemet.

When he got to the musty house on Ramona Palms, all he could think about was his father strung up like a skewered pig in a slaughter-house, hanging from the punch-bag hook in the corner of his bedroom. It was an image so clear in his mind it was like he was looking at a photograph. Everywhere he went for months he kept seeing it; his father's face drained of blood, eyes a'poppin', head hanging grotesquely to the side at an impossible angle.

Fearing for his safety and sanity, Mrs Ridings the next door neighbour contacted his mother Roseanna who'd left town after an affair with the insurance salesman. She'd moved forty miles east to Palm Springs, and it'd been more than a decade since she'd set eyes on her son.

When Frankie and Roseanna were reunited on the porch, the only one crying was old Mrs Ridings. Roseanna had thought about her son often but the lovelessness of her life had left her numb inside, unable to really feel anything. For Frankie, the reunion was just like everything else in his life; it just happened. His entire emotional system had been corrupted by a loveless childhood, by the adultery of his mother, his father's suicide, and by the Vietnam years, especially the last year when he found himself heading up Bleeding Dog Company. As the leader of a covert four-man Special Operations unit, Frankie'd found the bickering between two of his men so wearing that his ability to lead evaporated to the point where if the truth ever came out, the Bleeding Dogs would be labelled war criminals.

And it was his fault. His weakness allowed it to happen. He was the leader; he failed himself, his men and his country

The reunion with Roseanna saw her move back to Hemet in the spring of 1974. Though she came on a three week visit, she ended up staying two decades. She did everything for him but there was no intimacy, just co-existence. She completed the forms so his army and disability pensions could be collected from the local Post Office. It was the main source of household income; Frankie's attempts at work doomed to failure and guaranteed to bring on yet more depression.

After his mother's death in February 1994, old Mrs Ridings next door helped him with the cleaning, washing and ironing. But then, in October of the same year, death claimed Mrs Ridings too and Frankie was left helpless as a new born baby.

All alone, he didn't know which way to turn, so he did what he always did, nothing.

His pensions and allowances went uncollected and the bills piled up. Eight months after his mother passed away, the bank foreclosed on the mortgage. There was less than eight hundred dollars outstanding and just fifteen months left to run. But the mortgagors exploited Frankie's confusion and had him transfer the house into their ownership for less than four thousand dollars.

Without a roof over his head, Frankie began sleeping in Weston Park. His reputation and status as a Medal of Honor winner meant the officers of the Hemet Police Department left him alone to his park bench. Though he had whatever was left from the house sale stuffed into his pocket, he was never going to be mugged. He may have been a down-and-out down on his luck but he was still Frankie F and nobody in Hemet was foolish enough to think they could separate the man from his money.

When he was down to his last hundred dollars, he knew it was time to move on. If he wanted to eat or more importantly, if he wanted to get the wine he needed to lose himself, he would have to beg and that meant moving; so in the early summer of 1996 he upped sticks and moved west, to the City of the Angels.

The busyness of LA's Culver City bus station was a world apart to a man looking to hide, from himself and from his memories. Within a month, he'd found the solitude he was looking for: in Cardboard City, under the overpass where the 60 crosses the 710.

Sensing he was different to your run-of-the-mill hobo, residents gave him the space he craved. This was especially so after he battered three Hispanics who ventured into the overpass looking to do a bit of tramp-bashing. The incident fast-tracked him to the result he'd wanted all along, the right to be alone in the space he called "home."

As the last hours of the twentieth century ticked away, he was all alone at home, on his back looking up at the concrete slab that doubled as his bedroom ceiling, five feet above his face. Though the wine-induced haze was beginning to fall, he was fighting the battles he fought every night, his demons queuing up to bring him his failures in glorious Technicolor: his father hanging on a hook, that son-of-a-bitch Kingsbridge trying to kill McBride on the chopper and undermining his leadership at every turn. Then there was the crazed massacre of the Pathet Lao militia and the rape of the beautiful oriental girl by the river's edge.

Frankie should've stopped it all; but he didn't.

He was a failure and he knew that new millennium or no new millennium it wasn't going to change.

CHAPTER TWENTY:

"They must be the prettiest people on the planet!" one elegantly dressed sixty year old said to her friend sat next to her.

"He's drop-dead gorgeous, pure sex! And she, well, she's perfect!"

They were at the Four Seasons, for the three thousand dollar-a-head *Millennium Party of a Lifetime*. The guest list read like a who's who of Chicago's rich and famous. But even when mixing it with the windy city's high society, Rudi and Kay Kingsbridge were like royalty. Rudi was the outrageously handsome corporate mogul with the Midas touch, while his wife, formerly Kay Ferrano supermodel, was a global icon whose face had appeared on the cover of magazines in more than a hundred countries. They looked electric individually but together, as Chicago's highest profile couple, they were sensational, a team greater than just the sum of the parts.

They arrived late. It was no accident. Being late meant every eye would be on them as they walked to their seats. It was a strategy guaranteed to get tongues wagging all over the room.

Some let the superlatives roll off into the atmosphere, others just hung out in lust.

In every way, Rudi and Kay Kingsbridge were the beautiful people.

The son of legendary banker Jordan Kingsbridge and Hollywood actress Marlene Moorer, Rudi hat it all. 1999 may have seen in his fiftieth birthday but he looked at least ten years younger, testimony to his youthful vigorous look and to his being in amazing shape. His appearance on the front cover of *Men's Fitness* the previous month had everyone talking; stripped to the waist, his lithe muscular physique putting most super-fit twenty-five year olds to shame.

It also turned him into a gay icon.

His best friend and business partner Ulysses Maxwell, Max for short, ribbed him about the story when it first appeared. "What's it like being sex-on-legs to America's faggot community?" he chuckled, screwing his face up in disgust.

But nothing fazed Rudi. "I'm so handsome every pig in the pig-pen wants a piece of me!"

The two had met at Harvard in the mid-Seventies, shortly after Rudi returned from three-and-a-half years in Vietnam. Though a good looking boy himself, Max was a bit geeky: the type who wouldn't say boo to a goose. But rubbing shoulders with the likes of Rudi Kingsbridge has a way of changing a man: for the worse.

By the time they started their second year at Harvard they'd built a reputation as a sexual tag team. They were predators hunting as a combo and were so into themselves they thought they were doing the female population a favour. They were as insufferable as they were inseparable, the guys at Harvard giving them a wide berth. With Rudi oozing menace at the slightest challenge, even the big football stars and wrestlers had no option but to tolerate them. The word was everywhere Rudi had been Special Ops in Vietnam and no-one wanted to go hand-to-hand with a guy who once killed people hand-to-hand for a living.

Max had never been especially physical but in Rudi's shadow, he could lord it over the male population while taking his pick of the female of the species. He couldn't believe how good life could be. It was the start of a friendship that spanned the last quarter of the twentieth century and both men had risen through corporate America side-by-side.

Six years after graduating from Harvard, Rudi was Chief Operations Officer at the Kingsbridge Bank of Illinois. Jordan was still CEO and Rudi hated having to report to a father he despised. Four years into the role, he spotted his chance and made the decision that would change his life and Max's life forever.

Ever since he'd first met him, Max had predicted that communications would be *the next big thing*, convinced that one day, everyone would carry a personal telephone.

Rudi couldn't see it but Max ploughed on, investing time and money into his research.

When they left Harvard, Max joined the Corporate Research Team at Motorola. They shared his vision for the future but Ulysses Maxwell wanted a chunk of corporate America all to himself.

He knew exactly where he was going, how he'd get there and what he needed to reach his goal. Top of his needs list was Rudi Kingsbridge. KBI was a big-time investor and Max persuaded his friend that he had the investment opportunity of a lifetime. With Rudi shrewdly lobbying internally, Max's presentation to the bank's investment managers got a big green light and an even bigger thirty million dollar check. It cost Max forty per cent of the embryonic company he called *Maxucom*, *Max* short for Maxwell, *U* for Ulysses, and *com* short for communications.

By the end of '99, Maxucom was America's eighteenth most recognizable brand name. Max owned thirty-seven per cent of the business. He was one of America's richest men, a billionaire eight or nine times over. Though careful not to voice it anywhere, he loved being richer than Rudi; it was the only time he'd ever crossed the finishing line before him. Rudi may have hated it, but he didn't show it either. Though he would've preferred to be number one, rich is rich and Rudi had so much money he didn't know what to do with it.

Backing Maxucom strengthened his position and status within KBI and helped nudge Jordan towards a retirement that finally came to pass after a little blackmail, Rudi threatening to tell his mother about his thirty-year affair with Marsha Delano, the bank's former financial director. Jordan cut his losses, announced his retirement and named Rudi as his successor both as Chairman and CEO in the summer of 1983. The path was so well prepared there wasn't a dissenting voice on the board.

Despite being well into their thirties, Rudi and Max rampaged through life like spoiled hormonal teenagers: sex, parties, and drugs, especially cocaine, all part of their everyday lifestyle. Rudi thought the coke would be something he could control, just like everything else. But the power of the powder was such that *it* came to control *him*. At one point, it was costing him three thousand dollars-a-day but much more than the money which was neither here nor there, it was ruining his health and damaging his business expertise.

Then, at a 1986 Christmas party in Kenilworth, something burst, literally, blood cascading out the veins in his nostrils and even emerging out his tear ducts. Rudi wasn't the kind of man who frightened easily, but inside, he went ice cold, wondering if his time had come. It all looked like a cheap Seventies horror movie but there was nothing phony about it; it was real.

After being spirited away to a private medical centre that could be relied upon to be discreet, Rudi spent three months breaking a habit that very nearly snatched his life. He emerged clean and ever since, he'd been obsessive about his health. A regime of vigorous exercise and strict diet kept him in the kind of shape he enjoyed during his military days. He loved the sense of power his fitness and razor-sharp appearance gave him and he oozed confidence.

It was a cocktail the women couldn't resist.

Sex, sex and more sex became his entertainment and for a while he and Max, who dutifully relinquished his own desire for white powder in deference to his friend, were intent on reliving their sexual adventures at Harvard. This was despite both men now being in their late-thirties, though admittedly, both had retained their good looks.

But everything changed the day Rudi met Kay Ferrano at an exclusive fashion show at Chicago's Ritz Carlton Hotel. *Forbes Magazine* had already bestowed him with the title "Most Eligible Bachelor in Corporate America" and Kay Ferrano was, along with the likes of Cindy Crawford, Christy Brinkley and Jerry Hall, one of the original supermodels.

Rudi loved the way Kay looked and bizarrely, loved the way she repulsed his efforts to get her into bed. In the event, it took six months before the day came and by then, Rudi was hooked. Even though he consoled himself sexually elsewhere, he knew he felt different about Kay Ferrano. That was why he asked her to marry him. Kay said yes and the biggest celebrity wedding Chicago had ever seen took place in the spring of 1989.

Max was best man, Kay already three months pregnant.

Rudi's life and life-style changed dramatically.

But his sexual straying was far from over. It just became more calculated, more controlled.

Even before the wedding, he'd drawn up a long list of women whom he was considering for a special assignment.

He spent weeks deliberating before selecting just twelve, every one beautiful and all knowing how to keep a secret. Typically, he called them the *lucky dozen*. They were a varied bunch; there was nineteen year old Charmain Sinclaire, a cheerleader with the Chicago Bulls, Margot Remford who was four years his senior and wife of furniture mogul Jacob P. Remford. Then there was Maria Vander, his community affairs executive at KBI and Mary-Beth Benning, a thirty-four year old lifelong lesbian till Rudi persuaded her to change direction.

His harem cost him the best part of twelve million dollars-a-year but as he saw it, it was a small price to pay to ensure he could get quality sex on demand whenever he felt either the inclination or the need.

Conscience was never an issue; he didn't have one.

Though Kay had her suspicions, it was never more than a hunch. So she let it go. She loved him, loved the kids, and was happier than she'd ever been.

It was New Year's Eve 1999 at the Four Seasons and Rudi, king of the castle, looked like the cat that got the cream. Kay was to his left, looking a million dollars in a figure-hugging black dress set-off by three strings of white pearls tightly encircling her neck. On his right sat his friend and business partner Ulysses Maxwell and his wife Verdana who was a looker herself. Everyone was talking excitedly but though he nodded every now and then to give the impression he was listening, his thoughts had taken him back to his army days.

He'd loved the thrill of military life, especially the time he was part of the Special Ops team working under cover. He liked being able to do whatever he wanted: take, burn, rape, even kill, with all sense of deterrent removed. Truth be told, he loved playing God. It had all given a buzz that cocaine or sex hadn't even come close to. As his mind drifted, remembering some of the things he did, there was no twang of conscience. And then he remembered taking the amazingly beautiful oriental girl by the river's edge and again, there was no conscience, no regret, just a stirring in his pants under the immaculately adorned table.

He'd spent the first ten months after returning from Southeast Asia in hospital recovering from reconstructive surgery to his left shoulder which had been severely injured in a knife attack in his team's last mission on active service. He also had three separate operations to fix a badly broken nose and chipped eye socket. He told everyone the injuries happened hand-to-hand fighting with the North Vietnamese but the truth was, he'd come second fighting another member of the four-man Special Ops team otherwise known as Bleeding Dog Company.

He'd thought several times about *sending the boys round* to sort Michael McBride but he knew they'd have to be accurate enough to shoot him from a thousand yards. Any closer and the chances were McBride would get them first. He may have hated the son-of-a-bitch but he had to admit the guy was iron. But that didn't stop him dreaming about the day he'd get even, and one day, he intended getting even.

"What do you think Rudi?" he heard his wife say, bringing him back from his thoughts.

"Dunno!" he muttered, trying to cover himself. "What do you think?"

Kay, Max and Verdana laughed uproariously.

"You weren't listening were you?" Kay said indignantly, puffing out her cheeks in exasperation. "The new millennium starts in twenty minutes and we were talking about our wish-lists. What's your wish Rudi, for the twenty-first century I mean?"

"Me? I haven't got a wish. I've already got it all."

CHAPTER TWENTY-ONE:

The pretty town of Farmville, Virginia, looked almost unreal on New Year's Eve 1999, a fresh fall of snow making it look like something off a picture postcard.

In Room 34 at Southside Community Hospital, a gaunt grey old man peered at his TV, watching a spectacular fireworks display on Sydney Harbour Bridge, the Aussies among the first on the planet to welcome in the new millennium.

Sixty-nine year old Doug Miller knew he was a dead man and couldn't help wonder if he'd live long enough to see in Y2K. Diagnosed with cirrhosis of the liver six months earlier, it wasn't *if* the Grim Reaper would come, it was *when*.

But Doug Miller was no ordinary man waiting to die; he was a warrior to his bootlaces.

At midday his friends from Jumpin' Jack's, his favourite bar, called to see him. But Doug's speech was so slurred he was incoherent. He knew what he was saying but his lips and tongue wouldn't co-operate. It made conversation impossible so in his frustration, Doug feigned sleep, the visitors left, and minutes later, he was back to his thoughts.

After enlisting at eighteen and serving four years in Korea, he spent the next seventeen in Indo-China. It was a special time, the most memorable period of his life. He loved Vietnam, loved the Vietnam War. When he sat on his bar-stool at Jumpin' Jack's, it was what he talked about the most when he was with the guys and what he thought about the most when he was alone.

As he lay in his hospital bed waiting to die, his mind drifted to Vietnam as if searching for a final resting place. He was thinking about the men he'd served with and the men he helped form. He'd put together more than twenty Special Ops teams in his time and the Bleeding Dogs, though not quite fulfilling their potential, were the most effective of them all. They'd recorded an enormous enemy body count and left a trail of destruction everywhere they went. And until Kingsbridge had returned from the team's final mission with a nasty knife wound to the shoulder, the unit hadn't taken a single hit. Such a record was unprecedented. But their mentor knew they had more than just the warrior mentality; there was always an edge to them, something not quite right. And it added to the mystery that Miller had never been able to put his finger on what it was.

It was true to say that Doug Miller had spent much of the previous twenty-five years thinking about the Bleeding Dogs. As he watched TV, his eyes looking but not seeing, he wondered if any of the four would've come see him if they knew he was in a hospital bed waiting to die.

Miller spent his last five years of military service behind a desk. By the time he waved the Army goodbye, he'd been in for more than thirty years. It felt like a lifetime but he would've stayed in for another lifetime, subject to two conditions: America would have to go to war and he'd have to be able to serve in the darkest most secret part of it. Master Sergeant Doug Miller was the archetypal fighting man and assigning him a desk job was both plainly ridiculous and an appalling use of resources.

By the time he returned to Farmville in the spring of '82, his aging mother was in her late seventies and deteriorating fast. There was little love between a mother and son who'd seen each other just half-a-dozen times in three decades. Doug knew it was his fault. He knew long absences broken only by the occasional letter, was no way to treat someone with whom he'd once shared opposite ends of an umbilical cord. It gave him a profound sense of guilt.

Uncle Sam had always had him up to his neck in war and he'd never had time for the normal things of adult life:

marriage, home-building, kids and the like. He was always busy thinking about the next mission, next team; next death. But back in Farmville, domestic life with his mother was chaos. Jesting with the guys at Jumpin' Jack's, he'd say she wet the bed so much he'd find a rainbow in her ammonia-filled bedroom when he went in to open the curtains. They laughed. Doug did too but inside, it disgusted him. But bad as it was, it got worse still, one of the most fearsome military men in history bed-bathing and changing diapers for an incontinent mother who didn't know who he was. He hated it, only the call of duty keeping him from turning and running.

Mercifully, at eighty-one, his mother died in her sleep. It liberated him and allowed for a new routine. He'd spend most of his day reading down at the library, stroll home for some food before going back out to his favourite bar-stool at Jumpin' Jack's on Newman Street. From four till eight, seven-days-a-week, he'd get in some serious drinking and some equally serious talking.

Before he'd left for Korea thirty years earlier, teenage Doug had built himself a big reputation as a fighter who was more than a handful for the farm workers who'd stray into town on a Friday and Saturday night. But by the mid-Eighties, few in Farmville were old enough to remember the legends Doug inspired as a teenager. But one who could recollect with ease was Sheriff Bobby-Joe Rose, a former class-mate at Prince Edward High School.

One balmy June evening in 1982, the door to the Sheriff's office burst open.

"Sheriff; Sheriff!" panted the sixteen year old Bobby-Joe recognised as the grandson of one of his neighbours. "Come quick Sheriff!" the lad said, excitedly. "Doug Miller's hammering the crap out of some boys from out Burkeville way."

"Now listen to me son," the Sheriff said, not batting an eyelid, "If some tanked-up boys show such poor judgment as to pick a fight with Doug Miller, its time they learnt to have some respect, for history and for their elders."

"How'd you know it weren't him who started it?"

"Because Doug Miller don't pick fights boy, he finishes 'em. Always did, always will."

"Well, either way Sheriff, he's giving 'em boys a tuning! He'll kill 'em if you don't stop it. You are gonna stop it Sheriff, ain't yer?"

"No way son!" exclaimed the Sheriff, taking the boy and the two officers stood alongside him by surprise. "When Doug Miller's in full flow you best get out the way; you could call out the National Guard but even then it'll be too tight to call!"

Five young twenty-something's ended up in Southside Community Hospital that night and Sheriff Bobby-Joe Rose didn't think it especially a bad thing for the younger generation to experience the legend of Doug Miller first hand.

The altercation at Jumpin' Jack's was the last physical set-to Doug Miller ever had. No-one bothered him after that. He'd sip his Wild Turkey and chat away the hours with anyone who wanted to listen. He was a great story teller who rarely lacked an audience. Inevitably, he'd talk about his army days and the men he served with; it was all he knew. Locals would often hear him talk about "the Dogs" thinking he was commenting on the men's character rather than their collective name. Every story became an epic and though he'd change the names of the major players, not even the tiniest detail was made up; Doug Miller never needed to make anything up.

In three countries "the Dogs'" exploits bordered on the super-human. If it hadn't been for the covert nature of their missions they'd have all been household names, war heroes honoured in Washington and Hollywood. When he wobbled home just after eight each night, he'd chuckle to himself, convinced the world of Bleeding Dog Company would forever remain a closely guarded secret. He'd die never knowing how wrong he was.

He knew his daily routine was killing him but it wasn't enough to persuade him to change it. Jumpin' Jack's and a bottle of Wild Turkey night-after-night was an unsustainable diet that by the mid-Nineties had started to take a heavy toll. In June 1999 the situation became deadly serious when he was diagnosed with cirrhosis of the liver and given six months to live.

The doctor couldn't believe the way he took the news.

"Who gives a damn?" he said, "After a bottle of Turkey-a-day for fifteen years I half expected to be hollow inside!"

The stunned doctor even thought he winked at him before closing the door and heading off in the direction of Jumpin' Jack's.

In the six months since, Doug Miller had often wondered if he'd make it to the next century.

The way it turned out, he missed it by two hours. At 22:04 Eastern Time, he breathed his last breath. Alongside him were three of his Jumpin' Jack's buddies who, knowing their friend was struggling in the hospital, couldn't face drinking themselves, even if it was the New Year's Eve of a lifetime. As they saw it, he died peacefully. But the calm was just a veneer, on the outside only.

Inside, he was in agony; his shrunken liver, poisoned by years of alcohol abuse, finally imploding in on itself.

Even in death, Master Sergeant Doug Miller had kept one of his golden rules of life; never let the sons of bitches know how much you're hurting.

CHAPTER TWENTY-TWO:

Doug Miller wasn't the only one watching Australia celebrate the first new millennium in a thousand years.

Michael McBride had enormous respect for Miller. If he'd known he was waiting for death to snatch him from his hospital bed, he wouldn't have hesitated go see him even if he'd been on the other side of the world, let alone a few states away in Virginia. Even though they'd worked together for just nine or ten months nearly thirty years earlier, Miller had left an indelible mark on the man he nicknamed *Irish*. But in Foxboro Massachusetts, stretched out on the couch in front of the TV, Michael had no way of knowing that Doug Miller was on his deathbed. Though he'd thought many times about trying to contact "Kong," otherwise known as Eugene Sanders, he'd always baulked at the prospect, preferring instead to leave the past in the past. As a result, he'd had no contact with the team or with Miller.

By the time he returned to the United States in January 1975, Irish McBride had served Uncle Sam in Vietnam, Laos, Cambodia and Africa. Despite being away for one week short of six years, he couldn't bring himself to go home, or even to telephone to say he was back. Instead, he made his way to Yonkers, New York, where he spent three more years in the wilderness. They were years where basically, he fell apart. Without the adrenaline rush of combat he was bored stupid, constantly looking to test himself in dangerous situations, the more dangerous the better.

In a way, he found what he was looking for in uptown Yonkers. The area had two or three local gangs, the nastiest and meanest of which were the Sharks, a group of twenty or so mostly blacks with a few Hispanics and Latinos mixed in. People in the bars and clubs talked about the Sharks in hushed tones. Irish clocked it, filing it away for future reference.

Then, three months after he'd got to New York he got into a fight in one of the bars with two black guys who turned out to be Sharks. Much to the amazement of the bar staff and a hundred or so other people who happened to be in the bar, many of whom had already been abused by the two Sharks, Irish massacred them. After one had been taken away in an ambulance and the other shuffled bleeding and broken out the front door, he was a hero, everyone lauding him, buying him drinks, but secretly whispering the Sharks would be looking for revenge.

Irish heard the whispers, enjoyed them, saw it as a test.

Then he did what he'd been trained to do, he took the battle to the enemy. After keeping the Sharks headquarters under surveillance for a day or two, he worked out a plan. With his Bowie knife strapped to his calf, he calmly walked across the street at four in the afternoon looking like death itself, eyes blazing out his blackened face. It was a bizarre sight, as if from another world.

It was; the jungles of Southeast Asia had come to the streets of New York. And in a battle between black hoods and black ops there was only ever going to be one winner.

Nine sharks ended up in the hospital, slashed, beaten and humiliated, all nine owing their lives to just one thing: they were in the United States. Had their meeting with Irish McBride taken place in Southeast Asia they'd already be dead.

And just to underline his victory, he bent over the gang leader, a shaven-haired bruiser called Hezekiah Briggs. "Mess with Michael McBride and you're playing with death," he growled. "If we cross paths again it'll be me, my Bowie knife and you . . . and it won't be your leg I'll slice off."

Hezekiah had been around. The fact the intruder had told him his name so openly said it all; he was a man without fear. The gang leader motioned a nod indicating he understood, his spirit as broken as his body.

For the medical staff and the police who attended the incident, it was the stuff of legend, the kind of thing people couldn't wait to tell their kids and grandkids.

The warrior who'd wiped out the Sharks and the guy watching TV in his luxury home just hours before the onset of a new millennium, couldn't have looked more different. Though separated by nearly a quarter of a century, they were the same man. Despite his efforts to not go there, deliberately at least, Michael McBride was a man with a past.

Two-and-a-half years after taking on the Sharks, he decided the time had finally come to go home to his family. Ten years he'd been away, the decade starting when the death of Granddad Fergus ripped his heart out. Like the returning prodigal son, his family was so delighted they threw a big party. What they didn't know was that it was the first he'd been to in ten years that didn't end up with him fighting.

A few days after the party, he asked for a meeting with his Uncle Pat and Uncle Declan.

Cork Construction's impressive HQ was set in a hundred and fifty acres to the west of Sunset Lake, on the western side of Foxboro. It was a stunning location that would've had Fergus whistling in appreciation. Michael really liked it too but not as much as he liked the pretty receptionist.

"Hi Michael," she said with a toothy beaming smile that emerged from deep inside her. "We're all excited you're back. Your uncles are waiting for you."

It wasn't often Michael was rendered speechless but she left him catching flies.

His uncles welcomed him, obviously delighted their nephew was home. After shaking hands, Michael cleared his throat. "Uncle Pat, Uncle Declan, I've come to apologise. I want to apologise for my actions and for disappearing as I did and for not keeping in touch."

Both uncles nodded and conveyed firstly, that no apology was necessary and secondly, that if he insisted, the apology was accepted.

But Michael wasn't finished. "I had a bad ten years after Granddad died. I hated everyone and everything, God included. But something's changed. I can't explain it but it's like my anger's run its course. I want to draw a line under what's done and move forward into my future making good choices for a change. I know coming home was the first step."

Michael's uncles looked at one another, Pat speaking first. "Mikey, I can't believe how much like the old man you sound! It made me go goose-pimply because it felt like it was him talking not you."

Declan, the younger of the two, was nodding in agreement. "Pat and I were much younger than your Dad and we used to think he and Fergus were like supermen, didn't we Pat? I listened to you at the party and I've listened to you today, and every word you say makes me think you're the image of both your father and your grandfather. They were great men, Mike. Not a day passes without us remembering them in some way, without us missing them. You're of the same fighting stock Michael and you may not be aware of it just yet, but it's your destiny to walk in their footsteps."

Not knowing quite what to say, Michael stayed silent.

"You back for keeps Mike?"

"Yes Uncle Pat, I'm back to stay."

"What you planning on doing Mike? Can we do anything to help?"

Michael leaned backwards so he could reach into the pocket of his Levi's. "Here," he said, handing over a small folded piece of paper.

"What's this?" said Uncle Pat before unfolding it, smiling slightly and handing it to his brother.

"What's this about Mike?" said Uncle Declan, "Why you writing a check to Cork Construction for a quarter-million dollars?"

"That's what's left of my inheritance; I want to invest it in the company."

"It's an admirable gesture Mike but an unnecessary one," said Uncle Pat.

"It may be unnecessary Uncle Pat but it's what I want to do. Please feel free to use it for the company's benefit."

"Can we offer you anything in return Mike?"

"There is one thing I'd appreciate," Michael replied a little hesitantly, looking at both uncles in turn. "I'd like a job. No favours of course, just a job on one of the sites. Let me show you I'm back to stay and if you think I should dig holes for the rest of my life, I'll be happy to do as you say."

"Course we'll fix you a job Mike."

"Thanks Uncle Pat; thanks Uncle Declan. I won't let you down."

"We know you won't Mike. We're just glad to have you back, son," said Declan, his brother nodding in agreement by his side.

Michael knew they meant it. Being home with family was the first time he'd felt welcome anywhere for the best part of ten years. As he motioned to leave, he suddenly remembered there was something else. "Who's the girl in reception?" he asked.

The two brothers looked at each other, smiling.

"Her name's Madeline Lawrence, Mike," Uncle Pat replied, "But we call her Maddie. She's a great girl from a lovely church-going family."

Michael thanked his uncles and left. Seconds later, in reception, he exchanged smiles with Maddie and that was that: job done.

He'd gone to apologise, to pledge his allegiance to the family and to get himself a job. But while he'd achieved all three, he'd also found the woman he wanted to marry.

Although he'd been brought up to know better, Michael had used girls over the preceding ten years and not once had he desired relationship at anything deeper than superficial level. But instinctively, he knew everything would change for Maddie.

He found himself doing a lot of thinking. It was a time when many of his Granddad's life lessons came crashing back into his consciousness, bringing a deep sense of regret that he'd slipped so far. A battle raged in his head; the voice of Fergus speaking goodness and truth and another voice, a dark sinister voice, condemning him for his failings, his weakness, hissing, "What about the girl? What about the girl?" Michael knew *the girl* wasn't Maddie; it was the girl by the riverbank in Laos, the scene of his worst failing.

It was like a mental wrestling match and unlike during his ten-year wilderness period, he knew that this time, it had to be faced and there could be no hiding in his fighting or drinking, or from romping between the sheets with some woman he'd just met.

Madeline Lawrence was a committed Christian. She knew instantly that Michael was the man she'd been waiting for. She'd thought him handsome, warm and kind looking but he also had the "X" factor, the mysterious quality that sent her insides cart-wheeling down the street. Within a month, the two were an item. Everyone said they were made for each other and though it was a major battle, mentally more than physically, Michael fully respected one of the key conditions to courtship: no sex and no messing about. How he dealt with it helped convince him that there was a force at work looking over him and Maddie and looking over their relationship. He not only loved her, he respected her. He was impressed with her solidity and with the way in which her faith came through in everything she did. Hers was obviously no boring kind of churchy religion. As she explained many times, she didn't have religion she had relationship: relationship with Jesus, her Saviour.

Maddie was the first person he'd heard talk in such a way since Fergus and some of what she said, he'd heard from him first. He'd thought of himself as a Christian but he knew he wasn't where Maddie was or for that matter, where Fergus had been. He knew something was missing but couldn't admit that he wanted or needed whatever it was she had. But though he may not have known it, his moment of realization was on its way.

Over the preceding few months he'd become an avid reader. The book, *Who Moved the Stone?* by Frank Morison, deeply affected him and helped confirm a growing realization that the resurrection of Jesus was both fact and reality. It led him to study the lives of the disciples where he found a group of ordinary men who ended up leading extraordinary lives. And perhaps, even more significantly, most ended up dying horrific deaths; deaths they could have avoided.

Michael was fascinated with the stories in the Acts of the Apostles where the disciples ate, drank, conversed and met with Jesus *after* they'd followed him for more than three years and *after* he'd been nailed to a cross and died. His simplistic reasoning had him thinking that either they did do these things or they didn't; there could be no middle ground.

When the disciples preached the Gospel throughout the known world of their day, almost all of them ended up being tortured and dying agonizing deaths. Yet all they needed to do to make their pain go away and save themselves, was deny Jesus by saying that what they were preaching wasn't true. The problem was they couldn't. Why? Because they knew it was true. They'd eaten with Jesus, drank with him, conversed with him; and all *after* he'd died a death on the cross. The disciples were in the unique position of knowing that he really had been raised from the dead and therefore, really was who he said he was.

It was revelation that blew him away.

Michael had seen lots of death. He'd met, fought against and killed many men prepared to die for a cause. But all, he reasoned, were only prepared to die for that cause so long as they believed it to be true. None would have died knowing it to be a lie. Michael could see that the disciples were in the most unique of positions; there was no guesswork and no need for faith. Either they did see Jesus after he was crucified and killed or they didn't. And it was clear they did, otherwise they wouldn't have been able to endure death and torture.

Michael knew he was no theologian but he did understand the way men think, especially under pressure. If the resurrection hadn't happened, the disciples were in the perfect position to know it was a lie or a scam. Their enduring horrific deaths proved it couldn't have been either. It had to be true. The disciples really did eat, drink, and converse with Jesus *after* he was killed. Their subsequent deaths proved it.

He'd approached it much like a lawyer and he'd arrived at the conclusion that beyond all reasonable doubt, Jesus really was who he said he was.

It was a big deal for Michael, but still he felt as if something was missing.

Maddie smiled as he articulated his thoughts. "Don't worry Mike, one day it'll drop from your head to your heart."

He didn't understand, but he was destined to find out.

In the spring of 1982, world renowned evangelist Billy Graham was in New England for a series of crusades that opened with a rally in Providence Rhode Island.

Over eleven thousand people clapped him on stage, Michael one of them. He was immediately struck by the sixty-three year old's warmth, integrity and by the love that exuded from him.

"Some of you may be wondering why you're here tonight," he said from the platform. "Well, let me tell you, you're not here by accident. You're here for a purpose. Whoever you are, wherever you're from, whatever's in your past, Jesus wants you to know that He loves you and that He'll take you just as you are. You don't have to clean up your act to meet with Jesus. You just need to meet with Him. He'll see to the rest, in His time."

For Michael, it was like he was the only one there: just him, Billy Graham, and God.

When the great evangelist made his appeal after speaking for an hour, Michael suddenly had the clarity he'd been looking for. Billy Graham explained it perfectly. All a man had to do, he said, was acknowledge his sin, desire to walk from it, acknowledge his need for a saviour, see Jesus as his Saviour; and receive his forgiveness.

"If you've never said yes to Jesus," Billy Graham said from the platform, "Let me urge you to come forward; now's the time to make him your Lord and Saviour."

All over the room, nearly twelve hundred people left their seats. One of them was Michael McBride; the truth had dropped from his head to his heart.

He'd done some terrible things in his time and didn't need anyone to tell him he was a sinner. As Billy Graham prayed, the thirty-three year old man once known as *Irish* cried like a baby, shedding tears for the first time since his grandfather passed away fourteen years earlier.

Many times in the years to follow, Michael would describe the moment as the "the day the lights came on!" The change was as stark as it was immediate. Everyone noticed.

Maddie was thrilled and two months after the rally, Michael proposed.

It took her all of four seconds to say *yes*!

Two years after the wedding, they moved into the luxury lakeside home they had built on two acres of the family's land alongside Sunset Lake. By the time their first child, Joseph, arrived in 1987, they'd enjoyed a wonderful four years on their own. Joseph was followed by Ryan eighteen months later and then finally, by little Charlotte in 1991.

Michael knew how to be a father; he'd learned it from the master: Fergus.

Maddie was deliriously happy and would often say she'd waited for *Mr Right* and got *Mr Perfect*. Everyone agreed.

In 1985, Michael had become CEO of Cork Construction and overseen its growth into one of New England's most successful construction companies. By the early-Nineties the business employed over five hundred full-time staff, most of whom thought Michael such a good employer they nominated him for the *Wall Street Journal's* "Dream Boss" award.

When *Channel 5 News* anchor, Abbie Morales showed up unannounced to present him with his carved glass statuette, he told the beautiful reporter, "Of course I'm delighted Abbie but I'm sure there's hundreds of bosses out there equally as worthy as me."

The *Channel 5 News* report featured interviews with workers who all said how privileged they felt knowing and working for Michael and for Cork Construction. They were salt-of-the-earth construction workers and everyone could see they meant what they said. One of them, an older guy with forty years service to the company, said "Fergus and

Michael McBride are the two finest men I've ever met and I can honestly say it's been one of life's great privileges to call both men *boss*."

"Oooh Michael!" Maddie crooned.

But Michael knew it wasn't true. He knew he and Fergus weren't in the same league; the great man would never have done what he'd done.

Four years later the glamorous news anchor had her own primetime talk show, *Today with Abbie Morales*, Michael one of her very first guests. More than four million people from every corner of New England tuned in to hear him talk about his time in the military, his problems dealing with his Granddad's death, his rise from returning prodigal to company CEO, his love for his wife and family and climactically, how he became a Christian.

If the audience were transfixed, so was Abbie Morales. There may have been millions watching on live TV, but it didn't stop the beautiful hostess unashamedly coming onto him.

Watching at home Maddie was livid but she needn't have worried. Michael was the only one of four million to not even notice.

"She fancied you Michael," she blurted in disgust when he'd returned home. "She knew I'd be watching but she did it all the same. It's a good job you didn't go along with it or you'd be mincemeat mister. You may be ex-special forces but you're mine, all mine! You understand?"

Michael grunted, doing his best to swallow a smile.

The interview helped turn him into something of a New England celebrity, his story told in scores of interviews over the years. But there was no ego, no arrogance and everyone used words like wholesome, loyal, approachable, calm and confident to describe him. He was a man whose presence exuded strength, a genuinely all-round, really nice guy.

The only one who disagreed was Michael himself.

His wife would coo at the latest magazine article and though outwardly he'd smile at her obvious pride, inside he'd be bleeding as his mind raced him backwards to the day of his greatest weakness. As Maddie's voice sailed into the distance, reaching his ears all thick and muffled, somewhere in his brain somebody pressed the "Play" button. And up it would come again; the beautiful young girl, brutalized by a quartet of Bleeding Dogs.

Instead of doing what he knew to be right, what he knew Fergus would've done, he did what he did. He failed. Even worse, he participated. It was something he'd never shared with anyone, not even his pastor at church. Though he knew God had forgiven him it was the one transgression for which he'd never been able to forgive himself.

Despite the fact it didn't come to him as often as it once did, it was something he still had to battle with. And each time, he'd see the triumphant expression on Rudi Kingsbridge's face, gloating over his failure, his weakness.

He knew his Christian faith required forgiveness and in his better moments, he thought he'd forgiven Rudi Kingsbridge. But in his worst moments he couldn't see himself evangelizing his arch enemy from all those years ago; it was easier to imagine smashing his face to pulp.

When it invaded his thinking, he'd try to replace the thought with something more positive, telling himself it was over, behind him.

As he lay on his couch watching Australia celebrate the changeover from 1999 to 2000 he had no way of knowing that as well as being behind him in his past, it was also in front of him in his future; his immediate future.

CHAPTER TWENTY-THREE:

Dearborn Missouri is about as far from the sea as it gets in America.

"A little different to Dearborn darling!!?" he said with a smile.

"It's just beautiful!" she replied.

Bathed in glorious sunshine, Gus and Darlene O'Donnell were enjoying the last few hours of the twentieth century surrounded by a calm deep blue sea, their eyes hungrily devouring one of the most beautiful natural vistas in the world. The Pitons on the west coast of St. Lucia are a spectacular sight, immediately recognizable to the well-travelled. Visible from more than twenty miles out in the Caribbean Sea, Petit Piton and Gros Piton are two huge volcanic spires that majestically soar vertically out the waves crashing against their base.

Gus and Darlene were aboard the cruise ship Oriana, sat on the balcony outside their suite.

They'd been retired two weeks.

Though Gus had been a lawyer all his life, they were well-off rather than rich; rich pickings weren't easily accessible in a small town like Dearborn, even for a lawyer. The cruise cost Gus eighteen thousand dollars but Darlene had been hinting for years about taking a cruise and Gus thought she'd love the three-week *Millennium Treasures of the Caribbean* which took in both Christmas and the Millennium New Year's celebrations.

He was right; she loved it, revelling in the pomp and formality.

Gus enjoyed it too, especially having time to think. As his wife began getting ready for the New Year's Eve Gala Dinner, sixty-eight year old Gus was feeling pleased with himself; he'd come a long way from the tough suburbs of Kansas City where he'd been born and brought up. He worked hard at school and self-funded his way through years of study. After cutting his teeth with a city firm, he and Darlene upped sticks and moved thirty miles across the state-line to Dearborn where he opened *Angus P. O'Donnell & Associates*, the only law firm in town.

For nearly thirty years Gus worked alone then, in preparation for retirement, he took on a partner. The move was an investment and ten years later, just three weeks before the beginning of a new millennium, Gus reaped his harvest: selling the firm to his partner for three-quarters of a million dollars and a five-year, two-days-a-month consultancy at seventy grand-a-year.

As he sat enjoying the vista, Gus was looking forward to retirement.

He loved to fish, and had resolved that in anything but the foulest weather, he'd fish twice-a-week till the day he died. He also intended to travel. He and Darlene had been all round America but the cruise was their first jaunt outside the United States. It wouldn't be their last. They'd never had kids so were free to indulge themselves and he intended doing just that. They also didn't have family. Darlene was an only child, Gus the younger of two brothers. He'd been close to his brother William and with just eleven months between them, had idolized his big brother as they'd grown up. The two had done everything together and the day William told Gus he was leaving to join the military was the second saddest of his life, second only to the dark day in March 1983 when William agonizingly wheezed his last breath. Gus had maintained a day-and-night bedside vigil for months, heartbroken at watching his tough older brother slowly suffocate to death. The doctors explained that William's body had taken on lodgers during his time in Southeast Asia, scans showing hundreds of parasites crawling through his lungs, throat and bronchial canals.

Slowly but surely, they'd eaten away his insides.

William died in agony. It was death without glory for the West Point graduate who'd enjoyed an exemplary military career before ill-health forced early retirement and a move to Dearborn. Gus loved having him back, having him around. William wasn't just his big brother; he was his hero, a Medal of Honor winner in Korea who went on to become a Lieutenant Colonel.

Gus often thought about his big brother but in the last three weeks of the twentieth century William had been in his mind virtually non-stop. While clearing his desk and personal files during his last day at work, Gus came across a letter William had sent him years earlier. For nearly three decades it'd been locked away at the bottom of the office safe. Gus couldn't recall it arriving and when he picked it up, immediately sensed its mystery, its inexplicable aura.

"To be opened in the event of my death or before on my specific instructions, Lt. Col. William T. O'Donnell, U.S. Army," it said on the envelope. After carefully opening it, Gus gingerly removed two small pieces of blue lightly lined paper.

"My dearest Gus, I write with a heavy heart. I've been responsible, sometimes personally, for many awful things out here in this hell-hole and as if trying to trump what I'd done previously I somehow allowed a desire I held for several years to grip me. Don't ask me why but I always wanted to create a kind of all-star team that could pull off missions others couldn't even dream about. Last year, I was given the green light by my commanding officer General Matthew Kedenberg to establish the blackest of black ops teams. I called them the Bleeding Dogs. They were a four-man covert Special Ops team and in all my experience of warfare, I've never seen anything like them. Their track record is unparalleled and what they achieved set the enemies of the United States

back weeks, months, years even. This was the case even though they were together just nine months. Today they returned from their final mission and they've been decommissioned, erased to a point where they never existed.

Gus, these were men – and this is my reason for writing – that didn't have a problem stepping over a few lines; and I'm not talking about borders, though they crossed a few of those too! Cambodia and Laos were like second homes to them and even though Nixon's on record saying we'd send no ground troops into either, the Bleeding Dogs were like ghosts, moving in or out without anyone noticing. That's anyone apart from the enemy they encountered, who never lived long enough to tell the tale!!

Sorry I'm rambling Gus, but I'm tired. It's been a long day, long year, and my mind isn't quite as sharp as normal.

No Gus, these men crossed other lines too. I can't be specific but both myself and the men's trainer, a good man called Miller, one of the finest men I've had the pleasure to serve with, are convinced something's not right, something serious. Though we can't be sure what, we're as sure as dammit that something did take place.

So my reason for writing is to tell you that this last mission was a mission too far. Both Miller and I thought so. But we were overruled by Washington, by Kedenberg. I told him the Bleeding Dogs were all done in, but he flew to Kontum to meet with me a few days ago, on 13th June. The meeting was supposed to be "to discuss the situation," but there was no discussion! My advice was ignored, blanked. I was over-ruled and ordered to prepare the Bleeding Dogs for a last sortie, across the border into Southern Laos.

I asked Kedenberg to record my disagreement and the son-of-a-bitch told me to go to hell!

The men arrived back earlier today and both Miller and I feel something's not right. The team leader is on the edge of a breakdown, and the other three aren't saying dick. There's a big black fella, a Green Beret, tough as they come, but the other two hate each other. They been biting each other's butts for months and it's helped send the team leader round the bend. One of the two, the psycho with the film star looks, took a hit today – a nasty knife wound to the shoulder – but even that doesn't add up. This is a team that doesn't take hits. That knife wound is the first damage any of the four has taken in nine months – operating in places so dangerous the average soldier would be reaching for the toilet paper!

They were awesome Gus but there was a mean streak to them too. Something in my water tells me there could well be implications to all this somewhere down the line. As a result, it seemed prudent to write you this letter so you could keep it just in case my good name (it's not that good really!) gets besmirched in the process.

I know I can rely on you Gus. You've always been a great brother, a good friend and a wise legal counsel. I trust no-one more and, should the need arise there's no-one else I'd rather have look after me in this matter.

God bless you Gus and look forward to speaking to you soon."

Underneath, he'd signed and dated it: Lt. Col. William T. O'Donnell, June 17th 1972."

After reading it through for what must have been the hundredth time, Gus looked up at the Pitons, his eyes seeing but his mind elsewhere. The letter had a kind of power that was both disturbing and unnerving, its air of mystery somehow tangible. But given that William had never got in touch to tell him he needed to open it and never even mentioned it during the six years he'd lived with them, Gus figured the problem, whatever it was, had died a death and gone away.

He was wrong; it was searching for a crack, waiting to explode over an unsuspecting world.

CHAPTER TWENTY-FOUR:

Father Francois Mesnel, just a month off his seventieth birthday, was beginning the last day in a thousand years the same way he started every day: in prayer.

The devout Roman Catholic was an early riser, five-thirty early, and his first two hours each and every day were dedicated to prayer. And so it was on December 31st 1999. When he was done, he updated his journal, recording the innermost thoughts of mind and spirit. He'd kept a journal ever since the Church sent him to Laos as a missionary way back in 1961, dreaming that one day, a selection of his writings would be published.

After swilling his face, he glanced up at the forty or so brown leather-bound yearbooks on the shelves above his bed. They contained his life's work as a missionary, ministering comfort to the hurting and winning converts to the Roman Catholic Church. Having served Southern Laos for thirty-two years, he'd retired to a beautiful seventeenth century chateau overlooking the Garonne River in the Dordogne region of France. Chateau Chillon was a retirement home for priests, missionaries and staff members who'd faithfully served the Catholic Church.

As he sat in his room looking out the four-by-four window to the river, Father Mesnel felt the urge to reach up over the bed and pluck down a couple of journals from years gone by.

It was something he often did and the most thumbed were those from the early and mid-Seventies. They were his most challenging times, an era where Laos was squeezed by the Americans and used and abused by the Vietnamese, while on the inside, its population lived in fear of the indigenous Pathet Lao Communists. It was a time of so many memories, good and bad, and a time when he endured vast swings of emotion. For Father Mesnel, it was impossible to dwell on the period without thinking about his great but tragic friend Xiantha Dyong and his family from Ban Hatsati. Xiantha's wife had been murdered by the same American soldiers who so brutally raped his beautiful fifteen year old daughter Bian. The girl had fallen pregnant and fearing she'd be accused of collaborating with the enemy, Xiantha insisted she flee to Saigon along with the baby and the matriarchal Mai-Ly, his mother-in-law.

He was crying as he turned the pages to March 1973.

The family was blown apart. Xiantha never got over it. He hung himself from a tree in the corner of the family's largest rice field. It was Tong who found him. Father Mesnel picked up the pieces; helping restore Tong and helping him find solace in the Catholic faith.

Tong Tenh became a successful businessman and was one of the great successes of his years of service in Laos, the two keeping in touch by letter after he retired to France.

Father Mesnel dedicated much prayer to Tong and sometimes, to his beautiful sister Bian.

"Heavenly Father," he'd say, "This is a family that's seen a double portion of grief over the years. I pray grace and mercy upon them and if Bian did make it to safety, I pray that as you have restored life to Tong Tenh, you will restore to him the sister he misses so much."

On the surface it looked impossible but Father Mesnel was a man of great faith, a man with the power to believe for the impossible. As he sat by his desk engrossed in his journals, he had no way of knowing his prayer had been heard and that the answer was already on its way.

CHAPTER TWENTY-FIVE:

Fort Worth's *ClubZero*, on New Year's Eve 1999, was packed to bursting, hundreds of sweaty bodies gyrating to the music's vibrant hypnotic rhythm.

Half the people in the fashionable Texan nightspot were out on the dance floor, performing for the other half stood round and about. Hungry eyes roved the room: looking for a mate, people watching or just looking for titillation, looking to ogle. Many of the eyes were fixed on the big black guy and his dance partner. He was huge, dripping with sweat, the fabric of his skin-tight vest stretched tautly over his massive muscles and shimmering black skin. His size and athleticism exuded a kind of animal magnetism and it was like he and the music had become one, the rhythm almost part of his being, his personality. He wasn't especially good looking but hundreds of female eyes crawled over every inch of him while the guys looked on in awe.

He was impressive for certain, but if the revellers could've looked into his past, they'd have seen that Eugene Sanders was much more than just pleasing on the eye. He was the real deal.

Even at forty-eight, Sanders was so imposing he could make a man tremble just by looking at him. Violence had dominated much of his life but he'd been a new man for more than ten years, ever since his last spell in jail. His stretch started in bloody confrontation, when he took on and defeated the Mamas, the prison's ruling class. It ended with him dreaming of winning the Senior Mr Universe title. Body-building had been the love of his life ever since.

He'd gone down for fighting after it took an entire SWAT squad to drag him out of a Chinese restaurant when a group of young rowdies thought that because there were six of them, Eugene didn't have a chance. Some of the Chinese kitchen staff thought they should take their fight outside and waded in with meat cleavers and knives. Again, they thought their improvised weapons of war gave them the edge. It was a night where lots of people made lots of mistakes. And the biggest mistake of all was underestimating Eugene, "Kong," king of war.

His wife and dance partner Marlena, idolized him. They'd married three months earlier, in September '99, and Marlena loved thinking of herself as Mrs Sanders. As they gyrated their way towards a new millennium she couldn't have been happier. Eugene however, thought differently. To him, *happily ever after* was the stuff of fairy-tales. He was the ultimate survivor who'd learned to live with his circumstances, preferring to forget the past and especially the mistakes of his past. But sometimes his past would come hurtling into the present, just like it did earlier that New Year's Eve when he'd been watching Australia reach Y2K before almost everybody else on the planet.

As he watched the fireworks, he recalled his one and only visit to Australia and to Sydney when the shadowy Bleeding Dog Company he was part of, were on R & R. A fight in a club turned into full-on war, the battle for King's Cross, Sydney's red-light district. The bouncers and doormen from the area's bars and clubs took a severe pounding and Eugene couldn't help but smile at the way the memory gave him a warm glow. Like Charlie, the Aussie doormen found out the hard way that taking on Bleeding Dog Company was only for the very foolish or the very brave.

The whole Bleeding Dog thing had been one long adrenaline rush, the high point of five-years in the military. Twenty-five years later, he still missed it. For most of the time though, he did a good job of hiding his lack of inner contentment, his body-building, his job at Bell Helicopters and his relationship with Marlena all playing a part in helping him mask his innermost feelings.

Eugene wasn't especially philosophical but as the clock ticked towards midnight, he had two goals in his life, one longer-term, the other a little more immediate. He still dreamed of winning the Senior Mr Universe title but that was for the future. His present was dominated by Marlena and his desire to kick-off a new millennium with a passionate romp round the bedroom.

"You are looking hot tonight girl," he shouted above the loudness of the music.

"I'm yours; all yours!" she replied, throwing her head back suggestively.

"You got it girl; you're mine! But first, I need a leak!" he said, making a face.

She nodded and made off towards the bar as he headed for the men's room.

As he stood over the urinal, his track-suit bottoms pulled down below his buttocks, he heard the door open behind him and loud footsteps echo round the bathroom's tiled interior. An antennae vibrated somewhere in the dark recesses of his mind. He wondered if the man who'd moved alongside him was about to throw down a challenge.

"Hey man, you are some dancer," he said in as effeminate a voice as he'd ever heard. As the man unbuttoned his flies, he looked down to his left at Eugene emptying the contents of his bladder all over the urinal. "Oooh," he squealed, impressed. "Your muscles are awesome and that star-shaped birthmark on your butt is something else," he added, his eyes glued downwards.

Eugene turned towards him, noting his obvious excitement. He slowly raised his head until he was looking him eyeball-to-eyeball. A stream of profanity exited his lips like verbal razor blades, deadly menace stitched into every word, every phrase.

Shaking from head to toe, the young homosexual stuttered an apology. "Hey, sorry man," he whimpered, realising he'd come on to the wrong guy.

"You pathetic faggot!" Eugene snarled contemptuously before tidying himself up and leaving.

Even though there'd just been a few aggressive words and no physicals, Eugene experienced the rush fight-time always gave him. Back at the dance floor and with no sign of Marlena, he stood looking but not seeing, the adrenalin flooding his brain. Suddenly he was back in Australia fighting the bouncers. The thought was a trigger that had him wondering what had become of the other Bleeding Dogs. He'd heard nothing about Frankie the team leader or his mate Irish, though he had seen Rudi Kingsbridge, the man they called "Hollywood," on the front cover of a few magazines. He was a rich businessman from up north in Chicago but Eugene liked him the least and had never had any desire to get in touch.

"Fifteen minutes to go folks!" the DJ screamed, shaking him from his thoughts. It was the moment Eugene thought, "What will 2000 bring?" for the very first time.

He didn't notice Marlena return to his side.

"Hey baby, you OK?" she said, holding out his drink.

"Yeah," he said absent-mindedly, his head and his heart, somewhere far away.

For a few minutes at least, Eugene Sanders was back fighting Charlie in Southeast Asia.

As he'd watched TV that morning and thought so much about the Bleeding Dogs, he'd reached the conclusion he'd never see any of them ever again.

This time, it was the mighty Kong's turn to make the mistake.

CHAPTER TWENTY-SIX:

As the clock ticked towards the end of the second millennium, Tong Tenh was all alone working a rice paddy on the outskirts of Ban Hatsati. He was unaware it was party time and even if he'd known, he wouldn't have celebrated; he didn't do celebration.

Although his life had made a promising start, it took a disastrous turn one hot, humid day in June 1972. He was nine years old when it happened, when four American soldiers appeared from nowhere to invade his life: killing his mother, injuring his grandmother and brutally raping the older sister he idolized. It had devastating consequences, his family blown to pieces by circumstances beyond their control.

His mother and grandmother had tried to protect his sister, both suffering at the hands of the tall evil-looking one who wore black ties round his elbows. He'd been first and last to brutalize his sister. Though Tong could hide from it by day, at night he was at its mercy. He'd see his mother smashed in the face with a rifle before toppling over the riverbank out of sight. Then he'd watch his grandmother, the tiny Mai-Ly, clubbed to the ground and kicked and then, worse of all, he'd see the sister he loved so much, brutally violated. It was all hideous but the thing that haunted him the most was the pale star-shaped birthmark on the black man's backside. For years, it marked the moment he'd involuntarily urinate. And then there were the other two, bit part players in the ultra-personal video nasty. There was the one with the hawk-like nose and lumpy scar under his bottom lip and lastly, the fourth man, the one who looked as if he shouldn't be there, the one who looked guilty. Tong Tenh knew all four intimately; he'd slept with them most nights for twenty-eight years.

Bian had a baby as a result of the rape and she and Mai-Ly fled the village. Xiantha, his father, had never been the same after they'd gone. Conversation was rare; Tong happy to become a virtual mute. It wasn't that he couldn't speak, he just didn't want to. But things got even worse: his father hung himself. Tong found him, the trauma sending him even further into his shell, the agony making him contemplate suicide too. And if it hadn't been for Father Francois Mesnel, he'd probably have gone through with it. But the love he received helped rebuild his life and early in March 1983, he began to speak once again. It was eleven years after the incident.

With Father Mesnel's encouragement, his hard work in the fields saw him selling rice to the surrounding villages and to the bigger towns of Attapeu, Pakse, and Muang Paksong on the Bolovens Plateau. He became quite the businessman and by the time he married Shilong Dui who he'd met at market in Attapeu, the family's rice was even being exported down the Mekong River to Vietnam and Cambodia.

Father Mesnel had become his closest friend and a surrogate father. When he left for France and retirement in 1993, Tong had been desperately sad; his loss massaged only by the fact the two exchanged several letters every year.

But writing was a luxury inapplicable to the other person he missed so much, his sister Bian. He'd loved her with an all-consuming love and not a day could pass without him remembering their few short years together as brother and sister.

He ached for her and he despaired that he didn't even know if she was alive or dead.

On December 31st 1999, up to his knees in water tending his rice, Tong Tenh was convinced he'd never see either his sister or Father Francoise Mesnel in the flesh ever again.

He was wrong on both counts.

CHAPTER TWENTY-SEVEN:

Emotions were running high in Tarpon Springs and it was only partly because it was the New Year's Eve to trump all New Year's Eves.

"Oh darling, won't you reconsider?" Jeanette Templeman pleaded. She was talking to her forty-three year old daughter-in-law Bian, trying to persuade her to attend the party at the Tarpon Springs Country Club.

It was a big do. After all, Troy was Club President.

While mother and daughter-in-law had always been good friends, they'd become even closer following Randy Templeman's death in the mid-Nineties. Jeanette thought Bian would relent but ten minutes of effort got her nowhere.

"Sorry Jeanette but Thimay's home from university; I'm spending the evening with him," she said firmly.

Three months earlier, Troy had come home from work and sullenly declared he was moving into a rented apartment. It didn't catch her unawares; he'd been saying how unhappy he was for months, years. The three times they'd seen each other since, the atmosphere had been cool and Bian didn't want to spend New Year's Eve pretending to people that everything was alright when it most certainly wasn't.

As President of Tarpon Springs Country Club and managing partner of law firm *Robeson Boutwell Templeman*, Troy was one of the most respected men in town. He'd been hoping his mother could persuade Bian to attend the party but wasn't surprised when she phoned through the bad news.

He'd loved Bian ever since he'd first set eyes on her twenty-seven years earlier, in the hospital in Pleiku. But their evacuation from the U.S. Embassy went awry when Mai-Ly wasn't allowed to leave with them. Bian was devastated. Though she said she loved him they were like brother and sister: no real connection, no chemistry; no sex.

Then, early in 1978, she finally agreed to marry him. Things were better for a while but her lack of interest in the physical and sexual constantly undermined their relationship.

She'd never told him the full story and Troy's ignorance of what really happened meant he became a victim of his own imagination, convincing himself that his wife, even though she'd have been just fifteen or sixteen at the time, had been so attracted to an American GI as to want to sleep with him. It was a thought that ate away at him insidiously, his wife's ongoing lack of interest in him sexually, only serving to magnify his pain.

Years came and went and still the problem remained. They often slept apart, him on the couch downstairs, his wife alone in their bed. In many ways, it was a paradox. He had the woman he'd always desired, and even in her forties her beauty remained timelessly breathtaking. But she never really gave herself to him and it always felt like there was something in the way.

There was.

For Troy, it all became impossible. His problems at home made him even more driven at work. It was a kind of substitution thing, his burgeoning courtroom reputation somehow compensating for his lack of self-esteem in the matrimonial home and bedroom.

In court, he didn't have a care in the world; his charm and gentleness with judge and jury starkly contrasting with his brutal examination of opposition witnesses. The courtroom was the only place he got nasty, ruthless, and he liked nothing better than to take on insurance companies and the like and to ruin the testimony of their so-called expert witnesses.

It built him a profile as a feared courtroom litigator but still it didn't satisfy.

And it was the same with golf. Three years after playing his first round, he was club champion, playing off a handicap of five. He'd play three days-a-week and twice on Sunday. It kept him out of the house, camouflaged his pain, but still it couldn't deliver what he was looking for.

He had a period when he played out having an affair and the many pretty girls who worked in the firm's offices were fair game. He resisted it on every occasion except one, a disastrous one night stand that left him embarrassed and guilt ridden. The girl had been too bold. It intimidated him. It was his first and last dalliance outside marriage though the guilt hounded him for years.

Ignorant of his thoughts of philandering or his one night stand, Bian didn't mind his absence at work or playing golf. It released her from the pressure of having him around.

What both never really understood, Troy because he had no way of knowing and Bian because she refused to think about it, was that the most important thing in their relationship was something neither of them had any control over: the events and after effects of a few tragic minutes by the river in Southern Laos on June 17th 1972.

Though the separation gave Bian more time to think than she'd ever had, it'd made her lonely.

She missed her son. Thimay was a post-grad microbiology student at the University of Oregon. They spent hours on the phone and one particular conversation a month earlier had taken Bian into unchartered waters.

"I know you don't want me to ask but mother, I have a right to know."

Bian didn't need her son to say any more. But he did anyway.

"I want to know who my father is."

It caught her off-guard. Ten years had passed since the last time. She'd gotten very emotional then, and seeing tears streaming down her face had been enough for teenage Thimay to back off. This time though, it was different.

"Mother, I want to know who my father is," he repeated, conscious of her silence the other end of the line.

"Why is it so important?" she said, fighting back the tears.

"I love you mother. I don't want to upset you but I'm twenty-six years-old. It's time."

She couldn't argue; she knew it was. But she still couldn't bring herself to tell him the whole story. She simply said she'd been raped by an American soldier.

Four weeks later, Thimay arrived in Tarpon Springs for Christmas, Bian fully reconciled to answering his questions honestly and fully. But Thimay said nothing; hearing his mother and Troy had separated had been bad enough but discovering his real father was a rapist proved devastating.

Just as his mother had done, he shut the door on it.

Bian knew he was upset and spoiled him rotten. She knew she'd failed as a wife and didn't want to fail as a mother. Thimay had always been a model son, the kind every mother hopes for, thanks God for, and with no Troy around competing for attention, she was able to indulge his every need. It was a special time for both; mother and son had never been closer. It had her thinking about *family* and about Laos.

As the clock struck eight on New Year's Eve 1999, a smiling, hand-shaking Troy entered the main function room at Tarpon Springs Country Club. Immaculately dressed in a black tuxedo and bow-tie, he was ready to make the address that would officially get the party underway. The only thing missing was his wife, the wondrously beautiful Bian. He knew it would make for a few awkward questions but what could he do? Like everything relating to his wife, it was beyond his control.

At precisely the moment her husband began his New Year's Eve speech, Bian lay on the couch in front of the TV watching *Titanic* with Thimay.

But for all the film's considerable charms, it couldn't hold her concentration.

And it wasn't because she was thinking about Troy because she wasn't.

Though it made her uneasy, she was thinking about her family and about the life she'd left behind in Laos when she was just sixteen.

Bian Templeman, formerly Bian Nhu Dinh, was feeling one of the most primeval instincts of all; she had a stirring to go home. Laos was calling.

CHAPTER TWENTY-EIGHT:

"You'll need to go straight to Gate 37 madam; your flight's been called," the desk clerk said, his eyes fixed on the most beautiful woman he'd ever seen.

Bian smiled politely as Thimay took the paperwork. They'd both noticed the lingering looks but she dealt with it the way she'd always dealt with it, and pretended not to notice. Bian had been turning heads for decades and a casual observer couldn't have helped but smile as she walked through Tampa Airport late morning of January 7th 2000. Though Thimay was by her side, it was his mother who attracted the attention. As if caught under her spell every male in her immediate vicinity, did a rolling impression of a

Mexican Wave, as first one, then another, then another, turned their heads to give their eyes the chance to track her dark haired beauty for as long as possible. Even at forty-three she was still staggeringly beautiful. But rather than something to treasure, Bian saw her beauty as burdensome. She hated the way how she looked seemed to promise so much to men and she hated that for Troy, she'd found it impossible to deliver on the promises it made. Outwardly she may have looked like a woman who had it all, but inside, she'd been weeping for twenty-seven years.

And worse, now she was terrified as well.

The tears started when she was brutally raped as a wide-eyed fifteen year-old but the fear was new. It started New Year's Eve, seven days earlier. She'd refused to attend a party with Troy and stayed home with Thimay watching television. All night, one thought dominated her thinking. It wouldn't budge. It was calling her home to Laos, the country of her birth; the country she'd been forced to leave at sixteen.

She thought it would pass. But it didn't. For three days it hounded her, relenting only when she mentioned it to her son who surprised her by saying he wanted to go with her.

Seventy-two hours later, they were in the air.

Bian waited till the last minute before telling Jeanette she was flying with Thimay back to Portland and planned on taking a three-week vacation out on the West Coast. She didn't feel up to telling her the truth. The instant she hung up, Jeanette called Troy. As the taxi driver picked up Bian's bags, the telephone was ringing loudly behind her. She knew it was Troy; it was still ringing as she slammed the door. She'd taken twenty-five years to make the decision to go home and she wasn't going to let anyone or anything get in the way.

She didn't know what she'd find once she got to Laos. She had no idea if her father, her grandmother or her brother were still alive let alone still living in Ban Hatsati. The questions whizzed in and out her thoughts. What would she do if there was no trace of them at Ban Hatsati? What would she say if they were there? What would her Lao be like after having not spoken the language for decades? How would she explain her long absence and her never getting in touch? What would they think of her? Would they think she'd had it easy in the U.S. and just forgotten all about them?

It was never-ending.

As they flew across the Pacific, Bian told Thimay stories about the family he'd never met. Then suddenly, the "Fasten Your Seatbelts" sign flashed on with a ding above their heads. Bian reached for her son's hand seconds before catching her first glimpse of Laos in twenty-seven years. She wept as Thimay gently rubbed her shoulders.

Less than an hour after landing, mother and son checked-in to Vientiane's best hotel, the five-star Settha Palace. Bian had booked a three-day stay at the hotel, figuring she'd need time to compose herself for the last and most traumatic leg of the journey.

It proved a shrewd move and gradually she relaxed, enjoying chatting with the staff, pleased at how easily her Lao, her native tongue, returned.

On the fourth day, they took a fifty minute internal flight down to the tiny provincial airport at Pakse in Southern Laos.

Pakse is on the north-western rim of the Bolovens Plateau, ten to the hour on a clock-face with Ban Hatsati twenty past the hour, sixty miles away to the east. The journey by taxi was a slow one across the Plateau, past Paksong, before crossing the Se Kong on the Ban Sok river ferry, a floating raft able to convey no more than one vehicle and a few people at a time. When she saw the sign for Ban Sok her stomach churned; her roots and past just minutes away.

As she and Thimay watched the taxi pull away, its tires screeching on the dusty surface, Bian had never felt lonelier.

The two looked at one another nervously, picked up their bags and headed towards a row of single-storey huts. The village was quiet, a toddler peering over the bottom ledge of an unglazed window, the only sign of life. The boy waved at the mysterious visitors.

Bian greeted him. "Suh-bye-dee," she said smiling weakly before turning to Thimay. "The village is asleep; everyone takes a nap in the afternoon."

After a hundred yards of walking in-and-out the stilted brown and grey huts, they came to the small square where Bian played as a little girl. Her stomach was in knots, her arms shaking so much she had to put her bags down. She looked up at the house she was born in, grew up in, and saw a shadowy figure on the porch, wiping his face in a towel. She wondered if he'd seen her. She wondered if it was her father. Her heart beat so fast it felt it would burst.

"Yes?" asked the man in Lao, "Can I help you?"

As he stepped into the light, Bian recognised him immediately. Though he looked like Xiantha, it wasn't her father. It was Tong Tenh, the brother she'd left behind twenty-seven years earlier.

"Tong?" she said apprehensively.

"Bian?" he replied, unsure himself, his tone quiet and quizzical. But as he repeated her name over and over, he got louder, the intonation in his voice firstly incredulous, then triumphant. He leapt out the porch so he could run to her. Both were crying as they hugged a hug that had been stored up throughout most of three decades of separation.

The commotion woke the neighbours but lost in the emotion of a reunion they feared would never happen, Bian and Tong appeared unaware of anyone and everything. Bian sobbed uncontrollably, partly from emotion, partly from guilt while Tong just held her tight, his face above hers, tears rolling off his cheeks into her hair. Then he became aware of Nguyen Thimay and his wife Shilong Dui and their two children stood on the porch.

They all shared a look of baffled bewilderment.

"Mama," he said, beckoning his wife down to join them. "This is Bian . . . my sister," he added proudly, watching his wife and sister-in-law embrace. "And Bian . . . these are my children," Tong said, keen to involve the little ones.

"They're beautiful . . ." Bian said her eyes all puffy and watery.

"Xiantha is nine and . . ." he hesitated, "Bian was seven last week!"

The names went off like gunshots in Bian's head, tears streaming down her face as if someone turned on a tap. She opened her arms and beckoned her niece and nephew. Within seconds, both children were crying tight in the arms of the aunt they never knew they had.

Then, suddenly, Bian realised she'd not introduced or involved Thimay.

"Tong, this is Nguyen Thimay, the nephew you've not seen since he was three weeks old."

With everyone crying uncontrollably, it was the most intimate of intimate moments. Though it was very much a family occasion a few neighbours old enough to remember Bian also joined in, tears turning to yelps of delight as everyone realised it wasn't a dream.

It was real; Bian was back.

* * * * *

The call from his mother filled Troy with dread.

After clicking the phone dead, he said out loud, "What have I done?"

It was his turn to be gripped by fear.

Hearing Bian would be out on the West Coast for three weeks was a major shock. He thought there was more to it than met the eye, a sixth sense telling him there was a chance she'd never return. He was convinced there was something hidden, something unsaid, but there was nothing he could do save count down the days to her anticipated return.

* * * * *

Bian had gotten a welcome warmer than anything she could have ever imagined.

By the end of her first week in Ban Hatsati, she and Thimay were heartily enjoying the simplicity and peacefulness of village life.

Bian and Tong spent hours together, talking, chatting; sitting. Both Shilong Dui and Thimay were very understanding, Bian careful to involve them wherever she could.

"He's missed you so much," Shilong told her when she and Bian were alone, "When you went, a light went out inside him. These last few days, he's like a new man. His light is on again."

It was a catalyst to another half-day of uncontrollable sobbing and guilt.

Laos in January is warm and sunny with none of the over-bearing humidity of the long rainy season. With the sun high in the sky, Tong and Bian strolled out to the rice fields, brother intending to tell sister the truth about what'd happened to their father. The day Bian arrived in Ban Hatsati, she'd cried when she'd heard that Xiantha had died twenty years earlier and that Mai-Ly had never returned from their journey south. Tong knew he needed to tell her the full story but he didn't think their first day together in nearly thirty years the right time. That was why he'd walked her out to his rice fields.

The creamy brown shades of the rice paddy contrasted sharply with the verdant greenery of the tree-line, beyond which the staggering awesomeness of the Bolovens Plateau seemed to reach up to the sky itself. There were three people working the field. Tong proudly introduced them to his sister before leading her to an open-sided stilted hut in the paddy's far left corner.

"We use this as a rest-place when the sun gets too hot," he said before steering the conversation round to the horror story concerning their father.

The unexpectedness caught Bian unawares. She was consumed with guilt, weeping uncontrollably at the unending pain. But her spirits lifted when she heard how Father Mesnel helped Tong cope. It made her even more convinced that he was an angel of God.

"Do you want to see where father died?" Tong asked, surprised when she nodded.

They walked to the tree, embraced, cried, as Tong said a prayer.

As they walked back to Ban Hatsati, Bian experienced a sense of release in having finally found out the truth regarding Xiantha's fate. It felt like she'd taken on her fear, closing the door on something in the process. It must have acted like a trigger.

"Have you ever been back *there*?" she asked, unpeeling in a sentence decades of denial that there was a there.

Tong didn't need any explanation; he knew instinctively where *there* was.

"No!" he said curtly, his turn to be surprised by the unexpected.

But Bian didn't back off. She sensed the time to confront the real demon was fast approaching and she had no intention of letting her brother's reluctance get in the way. Deep-down she suspected it was the real reason for her travelling half-way around the world and once again, she was overcome by guilt at her selfishness.

"I think I want to go *there*," she said, before adding by way of concession, "But we don't have to do it today."

Brother and sister walked back to Ban Hatsati in silence, Bian certain she was ready to confront the past, Tong sure he wanted nothing less.

It was all he could do to stop himself making a run for it.

* * * * *

"Have you been ringing her?"

"Troy, I've rung every hour on the hour, just as you said."

"Three weeks from the date she went is yesterday mother!"

"She'll be back dear; don't you go getting yourself all worked up now."

"But even with travel time back from LA, she should've been home by now."

"I'll keep trying," his mother said, not knowing what else she could say or do.

"Thanks," Troy said before hanging up abruptly.

He was in no mood for conversation. Ever since his mother had rung to say Bian was going away, he'd been beset with worry she wouldn't return, in three weeks, or perhaps, ever.

* * * * *

Two weeks had passed since Bian and Tong first spoke about *there*.

She'd been careful to bring the matter up only when they were alone and each time he'd blanked her, quickly changing the topic or simply walking away.

But this time it was different; she wasn't going to be put off.

"Tong, we must!" she said forcefully, sounding like the older sister she was.

Despite his reluctance, later that same afternoon, the two slowly walked the mile or so to the riverbank. Bian had imagined the place to be stony silent, as if paying timeless homage to the evil that'd taken place there. But as they turned the corner they heard children splashing about in the river, just like they'd done with their father and mother years earlier.

Seeing the children having fun helped her relax but unlike his sister, Tong was tense, a taut deadpan expression fixed to his face.

"Shall we come back when the kids have gone?" he asked, looking for an out.

"No, it's good they're here. Let's find ourselves a place to sit up there," she said pointing. "We can look down on the scene and talk everything through."

She was in charge and Tong was in no mood to challenge either her leadership or seniority.

Their high rocky vantage point gave them a panoramic view over the trees and across the river to the Bolovens Plateau beyond. But they both knew they weren't there to take in the vista. It was time; time to exorcise their demons.

For Bian, it'd been a long time coming and in a strange way, she was looking forward to being released from the chains of the past. She loved her little brother and hated the fact that something that happened to her had so negatively affected his life. Though she didn't want to see him hurt again, she knew freedom from bondage was waiting for them like a pot of gold at the end of the proverbial rainbow. But she was under no illusions; it would be tough, a time where both would need to plumb hidden depths of courage.

But she was determined and if her little brother couldn't summon up the bravery for himself, she'd be brave for him.

In front of them, a hundred yards away, was the bend the men had emerged from. Below their feet was the clearing where they'd been doing the family's laundry. Forty yards to their left was the promontory that stuck out into the river and more importantly, the path that took the men out of sight as they exited the scene of shame.

"Where were you hiding?"

"I was there," he replied, pointing to a big grey rock below and to the right of where they sat. "You can't see it from up here, but there's a sort of a natural alcove low down. I hid in it and peeped round the corner, with my face low to the ground."

Bian gently patted Tong's back as he talked, much like a mother consoling an upset child.

"I looked over to the spot when we arrived and it was like I was still there," he said with a shudder, lifting his hand to the side of his head as if trying to clear an unwanted image from his mind. Bian pulled him tight into her shoulder. He cried like a baby, weeping sorrowful sobs as memories stored up for so long came crashing to the surface.

They held the position for over an hour, only the weeping breaking the silence.

With the sun lowering towards the horizon, it was Bian who noticed the children had finished playing and left. "Look," she said, "The children have gone. It's time we went down."

Tong reluctantly stood to his feet and the two scrambled down to the riverbank.

Thirty paces to the right and they were there, right where it all happened.

Bian knew she needed to speak first. "The men came from there," she said pointing to the far bend, beyond which lay Ban Hatsati. "We were putting the clothes away when we saw the first two. Before we knew it, they'd passed us and disappeared round the promontory. We thought the danger had passed but then I heard mother shouting and swearing. I'd never heard her swear before. It shocked me. I saw her head off the tall soldier who'd passed us last. I knew he was coming for me. I remember him as handsome but evil looking, his face full of hate. He smashed mother in the face with a rifle. The noise was horrible. She rolled backwards and disappeared over the riverbank. Then he came for me, turned me round, shoved me on the floor, pulled my skirt up . . ."

She hesitated slightly before going on.

"It hurt so much. Then I heard him scream and pull away. I turned my head and saw him stomp on Ma'ma. I heard her bones breaking. She didn't move. I was sure she was dead." She broke down in tears, her left arm clinging tightly to her brother. After a pause, she continued. "Then I saw the big black man shout at the first man and then it started all over again. I felt numb; it was like I was paralyzed. I think I must have blacked-out because I don't remember anything about what happened after that except that I kept wondering where you were, hoping you were safe. The next thing I remember was someone pulling my hair. They were so strong. I felt helpless. Then I felt my back hurt, a burning kind of pain like something really hot behind my shoulder. I must've blacked out again because when I woke, you were there, and we were both snuggling into Ma'ma. That's all I remember."

Bian's last sentence was meant to be a door-opener for her brother. But he stayed silent.

"Tell me how *you* saw it," she added, the gentle reassuring tone in her voice massaging his fear. "But first, show me where you were hiding."

"It was over there," he said quietly, pointing.

Bian led him to the spot. "Was that where you were hiding?"

"Yes," he said, not wanting to offer anything more.

"Tong, you *must* tell me. It's important for me to know and just as important for you to voice what you saw," she said gently but firmly. She could sense her little brother was on the point of breakdown but she knew that for both of them, it was vital they kept going. It had to be faced. "You have to tell me what you remember," she repeated, even more firmly.

"I was playing back there when I heard mother cursing. I crawled forward and peeped round the corner to see her rolling backwards before dropping out of sight. I was so frightened. You were on the floor and the man was behind you. Then I saw Ma'ma hit him with a rock. He got up and hit her. He was very angry and he looked huge next to Ma'ma. I remember he had black ties around his arms and he was muscular, but not as muscular as the black man. Mama was on the floor. I was sure she was dead. Then he got behind you again before changing places with the black man. The black man pulled his trousers down and started moving. It was then I noticed a strange birthmark on his bum. It was nearly white, and star-shaped. I remember staring at it. I couldn't take my eyes off it."

Tong shook from head to toe.

"That birthmark terrified me," he said. "It was always the place in my dream that made me pee. Then I'd sort of half wake up before falling back to sleep. And somehow the dream always restarted in the same place, like as if I hadn't woken up."

"Oh Tong, I'm so sorry you had to be part of this."

They were both crying again.

"For years it happened," he said. "And I still have the dream from time to time and it still wakes me up with terror and panic."

Bian squeezed him gently. "What happened next?" she asked.

"While I was watching the black man, I became aware of two other men who came into view from my right. One of the two had a big nose that was sort of hook-shaped and he had a fat pink scar under his lip. The other was strange looking, like as if he wasn't supposed to be there. They both got behind you after the black man had finished, first the man with the hook nose then the other one, the guilty looking one."

"And that was it?"

"No, that was when the tall evil one started all over again. He yelled, grabbed your hair, pulled your head back and then he . . ."

"He what?"

"He . . ."

"He what? Tong, you must tell me."

"He . . . bit you on the shoulder."

"What?"

"The burning pain you felt was him biting you; so hard he bit out a chunk of flesh. He shrieked like an animal, you screamed in pain and suddenly the guilty looking one kicked him in the side of the head. It looked like they'd fight when the hook-nosed man, I think he was their leader, fired his gun before yelling at them. Then, in a flash, they were gone," Tong paused, stunned by the power of his own words. "I waited a few minutes and then ran to you. You were bleeding and shaking and I covered up your bum. I felt awful."

Again he broke down and it was several minutes before he could continue. "I was so angry. I was angry at them but most of all I was angry at myself for being so weak. I wanted to protect you but all I could do was hide away, wet myself and wait for them to go!"

"It's OK Tong. You were so young, so small. You mustn't blame yourself."

Listening to Tong had helped Bian. The agonizing pain to her shoulder had been explained and her brother's insight on the man who looked as if he shouldn't have been there was helpful too. Bian thought she remembered seeing him look back as she lay on the ground. In a hazy kind of way, she remembered having eye contact with him, sort of connecting with him. She too had the feeling he didn't look as if he should've been there. In her mind's eye she'd thought he hadn't taken part and was surprised to hear he had. Somehow, it disappointed her and she didn't know why.

"Tong, don't blame yourself; you did nothing wrong," she said softly. "You were and are, a wonderful little brother that I've always loved with all my heart. I'm sorry it's taken me all these years to come see you. I was frightened of facing all this but now we have, I realise it was something to be faced not feared. I should've come back years ago. Please forgive me."

"I love you too Bian; there's nothing to forgive. I'm just glad you're here."

With their faces pressed into one another's shoulder, they wept once more.

Sat with their legs dangling over the edge of the riverbank, they were completely unaware their feet were just inches above the grey flat rock onto which their mother had fallen and died.

But purged of their demons Bian and Tong sat looking out over an idyllic scene. The low January sun had turned everything a shade of orange and the last hour of sunlight cast strange almost surreal shadows across the spectacularly beautiful landscape. Three of the small children who'd been playing in the river earlier had returned unnoticed, and were stood at the end of the promontory. Their chattering laughter danced across the water as they tossed stones into the gentle current. Like the rocks and the mountains beyond them, the children were visible only as silhouettes as the orangey sunset played out its nightly ritual with the horizon.

The sun was going down at the close of another day, something ending as something else, a new day, was about to begin.

It was as true for Bian and Tong Tenh as it was for Mother Nature herself.

CHAPTER TWENTY-NINE:

"It's been five weeks mother! She's gone!! I never believed that crap about her going to LA."

"Don't be crude Troy. It was you who forced the separation remember. She'll be back; she just needs time to think about what comes next."

Troy didn't need reminding it was *him* who'd moved out. "I have to go to London on business next week," he said, trying to change the subject. "And if there's no news by the time I'm back, I'm going to hire a private detective firm we use at work."

"Will that be necessary dear? I'm sure she's OK and it was you who left her."

"Mother, do you have to rub salt in my wound?"

"I'm sorry dear. It's just I can't understand why you did it. You know you're besotted with her; always have been."

"Yes mother," he sighed, resigned to the fact she was right even if she didn't know the full story. After all, how could he tell his own mother that when it came to the bedroom and to the sexual side of life, the daughter-in-law she loved with all her heart had not a flicker of interest in the son she loved just as much?

But the conversation served another purpose too: triggering the idea of employing private detectives. Several times over the previous few weeks Troy had wondered if his wife had left to pursue a relationship with someone else. It ate away at him and in the end he gave in to his burning curiosity and drove round to Bayshore Drive.

He still had a key. He didn't see it as snooping, preferring instead to rationalize it as a healthy need to know the wife he loved was safe. It didn't take him long to find what he was looking for. In the writing bureau in the den he found a letter from a local travel firm outlining an itinerary that nearly knocked him off his feet.

"She's gone back to Laos!!" he exclaimed. "And Thimay's gone with her!"

Not for one second did he imagine she'd go *home*. He thought thirty years in America had separated her from Southeast Asia forever. But the thing that most concerned him wasn't where she was; it was that she'd not returned, the itinerary listing the return leg as beginning January 28th out of Vientiane.

"As it's now the 12th of February, she's obviously missed her plane!" he said sarcastically, slamming the front door behind him. Troy was shaken, his head filled with questions. How would he find her in a country so completely alien to him? Assuming he did find her, would she be pleased to see him? Would he find her shacked up with a handsome home-grown stud? But the biggest mystery of all was the one that'd been troubling him for weeks: whatever possessed him to walk away in the first place?

Troy may have thought himself a fool but he was determined to find her; his wife was not going to be the *ex* Mrs Templeman.

* * * * *

A week later, he was at the BA desk at Heathrow Airport.

His London meetings had gone well but he was plagued by images of his wife. Bizarrely, she was sat astride a lithe Laotian farm worker in the middle of a rice paddy. He knew few things were more unlikely but . . .

"Your ticket and passport please?" the clerk said interrupting his thoughts.

"Does BA fly to Laos?"

"I'm not sure about Laos Mr Templeman but we certainly fly to Bangkok."

"How would I find out?"

"The BA services desk; they'll have all the information you need."

Two hours later, Troy was in the air on a one-way first-class ticket to Thailand. It cost him seven thousand dollars but he was determined to go get his wife.

Even before the "fasten your seatbelts" sign had gone off, he'd pulled out a writing pad and written Bangkok at the top of the page. Half-hour later, he'd gone as far as he could.

"Not bad, considering all I had to go on are two place names – Ban Hatsati and Attapeu!" he said to himself. Troy remembered Bian say many times that she hoped Mai-Ly had "made it back to *Ban Hatsati*." He also remembered her saying that there was a Catholic priest who visited her father from *Attapeu*, "which wasn't very far away."

Attapeu was on the map in the back of his diary but Ban Hatsati wasn't listed. He suspected a Catholic priest in Laos in the early-Seventies would be operating on foot or by bicycle and concluded Ban Hatsati was probably within ten or twelve miles of Attapeu, with the most likely direction north because south was Cambodia, east was Vietnam and west was blocked off by the Bolovens Plateau.

Bangkok was three hundred miles as the crow flies from Southern Laos and Troy figured that even if he couldn't get a plane to fly him closer, he could hire a four-wheel drive.

Feeling confident, he dropped off to sleep. He woke wondering what Bian would say when he showed up. What would her reaction be? Would she be impressed at his devotion or would she feel her space was being invaded? As was always the case whenever he thought about his wife, there were no definitive answers, just more questions.

At Bangkok, he made his way to BA's first class lounge reasoning his ticket status would get him the help he needed. He was right. The lounge attendant spent twenty minutes making phone calls. She was a pretty girl in her mid-twenties and as Troy watched her chattering away into the telephone, he yearned to see his wife again.

"Right Mr Templeman, this is what I've found out for you," she said, surprising him by suddenly switching from the sharp staccato of Thai to a purring almost perfect English while at the same time unfolding a map of Southeast Asia. "Bangkok is here and Attapeu is here," she said, pointing to both places and running her finger between the two. "The nearest Thai airport is Ubon Ratchathani, which is . . . here! Thai Airways has three flights a week to Ubon but the next isn't until day after tomorrow. So I spoke with a man called Mr Ratana who has his own plane. He operates a bit like a taxi, flying people round Thailand."

"That sounds interesting."

"He'll be here in ten minutes," she said, "Now, if you don't like what he's got to offer, just say no to him and we'll look at other options."

When Troy met Mr Ratana he was amazed at how many wrinkles lined his face. "He can't be a day less than a hundred and twenty!!" he said quietly to himself.

Twenty minutes later, Troy and Mr Ratana were sat in the old man's battered Nissan headed for his hangar. If Mr Ratana looked the most unlikely pilot Troy had ever seen and the Nissan was the cronkiest car he'd ever sat in, then Mr Ratana's tiny Cessna looked positively terrifying.

"You're kidding?" Troy said incredulously.

"She fly like bird," Mr Ratana replied through a big grin.

Aboard, Troy said a silent prayer, shut his eyes and dozed off. An hour later, Mr Ratana aimed an elbow at his ribs, "Ubon close, reeel close!"

He woke from his dream with a start, sensing he'd finally reached the place where he'd be happy to take his wife just the way she was; even if it meant a sleepless night or two on the couch.

As Mr Ratana battled with the controls and the ground moved ever closer, Troy genuinely feared for his life. To take his mind off it, he looked out the window hoping he'd live long enough to see his wife. Would she rebuff him or would he get the reconciliation he hoped for? He had no way of knowing what the outcome was going to be. He had no way of knowing that their relationship had been dominated by an incident he didn't even know had taken place. And he had no way of knowing the four men responsible had spent their first week together in the airfield storage hut four hundred feet below where he sat.

* * * * *

The slapping rain woke Bian from her afternoon sleep.

Troy was in her mind as she came round. She'd started to miss him and several times she'd wondered if *he* was missing *her*. Even though she'd always loved him, she knew she'd hurt him badly over the years. But she'd felt a sense of liberation ever since she and Tong had visited the riverbank; it was like she'd been set free from the thing that had always haunted her.

It had made her thoughtfully reflective, and somehow, everything seemed to make more sense. What'd happened on the riverbank had made her fear, fear men's sexuality and fear the way her beauty affected the opposite sex. She'd paid a heavy price but so had many others: her father, Tong, Mai-Ly and Troy. If less tragic than the others, Troy was possibly the most innocent of all, given he was totally ignorant of the events that lay behind his misery.

Though she'd loved staying with Tong and his family, she knew her time in Ban Hatsati was nearing its end. She was keen to tell Troy the truth and she and Thimay had discussed returning to the U.S. the following week. She wondered if her marriage could be salvaged, whether Troy would want to try again. And most of all she wondered whether her feeling so free and liberated would make any difference to their relationship, particularly the way they connected sexually. As she lay on her bed listening to the rain, she resolved that if Troy gave her the chance to make it up to him, she'd give him everything she had.

She played through a variety of scenarios of *how* she'd tell him and *where* she'd tell him.

But in each case she got it completely wrong.

As the heavens opened above Ban Hatsati she had no idea Troy was just eighty miles away, closing by the minute in the huge Toyota he'd hired at Ubon Ratchathani Airport.

Bian had thought she'd go to Troy. She never imagined he could come to her.

Telling him would be her last demon and confronting it was going to happen sooner than she thought.

CHAPTER THIRTY:

The Toyota Landcruiser is a beast of a four-wheel drive.

It wasn't often that Ban Hatsati saw such a vehicle, so when it's huge tires skidded noisily to a halt on the northern outskirts of the village it was quickly surrounded by excited children.

The midday sun was high in the sky as Troy stepped out its air-conditioned interior, the clinging humidity enveloping him in what felt like a heavy steaming overcoat.

As he walked slowly in and out the houses, he was filled with fear. Would he find his wife? Would she see him as a welcome visitor or gatecrasher? And would she be shacked up with the sinewy Laotian farmer who'd been haunting him for weeks?

Just as his hopes began to wane, Troy saw a young girl run from between two houses into a small square. She was a pretty thing, smiling from ear-to-ear. But it wasn't the girl that gave him hope; it was her name. "Bian, Bian," someone called, stopping her dead thirty feet from where he stood. When he stepped into the square he saw a woman, brush in hand, standing outside one of the stilted huts.

Shilong Dui and Troy Templeman had never met but instinctively she knew he was looking for Bian. He smiled nervously as she turned and said something to whoever was in the house behind her. Four or five seconds later a man came onto the porch and then, just behind him, Troy glimpsed the woman he feared he'd never see again. Though she wasn't fully visible, he knew it was her. His emotions swung wildly between elation and fear, his heart wanting to love his wife, his legs wanting to run.

"Bian!" he said, the boldness of tone belying the panic he felt inside.

"Troy?" she said, as if convinced she was dreaming. "Troy!" she repeated over and over, the tears streaming down both cheeks as she scampered the six or eight steps into his outstretched arms. "I was just thinking about you," she blubbered, locking her arms behind his neck. "I was wondering where you were and wondering if you were missing me, and now . . . you're here!!"

"Wondering if I was missing you?!!"

"Yes. You came to find me! Oooooh Troy!"

"I love you Bian. I missed you so much. I *had* to come find you."

"I'm so glad you did. I've missed you too," she replied, her words and warmth taking Troy to a place he'd never been before. "And Troy, I love you."

It was his turn to cry.

"Oh Troy," she said as Thimay leapt down the ladder so he could warmly embrace his step-father. It was then Bian saw Tong and his family on the porch, all looking slightly bemused.

"Troy, this is my brother and my sister-in-law," she said, careful to speak in both Lao and English. "And this is my nephew and niece. Xiantha's named after my father, and Bian, well, I'm not sure who she's named after!"

When they went inside the house, Troy didn't feel at all awkward. He was deliriously happy. Not only was he reunited with his wife and step-son who were obviously pleased to see him, there was no sign of the sinewy Laotian farmer or any evidence to suggest he existed anywhere but in his own imagination.

Bian fussed about excitedly all afternoon, telling Troy about how she felt so much better for visiting Laos and for reconnecting with her brother and then telling Tong and Shilong Dui, stories about America.

Troy noticed Bian was different as early as their first moments together. She was warm, open and tactile. She held his hand, put her hand on his back and shoulders, touched the back of his neck and let her hand stray to his thigh. Troy loved it. It was like a giant weight had lifted off her. It made her even more attractive.

Late in the afternoon Tong suggested he and Thimay went for a walk and beckoned Shilong Dui and the children to join them.

After waiting a few minutes to make sure they'd gone, Bian looked at Troy, smiled the most incredibly perfect smile and held out her hand. "Come with me," she said, her eyes locked on his. Troy melted. If she'd asked him to run barefoot over broken glass he wouldn't have hesitated. But there was to be no pain where he was going. As he basked in the love and attention he'd always craved, he couldn't help wondering how it was possible. The cynical part of him said it was only because she'd not had any sex in five months.

But it went deeper than sexual hunger. They had finally connected.

"Bian, you're amazing" he said as they lay side-by-side. "How could I have left you? I must have been insane. Yes, that's my plea," he said in his courtroom voice, "Temporary insanity!"

Bian smiled. "I don't blame you one bit," she said playing idly with her dark hair as it splayed over his chest. "The way I treated you was unforgivable. I am so sorry. I always loved you Troy; I just didn't know how to show it. But finally, I know I can love you like you always wanted."

"It wasn't unforgivable Bian. I forgive you," he said turning a smile into a broad grin in an effort to lighten the intensity.

"No, what I did was wrong. But now, I'm going to be the wife I always wanted to be and you, the kindest, most handsome, most generous and sexiest man on the planet, are going to get the wife you always wanted."

It was like a dream come true for Troy.

As she said the word "sexiest," she reached under the thin sheet. Troy thought it was a lost cause but couldn't help marvel at the transformation in his wife.

"Bian, what's happened to you?" he said, unable to stop the thought dropping to his lips.

"Shhhhhhh . . . You just relax," she replied smiling, the same time she put her index finger to his lips.

"But Bian . . ."

"Tomorrow."

"But . . ."

"Tomorrow," she whispered, a second time.

* * * * *

Bian too, was in the theatre of dreams.

Laos had been good for her. She'd felt a sense of release the moment she and Tong off-loaded their trauma on one another. It went further than liberation. She felt transformed, renewed. And Troy's unexpected arrival helped confirm that what she felt was real.

It was Bian who woke first next day. She looked at Troy asleep beside her sorry he'd suffered so much and paid such a heavy price. She wanted to make it up to him and she knew he was the key to her achieving the peace and fulfilment she was seeking for herself.

A few moments later she was sat on the porch praying, acutely aware she needed all the help she could get. It wasn't just Troy that needed to be told, Thimay had to know too. Bian and Tong had agreed their strategy. She'd lead her husband to the riverbank while her brother took Thimay to the sun shelter in the rice paddy. If things went to plan, the two most important men in her life would be told the horror story at precisely the same time. She knew that unlike with Tong, the horror would come as a total surprise to both; she prayed they'd be able to handle it. And she prayed Troy would give her the chance to put right the years of denial and deceit. How she wished Father Mesnel could've been by her side, praying with her. But what she didn't know was that he'd been in deep prayer for her for the previous four days, ever since he got Tong's letter to say she and her son were in Ban Hatsati and that sister and brother had faced their fears, visited the riverbank and unloaded each other's pain on one another. Though he was thousands of miles away in France, the wise priest sensed there was still some way to go before the family was freed from its past.

While she had no idea Father Mesnel was praying for her, she did sense a level of calmness and confidence that seemed strangely out of place.

"Morning Troy . . . and welcome to Laos!" she said, gently kissing him on the lips.

"Morning honey."

"I've brought you coffee," she said, making a mug appear as if by magic.

"Thanks," he said, kissing her again, wondering how it was possible for someone to look so perfectly beautiful so early in the morning.

"When you're ready Troy, we'll go for a walk down to the river," she said. "It's the best time, before it gets too hot and sticky."

"OK, be with you in a minute," he said, looking forward to strolling hand in hand with his wife.

Had he known what he was walking into, he'd have thought differently.

* * * * *

"It's so beautiful it's breathtaking!" Troy said as he looked out across the trees and river to the Bolovens Plateau that rose dramatically out of the flatlands a mile or so in the distance. The sky was a light shade of azure blue and there wasn't a cloud anywhere to be seen.

"Yes, it is beautiful isn't it?" Bian said, knowing the moment of truth had arrived.

The two sat holding hands in the same place Bian and Tong had sat a few weeks earlier.

"I love Laos Troy. I love Ban Hansati and Troy . . . I love you."

The tone in her voice suddenly had Troy realising there was a purpose, a reason they were sat where they were.

"What's up Bian?"

"Troy, I really do love you and I'm so sorry for not being what I should've been for you," she said, her eyes filling up as she spoke.

"It's OK Bian. That's behind us now. It's time to move on," he said, doing all he could to hide his sudden nervousness. He wondered what was in store. Was she going to tell him it was over? Was he about to be told the truth about the lithe Laotian farmer?

"Yes Troy, it is time to move on. But first I need to share something with you, something I should've shared a long time ago. Please forgive me for not having done so."

"Bian: what you talking about?"

Then she started. "Troy . . . more than twenty-seven years ago, down there . . ."

Just under an hour later she stopped talking. Early on he'd tried once or twice to interject, to ask a question, and each time she gently put a finger to his lips. He got the message and had no choice but to endure the most difficult hour of his life.

Inside, he felt like death: inadequate, frustrated, guilty his ignorance had made him so lack in understanding.

He was amazed at Bian's bravery as she explained how she and Tong had sat in the same place just a few weeks earlier.

"Troy, I know I needed to tell you this. I know my not telling you before was unfair on you but I had to come to Ban Hatsati to face my fear, face the past. I hope you understand. I love you so much. In fact, I love you more today than ever and having been through this, I now know I can love you the way both of us have always wanted."

She was crying so much, the last few words barely made it out.

Troy put his arm round her, squeezing her tight. His legal training had taught him that it never paid to think aloud and he knew the wrong words at the wrong time had the potential to do irreparable damage. While he hated the thought of the men abusing his wife, many things he'd wondered about for years had suddenly fallen into place.

"What about Thimay? Does he know?" he asked, needing confirmation.

"He asked me about his father for the first time for years just before Christmas. I told him I'd been raped. But he didn't know the full story till now. He's been with Tong this morning."

"One of the three white men was his father?"

"I guess," Bian said, shutting her eyes as if to avoid taking the truth head-on.

"Don't worry Bian, we'll put this behind us and move on," he said careful to say the right thing, what he knew his wife needed to hear. Inside though, he wasn't so sure. He needed time to think but that would have to come later.

"Oh Troy: I love you so much."

* * * * *

When Troy and Bian arrived back at the house, Tong and Thimay were sat silently in the sitting area. Both had obviously been crying.

The three men exchanged looks. It was an intimate moment; a moment the macho spirit of the male psyche rarely allows. Sensing one another's pain, the three men embraced, each feeling inadequate and helpless in the face of such gross injustice. In their different ways, they were a trio in love with the same woman, the victim of an injustice so vast it made them victims too.

Conversation wasn't easy and several hours and half-a-dozen coffees later, Troy quietly whispered to Bian, "I'm going to the car a minute. I need some time . . ."

"I understand," she said, gripped with fear but trying not to show it. "We've got chicken for dinner," she added, somehow hoping her words would anchor him in the event he was thinking of not coming back.

"OK; see you later," he said pecking her gently on the cheek.

Two miles south of Ban Hatsati, on the road to Saisettha, he pulled over hoping to clear his head. Within seconds, the brightness of the sun disappeared as a thick belt of dark cloud descended over the stationery vehicle. The sudden gloom was followed by an impossibly loud thunder clap and three forked lightening blasts that lit up the sky for miles.

Then the rain started.

Troy switched on the wipers and gazed southwards across the marshy flatlands, his eyes fixed on two trees four hundred yards to his left. They looked strangely out of place, surrounded by a characterless landscape that was totally flat. They fascinated him. He didn't know why and he had no way of knowing how significant they were.

If he'd been able to take a ride in a time machine and switched the dial to June 17th 1972, twenty-seven years and nine months earlier, he'd have seen two Cobra helicopters guarding the skies while a third chopper, a Huey, descended to within a few feet of the ground. In effect, the Huey was like the getaway car in a robbery. But it wasn't a robbery in the conventional sense. No jewellery store had lost its gems, no bank separated from its money. Instead, the victim was a stunningly beautiful fifteen year old village girl robbed of both her virginity and her innocence.

* * * * *

Bian looked relieved as Troy climbed into the porch.

"It's OK, it's going to be OK," he said hugging her, the same time he shot reassuring glances to Tong and Thimay.

Buoyed by his return, Bian busied herself with dinner.

"This is Tong's rice, the sweetest rice in all Southeast Asia" she declared proudly.

Later the same evening he appeared disinterested as she nuzzled into him. She thought the worst but her worries lasted no more than a few minutes as he began to respond.

"We'll have to be quiet," she whispered. "Tong and Shilong are only a thin partition away."

As she spoke, she climbed on top of him. He gasped lightly at her eagerness. Fifteen minutes later she was done but poor Troy was too tense.

"Its knowing I have to be so quiet," he whispered.

"That's OK, leave it to me," she said, lifting the sheet.

Five minutes was all it took. It would have been perfect, idyllic even, except Troy couldn't get the picture of his wife out of his mind. It was a photo wholly unsuited for the family album, his fully clothed wife on her knees being taken by a faceless soldier.

Worse still, Troy could see the queue behind him, the other soldiers waiting their turn.

* * * * *

Just over a week later, Troy, Bian and Thimay flew into Tampa.

Saying goodbye had been hard but aside from one bout of weeping as they drove away, Bian held it together. Troy knew he was lucky. He'd got his wife back, transformed for the better in every way. The only downside was the images that plagued him by day and the nightmares that refused to go at night, the subject matter always the same: his wife being abused by a quartet of faceless soldiers.

By the time they arrived home, they were completely exhausted. Even though it was close to midnight, Troy called the office to leave an answer-phone message saying he'd be in lunchtime next day.

"They'll be very concerned; I was due back ages ago," he said loudly from the bathroom.

But Bian wasn't listening; she was already asleep.

After showering, Troy climbed in beside her, gently stroking her thick black hair as it splayed over her shoulder and down onto the pillow. She looked like sleeping beauty as he carefully brushed a few stray hairs off her face before pecking her on the cheek and then, on the point of her shoulder. The scar came into view.

Now that he knew the story of how she got it, it filled him with silent rage.

"How could anyone want to hurt anything so beautiful?" he whispered, the anger bubbling inside him. It was the trigger to his head filling once again, with imagined images of his beloved Bian being violated by faceless soldiers.

"Sleep tight my precious. You're safe now," he said, before turning over and dozing off; for his own appointment with the soldiers.

Two hours later he woke suddenly, swimming in a sea of sweat.

"Sons of bitches!" he screamed as he sat bolt upright. He shook his head, realising it was a dream, a bad dream. He went downstairs, made himself a coffee and moved into the den sensing he'd reached a pivotal, life-changing moment. He knew it was time: time to dedicate his life to destroying four men who robbed his wife of her virginity.

The fact it all happened before Troy and Bian met, didn't lessen how he felt. "You picked the wrong girl you faceless sons of bitches!" he said out loud. "You gonna pay for what you done."

After two hours scribbling notes, he went back to bed.

"You OK, honey?" Bian mumbled.

"I'm fine; you go back to sleep now," he whispered before kissing her gently on the forehead.

And he was fine. In fact, he hadn't felt better since the day Bian had taken him to the river.

His two hours in the den had changed things. He'd reached a place of decision and Troy Templeman always operated better when he knew where he was going.

He had just one thing on his mind, the "V" word: VENGEANCE!!

PART THREE

VENGEANCE AND JUSTICE

Early summer 2002

CHAPTER THIRTY-ONE:

Gabriel Tyner was the archetypal newspaper man.

The Senior Editor at *Tampa Bay Today*, he'd been in the business forty-six years.

Tampa Bay Today was one of America's few remaining family owned broadsheets and the Bailey Family, who had interests in everything from Venezuelan oil to South African diamonds, was a major corporate client of *Robeson Boutwell Templeman*.

Over two years had passed since Troy and Bian had returned from Laos and despite many setbacks and closed doors, Troy's determination to bring the four perpetrators to justice was stronger than ever. It was the reason he was sat waiting in Tyner's office.

Even at sixty-two, Gabriel Tyner was a veritable tornado of a man, exuding energy and dynamism in everything he said and did.

"Good to meet you Troy," he bellowed, hand extended out in front of him. "Jim Bailey speaks highly of you. Saved him a mill or two in the courtroom I understand; always a good way to get on the right side of Jim!"

Troy wasn't really listening. All he could think about was freeing his right hand before Tyner crushed his fingers to powder.

With a powerful twenty-inch neck squashed between his huge bald head and a pair of shoulders that easily filled his sleeveless shirt, Tyner was built like a bull. As he rested his massive forearms on the desk, Troy could see why the handshake had been so crippling: Tyner had the biggest spade-like hands he'd ever seen, his fingers thick as German sausages.

"I need some advice Mr Tyner . . ."

"OK Troy, how can I help?"

It was twenty-five minutes before Tyner spoke again. "That's a helluva story Troy," he said puffing out his cheeks. "I spent ten months in Nam in '69, reporting for the *LA Times*. If we reported half what we saw, it would've put Middle America off her food forever! Part of me thinks you should let this go but I can see why you need to pursue it."

"Every door's been shut in my face Mr Tyner. The military, the government, they all deny there were military personnel in Southern Laos in June '72. In effect, they're saying my wife imagined the whole thing! It makes my blood boil!"

"Steady now son," Tyner said calmly. "Get your lawyer's head back-on. Clear thinking's a must in situations like this."

"I know; sorry Mr Tyner."

"Call me Tiny, son, like the rest of the planet."

"OK Tiny; so what you think?"

"You're stirring a storm son and officialdom will not want you to find the truth! That's why the doors close in your face."

"So where does that leave me?" Troy said interrupting.

"Let me finish," Tyner replied abruptly, making Troy wish he'd stayed quiet. "I don't think this is a story for a daily like *Tampa Bay Today*. It's more human interest than mainstream, more magazine than newspaper. So what I suggest is we meet again in three months. I'll make inquiries myself and I'll also think about which magazine we approach. We need a national than can cause ripples coast to coast. And another thing Troy; doesn't next month mark the thirtieth anniversary of the incident?"

"Yeah, it'll be thirty years on 17th June."

"Holy cow Troy: 17th June?!! 1972?!!'"

"Yeah, that's right. Why?"

"Son, June 17th 1972 was the date of the Watergate break-in! You know what that means?" Tyner said before answering his own question amid a string of excited expletives, "A newspaperman's dream-come-true! What an opening for our story!"

Troy looked puzzled.

"Every story needs a start-point Troy, a hook. Your story's thin on evidence but historically, the time-line's pretty damn awesome! Trust me son, every editor we talk to will be excited by the connection."

"OK, so why wait three months?"

Tyner looked at his watch impatiently; it was the fifth time in five minutes.

"Troy, you came here for advice so let me give you some. You spent two years running up your own butt and all you got to show for it is a brown nose. Three more months won't matter. You want a result right? Well, a case like this is more tortoise than hare; long haul. I can help you Troy, but don't push me son. I ain't the sort who responds to being pushed."

Troy had the thought it hadn't been one of his better meetings. "Sorry," he said sheepishly.

"Good Troy. Now, I'm three minutes late. One other thing quickly; after thirty years most government and military paperwork falls into the public domain so you hunt about, see if you can get us a lead or two. OK? See you in August."

"Thanks Tiny," was all Troy could manage before Tyner disappeared down the stairs at a pace that should've been way beyond a sixty-two year old.

Troy was excited. He felt he'd finally found someone with both the expertise and desire to help and justice and incarceration for the men who dared paw his wife somehow felt that bit nearer.

All that remained was letting Bian in on what he was up to; the most difficult bit left to last.

* * * * *

Troy had been accused of being manipulative since his teens and deep down, he knew it was true. Two weeks after the meeting with Tyner, he planned on aiming all his powers of manipulation in his wife's direction. He knew he was being selfish. Bian had let it go but he couldn't. Four men had got to his wife first, before he did, and dared steal her virginity. Now they had to pay. He hated the fact his wife's happiness and contentment came a poor second to his lust for vengeance. He wasn't proud of himself but it didn't matter. He intended convincing Bian that bringing the four to justice was the right, proper and *only* thing to do.

He chose Luigi's, their favourite restaurant, as the place to start the ball rolling.

As they were shown to their seats, every male in the restaurant looked their way.

It didn't get to Troy like it used to. "You make me so proud Bian; I'm so lucky," he whispered as they settled into a booth.

"Oh shush Troy. It's me that's lucky. You stuck by me when no-one could've blamed you for walking away. I want to be the wife you've always wanted and you know what, I'm even going to buy you dinner!"

She laughed and all the men's heads turned her way once again.

As the first course arrived, Troy took a deep breath. "Darling?" he said, hesitating.

"Yes," she replied lifting her eyes from the table.

"There's something I been meaning to talk to you about for some time but I don't really know where to start."

"As you say Troy, just talk!"

"It's not easy. It's something I feel strongly about. But I'm not sure you'll see it the same way."

"C'mon Troy, just tell me!" Bian said, feigning exasperation.

"Well, I've been thinking about what happened to you. I think the men responsible should be brought to justice. It's the right and proper thing to do."

Bian looked stunned. She put down her knife and fork. "But Troy, it's over. Surely it's better to leave the past in the past?"

"They crossed a line Bian. They were soldiers who discredited their uniform and their country. What they did was a disgrace. It's not right they should live their lives as if they didn't do anything wrong."

"But Troy, it was thirty years ago. I thought it was over."

"It is in a sense. We've done the hard bit; now it should be about justice."

Troy knew he was playing a dangerous game but there was no going back. "Bian, I love you more than anything in the world. What these men did caused such pain. You and your family bore it directly but me, I lived with it without even knowing it was there," he said lowering his eyes which had filled up slightly. "It's not right they should get away with such a thing."

"Troy, I know you've suffered. It breaks my heart I couldn't tell you earlier but we are so happy now." Then, as if overwhelmed by a moment of self-doubt, she added, "You are happy Troy, aren't you?"

"Of course I'm happy Bian."

"Good, because after being such a rubbish wife I know I'd do anything to make you happy."

Without even being aware of it, she'd backed herself into a check-mate position.

"Then, stand with me in this Bian. These men should be brought to justice. In any other walk of life, when people cross a line they pay. Why should it be different because it was you? Or because it happened in Laos?"

"But . . ."

"No buts Bian. It's not right."

"OK Troy, I'll stand with you," she said defeated.

"Good," said Troy trying hard to conceal his delight.

When they got into bed later that night Troy sensed she was on edge. He cuddled in behind her, whispering, "It'll be OK Bian. We're doing what's right. It'll finally put it to rest, you'll see."

She didn't believe it for a second.

The way they slept couldn't have been more different; Bian on pins, Troy snoring lightly, left to dream of watching four men pronounced guilty before being led off to prison. As each man looks across the courtroom at him, Troy mimes, "You picked the wrong girl!"

Who said revenge isn't sweet?

* * * * *

Troy Templeman never had a problem with commitment.

His co-partners had been sympathetic to his cause, his revised engagement terms agreed at just one meeting. It left Troy free to focus on his mission and all summer he burned the midnight oil, thankful the older he got the less sleep he needed.

On August 22nd 2002 he stood in Gabriel Tyner's office for the second time.

"Tiny, this is Bian," he said proudly.

"Good to meet you Mrs Templeman," Tyner said warmly, his eyes enjoying her beauty without betraying any kind of lust. Within seconds he was down to business, posing five or six questions in quick succession. "OK, that's great," he said, "So next up, I want us to write down everything you remember about the four soldiers?"

"But it was such a long time ago," Bian replied nervously.

"Of course, and there'll be lots of things we don't have answers for. But let's concentrate on what we *do* know."

After twenty minutes brainstorming, Troy was looking at a sheet of paper split into four columns with notes scribbled under the headings: *Mr Evil*, *Mr Blackman*, *Mr Leaderman* and *Mr Out-of-Place*.

"That's a great start. Well done Mrs Templeman! Do you think we could send this list to your brother and ask him to add his thoughts?"

"Yes," Bian said quietly, "Tong saw things I didn't."

"OK," said Tyner turning to Troy. "You get any leads from the Public Records Office?"

Troy reached for his attaché case. "Not a lot. But I did find an ex Special Forces guy called Matt Kallins, who led a search and destroy team that worked with pro-government forces in Cambodia throughout 1971 and wait for this . . . well into '72."

"Well if Kallins was in Cambodia when he wasn't supposed to be, our boys could just as easily have been in Laos. Anything else Troy?"

"Just this," he replied passing Tyner another print-out from a web-site.

It was an obscure reference to an assassination attempt on a Khmer Rouge commander called Ke Pauk who, the article alleged, had been in Southern Laos in June 1972 for a meeting with Pathet Lao leaders. Troy had highlighted the relevant sections so Tyner could speed-read the article which majored on collaboration by anti-government forces in Cambodia and Laos and how it hastened the fall of the Cambodian government in Phnom Penh.

"It's interesting isn't it?" Troy said as Tyner read. "Southern Laos includes Ban Hatsati of course so, if the report is accurate, those behind the assassination attempt could've been Special Ops. So if the assassins were our guys, this incident both puts them in the vicinity and inside the time-line."

"You're quite the investigative journalist Troy! OK, now it's my turn," he said rubbing his giant hands vigorously. "As expected, I got zip from my sources except denial that there were any troops in either Laos or Cambodia after 1st January 1972!! That means, and you've already established this through your web-site cuttings, that any U.S. combat soldiers in either of these countries in '72 would be covert, undercover, and that means Special Ops."

"But that gets us nowhere!"

"We're a long way from nowhere Troy. We know what category of soldier we're looking for and we know something about each of them. That's not nothing son; that's a beginning point."

"Sorry," Troy said feebly.

Tyner nodded; apology accepted.

"And Troy, Bian, you'll be glad to hear we have a magazine interest."

"That's great news; is it Newsweek?"

"No, it's not Newsweek Troy, though they were quite interested."

"Who then?"

"*American Dream*."

"*American Dream*? That's my favourite magazine!" Bian exclaimed.

"Good; coz my guess is, you're going be in it!"

"What?" Bian said glancing at Troy, her face a mix of confusion and panic.

Tyner pretended not to notice. "Troy, you come back to me as soon as you hear back from your brother-in-law. I need that list soon as."

"And what happens then?" Troy asked, unable to help himself.

"We go see Claudia Kaplan at *American Dream!*"

* * * * *

In the event, it was six months before they finally got the plane to Colorado Springs.

Bian insisted on taking the list to Tong Tenh in person, spending two months in Laos and stopping off in France to see Father Mesnel on the way home.

Seven weeks into her visit, Troy decided to join her.

Tyner was all for it, especially after Troy told him he'd bought a broadcast quality video camera and intended recording interviews with Tong and Father Mesnel. Next day, Troy had an e-mail from Tyner and a long list of questions to put to his two subjects.

The interview with Tong was especially harrowing. Tyner had instructed that any tears needed to be filmed so despite the risk of alienating his brother-in-law, Troy kept the cameras rolling.

And there were more tears with Father Mesnel but this time the tears were Bian's, who was overjoyed at seeing him again. The Catholic priest had become aware of the original incident when he and Xiantha, Bian's father, became close friends in the autumn of 1972. As a result, he was uniquely positioned to provide a kind of after-the-fact type context to the entire tragedy.

Tyner was delighted with the video footage.

"This is gold Troy," he declared excitedly. "Father Mesnel is like the most credible witness of all time!!"

Troy however, seemed less sure.

"Come on Troy; trust me on this. When Claudia Kaplan chucks her boulder into the water the ripples will make waves big enough to wash away the Eastern seaboard!"

"What'd you mean?"

"You're the lawyer Troy. How often you asked a question pretending you already had the answer?"

"All the time I guess."

"That's my point exactly. That's what this is all about. Once we show Claudia Kaplan we have a case and more importantly, she has a story, she'll have her people sniffing all over the planet and then, when she's ready, she'll publish a story that'll look as if she's already got all the answers. Twenty million people will read it and something will come crawling out the woodwork. You mark my words son; our perps will have nowhere to hide."

"Is that the way it's done?"

"Aye, just like you legal boys Troy; we make it look like we know the answer, then we watch the sons of bitches hang 'emselves!"

CHAPTER THIRTY-TWO:

Though each knew who the other was, Gabriel Tyner and Claudia Kaplan had never met.

While both were in the news reporting business, it was the only thing they had in common. Claudia Kaplan was thirty-eight years-old, tall, elegant, beautiful and blonde. She also happened to be a lesbian. Even her office was like a different world to Tyner's; six times the size, with so many plants it looked like a public botanical garden.

"Good to meet you Claudia; Jim Bailey asked me to pass on his best wishes."

"It's good to meet you too Gabriel. How is Jim?"

"He's well and probably a hundred million richer than when you last ran into him!"

"Yes, Jim's always been a passionate accumulator of wealth. I wonder when enough will be enough?"

"I reckon he's a way to go yet!" Tyner replied, raising his thick eyebrows.

"He was good to me though," Claudia said. "It's not often you tell a boss you're off to set up a competitor magazine and he gives you two million to help you on your way."

"Did he really?"

"Yeah he did! It bought him ten per cent of the company and today, it's worth over thirty million so it was a good investment!" she said, without boasting.

Having answered the question, she turned to Troy and Bian.

"Now, you must be Bian . . . and from what I hear Bian, you have a helluva story to tell."

* * * * *

Gabriel Tyner had done an excellent job selling the story to Claudia.

At his suggestion, she'd blanked off the entire afternoon and even made an allowance for lunch. Tyner was pleased with the respect afforded him and his guests and mentally made a note to reciprocate first chance he got.

Claudia Kaplan was an experienced reporter who'd devoted her life to exploiting the news business for her own benefit. The day she'd left the University of Southern California she'd confided to her then girlfriend that she'd be worth forty million dollars by her fortieth birthday.

The girlfriend may have been dumped soon after but Claudia achieved her goal with six years to spare.

Her beauty hid a hard centre. She was a shrewd businesswoman, queen of both her media empire and her boardroom. She had six years at *Newsweek*, the last two as executive editor, and won the MATRIX Award for outstanding woman in the field of communications. It was at the award ceremony that she met Jim Bailey.

"You head-hunting me or coming on to me?" she'd said by way of an opening line.

"What would your answer be if I were?" Bailey replied, cleverly answering a question with a question.

"On the first there's a possibility but regarding the second, you're not my type!"

It was the start of a mutually beneficial relationship that saw Claudia climb towards her goals and Bailey get the talented straight-talking editor he needed if his three ailing magazine titles were to survive. Four years later, with all three magazine titles in pole position in their respective categories, Bailey wasn't surprised when she told him she was moving on.

He knew whatever she decided to do she was going to do; she was that kind of woman.

"Are you sure about this?" he asked as he reached for his check-book.

"What's this for?" she asked in amazement.

"Ten per cent of your business!" he replied.

In such a cash rich position, Claudia estimated the two million probably accelerated her plans by five years. It helped *American Dream* quickly establish itself as the fastest growing magazine of any category in the United States. The meteoric rise had been underlined the previous month when sales had broken nine million for the first time.

As Bian, Troy and Gabriel Tyner sat down, it was clear she was the one in charge. She knew Bian was the key to the story, if there was a story. She looked straight at her. "Bian, *American Dream* likes substance to its stories and I believe the American people want substance too. We want stories that focus on the best and worst humanity has to offer. We want to promote what's right and make a mark on every reader's heart. Now Bian, I'm told you have such a story. I know it'll be difficult but I need to hear it; we can't go any further till I do. So, are you up to it?"

It was an impressive introduction.

With Troy stroking her hand, Bian nodded, albeit a little reluctantly.

"OK; now Troy, Gabriel, I only want to hear Bian's voice. I want this taped with no interruptions. If you want to make a point or add anything, make a note and we'll talk later."

Troy looked at his wife, noted the trepidation in her eyes. He may have felt guilty but he didn't feel guilty enough to say stop. "It's OK," he whispered, gently squeezing her hand.

Bian knew it wasn't; but she knew she had to go through with it.

Forty-five minutes later she'd given a full and graphic account.

"Sons of bitches; men are the absolute pits!" Claudia exclaimed, making no apology that Troy and Tyner fitted the profile and could've taken offense. "Don't you worry Bian, we'll get these low-lifes and when we do, they're mincemeat!"

The words emerged from her beautiful lips like music to Troy's ears.

He reached for his attaché case, unable to hide a smile.

"Everything we know about them is in this document Claudia, and these are DVD's of the interviews with Bian's brother and Father Mesnel."

"Excellent," she said, flicking the pages before glancing at her watch. "I think we'll call it a day. We've booked you into the Broadmoor. I'm sorry I can't join you for dinner but everything's on us so please feel free to indulge; it's by far the best hotel in town. Troy, I understand you like your golf. Well tomorrow morning, you're playing the East Course with the hotel's professional. Bian, for you, we've arranged a full body massage, a facial and a manicure. You'll be spoiled rotten! And Gabriel, we've booked you a business suite so you can get some work done. I know how busy it is in the newspaper business."

Claudia had thought of everything. But she wasn't finished. "I've scheduled a second meeting for two-thirty tomorrow when we'll discuss strategy. We'll be done by five and have you at the airport in plenty of time for your flight back to Tampa."

"Dynamite: she's absolute dynamite!" Troy exclaimed as the chauffeur-driven limo headed for the Broadmoor.

"She's a crackerjack alright!" Tyner grunted in agreement.

Only Bian said nothing.

Troy was so excited he didn't notice his wife's silence. All he could think about was the mental rush threatening to overwhelm him. Everything he'd seen and heard pointed the same way; *the enemy* were going to pay for what they did to his wife and for what they did to him.

* * * * *

Set amidst breathtaking scenery, the Broadmoor was sensational.

Troy had headed the club pro all the way to the par five seventeenth where a sliced three wood second shot put him in the trees. The competitor in him knew he'd blown it but he took solace in the fact he only lost by a shot to someone who played golf for a living.

As he sat in the limo deep in thought, he wondered what Claudia's next step would be.

"What you thinking Troy?" Bian said quietly, shaking him from the mental image of four men watching their jailer throw away the key.

"Nothing," he replied, lying.

"What's going to happen with this next meeting?" she continued.

"Claudia Kaplan's gonna tell us what her plans are," interrupted Tyner. "And my guess is we're about to find out how seriously she's taking us."

Bian would've preferred Troy to have answered. She didn't like the way he'd become distracted. But just as she suspected, he was totally oblivious to her feelings.

"I'm looking forward to the meeting," he said to neither Bian nor Tyner. "I have a feeling Claudia's going to come through big-time. I sure as hell wouldn't want her on my tail."

Bian was wounded by his lack of sensitivity, her silence opening the door for Tyner.

Just as insensitively, he said, "You're right Troy; she's a high-powered bitch who knows how to go for the throat."

It didn't help Bian one bit, but once again, it was music to Troy's ears.

* * * * *

"How was your morning?" Claudia said chirpily, rising to greet her guests as they were shown into *American Dream's* sumptuous boardroom.

"Why'd you think we're meeting in here?" Troy whispered to Tyner as they were ushered one side the massive walnut table, opposite Claudia and two men.

"Because we just leapt up the food chain son!"

"Bian, Troy, Gabriel: let me introduce Phil Woodcock and Brett Jameson. Phil is Legal Affairs Editor and BJ is one of four associate editors. They'll be working with us on the story. After careful review, *American Dream* is keen to run Bian's story. This is why the guys are here."

Claudia was already talking team and her terminology wasn't wasted on Tyner or Troy.

"Like I said Troy, they're taking this very seriously!" Tyner whispered.

"Phil's drawn up a contract which Bian needs to sign. I'm sure you'll find its terms favourable. Let me bring Phil in here; he can elaborate."

"Thanks Claudia," he said sitting up out his seat so he could push a buff folder across the table. "It's an easy to read two-pager which perhaps, I should summarise. The agreement gives *American Dream* exclusivity without time limit. While there's no guarantee, the magazine will deploy unlimited people, time and finance to locating the four men and bringing them to justice."

While his wife looked uncertain and nervous, Troy had the thought that life had never been better.

"In addition Mrs Templeman, the magazine is prepared to offer you a financial consideration in advance of the first story. You'll find a bankers draft attached to the rear of the contract."

"You're paying us one hundred thousand dollars?" Bian said incredulously.

"Of course we're paying you Mrs Templeman," said BJ speaking for the first time. "While we have a very real interest in seeing justice done, this ultimately, is a commercial decision. But to avoid any accusations you're telling your story for money, the agreed remuneration will be paid into a special trust fund we've set up on your behalf."

BJ's words hid his surprise. He wasn't prepared for the fact the beautiful woman opposite wasn't there to make money; it just wasn't normal in twenty-first century America.

Claudia was less surprised. "If things go as we expect Bian," she said, "The story will launch big and finish bigger, with several updates in between. The hundred thousand is simply a gesture of goodwill on our part. The package is linked to sales and it's perfectly feasible that by the time it's over, you could be sitting on two-and-a-half million dollars or more, subject of course, to a successful prosecution."

Claudia paused for a second, her eyes fixed on Bian. "While this is a commercial decision Bian, I need you to know that I want these men found and I want them brought to justice. In fact, at this precise moment, there are few things in my life I want more."

There was an unmissable bite to her words, a bite reinforced by the silence that followed.

"Right," said Phil Woodcock sensing Claudia was in danger of blurring the lines. "Why don't we take a twenty-minute break for you to look over the agreement?" he said, glancing at his boss hoping he'd called it right. He had.

"That's good thinking Phil," Claudia said, before adding, "Oh, there's one other thing. This story will be the first in four years to appear in my name."

"Wow: they *are* taking this seriously!" Tyner said as the *American Dream* trio left the room.

"She'd never risk her reputation if she wasn't supremely confident," Troy said, glancing over at his wife as she scanned the contract.

"There'll be no halfway ground Troy; it'll be victory or nothing. She'll have BJ do all the work, tweak it a little and drape her name all over it."

"I don't give a damn as long as the sons of bitches are made to pay," Troy responded, once again demonstrating his ability to focus.

While making money may not have entered Bian's head, it had crossed Troy's mind. But money-making didn't figure on his list of reasons for pursuing the case. If he'd written his motives down on a piece of paper, at the top would've been the word "vengeance," in capital letters, and below it there'd have been nothing but white space. Nothing else counted.

"You're the lawyer Troy, what'd you think?" Tyner said as he looked over the contract.

"It's short, snappy and well-drafted . . ."

"Shall I sign it?" Bian said timidly.

"If you're sure you want to go through with this?" Troy replied, momentarily panicking she might say *no*.

"It's what you want isn't it darling?"

"I want what you want dear," Troy replied, convincing no-one.

"OK," Bian said quietly. She scribbled her signature just as the boardroom door opened.

"We have a deal then; so let's push on," Claudia said as BJ handed a wire-bound document to each person in the room. On the front cover, it said, "*Subject* – Bian Templeman. *Incident* – Laos, June 17th 1972. *Objective* – Identify & Locate Four Perpetrators, all assumed to be U.S. citizens."

As Claudia led them through the contents of the report, Tyner marvelled at how such detailed analyses could've been prepared in the few hours between meetings. "It's no wonder she couldn't come to dinner!" he said quietly to Troy.

But Troy couldn't think. His mind was surfing a sea of adrenaline, the excitement threatening to burst his veins. The four men, the focus of his life for three years, may have been Black Ops, Special Forces or suchlike but it counted for nothing. Being the toughest men in the world was meaningless if you had a man-hater like Claudia Kaplan on your tail. Now it was their turn, Troy thought. The predators who'd hunted his wife had now become the hunted.

They would become the focus of the largest, most costly investigation ever undertaken by an American magazine and were about to find themselves hunted by the female of the species who was anything but submissive.

In the spotlight, there'd be nowhere to run, nowhere to hide.

CHAPTER THIRTY-THREE:

As its founder, Claudia Kaplan was the inspiration behind the meteoric rise of *American Dream*.

"Preparation is always the key to a good magazine story," she'd often say in interviews. And another of her oft quoted lines was, "Newspaper reporting may be all about immediacy but a magazine story requires the right angle, the right timing and has to press the reader's hot button."

The New Year opened with her becoming just the second woman to be named *Adweek's* Editor of the Year. At the summit of her profession, Claudia rarely called it wrong. From the first meeting, she'd been convinced Bian's story would be huge and she'd overseen everything, down to the last detail. So when it finally hit the news-stands in the spring of 2004, it did so with the seismic force of an atomic bomb.

The front cover was sensational. As usual, top right was the magazine's logo underpinned with the words, *Bringing the Heart of the Story to the American People*. But the main feature, top billing if you like, was Bian's face in ultra close-up. She looked stunning in a jet black top with oriental type collar. Running across the blackness of her neck and shoulders in heavy gold lettering was the headline, *Atrocity in Southeast Asia!*

The magazine flew off the shelves.

"Congratulations Claudia! We're already twelve per cent up on our previous best first day sales figures," BJ exclaimed excitedly.

"I told you that face would put two million on our sales figures didn't I?" his boss replied triumphantly, her eyes fixed on the magazine in front of her.

"Yeah: but what about the story? It's a gem, even if it's got your name on it!"

"Now don't go all sulky on me BJ!" Claudia teased. "You'll get your reward in heaven! Seriously though, the story is good. You did well. Our pebble's been tossed into the water and even as we speak, the ripples are going far and wide. I reckon the first wave's about to hit the beach!"

As with everything else in the magazine business, the founding editor of *American Dream* was about to be proven right once again.

* * * * *

Monday, Tuesday, Thursday and Friday always started the same for Eugene Sanders.

From six to seven forty-five he'd be at the gym and by eight-thirty he'd drive through the main gates at Bell Helicopters.

He was very much a man of routine, nine sessions a week with four early starts. Finishing his session as most were starting or still contemplating theirs gave him special pleasure. Mentally it gave him an edge and even though he didn't think like he used to, he still liked to have an edge.

He loved Mondays and Thursdays. They were chest/shoulders/traps days and that meant his two favourite exercises, bench press and lateral raises. Thursday was his heavy day and this particular Thursday had seen some solid bench, over four hundred for reps, and something close to his best for lateral raises. Many men can't lift a hundred and twenty-eight pound dumbbell off the floor but then again, the description "ordinary man" never quite fitted Eugene Sanders.

As he emerged from the showers into the spacious locker room he was feeling well-pleased with himself. Sitting round about in various states of undress, were three or four other guys who all looked as if they were about to start their session.

"Hey dude?" said one guy from behind him, "That's the strangest birthmark I ever seen."

"Yeah man; drives my woman crazy," Eugene replied nonchalantly, the same time he flexed and unflexed his buttocks, making the birthmark dance a jig up and down his right glute.

All three men laughed.

Eugene was used to attracting eyes when he was naked but this time he sensed something was different. His first thought was that the two guys were queer. As he towelled himself down, he glanced round. One of the guys was white, the other black, and they were furtively whispering to one another. The black guy was tying his shoe laces, while the white guy, appeared to be reading a magazine.

In days gone by, he would've bristled aggression at having his space invaded, even if it was just with words, but his self-control had increased with age. But the whispering irritated him and there was only one way to deal with it, front on. That hadn't changed.

"Hey, what's up man?" he said directly, turning to see the black guy slip his Nike training top over his head.

"Nothing dude; we just looking at this magazine," the man responded with a sly smile curling up his lips.

"Yeah man; perhaps you'd like to have a look at it?" chirped the white guy suddenly throwing the magazine like a Frisbee across three or four benches separating him and his friend from Eugene.

"I don't look at magazines," Eugene snapped, his patience stretched to the limit.

"Trust me man, I think you might be interested in this one!" said the white guy smirking, the two men already heading towards the safety of the locker room door.

* * * * *

Gus O'Donnell liked being retired.

He and Darlene had always promised themselves they'd travel in retirement and in four short years they'd done just that. They'd sailed the Caribbean, visited Hawaii, Bermuda and the Bahamas, taken another cruise up the West Coast to Alaska and visited Europe spending a week in each of five capital cities: London, Paris, Berlin, Brussels and Prague.

Another promise Gus made to himself was that he'd fish twice-a-week till the day he died.

Darlene always went with him, anxious they squeeze maximum value from their time left together. As Gus fished, she liked to sit and read or lie out in the sun catching rays.

But the April chill meant that as Gus cast his fishing line, Darlene's backside was being gently toasted by the heated leather seats in their silver grey Lincoln Town Car. Darlene had tilted her seat back slightly and pulled the car rug across her lap. In her hands she held *American Dream* magazine and was so lost in the lead feature, a harrowing story of rape and brutality, she hadn't noticed that it was raining.

She jumped as Gus opened the car door and climbed in, cursing the rain. He stopped abruptly when he realised his wife was crying.

"What's up dear?" he said surprised and concerned.

"It's this story. It amazes me how people can be so cruel?"

Gus grunted, doing his best to fake an interest. But when Darlene closed the magazine a little so he could see what she was reading, the need for faking disappeared. He'd often seen his wife reading *American Dream*. He thought it was a woman's magazine; ignorant that forty-two per cent of its readership was male.

Either way, the cover caught his attention.

"What an incredibly beautiful woman," he thought, battling to stop it dropping to his lips.

As he drove, Darlene explained the gist of the story.

"It seems there were four soldiers, one black, three white. They were in Southern Laos at the end of the Vietnam War and on June 17th 1972 a date which incidentally, was the same day as the Watergate break-in, they raped a young girl, murdered her mother, and seriously assaulted her grandmother. The magazine thinks they were some kind of covert team, Special Forces or something, working undercover."

Darlene continued talking but Gus wasn't listening. He'd heard it before. It may have been a while since he'd last read his brother's letter but its contents were etched into his memory. He'd read it a thousand times, knew it by heart, and all the way home, it was like Darlene was reading it aloud.

As he opened the front door into their sitting room, Gus O'Donnell's heart rate had been working at close to double speed for the previous half-hour. With *American Dream* magazine in his hand, he rushed to his study knowing his brother's nightmare scenario had made the quantum leap from covert black ops all the way into the public domain.

Though the woman on the front cover was beautiful and he regretted what had happened to her, it wasn't her or even justice that Gus O'Donnell cared about. The only objective that mattered was preserving the good name of the dead brother he idolized, Lieutenant Colonel William T. O'Donnell.

And for *that*, he'd do anything.

"Where's that damn letter?" he said sharply, his fingers rifling through his desk drawer.

* * * * *

Marlene Moorer loved Chateau Chantalle in the spring, the gardens and the colour merging seamlessly with the shimmering waters of Lake Michigan.

In fifty-five years of residence, she'd come to love the house, especially since her husband's death fifteen years earlier. Marriage to Jordan Kingsbridge turned her into a bitter and emotionally unstable woman, swinging like a pendulum from downright unhappy to manically depressed. She blamed Jordan for robbing her of her potential and for the first few years after he was gone, she'd often reflect that watching him wheeze his way to an angina-ridden death was the high point of their loveless relationship.

At eighty-two, she'd mellowed and learning to appreciate Chateau Chantalle was a key factor to her enjoying the twilight period of her life. She spent most mornings in the large conservatory that looked out onto the Lake; it was her favourite part of the house. It was her son Rudi who'd had it built but Marlene never strayed into the conservatory when he was home; they may have both loved the beautiful glass structure but they didn't love each other. Theirs was another loveless inter-Kingsbridge relationship and the less she saw of him the more she liked it.

Marlene liked to sit in her favourite chair, the sun on her back, enjoying the richness of the expensive curtains and the lovely furnishings all of which had been chosen by Kay, her ex-model daughter-in-law. Kay's influence could be seen all over the conservatory and the only thing Marlene would've changed had she had the power to do so, would've been the war memorabilia and photographs; not because she had anything against war but because they all featured her son and she had plenty against him.

With Rudi out of town on a business trip and Kay at a meeting, she had the house and the conservatory to herself. As she looked out across the grounds sipping a coffee, one of the maids gently coughed behind her.

"Madam; the mail is here," she said in a whisper.

"Leave it on the table Victoria."

Most was for Rudi and for Kay; only one item for her.

"Oh good," she said out loud, "American Dream!"

She'd been a fan over a year, enrolling as an annual subscriber three months earlier.

"What a beautiful girl!" she said to herself, as she slid the magazine out its polythene envelope. Twenty minutes later she was engrossed in the lead feature, a story about an atrocity committed by four men in Southeast Asia at the end of the Vietnam War. The implication was that the perpetrators were U.S. soldiers on some kind of covert mission and all through, Marlene had a sense that though the incident had happened decades earlier and thousands of miles away it all somehow felt closer to home.

Then she turned the page and found out why.

At five thousand words and twelve pages, the article was a long one. It was gripping reading: personal, brutal, compelling. But its last two pages had the former Hollywood actress on the edge of her seat. There were four hand-sketched featureless head outlines, three white one black, with each having a kind of pen portrait underneath it. Marlene didn't get past pen portrait *No.1*. "Very handsome but cruel, evil even; tall, well-built and muscular," it said, adding, "Wore black straps round his arms, tied just above the elbows."

An alarm bell suddenly went off in Marlene Moorer's head, the magazine dropping to the floor.

Fifteen seconds later, she was dead.

When a plane goes down the first thing accident investigators look for is the *black box*. Inside is a microcomputer that can shed light on the events leading up to the crash, identifying what decisions were made by the pilot, how the instruments performed and suchlike.

It's an invaluable tool.

Alas, for human beings, there's no black box equivalent. The verdict on Marlene Moorer's death certificate may have stated *Massive Cardioembolic Stroke* but had there been a black box or video tape of her last moments, the pathologist could've called it differently, recording instead, her son Rudi Kingsbridge as the cause of death.

In the last seconds of her life, the video tape would have pictured Marlene reading the pen portrait of *No.1*. It would've shown her reaching the part that said about him wearing black ties round his arms. It would've recorded the look of dreadful realization as her face drained of blood. Then finally, a split second later, it would've captured her looking up at the war pictures on the wall confirming what she already knew; that in all six she could see from where she sat, her son Rudi had black ties around his arms, fixed just above the elbows.

Assuming it could record sound, the video would also have preserved her last words.

"You really are a bastard!" she said, her eyes locked on the nearest photo of her illegitimately conceived son.

* * * * *

Seventy-four year old Bobby-Joe Rose was a Virginian to his bootstraps.

Being the former sheriff of Prince Edward County gave him status, even in retirement, and all his life Bobby-Joe had liked being a big fish in a small pond.

He was supremely fit for a man his age and his mind too, was razor sharp. The slowness of retirement was something he constantly battled with. He desperately missed his beloved wife Suzie, their forty-two year marriage ended by cancer the year before he retired. Alone and bored, he'd taken to spending a couple of hours each afternoon at Jumpin' Jack's, a bar in the centre of Farmville. He'd play dominoes, cards, or just while away the hours telling or listening to stories with the likes of Mo Costello and Ernie Troyer who, like him, were well into their seventies.

Bobby-Joe, Mo and Ernie had been at Doug Miller's bedside the night he died, New Year's Eve '99. He and Doug had been friends since High School. Bobby-Joe thought the world of him and was honoured when, breathing pretty much his last breath, Doug bequeathed him his bar-stool at Jumpin' Jack's. It was one of the proudest moments of Bobby-Joe's life.

Doug Miller was a real-life war hero, a Master Sergeant in the U.S. Army who'd seen active service in Korea and Vietnam. He also happened to be a legend in Farmville. Bobby-Joe's dedication to law enforcement had won him many commendations but nothing gave him a greater sense of lifetime achievement than being thought of as Doug Miller's friend.

In April 2004, sat on Doug's former bar-stool, Bobby-Joe was looking agitated as he waited for Mo and Ernie. In his left hand was a glass of Wild Turkey, while in his right was a magazine he had no choice but to buy, the girl on the front cover so breathtakingly beautiful she virtually demanded he spend five bucks purchasing her.

It was forty-five minutes later when Mo and Ernie finally showed up, both donning neatly trimmed haircuts.

"Sorry we late Bobby-Joe," Mo said apologetically.

"What's that you looking at?" Ernie asked, noticing Bobby-Joe was on edge.

"*American Dream* . . . and believe me, this is a girl with a helluva tale to tell!" Bobby-Joe replied, slightly closing the magazine so both men could glimpse the front cover.

"She's a looker all right," said Mo, puckering his lips, "So why's her story so special?"

"Why? Because it sounds like one of Doug Miller's!!"

* * * * *

"Hi Mike, where are you?" Maddie asked, speaking softly into her cellphone.

"I'm in the car, hun. The meetings went well. Be home in an hour."

"Oh good, I missed you. I hate it when you have to stop away overnight but I am glad the meetings went well. The kids are at your mother's so I got you all to myself!"

"That's great baby. We can curl up in front of the fire."

After she hung up, Maddie put an extra couple of logs on the fire, made a coffee, and settled down on the biggest of the room's three leather sofas. She was looking forward to seeing Michael who, even after more than twenty-five years together, was still her *Mr Perfect*.

Idly, she reached for something to help pass the time and picked up the magazine she'd bought while shopping earlier in the day.

She wasn't really into magazines but at the Wal-Mart check-out, she'd found her eyes inexplicably drawn to the stunning oriental woman on the front cover of *American Dream*. While her face was picture perfect it was also strangely captivating, somehow making the magazine leap off the shelf shouting "Buy me!!"

Throughout the fifteen minute drive home, Maddie found herself repeatedly glancing at the face looking up at her from the front passenger seat. For several months she'd been having a slight crisis of confidence and for the first time in her life she'd started to fret about how she looked. At first it was noticing the odd wrinkle around her eyes. Then it was the grey hair. More recently it was wondering if *Mr Perfect* still found her attractive. She wondered if she'd been drawn to the magazine because of her insecurities and because the woman was so beautiful. Maddie guessed they were the same sort of age; so why couldn't she look so perfect?

It was a thought, a question that had troubled her all day.

"How dare I be so ungrateful!" she said out loud as she snuggled up on the couch, placing the magazine on the glass coffee table beside her. She did intend reading it, cover-to-cover, but she was looking forward to seeing her husband and wasn't in the mood. She yawned and her hand fell off the magazine.

By the time Michael opened the front door, she was sound asleep.

"Maddie? Baby? I'm home," he said, removing his jacket. "Maddie?" he repeated, wondering why his wife wasn't answering. As he looked over to the sitting area he saw her long brown hair hanging over the arm of the sofa. He smiled as he stepped lightly up behind her before squatting down on his haunches so that if she wasn't asleep, she wouldn't see him. He wanted to kiss her awake, whispering "I love you" as he did so.

But this time it was going to be more difficult than usual, not because he loved her any less but because something unexpected was lying in wait for him.

As he edged forward, the scope of his eye-line increased with each shuffle. When the coffee table and the front cover of *American Dream* magazine came into view, there was an explosion deep inside his brain so loud he thought it'd wake his sleeping wife. It was an intense life-draining moment that caught him so unawares he found it hard to breathe and almost lost his balance.

She may have been thirty years older but there was no doubting it was her. And unlike the cheerleader he'd seen three months earlier, the night of Super Bowl XXXVIII, the girl looking at him from his coffee table was the real thing.

Michael McBride had never been a man to scare easily; raw fear was new ground.

* * * * *

It was a glorious Saturday early morning as the board gathered expectantly.

While many executives may have reasonably expected to be at home with their families, those who worked for Claudia Kaplan knew better. Like a dog with a bone, she was focused on her game plan and anyone who worked for her was expected to show similar commitment.

It was strictly her way or the highway.

"OK guys, let me start by expressing my appreciation of the great work BJ did in getting our big story ready. Top job BJ; thanks!"

Bernard Jameson glowed at the affirmation, Claudia once again demonstrating why people like him were so keen to work for a boss like her.

"We got a three-point agenda – sales, finance and feedback – so, hopefully, we'll all be on our way home in an hour," she said, careful to engage eye contact with every one of the five men and three women who made up her board.

"Now, we all know there's more to *American Dream* than just one story, but this one can launch us into the stratosphere! So while we're always talking magazine, our main focus today is our Southeast Asia story. It's been forty-eight hours since we hit the news-stands so Jess, can we have an update please?"

At twenty-nine, Jessica Bell was the youngest person in the room.

"Thanks Claudia. After our best ever first-day sales, I'm pleased to report that things have got better still," she said smiling the same time she handed out a one-page report highlighting the key numbers. "As of 7:00 AM this morning, we're showing a seventeen per cent increase on our best ever forty-eight hour sales figures. As we speak, we have more than seven million copies already with our customers and, with plenty of stock with retailers and good levels at the warehouse, we have a great chance of breaking ten million for the first time."

Jess smiled demurely as the room erupted.

"Thank you Jess, that's excellent," Claudia said beaming, "Finance is next: *Maureese*?"

Maurice, pronounced Maureese, Farrell was the financial director and least popular person in the room. A number cruncher with little sympathy for the magazine business, he was known as *Poodle*, partly because of his squeaky voice and partly because he was seen as Claudia's too-eager-to-please pet dog. But there was no shrewder judge of people than Claudia Kaplan. She'd heard the whispers, knew the nicknames, knew that he'd seemingly had his personality sucked out and even knew he didn't understand the magazine business. But it didn't matter; Claudia didn't care. Maureeese Farrell was a master of his world and the best company accountant she'd ever come across. It was the reason she headhunted him from Hewlett Packard and the reason why, after herself, he was the highest paid person in the room.

Mercifully, his report didn't take long; awash with cash *American Dream* was on a roll.

"Thank you *Maureeese*. And that brings us nicely to the bit we've all been waiting for. We been live for forty-eight hours, we're in eight million homes so tell us Marcia, does anyone give a damn about our girl?"

Marcia Sullivan was customer services director and in a story like Bian's she was the person with the most vital role of all. The entire article had been presented so as to encourage readers to supply information. Like Bian's face, the *Atrocity in Southeast Asia* headline was just a hook, a taster to get readers to want to know more. Inside, the article appeared under a headline that declared *Justice Demands These Monsters Are Found!!* It made the magazine's position crystal clear: locate the men, bring them to trial.

Under the pen portraits and head outlines, *American Dream* urged readers to telephone the hotline if they had any information.

With the implied promise of an unspecified reward, it was a package guaranteed to generate a response.

"The feedback's been excellent," Marcia stated confidently. "We've had over seven thousand calls and four thousand e-mails! Most are crap of course but you'll be interested to know that half of America's female population reckons they're already married to *Mr Evil* and the other half wants to be!" Troy's name for *No.1* had stuck.

After waiting for the room to quiet, Marcia continued. "Bottom line? We have eighty-four solid looking leads, twelve currently sat in the personal visit category and six or seven looking truly blue-chip."

"Like what?" asked Claudia, her two-word question direct and to the point.

"It seems we have several leads on the star-shaped birthmark. We've had three calls from the Dallas area. There's no positive ID as yet but all three point to a gym in Fort Worth."

"That sounds interesting Marcia. Anything else?"

"Yes Claudia, there's two other leads that look really strong. We've had a call from someone in New York who says *No.3*, the leader, is her ex; says he's a former Marine, with a big nose and scar across his bottom lip."

"From what I know of New York that description fits half the male population!" Claudia quipped. With two or three of her directors nodding their heads in agreement and her pet poodle laughing uproariously, she added, "You said two more, Marcia?"

"Yeah, this one looks to be the most interesting of all. A retired lawyer from Missouri reckons he's in possession of a letter from his brother; a former Lieutenant Colonel now deceased. The letter refers to a Special Ops team he headed or oversaw or something. He says he's sure the letter and our article refer to the same incident, apparently everything fits."

"Has he faxed us a copy?" Claudia asked, interrupting.

"No, he won't. He said we should send someone to interview him and he's promised to show them the letter. It looks genuine and he's not chasing money."

"Who've we instructed to do the follow-up?"

"We're using *Aldrich Matthias & Lyman*."

"That's one firm of private detectives who really know what they're about," Claudia said, approvingly. "Great report Marcia; keep it up."

Marcia smiled politely and nodded as every eye fixed on Claudia.

"We all know that when you toss a pebble into the water, anything can happen. We're off to a great start guys. Have a great weekend."

Claudia was delighted with the way the meeting had gone, but she wasn't finished.

"Can I have a word please BJ?" she said quietly as the others were leaving.

"Sure Claudia; what's up?"

"I want you ready with a follow-up for the next issue BJ. Stick close to Marcia and ring *Aldrich Matthias & Lyman* every hour on the hour. We'll reserve a double page spread and keep it open till the last second."

"But I thought we were talking about a two-issue gap before we did a follow up?"

"I know, but I got a hunch. I reckon this'll break quicker than we thought. I sense the net tightening even as we speak."

* * * * *

Barney Mayer had been Rudi Kingsbridge's personal assistant for twelve years.

While he may not have especially liked his boss, he was intensely loyal, partly due to the fact loyalty was in his nature and partly because no other PA he knew was paid anything close to the half-million-a-year he was paid.

He'd already heard his boss' mother, ex-Hollywood actress Marlene Moorer, had died suddenly at Chateau Chantalle and he knew the funeral arrangements would be down to him. He was thankful though that with Rudi out on the West Coast on business, telecoms billionaire Ulysses Maxwell would be the one to break the news.

"Hey Rudi: it's Max."

"What's up Max?"

"I got some bad news. It's your mother."

"What about the bitch?"

"She's dead man; died suddenly this morning in the conservatory at Chateau Chantalle."

"She what? That bitch always had a great sense of timing!" he said as if unwittingly speaking out a perverse epitaph for her gravestone.

"Don't worry about Kay," Max said, ignoring his friend's lack of sensitivity and overlooking the fact he hadn't mentioned his wife. "She's with Verdana at our place. Will you be coming back tonight?"

"Not a chance! I been looking forward to this weekend for months and there's no way I'm gonna let my bitch mother screw it up. Tell Kay I'll ring tonight. Thanks for the call Max."

Before Max could say another word, the line clicked dead.

Rudi may have been in Silicon Valley on business but he always saw the chance of getting away for a few days more as vacation than business.

Barney made all the arrangements and when it came to planning, there was no-one better than Barney Mayer. The five-star Stanford Park Hotel, the chauffeur driven S600 Mercedes and an itinerary that included meetings with the likes of Apple, Sun Microsystems, Novell and Bank of America were all nailed down weeks in advance.

The only bit Barney left to last minute was Rudi's choice of travelling companion. When he stayed out of town, his boss never slept alone and it wasn't until three days before he left that Rudi told him which of the "lucky dozen" had won star prize.

Thirty-eight year old Teresa Chesley first met Rudi Kingsbridge at a high society party in Kenilworth in the late-Eighties. Being married at the time didn't inhibit her at all and since separating from her husband five years earlier, she'd been more than happy to lead a single life. Rudi didn't mind what she did or who she did it with, as long as she came running the minute he called. Teresa didn't find the pre-conditions unduly onerous and given that her ex-husband wasn't honouring their divorce settlement, Rudi was the sole source of the lifestyle she'd craved since her teens. As a result, she was his whenever he wanted, how he wanted, and where he wanted. Truth be told, it wasn't difficult; she was quite happy to be his puppet and to dance when he pulled her strings. It also helped he was drop dead gorgeous and great in bed.

When he made hotel reservations, Barney always booked two adjoining suites, one in his name, the other in KBI's, as a kind of insurance policy against Kay engaging the services of a private detective. Rudi didn't mind paying twice the rate; he could afford it.

Meals were always taken in their room and when his partner wanted to see the local sights or go shopping, she did so alone. It was the way he wanted it and therefore, it was the way it was.

It was seven o'clock by the time he got back to the hotel on the Thursday night. Aside from the news about his mother, the day had gone well. He was in buoyant mood as he opened the inter-connecting door that linked the two suites.

"Rudi!!" Teresa said excitedly.

"Not yet babe," he said, fending her off as she grabbed for him. "My mother died this morning so I got some phone calls to make."

"Hey, I'm so sorry baby."

"Don't worry yourself; I hated the bitch. Make me a coffee and bring it next door," he said, not bothering to say please.

Ten minutes later, Teresa Chesley waltzed into his suite to find Rudi on the phone. Kay was obviously crying the other end as Rudi tried to console her. "It's OK darling. It's a big shock I know, but don't you worry baby, it'll be alright."

Teresa wanted to stick her fingers down her throat she felt so sick. She probably would have if Rudi hadn't made it obvious he had something else in mind. Unzipping his flies, it wasn't a tough one to work out. And all through, bereaved son Rudi chatted away to his wife the other end of the line sounding like the caring, dutiful husband.

"Barney'll make the arrangements hun. You go rest up and don't worry about a thing."

Kay must've said she loved him because Rudi said, "I love you too, baby" before ringing off.

"Don't stop. Stay there," he said rolling his eyes as he looked down at Teresa on her knees in front of him. "One more call to make then I'm all yours."

"Hi boss; sorry about your mother."

"Yeah: no problem Barney. If you phone Max he'll tell you where the bitch is. Once you find out, use the same people we used for my father."

"OK boss it's done. Anything else? Hotel OK?"

"Yeah, the hotel's great. There's great room service too!" he said glancing down at Teresa. "Any messages?" he added.

"Not really boss. Just the usual stuff," Barney replied before suddenly remembering there was something. "Yeah boss, there was one thing."

"What?"

"Someone called Eugene Sanders rang for you. He said he knew you; you'd once worked together or something? He said it was urgent and that you'd know what it's about. I told him you were unavailable till Monday; he said he'd call first thing Tuesday."

Barney Mayer's boss hadn't spoken to the mighty Kong since the day he'd left Vietnam almost thirty-two years earlier. Despite Teresa Chesley's efforts to command his full attention, he couldn't help wondering why he'd be trying to reach him after such a long time.

Rudi Kingsbridge may have been completely unaware of it but in the words of the editor of one of America's best-selling magazines, "The net was tightening."

CHAPTER THIRTY-FOUR:

"You look amazing Bian!"

"Oh shush."

"You do. You really do," he said looking first at his wife, then at her photo on the magazine cover on the kitchen table in front of him.

"You always say that Troy! You even say it when I get out of bed in the morning!!"

"It's true . . ." he said as the phone interrupted him.

"Hi Troy, this is Claudia Kaplan from *American Dream* magazine."

"Hey Claudia," Troy replied, wondering if she thought he knew two Claudia Kaplan's.

"You get the magazine?"

"Yeah, we got it."

"Did you like it? Did Bian like it?"

"Yeah, we both liked it."

"Good," she said, pleased and slightly relieved. "I've just come from a board meeting where we discussed your story. We've certainly stirred the waters Troy."

"Anything solid?"

"Yes, we've had a few bites and a couple look blue-chip," Claudia replied before briefing him from the notes she'd made a few minutes earlier at the board meeting. "We're putting a lot into this Troy; we got forty telephone operators working round the clock, twenty administrators handling e-mails, and a management team to collate the information. Our customer services director Marcia Sullivan heads the operation and reports directly to me. It's a big deal Troy and that's just the internals. Externally, we're using *Aldrich Matthias & Lyman*, a firm of . . ."

"Private detectives," Troy said interrupting. "I know them; they have a big reputation."

"*Aldrich Matthias & Lyman* are like the Canadian Mounties Troy; they *always* get their man!"

"Are you *that* sure Claudia?"

"Troy, I'm absolutely positive!"

Troy didn't respond, verbally at least. Bian's eyes hadn't left him since he'd picked up the phone. But in the short pause after his last question, she knew Claudia had given him an answer he liked, because he puffed out his cheeks in a kind of perma-grin.

"And Troy, I think we're going to do an immediate follow-up."

"How immediate?"

"Next issue immediate!

"That's great news Claudia!"

"I'm glad you're pleased; I'll be in touch in the next day or two."

"Thanks," he said, trying his best to hide his excitement from both Claudia and Bian.

"There *was* one other thing Troy. Our competitors will be scouring the country for Bian so if anyone calls, don't forget, no interviews. That's the deal remember?"

"No problem," Troy said, sure they'd do nothing to jeopardise the client/magazine relationship.

"Oh and Troy, we *are* going to get these guys."

"I know," Troy replied. But it was too late; Claudia had rung off.

"Now, where was I?" he asked, his eyes fixing on his wife. "Oh, I remember . . . Bian, you look amazing!"

* * * * *

Two minutes past nine, Tuesday morning, the phone rang on Barney Meyer's desk.

"Good morning Mr Sanders, Mr Kingsbridge is expecting you."

Rudi was convinced that Eugene had seen his handsome features in a magazine or on TV and was probably chasing money. But it wasn't Rudi's face Eugene Sanders had seen on a magazine cover.

"Hey Kong: how you doing man?"

"I was doing fine till last week; but I got plenty of problems now."

"Why? What happened last week?"

"You ain't seen *American Dream* magazine then?"

"I stopped getting off on magazines when they invented video!"

"Trust me man, I ain't laughing. Go and get a copy and I'll call you back this afternoon," he said before abruptly hanging up.

Five hours later, the two former Bleeding Dogs had their second conversation in thirty-two years, Rudi in no doubt about the reason for the call.

"You see it?"

"Yeah, I seen it," Rudi replied. Seeing the girl's face was something of a shaker, and he'd been thinking furiously ever since.

"Well, what we gonna do about it? The gym's off limits and I got people on my tail, every last one of them trying to get a glimpse of my shiny black ass!"

"Don't worry man, it's gonna be OK."

"That's easy for you to say man. It's my butt that's in the mouse-trap not yours. But Kingsbridge, understand now, if they get me; first thing I'm giving them is your telephone number. You hearing me man?"

"I can't see that whining at me helps much but yeah, I hear you, you black son-of-a-bitch," Rudi snapped, glad two thousand miles separated them. After a pause, he added, "Where you work?"

"What? This ain't a social call dammit. What'd you wanna know where I work for?"

"Because I reckon it's time you did some travelling. You got vacation time owing?"

"I work at Bell Helicopters. I got plenty of time due me but no friggin' money; we just moved."

"Who's the 'we'? You married?"

"Yeah."

"What's her name?"

"Marlena," Eugene said impatiently. "What the hell is this man?"

"Just shut up for a minute will you? Let me think. OK, here's the deal. I'll have ten grand deposited into your bank account this afternoon and my PA will call you with the arrangements once he's fixed an itinerary."

"Arrangements? Itinerary? What you talking about?"

"Your travel itinerary; you and Marlena are going on vacation. How's the Caribbean sound?"

"Sounds great but . . ."

"Good, now call Bell; tell 'em you're sick and want to take all the time-off due you at once. Is it two weeks, three weeks or what?"

"Three weeks I think, maybe three-and-a-half," said Eugene, still sounding bemused.

"That's sorted then. Three weeks out of the spotlight will give us time to come up with a game plan. One other thing, you have any contact with the Corporal or McBride about this?"

"No, I ain't seen Frankie since the summer of '72 and me and Irish haven't spoken since we got back from Africa, January 1975."

"Africa! How'd you end up there?"

"Neither of us wanted to come home I guess. Why'd you wanna know if I spoke to them?"

"Because it's obvious that at some point, the four of us will need to meet," Rudi replied, wondering how it was possible for another human being to be so stupid. "But don't worry about it. I'll track the others down and be in touch. Enjoy your vacation."

With the unwanted conversation over, Rudi Kingsbridge stared down at the reason for it: the magazine. "You Gook bitch!" he hissed, speaking to no-one except himself, and Bian.

Several seconds later he lifted his head slightly, the colour drained from his face.

"Barney!!!" he screamed, not bothering to use the intercom.

* * * * *

At pretty much the same time as Rudi Kingsbridge was screaming for his PA, Michael McBride was at home meeting with his pastor, Rev. Bill Pickard.

The fact that Pastor Bill, who never used the "Reverend" bit of his title, was a close personal friend as well as his pastor didn't help in the slightest. Michael didn't need anyone to tell him the meeting would be the most uncomfortable of his life. And the worse thing was he knew it could've been avoided; if only he'd made the right choice.

By nature he was an analytical man and he'd been brutally honest with himself, concluding he'd buried rather than dealt with the moment of his greatest weakness. It was a big mistake and it'd come back to bite him with a vengeance. He'd run from it instead of facing it on his terms so, as a result, it was dictating the terms. He stood to lose everything.

"Sorry I couldn't meet sooner Mike. It's been real busy. But tell me, how can I help?"

Michael had never felt so nervous; his stomach churning at the thought of having a conversation he should've had twenty years earlier. But there could be no more running.

He cried repeatedly as he peeled away the layers, revealing the ugliness of what he'd gotten involved in, what he'd done, thirty-two years earlier in Southern Laos.

At the end both men cried together arm-in-arm, Michael spluttering, "I'm sorry to drop this on you Bill, without any notice."

"No matter Mike, that's one you needn't worry about. You told me a story that's been hard to listen to and even harder to tell no doubt, but know this Mike, I'm still your pastor and I'm still your friend. But Mike, we gotta face this and do what's right. You've heard me speak a thousand times. You cannot conquer what you will not confront. We have to take it on. But before we do that, let me make a point or two."

"Sure Bill, whatever you say."

"OK . . . Right . . ." he said, delaying slightly so he could gather his thoughts. "Mike, when you were a boy you lived with a great man, a great Christian man. Fergus taught you much and tried to prepare you for life in what he knew was a big bad world. He constantly pointed you to Jesus but there was something in the way and the penny didn't quite drop. Though you knew it was the truth, the right way, you couldn't somehow get yourself to commit to it. That's right isn't it?"

"Yes," said Michael, lifting his head slightly to answer.

"Then Fergus died and you reacted badly, blaming people, blaming life and most of all, blaming God. You basically fell apart, went off to Vietnam and violence became the dominating influence in your life. Even when you returned, your wilderness period continued. You weren't a Christian then. You knew Christian values, they'd influenced you, but you hadn't reached the place we all have to come to, the place where we make a heartfelt commitment to Jesus. Reaching that place anchors you, stops you from being tossed here, there and everywhere, by life and by circumstance. Without that anchor you meander-ed, causing mayhem wherever you went, hurting people, sinning. You didn't need anyone to tell you that you were a sinner did you?"

"No," said Michael, making another one-word contrib.-ution.

"Exactly Mike, but then praise God, you reunite with your family, meet the wonderful Maddie, work hard and suddenly with the help of the great Billy Graham, the blindfold is removed; you give your heart to Jesus. It was then and only then that you became a Christian and were born-again. Praise the Lord, huh? But at that moment all of what you did in the bad days didn't disappear. It still happened but now because you've made Jesus Lord of your life, the blood he shed on the cross for you personally, washes away your sin. Now let me explain that one. It's not that what you did goes unpunished; it's just that Jesus takes the punishment for you. His blood covers your sin and you know what Mike, the bigger the sin the bigger God's grace. What a Gospel, huh? It's no wonder I love my job lad with the boss I got!!"

Michael smiled weakly. It was the best he could do.

"So, when we make the decision to become a Christian, especially when we do so as adults as you and I did, it's inevitable that we bring with us a whole sack-full of baggage. And Mike, you brought enough to fill a couple of delivery trucks!"

"Aye," he said ruefully, nodding his head.

But Pastor Bill wasn't finished. "Now because God is love and love keeps no record of wrongs, to him, what you did, however bad, has gone: erased to a point where it never happened! The problem is however, that before you became a Christian you crossed a line, someone got hurt and though God has forgiven you, what you did has consequences that run and run. And this is the nub of the issue; though God's grace is boundless, some sin, like your sin in this instance, is a criminal act that potentially carries criminal implications. Now, the consequences of what you did include this girl telling her story. It's a big shock but Mike, get this one and get it good, God is still God! He's in control. And Mike, grasp this one too, you are still Michael McBride, mighty man of God, born-again Christian saved into eternal life. In other words Mike, nothing's changed except your circumstances. Now some of those circumstances may cause some pain, for you and for others, but viewed from the eternal perspective it literally isn't the end of the world."

"Thanks Bill, I really appreciate your help with this."

"Good Mike, but sorry lad, I've still not finished. This is where it gets toughest because we have to take things forward. I'd love to pray and have the whole thing vanish but we both know it isn't like that."

Michael reluctantly shook his head, dreading what came next.

"Now Mike, you want my advice don't you?"

"Yeah, course Bill," Michael replied, battling to stop himself vomiting as the words left his lips.

"Well, I'm assuming you've not told Maddie yet."

"No" said Michael shaking his head, wanting to curl up and die.

"You know you have to don't you?"

"I guess."

"Mike, you have to, and Mike, you need to do it sooner rather than later."

"OK, I'll tell her soon as I can."

"Don't put it off mind."

"I won't; I'll tell her."

"Good, and once Maddie knows you'll need to tell the family."

"But what if the article is the end of it?" Michael spluttered knowing he was grasping at straws.

"Don't kid yourself Mike, neither of us knows where the end is but we both know this magazine story is more likely beginning than end. And in any case Mike, Maddie needs to know."

"Yeah," said Michael, returning to one word answers.

"And the other key issue is making sure you get good legal advice Mike. You need to see your lawyer, give him time to get used to the idea, prepare and the like, just in case things get more serious, more public."

Michael began to physically retch; glad he'd not eaten since the previous day.

"Come on Mike, hold it together," Pastor Bill said gently patting his friend on the back. "Look Mike, the bottom line is that you have to do the right thing. That was always gonna be my advice. You knew that anyway didn't you?"

"Yeah, course."

"Mike, whatever happens, wherever this goes, whatever the cost, you have to do what's right. That means telling the truth. There'll be plenty of voices trying to convince you otherwise, some from people, some just in your head. Ignore them. Get yourself into intimate relationship with God, up your prayer life and do everything the right way, his way. You will come through this and somewhere down the line there will be a day when you'll be able to say it worked for your good. How can I be so sure? Because the Bible promises it: 'in all things God works for the good of those who love him'? It's time to claim it for your own life Mike; make it personal."

"That's great Bill. I really appreciate it. I'm sorry I never came to you sooner when the pressure would've been so much less. Not brave enough I guess! I will learn from this though. I know it'll be tough but I'll not be lying about it to anyone. It's time to look my failure in the eye."

"I'll bid you good night then Mike. Gimme a call if you need me," Bill said as he got up to go. "And Mike, I'll be on my knees praying for you."

"Thanks Bill, I know."

After he'd left, Michael stretched out on the sofa.

"Lord please forgive me; I'm so sorry for getting you into this!" he said out loud.

Pastor Bill wasn't the first to counsel that he do the right thing. After seeing the girl's picture five days earlier, he'd heard his Granddad's voice rise up from deep inside him.

"Lies are malignant boy, they contaminate yer soul. Don't give 'em a hold lad; it's time to do what's right and tell the truth."

Michael McBride's choice was no choice and it had already been made.

* * * * *

It was late Wednesday when the silver Mercedes pulled into the long drive.

Eugene Sanders was grinning from ear-to-ear. "What'd you think doll?" Does this scratch your itch?"

"It's amazing!" his wife replied shaking her head in disbelief. "Who is Rudi Kingsbridge?" she queried yet again as the car finally came to a stop alongside a huge fountain directly in front of the magnificent floodlit villa.

"I told you woman, your stud's connected!"

"You're telling me you spoke to him yesterday for the first time in years and just like that, he sends us on a luxury vacation, all-expenses paid? Somehow I don't think so!"

Eugene knew he'd have to tell her. And it wasn't just because she was suspicious. Barney Mayer made it clear they weren't to leave the villa; it was the one condition of making the trip.

When he'd rung with the details, Eugene was dumbstruck. "But neither of us have a passport," he said.

"Don't you worry Mr Sanders; friends of Rudi Kingsbridge don't need passports. You just relax; we'll take care of everything."

They did.

The Cadillac showed up at precisely two fifteen that afternoon, before driving them to an obscure airstrip thirty miles west of Waco. There they boarded KBI's Gulfstream jet waiting for them on the sun-bleached concrete before flying two thousand miles southeast across the Gulf of Mexico to Antigua and to another tiny airstrip five miles northwest of Freetown. As the plane taxied to a halt, a silver Mercedes pulled alongside. Half-hour later, the driver pulled up outside the villa atop Cherry Hill. From the minute they'd left they'd not seen a single person from the outside world and it had been luxury all the way; just as Rudi Kingsbridge ordained.

"The villa's fabulous," Barney said. "It comes fully staffed: a cook, maid, gardener and butler. You won't have to do a thing except sit back and enjoy." Then as if remembering something he was in danger of forgetting, he added, "But don't forget now, you don't leave the villa."

It was the third or fourth time he'd mentioned it and Eugene knew that once she'd seen the vista in the daylight, Marlena was going to want to see the sights.

Eugene Sanders had no option; his wife was due an explanation.

* * * * *

"Maddie, can you come here please?"

"OK baby, gimme a minute," his wife replied from the kitchen.

Michael was dreading the moment, fearing his wife might walk away from their twenty-two year marriage. As she walked into the sitting room, he was already in tears.

"Michael. What's wrong? What's the matter?"

"It's this story?" he said, nodding towards *American Dream* on the coffee table.

"Yeah, it's awful isn't it?" Maddie said, thinking he'd been upset by the article.

"Yes, it is awful," he replied picking the magazine up. As he flicked through the pages, his fingers found what he was looking for. He forced both leaves backwards so it stayed open on the double-page spread with the four featureless head outlines and short pen portraits.

"Mike? What you doing? You're scaring me," she said confused, suddenly realising there was more to what he was doing than just getting upset at a harrowing magazine article.

"Maddie, I'm so sorry."

"What Michael? Tell me!"

"I'm *No.4*," he said, nodding towards the open magazine, tears streaming down his cheeks before dripping off his chin onto his jumper.

"What?" she screeched, her eyes filling instantly to overflow. "You can't be Michael. Is this some kind of sick joke or something?"

"I wish it were, but it's true. I'm so sorry Maddie."

As he spoke he extended his arm round her. She flinched and pulled away.

"No Michael, don't touch me. I need time to think."

"I understand," he said, not really knowing what to say.

"You understand! No you don't Michael. You don't understand. You can't. How can you? Who are you Michael? How could you do this to me? How could you do this to *her*?" she snapped, looking straight at Bian whose face had come into view after the magazine had magically closed itself on the coffee table.

If only the whole chapter would close, Michael thought, hanging his head in shame.

"Give me space Michael. Don't come to me. I'll come to you . . . *if* and *when* I'm ready!"

Madeline McBride felt like she'd crashed at speed into a brick wall.

She'd found out the hard way that contrary to what she'd believed for so long, her husband was no *Mr Perfect*.

* * * * *

Eugene didn't sleep a wink that first night in Antigua.

He was so worried he even turned down his wife's efforts to celebrate their first night of luxury with a romp round the bedroom.

As darkness turned to the first watery light of day, he quietly opened the bedroom door into the enormous sitting room which was glazed all down one side. The villa was perched on the edge of the mountain, twelve hundred feet above the ocean, harbour and four beautiful golden beaches.

The view was incredible. "Holy cow, one look at that picture postcard and she'll want to take off immediately!"

Three hours later, he and Marlena sat out on the suspended wooden decking taking in the view. The cook, a cube of a woman, brought them a pot of sweet smelling coffee, lots of toast, and two plates of scrambled eggs, tomato and bacon. Normally Eugene would have wolfed the lot and more, but knowing what was to come had robbed him of an appetite.

"This is wonderful baby," Marlena said, basking in the luxury. "Remind me to drop a thank you note to your nice friend Rudi."

"Sorry to disappoint you hun, but Rudi Kingsbridge is neither nice nor my friend. We knew each other once that's all."

"From where I'm sitting that sounds like the most ungrateful thing I ever heard!"

"Baby, I need to tell you something and it's not going to be easy."

Within seconds Marlena was consumed by fear, expecting him to say he was leaving her. As he spoke, she realised that what he was unloading, though horrendous, was far from her worst nightmare.

"You son-of-a-bitch! How dare you! How could you? She wasn't even sixteen!"

"Hey baby, I'm sorry but you must understand it was a crazy time. We was pumped so full of adrenaline we didn't have a clue what day it was. We'd just been in fight situation that was like hell itself. I know it don't make it right baby and yes, I wish I could go back and change it all. But I can't. It's like I say, life's a bitch and then you die."

Marlena pulled her hand away as he reached for it.

"It was Kingsbridge who started the whole thing," he added, "And somehow I got sucked in. That's the way it was and there's zip I can do about it now."

"I still think you're a son-of-a-bitch to have gotten involved!"

"I'm sorry baby"

"So what do we do now?" she asked.

"I guess we'll have to take it one day at a time."

"I suppose I can live with that," Marlena said, mellowing slightly. She *was* angry but deep down, he was still her man and that was the most important thing in the world to her. "I'm not happy about what you did Eugene but it was a long time before I met you. You know I'm crazy 'bout you and no matter what, I'm gonna stand by you."

"Thanks baby," he replied, relieved to have shared the burden.

"If we gonna live one day at a time as prisoners in this mean old jail," she said, with a weak smile, "We may as well make the most of it. I've always wanted to live like we were rich and famous, like celebrities!"

"OK honey, whatever you say," Eugene said vaguely.

He could handle the rich bit but something told him he was going to be much more famous than he wanted. Famous was one thing, infamous another, and Eugene sensed there'd be no adulation in the kind of celebrity headed his way.

* * * * *

"It's good to see you Mike," Robert O'Meara said from the other side of the desk.

"Thanks for seeing me so early Robert; and for rearranging your diary at such short notice."

"It's no problem Mike. Our families go back a long way and it's a privilege for O'Meara and Sons to be lawyers to Cork Construction and for me and my family to be able to call the McBride's our friends."

"Aye Robert, there is indeed some history between us, history that started with our grandfathers and stretches all the way back to County Cork and the old country. But Robert, I'm not here on company business or even family business. This is strictly personal and believe you me it's not going to be easy. I've been such a fool."

"You just talk Mike; say what needs to be said," Robert said, trying to make it as easy as he could for his friend.

Twenty minutes later, it was out.

Robert O'Meara looked ashen. "Oh Mike, what can I say? You've come to me for advice but I'm going to need a few weeks to think this through."

Michael left the Boston office of O'Meara & Sons knowing that his was a life where the reality didn't match the hype. Robert O'Meara had known Fergus McBride and he'd been one of the many who thought Michael and Fergus were one and the same.

He now knew they weren't.

Michael walked back to his car humiliated, his head hanging in shame.

CHAPTER THIRTY-FIVE:

Claudia Kaplan was looking forward to the board meeting.

"OK guys, let's get going. As of tomorrow, I'm forming a war cabinet to take our story forward. It'll comprise me, BJ, Phil, and Marcia."

She knew it was her call, a privilege of position. BJ was her runner and writer, Phil ensuring their reporting didn't land them in court. Marcia was the engine for the investigative campaign and she, Claudia, was the glue, sat in the middle pulling everything towards the centre.

It was leaner, meaner and tighter; just like she wanted.

"First-up, let's start with a sales report. Where are we Jess?"

"As at this morning Claudia, sales are showing ten point two-eight million: a new magazine record!" The sales director paused for the cheering to subside. "Shelf stock has fallen to dangerous levels and a further one point five million copies are on the press as I speak. In addition, advertiser feedback is at unprecedented levels and four of our blue-chip clients have signed extended contracts for up to three years."

"What's the projection Jess?" Claudia asked.

"Eleven million for certain, twelve is likely, and thirteen a good outside bet."

"Fantastic!" said Claudia before turning towards her customer services director. "Your turn Marcia; what we got?"

"I'll start with a negative. Remember the woman from New York who thought her ex was our leader? It was a hoax, some kind of domestic spat that we somehow got sucked into! But there's better news on Mr Muscles, the black guy," Marcia declared enthusiastically. "While he and his birthmark seem to have disappeared off the planet, we now know who he is; though I must say, I wanna look at that tight ass myself before I confirm it for certain!"

Pausing for the giggles to dissipate, she added, "Seriously though, unless that star-shaped birthmark turns out to be a tattoo, *Mr Blackman* is fifty-four year old Eugene Sanders who we've tracked down to an address a few miles southwest of Fort Worth. He's married to Marlena, no kids; works at Bell Helicopters. He's a Vietnam vet but we've yet to confirm he was in Southeast Asia at the time of the incident. He's not answering his phone, hasn't been seen at the gym, and Bell inform us he's phoned in sick. My guess is he's hiding somewhere, possibly out-of-country, hoping we'll back off.

"He's our boy alright; I can feel it in my bones," Claudia exclaimed, "And he's got a helluva shock coming if he thinks we'll back off! What about the lawyer Marcia, the guy with the letter? Where's he from now?"

"Dearborn, Missouri. His name's Angus P. O'Donnell. He's the guy who phoned to say he'd received a letter from his brother in July '72. The brother turned out to be Lieutenant Colonel William T. O'Donnell, a distinguished war hero and real-life John Wayne, who died 1986. His brother wouldn't show us the letter till we signed an affidavit pledging that our reporting would stress William T's honourable character and that we'd exonerate him from any responsibility, vicarious or otherwise, for what the men did to Bian."

"How can he be so sure his brother should be absolved of responsibility?" asked associate editor Jake Helmich.

"That becomes apparent from the letter," Marcia said as she handed out copies.

You could've heard a pin drop.

"Holy moley Claudia, it's them; the Bleeding Dogs!" exclaimed Chuck Sherman, one of the magazine's associate editors.

"You're right Chuck, they're our boys alright. Phil's advised us to not mention Master Sergeant Doug Miller or General Matthew Kedenberg at this stage but other than that we're going live with a follow-up in the next issue which will be signed-off in . . ." she hesitated so she could look at her watch, "Precisely one hour and forty-seven minutes!"

The pronouncement sent a buzz round the room.

Despite BJ's many drafts, Claudia had written the follow-up herself. At nearly eight hundred words, it was a hard-hitting piece that made the magazine's position crystal clear.

"Here's the copy . . ."

On a Mission – To find the Bleedings Dogs!!
by Claudia Kaplan

In last month's issue we told you the heart-breaking story of Bian Nhu Dinh, a fifteen year old village girl from Southern Laos who was brutally raped by four men, believed to be U.S. military personnel on active service.

During the incident, which took place on June 17th 1972, Bian's mother was murdered and her grandmother subjected to a vicious physical assault.

If the date somehow seems vaguely familiar it's probably because James W. McCord and his colleagues chose that very same day to break into the offices of the Democratic National Committee at the Watergate hotel and office complex in Washington, D.C. And we all know where that led.

The level of feedback from last month's article from you, our readers, suggests that Bian Nhu Dinh's story has caught the imagination like never before. Where this will lead, no-one yet knows.

What we do know is that *American Dream* is committed to seeing justice done and that means seeing the four men who crossed the line of common decency in Laos thirty-two years ago, found and brought to trial. Bian Nhu Dinh has been living in the United States since 1975. She is happily married and has been a U.S. citizen for twenty-five years. Justice is the least she deserves.

American Dream magazine is not against war. Our support for our government's foreign policy including the sending of troops into Afghanistan and Iraq is both well-documented and in direct contrast to many of our colleagues in the media. What we are against is people playing God, from people acting as individuals to entire governments and everything in between. In their corrupt hands power becomes absolute power and they propagate their evil outside of natural law, unfettered by deterrent, detection or any sense of higher authority.

What happened on the outskirts of a little village in Southern Laos more than three decades ago was exactly this, men playing God. They murdered, assaulted and abused three village women who were in no position to stop them or to fight back.

American Dream considers this abhorrent and an affront to mankind.

We stand for the underdog and cannot and will not stand idly by, passively looking the other way. As someone once said, "The only thing evil requires in order to prosper is for good men to do nothing."

Well, *American Dream* refuses to do nothing. We make our stand and we know from your feedback that it's a stand you agree with.

We hadn't intended to follow-up on last month's article quite so quickly but the strength of feeling you've communicated to us has prompted a change to our original thinking. As a result, I'm pleased to inform you that we have some news.

Our investigations have revealed that at the time in question, the four men were part of a covert Special Operations team called the Bleeding Dogs, a team assembled with a view to causing maximum damage deep behind enemy lines.

The unit worked together for nine months, from October 1971, causing mayhem in Vietnam, Cambodia and Laos.

We know the formation of Bleeding Dog Company was the idea of Lieutenant Colonel William T. O'Donnell, a Medal of Honor winner with a distinguished record of service.

Crucially, the Lieutenant Colonel's advice that the Bleeding Dogs should not be given the mission to Southern Laos was ignored and he found himself over-ruled by his commanding officer in Washington.

The mission went ahead and Bian Nhu Dinh and her family somehow got caught in the crossfire. It was the Bleeding Dogs last mission. But the four men crossed a line.

The unit was immediately decommissioned upon their return to base camp where their existence, memory and trail was erased to the point where they never existed. Our government, the Department of Defense and the U.S. military all agree: the Bleeding Dogs never were! They'd have us believe they are figments of someone's imagination but Bian Nhu Dinh carries the physical and mental scars to prove they were real not imagined.

So the big question is where are they now? We don't know but we certainly intend to find out.

Knowing that millions of Americans will be listening into the conversation, we want to speak directly to the four men of Bleeding Dog Company.

Gentlemen, know this, *American Dream* magazine is coming for you.

Look over your shoulders because we *will* find you and once we do, we intend doing everything within our power to see you brought to trial for what you've done.

Justice *will* be served.

"Wow Claudia, that's incredible; brilliant!" Chuck Sherman said appreciatively, reflecting the thoughts of the room.

Claudia nodded and smiled before closing the meeting as BJ made a bee-line for his boss.

"Claudia, that *really* is a wonderful piece. It made me go goose-pimply more than once! You're really going for this aren't you?"

"Too true BJ! The sons of bitches are gonna pay for what they did."

"Excuse my crudeness," he said, "But I bet these guys are dumpin' in their pants."

"I hope so BJ; I hope so."

CHAPTER THIRTY-SIX:

Four o'clock in the afternoon is about as quiet as it gets at Jumpin' Jack's.

At seventy-four, Bobby-Joe Rose had been the ex-Sheriff of Edward County for almost ten years and the last thing he craved was noise and excitement. He enjoyed the couple of hours he spent in the bar each afternoon, a large Wild Turkey helping him relax before a night in front the TV. Retirement had promised more but when Suzie his wife of forty-two years, fell victim to cancer the year before he retired, he knew his options had taken a serious dive towards zero.

"Any sign of Mo and Ernie?" Bobby-Joe asked the barman as he climbed onto the barstool bequeathed him by Doug Miller.

"Not yet," the barman replied, already reaching for the Wild Turkey. "What you looking at?" he added, as he poured the golden liquid.

"*American Dream* magazine; they had a gripping story in last month's issue."

"Oh yeah: what kind'a story?"

"A young girl was raped by four American soldiers at the end of the Vietnam War. It had me wondering if they'd do a follow-up."

"Well have they?"

"I dunno. I only just bought it." said Bobby-Joe, spreading the magazine on the bar-top.

On pages sixteen and seventeen he saw the words "Bleedings Dogs" in the headline, and nearly fell of his barstool.

"Hell fire! They're real people; the Bleeding Dogs were real people!!" he said out loud. "And we thought it was a Doug Miller play on words!!"

Bobby-Joe was stunned. A bell rang in his head when he'd seen the first article because it sounded so much like one of Doug's stories but reading the follow-up was like hearing his great friend speak from beyond the grave.

"What's up Bobby-Joe? You look like you seen a ghost," the barman said, closer to the truth than he could ever have known.

Bobby-Joe didn't answer; he was already headed for the phone booth at the back of the bar.

"*American Dream* feedback centre."

"I got some information regarding the story about the girl who got raped."

After a few standard questions, the telephone operator identified that Bobby-Joe needed to speak to someone further up the food chain. "Thank you Mr Rose, we'll call you back in a few minutes," she said trying to hide her excitement.

As he got back to the bar, Mo and Ernie walked in.

"What's up Bobby-Joe?" they said in harmony.

Bobby-Joe didn't answer. He simply slid the open magazine across the bar-top; his weight inch perfect as it slid to a halt between the two men who'd already mounted their barstools.

"There's that girl again," said Mo appreciatively. "She's a real looker ain't she?"

"Just read the story," Bobby-Joe said impatiently.

Seconds later, it was Mo and Ernie's turn to look stunned.

"See, the Bleeding Dogs were real," Bobby Joe declared. "It's like Doug's telling the story in it? We always thought he was describing some mean dudes he trained, didn't we? We never thought he was in charge of something actually called Bleeding Dogs! And didn't he mention his boss O'Donnell?"

Before Mo and Ernie could answer, the telephone rang.

"That'll be the magazine calling me back," Bobby-Joe said leaping from his stool.

"Mr Rose? This is Marcia Sullivan, *American Dream* magazine. I understand you have some information you think may be of use to us," she said, her eyes fixed on the query sheet across the top of which the telephonist had scrawled "Top Priority!!" Ten minutes later she hung up, not bothering to put the phone down. Instead she just clicked it dead and dialled *Aldrich Matthias & Lyman*.

"I got a name for you . . . Master Sergeant Doug Miller."

The next hour felt like four. Then the phone rang. For five minutes, she listened without speaking, frantically scribbling notes.

"That's incredible. Yeah, I got everything. Thanks," she said and rang off, once again choosing not to return the receiver to its cradle.

"Claudia, I need to see you . . . like now!"

Two minutes later, she knocked her boss' door.

"We've had a breakthrough Claudia. Remember 'Miller,' the trainer O'Donnell mentions in his letter? Well, we tracked him down. He's Master Sergeant Doug Miller, from Farmville, Virginia."

"That's wonderful news Marcia. Have we talked to him yet?"

"He's dead; died New Year's Eve 1999, missed the new millennium by a whisker apparently. But you'll never guess what?" Marcia added mysteriously.

"What?"

"Well, the U.S. Army agrees he's dead but listen to this: his name's on the Vietnam War Memorial in DC!! He's listed as being KIA, Quang Tri Province . . . October 1967!!"

"Wow; that *is* spooky!! These guys are like something out the twilight zone!"

* * * * *

Madeline McBride wasn't used to pain.

Her parents were honest God-fearing folk who knew how to love and protect their children. Maddie had no experience of disaster, violence or brutality; indeed the most traumatic moment she could remember was waving her eldest sister off to Brown University down in Providence Rhode Island, thirty miles away. It hardly qualified as personal tragedy.

But her husband's revelation had rocked her world; finding out he wasn't who or what she thought he was, proving a bitter pill to swallow.

Three times she'd met with Pastor Bill Pickard. Each time, he played it straight down the line, same as he had with her husband. "Now Maddie, I know it's been tough," he said, "But like I told Michael he has to do the right thing, I have to tell you the same and the key for you is to forgive him. You know what we teach Maddie, the Bible makes it clear, you must forgive lest your Father in heaven cannot forgive you."

Maddie emerged from the meetings determined to lean on her Christian faith.

Pastor Bill suggested she read and reread the magazine article. It was the start point to her forgiving her husband. It was a harrowing story and though she continually wondered how such a righteous man could've allowed himself to get involved, she took refuge in the fact that as *No.4*, he'd clearly been a reluctant bit part player in the whole sorry episode.

No.4's pen portrait said he was "tough looking, brutal even, but with an air of gentleness that seemed out of place." It went on to say that "he was handsome, with dark hair and blazing yet gentle eyes." She thought this sentence was one she could've written herself but the words that helped the most were, "he looked as if he didn't want to be there."

Michael also explained how he'd been scrambled by the fighting immediately prior to the incident and though Maddie couldn't imagine what it was like to be in a kill-or-be-killed situation, she desperately wanted to give him the benefit of the doubt. He told her about the feud with *No.1*, who seemed to be the primary instigator of the incident. It also helped that *No.4*, "kicked the tall one, *No.1*, in the head as he was taking the girl a second time."

After repeatedly reading the article, Maddie arrived at the place she needed to be; though her husband was guilty, he was less guilty than the others. It accelerated the forgiveness process and ended his exile to the sitting room couch. But the reconciliation couldn't change her conviction that there was only one end in sight: her husband was going to jail.

Michael McBride agreed.

It had always been an impossible task living up to *Mr Perfect* and since his wife had realised he wasn't and he couldn't, he too, had nothing to fall back on but his Christian faith.

Like Maddie, he directed his thanks heavenwards and rejoiced that his wife had found the strength to forgive him.

It was one less thing to worry about.

* * * * *

Thirty-two year old Paul Lehmann had been a private investigator with *Softly Softly* for nearly seven years. He loved his job, the occasions it was mundane and routine more than compensated by times, like the last three weeks, when it felt like something out of a movie.

Lehmann loved a challenge and Rudi Kingsbridge, Softly Softly's number one client, was certainly a challenge. He demanded solutions, like when Lehmann was told to fly the black man and his wife to the safe house in Antigua and told to avoid airports.

He'd just got off the phone and was staring at a piece of paper on which he'd scribbled Kingsbridge's latest instructions: fly the two he'd sent to Antigua back home, track down a man called Michael McBride in Boston and a second guy called Frankie Fernando in California, and identify a safe public place for a very private meeting.

The geography alone was daunting and he only had a week to deliver. But he was puzzled. Despite Kingsbridge giving only the sketchiest background, he chose to labour the point that he wasn't to tackle McBride or Fernando physically or one-to-one under any circumstances.

"They may appear old men to a young buck like you," he said, "But don't be fooled; appearances can be deceptive."

Lehmann was ex-CIA and a martial arts expert. It was difficult for him to imagine coming off second best to anyone, least of all to a middle-aged fifty something. He thought Kingsbridge was just being cautious but either way, Paul Lehmann knew he was going to be a busy boy.

He called his wife to let her know he wouldn't be home for a few days.

* * * * *

In the scheming mind of Rudi Kingsbridge it was always going to be the mighty Kong that would contact McBride.

Three days after returning from Antigua, Kong was on the phone to Barney Meyer.

"Gimme your boss."

"How was the villa?" Barney asked, ignoring Kong's lack of civility.

"Great: now gimme your boss."

"What's up?" said Kingsbridge.

"I'll tell you wassup; I just opened my door on two dudes from *American Dream* magazine. They said they wanted to ask me a few questions but really they just want me to drop my pants!!"

"Hey, calm down."

"I am calm. You should see me when I'm angry!"

"Have they gone? The magazine people I mean."

"Yeah man I got rid of them," Eugene replied, not bothering to elaborate. "But they'll be back. This isn't going away. How can I go back to work now?"

"You don't need to work. Check your bank account. I'll wager it's never been so flush!"

"Am I supposed to say thank you?"

"Well, it would be nice!" replied Kingsbridge sarcastically.

"OK, thank you. Now, what's the next step in your master plan?"

"It's time you called McBride."

* * * * *

As he punched in the numbers, Eugene wondered what he'd say to his old friend.

"Hey man it's me, the mighty Kong," he said after being put through, "How you doing man? Long time no speak, huh?"

Michael McBride was surprised that he wasn't surprised by the phone call.

"Till recently, I was doing great; I mean really great. But anyway it's good to hear your voice again Eugene."

"You've seen the magazine then?"

"Yeah: I seen it. It's been like a war zone man. My wife took it badly but things have eased a little over the last few days."

"You seen the follow-up?"

"Follow-up?" queried Michael.

"We're splashed all over this month's issue as well. Not as big as last month but very pointed. They coming after us man," Realising how negative he must've sounded, Eugene tried to change the subject. "I thought about getting in touch hundreds of times and can't believe I waited till now to actually do it. I missed you Irish."

Michael flinched. He hadn't been called *Irish* for the best part of thirty years.

"I thought about it a lot too," he said, scribbling *magazine* on his notepad before underlining it. "But something always held me back. Maybe it was this, this thing that's blown up in our faces. Have you been in touch with the others?"

"That's one of the reasons I called. We're meeting next week. Will you come? I know how much you hate that posing son-of-a-bitch Kingsbridge, but we do need to talk."

"Don't worry about that; the fire went out on my anger a long time ago," Michael said more in hope than anything else. Hearing Kingsbridge's name out loud for the first time in three decades wasn't easy. It surprised him that it still had the power to press a few buttons. He knew seeing him face-to-face was going to be his greatest test. He hoped he'd come through; but only time would tell.

"You're OK to meet then?"

"I guess. When and where?"

"A week today but we haven't nailed down a venue yet. Soon as we do, I'll call."

Two or three minutes chat, and their conversation was over.

Kong had picked up that there was something different about his friend long before he said his anger was gone. He'd been surprised by his gentleness, never expecting him to agree so readily to the meeting or to be so calm when he'd mentioned Kingsbridge.

"Yes," he said to himself quietly, "There's something different about my mate Irish."

* * * * *

"What's up Marcia?"

"Claudia, I've just had *Aldrich Matthias & Lyman* on the line."

"And?"

"You know I told you that Eugene Sanders and his wife are back from wherever they've been and that they won't talk to us directly? Well, guess what, we got their phone records."

"Strictly legally I hope," Claudia said, her tone thick with doubt.

"Oh, I'm sure," said Marcia. "*Aldrich Matthias & Lyman* always do things the right way!"

"So what we got?"

"Nothing solid as yet, except that he's only called four numbers outside Fort Worth. Two look innocent enough but the third was to a building company near Boston and the fourth to a bank in Chicago."

"What's he calling them for?" asked Claudia thinking out loud.

"I don't know but he's called the building company twice and the bank seven times."

"Perhaps he wants to take out a loan for some house renovations!" Claudia quipped before adding, "Thanks Marcia. Keep me informed."

Claudia couldn't help but smile; not at what she'd said, though she did think it funny. She smiled because she felt the men gag as the noose round their necks tightened a notch or two.

CHAPTER THIRTY-SEVEN:

"Can you check the mail please Bian?" Troy shouted down the stairs.

"Sure dear."

"Anything interesting?"

"There's one with a Colorado Springs postmark."

"It'll probably be Claudia Kaplan looking for feedback on the second article."

"Troy . . . they've put five hundred thousand into the trust fund!"

"Wow! You're beautiful *and* rich! But I can't love you any the more because it doesn't get more than etern-a-zillions!"

"You can be smooth as glass sometimes Troy."

With the quest for justice now in the hands of others, Troy was more relaxed and Bian loved the fact her husband was less distracted. It made her feel less alone.

"What'll you spend it on?" Troy asked, not expecting her to have the slightest idea.

But she'd thought about it many times.

"Assuming he'd accept, I'd like to buy Thimay his first house and his first car so he can start life debt free."

Her son hadn't reacted well when he heard his parents were talking to *American Dream*.

"He'll come round you'll see."

"It's been tough on him Troy, and it doesn't help he's so far away in Oregon. I miss him so much."

"What else will you do with your trust fund?" Troy asked trying to change the subject.

"I'd like to bless Tong Tenh, Father Mesnel and the village of Ban Hatsati."

"What you got in mind?"

"Well sometime soon I want to invest in Tong's rice business and help him achieve everything he's ever dreamed of. And I'd like to help Father Mesnel publish his memoirs."

"Bian, that's wonderful."

"And Troy, I'd like to establish the Mesnel Medical Centre in Ban Hatsati."

"Sounds wonderful dear," Troy said, marvelling at his wife's plans and at the unselfish nature of what she had in mind.

How he wished he was more like her, self-interest noticeable only by its absence.

* * * * *

Sat in his Hemet hotel room, Paul Lehmann was feeling well-pleased with himself.

Three of the four tasks set him were already done and dusted. He'd successfully flown Eugene Sanders and his wife in from Antigua; he'd tracked Michael McBride to a building company called Cork Construction operating out of Foxboro Massachusetts; and he'd identified the Royal Plaza Hotel, Las Vegas as a safe place for a clandestine meeting.

All that remained was task number four: find Frankie Fernando and ensure he attended the Vegas meeting. That was why he was in Hemet.

The brief from Kingsbridge couldn't have been sketchier. All Lehmann had to go on was an old photo from the early-Seventies and a few scribbled notes to say Frankie was a war hero from Hemet, a Medal of Honor winner no less. It was the briefest of briefs but Lehmann knew there was no margin for error. Frankie had to be found; Kingsbridge had said so.

His first stop was the Hemet Police Department where everyone over forty knew Frankie, or knew of him. Lehmann pieced together the story. A war hero of few words, he'd returned from Vietnam deeply depressed. His father had committed suicide when Frankie was still in his teens and when his mother passed away years later, the bank foreclosed and he was homeless. At first he slept rough in the local park then, in the mid or late-Nineties, he left Hemet for LA.

By noon, Paul Lehmann was in his rental car heading west. On the seat alongside him was a list of city sites most popular with LA's hobo community. A day-and-a-half later, he'd reached the third place on the list, the overpass where the 60 crosses the 710 in Central City East.

"You know this guy?" he said to an old tramp with a filthy tobacco-stained beard. "It's an old photo. He'd be in his late fifties now. He's got a nasty scar under his lip." It was a script he'd delivered over five hundred times. He'd heard so many grunts and seen so many shakes of the head he was on auto-pilot, a positive response the last thing he expected.

"Yeah, I know him, and I know where you'll find him," the tramp said smiling, opening up a gap between beard and moustache, revealing two teeth, one top one bottom, both rotten.

"You do? Where?"

"What's in it for me mister?" said the tramp, the smile starting to look permanent. It wasn't often pay-day came round and he intended making the most of it.

Lehmann flashed a twenty dollar bill.

The hobo snorted in disgust, so Lehmann tried again; this time with a fifty.

"Double it!" he declared confidently.

"OK, hundred bucks it is; where is he?"

"We call him *Frankie F* and you'll find him sat on a bench by the statue in Obregon Park, two blocks from here," he said, carefully folding the two fifty dollar bills and tucking them deep inside his filthy clothing. "Oh, and mister, there's one other thing . . ."

"What?"

"Be careful!" the hobo added with a loud chuckle.

Ten minutes later, Lehmann opened the gate into Obregon Park. Around the statue were four benches, equidistantly spaced. Frankie was on the one nearest the gate; his head slumped forward as if he were asleep. Even from forty yards, Lehmann could make out the bulbous scar under his lip and hook-like nose.

As he moved closer, he suddenly recollected the warning from Kingsbridge before he left Chicago and from the old hobo who'd said much the same thing just twenty minutes earlier. He wondered what there was to be careful about.

Dozing in the late afternoon sun, Frankie looked the picture of harmlessness; but so does a cup of coffee laced with strychnine. He wasn't asleep. He'd clocked Paul Lehmann the moment he'd stepped into the Park and tracked his every step.

"Hey, old man," Lehmann said bending forward slightly to nudge Frankie on the shoulder.

Frankie may have been just a year or so off his sixtieth birthday and he may've found himself in the sitting position but he could still generate enough speed, power and timing to send the young private detective crashing down onto his back and floating into unconsciousness. In a blur of movement, Frankie's right hand exploded upwards into Paul Lehmann's unsuspecting face, and down he went. It was a harsh lesson, proof that things are not always what they seem. By the time he came round, his cut right eye was closed and more importantly, Frankie was gone.

It preceded an embarrassing call into the office.

"I've found him, but I lost him," he said to Bob Pike, *Softly Softly's* desk controller.

"You got out-run by an old hobo?!!"

"He's no ordinary hobo," said Lehmann defensively.

"You in the right job Paul? Perhaps we need to get you behind a desk, for your own safety? What'd you think?"

The loud laughter alerted Lehmann that the desk controller had him on speaker.

"Screw you Pike. What do you know anyway? You never spent a single day in the field."

"Don't be so touchy Lehmann. Just go find our rough tough hobo before the client bites our butt!"

"Like I said Pike; screw you!"

He put his cellphone back in his pocket and took out a handkerchief to dab his sore eye.

His head hurt and so did his pride. He wished he'd been more careful.

* * * * *

"Well, do you approve?" Bian asked, looking across the kitchen table at her husband.

"Of course; it's wonderfully generous and confirms what I already knew."

"What's that?"

"That you are Mrs Wonderful!"

"Oh Troy: you are such a sweetie," Bian said, grinning.

"You . . ."

Whatever Troy was going to say was interrupted by the front door bell. "I'll get it," he said.

A split second later Troy was face-to-face with Michael McBride.

Michael knew he was taking a risk but after talking it through with both his pastor and lawyer, he decided that risk, however big, had to come second to doing the right thing. He needed to apologise to Bian and he needed to do it in person. He had no idea how they got it but O'Meara & Sons furnished him with the address.

Michael hoped it would be Bian who answered the door. It wasn't.

"Morning," he said managing just the tiniest hint of a smile.

It was like Troy already knew him. He had no idea how, but he knew he was *No.4*.

"You're one of them aren't you? You son-of-a-bitch; you got some cheek coming here."

"Troy?" Bian said from behind him, his name posed as a question. "Who is it dear?" she said, moving forward into the porch, linking her arm with his.

It gave Michael his first glimpse of the woman who'd suffered at his hands as a young girl. She looked beautiful on the magazine cover but she looked even more attractive in person.

Michael felt so guilty, he wanted to cry.

But she'd recognised him too, instantly.

"What do you want?" Troy asked sharply. "If you think we'll be intimidated you've got another thing coming. You're going to pay for what you did you son-of-a-bitch."

"I haven't come to try to intimidate you," Michael said, his calm outward appearance belying a rocketing heartbeat.

"So what have you come for?"

"Actually, I've come to apologise." he said looking straight at Bian. "I know it's a bit late and given what you been through, a word of apology can't right the wrong, but it still needs to be said all the same. I really am sorry."

Troy was surprised and relieved at the same time, his courage soaring at his passivity and obvious lack of aggression. "It won't help you. You're still gonna fry."

"Troy! Please. Don't," Bian said, speaking for the first time.

"OK, you've apologised, so get the hell out'a here!"

"Troy!!" Bian said scowling before turning to look at Michael. "You were never part of it were you? I knew that when I looked at you afterwards, after it'd happened."

"I *was* part of it. I should've stopped it. But I didn't. I got sucked in because of my own weakness and it's something I've regretted every day since."

"You bet you gonna regret it," Troy said, alarmed at the sympathy his wife seemed to have for one of the men he'd spent four years thinking about, hating, hunting.

Bian scowled at him again.

"I am so sorry," Michael said ignoring Troy's threat.

"Where've you come from?" she asked.

"Boston."

"Boston! You mean you've travelled all this way just to say sorry."

"Like I said, I thought it important I apologise face-to-face."

"OK Bian, that's enough. He's said what he came to say," Troy said, his turn to be firm.

In no mood to argue, Bian turned to go back inside the house.

"You picked the wrong girl soldier! You are gonna burn," Troy said sharply, safe in the knowledge his wife was out of earshot.

He'd dreamt of miming a parting shot across the courtroom as the men are led off to jail. He especially enjoyed saying it to *No.4* face-to-face.

But Michael's response surprised him.

"That's no less than I deserve; sorry again." And with that, he was gone.

CHAPTER THIRTY-EIGHT:

Paul Lehmann was beginning to get worried; the meeting in Vegas was rapidly approaching and there was no sign of Frankie.

He'd spent two whole days hiding in the heavily treed corner of the Park and then, on the third day, after a flurry of dog walkers and joggers, in he shuffled.

"You can't fool me with that old man shuffle; I seen you in action Frankie!"

Lehmann called the office. "I found him," he said quietly.

"OK," Pike replied. "I'll get instructions and call back in half-hour."

Twenty-nine minutes later Lehmann's cellphone vibrated in his pocket.

"This is from the very top Lehmann, from Monroe himself. Do not tackle Fernando alone. Beattie, Grimaldi and Hutchinson leave O'Hare at midnight. They'll pick up a rented SUV at the airport and when they get to you, then and only then, do you approach Mr Fernando. He will be persuaded he needs a lift and the four of you are to deliver him to Vegas in time for his meeting with the client. And Lehmann," Pike added, "Monroe's told me to tell you that he'll be very upset if you mess up!"

Marcus Monroe was both the brains and the energy behind *Softly Softly*. Ex high level CIA, Lehmann knew the lives of many human beings had been terminated either by Monroe personally or by men who took their orders directly from him. His boss wasn't a man to be trifled with. Failure was never an option when it came to the client, especially if the client was Rudi Kingsbridge.

All day Lehmann watched Frankie sit on his bench, slouched and motionless till someone came within begging distance. "Who are you old man?" he said quietly, wondering what the link could be between one of America's richest men and a hobo shaking his glass jar at passers-by. And what was the link to the black guy from Texas and the company CEO from Boston?

They were thoughts without answers.

At the end of the afternoon, Frankie rose from his seat and set off for the gate. From eighty yards back, Lehmann watched him enter the 7/11 store empty-handed and come out with two carrier bags containing some bottles. He guessed it wasn't Pepsi. He followed him into the overpass, letting the distance between them increase before hiding away to wait for his back-up to arrive. Every few minutes he squinted through his pocket-sized binoculars, scanning the scene though his one good eye. But all he could see in the fading light was the occasional glimpse of a bottle being raised up as Frankie supped its contents out the other end.

It was close to midnight when Pike called a second time.

"You still with Fernando?"

"Yeah, he's out cold; drunk himself into a stupor."

"The plane's been delayed an hour. They should be with you in five hours or so. Where do I send them?"

Lehmann gave the specific location knowing that Pike would use the office's GPS tracking system to direct the SUV to within inches of where he sat.

"And Lehmann, Mr Monroe sends his love!" Pike quipped convinced he was the funniest man in the world.

* * * * *

Michael McBride flew in from Providence Rhode Island via Chicago. He was a seasoned traveller but he'd never been to Las Vegas. It wasn't his kind of town.

Three days earlier, Eugene called to let him know the venue.

"Hey man, we staying overnight so we got plenty of time to talk. The hotel, your flight, everything, is all on Hollywood."

"Thanks, but I'll pay my own way. And Eugene, I'll be flying in and out on the Tuesday."

"OK man, no problem. Let me know what time you in and I'll meet you off the plane."

Four days later at McCarran International Airport, the two men came face-to-face for the first time in twenty-nine years. It was an emotional moment, Eugene even filling-up at one point. For Michael it was a strange feeling. He'd loved Eugene but the huge black man was part of a past he'd walked from and tried hard to forget. It was also made more difficult by the fact that even if he himself didn't realise it, Eugene was Rudi Kingsbridge's puppet.

"How you doing man? You look great, just like you did in 'Nam," Eugene said

"You look good too; you must be living in the gym!" Michael replied, trying to match his friend's warmth.

"I was, till all this crap blew up. I was on course for the Senior Universe title but it looks as if I'll have to let it pass this time. It was on too. I could've done it!" As he spoke, he lifted both arms so his massive biceps and shoulders exploded out his T-shirt. It brought the airport to a standstill, some chattering Japanese tourists even snapping pictures. "Just like 'Nam huh? Little yella fellas everywhere!!" he joked, dying to reminisce with his former partner.

Michael just grunted but Eugene was unperturbed as he jumped behind the wheel of the S-class Mercedes and fired up the six-litre engine.

"We got a few hours to kill before we pick Frankie up at eleven-thirty. It'll be good to see the Corporal again won't it? I'll drive you to the hotel so you can get cleaned up. What time's your flight?"

"Six thirty-five," said Michael declining to answer most of his friend's questions.

It set a pattern for the rest of their twenty minute journey: Eugene chattering away, Michael saying as little as possible.

When they pulled up outside the Royal Plaza there was a quartet of bikini clad showgirls handing out promo leaflets to the various shows.

"This city's built on sex! There's so much flesh on display it makes you dizzy!" Eugene said his eyes full of lust. "Seeing these chicks on the street reminds me of Australia, Sydney. Remember that fight we got into man?"

"Yeah I remember, but I try to forget."

They took the private lift to the Royal Plaza's skyloft suite situated on the two topmost floors, the fourteenth and fifteenth. Opulently decorated like something from a Roman Empire big screen epic, the suite was a little garish and over-the-top for Michael's taste.

"It's got Kingsbridge's fingerprints all over it," he said, realising it was the first time he'd said his old enemy's name out loud in over three decades.

"Yeah I guess. But to a poor black boy from Texas, it's pretty damn amazing!"

Eugene had picked up on Michael's reluctance. Like his lack of enthusiasm for reminiscing, it pointed to the fact that the man he'd once known as "Irish," had changed big-time.

* * * * *

It was just getting light when Beattie, Grimaldi and Hutchinson arrived. After the briefest of handshakes, four burly men, none older than forty, silently approached the place where the old hobo had been partying several hours earlier.

Of the four, only Paul Lehmann expected the unexpected.

Joss Grimaldi edged ahead of the others. In his hand was a plastic bag. He slipped it down and over Frankie's face and pulled its drawstring tight round his throat. The first breath he took that failed to get the required air into his lungs woke him into sudden panic-ridden consciousness. His eyes opened impossibly wide and then, all hell broke loose: kicking, flailing, arms everywhere. But it was a hopeless effort, not because he was outnumbered four to one but because without oxygen, the human body ceases to function.

Unconscious, Frankie began twitching and retching.

"Awww my God; he's thrown-up!!"

"Take it off, before he chokes."

Grimaldi pulled a second bag, a black canvas one, from the thigh pocket of his combat trousers and slipped it over Frankie's head.

"Tie his hands; he can be dangerous," Lehmann said speaking out of experience.

"Is that how you got the eye?" Hutchinson asked, not even trying to hide a smirk.

Lehmann ignored the jibe as the four manhandled Frankie the two hundred yards to the Ford Explorer before bundling him into the back seat. Beattie and Lehmann climbed in either side of him, while Grimaldi and Hutchinson sat up front, Hutchinson driving.

Once they checked in with Pike, they settled down for the three hundred mile drive up Interstate 15 to Vegas. Frankie said nothing; but his silence didn't mean he wasn't with it or there was nothing happening. He was listening intently for clues, for information that would give him an edge somewhere in his immediate future.

Two hours into the journey, he spoke for the first time.

"I need a leak," he said, provoking a flurry of conversation.

"Do we take his hood off?" Beattie asked.

"What about the cuffs?" Grimaldi said, looking at the others. "If we don't free his hands, one of us is going to have to get it out for him!"

"I ain't doing it," Marty Hutchinson exclaimed, nearly choking as he said it.

It may've brought a smile to proceedings but it also confirmed the cuffs were coming off!

What they didn't know was that their captive had a plan though Frankie would've been first to admit it wasn't much of one. Once the cuffs were off, he intended hitting anything in range before legging it. He had no idea where he'd run, but he thought he'd think that one through later.

As the SUV pulled up at the side of the road, Frankie expected them to free his hands but leave the hood on.

But Mick Beattie, who was sat in the back seat alongside him, unexpectedly removed the hood. Despite his hands still being firmly tied behind his back, Frankie couldn't resist it. The second the hood lifted past his eye-line was the same second the Ford Explorer became the Ford Exploder. Frankie's first view was of Joss Grimaldi sat in the front passenger seat, turning to his left to see what was going on behind him. Frankie lurched forward slamming his head straight into his unsuspecting face, Grimaldi screaming as the head butt landed with a sickening splat. Beattie and Lehmann, sat on Frankie's left and right, instinctively tried to pull him back onto his seat. Beattie pulled harder than Lehmann, rotating him towards himself. Frankie aimed a head butt, missed, and it sailed wide. But with his face up tight to Beattie, Frankie opened his mouth wide and fixed a bite on his cheek. It wasn't a position new to Frankie, he'd been there before. Beattie wailed like a banshee, his three colleagues doing their best to slam blows into their prisoner. One blow caught him on the temple. Frankie let go his bite and slumped back into his seat.

"You stinking son-of-a-bitch," Beattie wailed, his hands clutching at his bleeding face. "Get the bag back on him. You wanna leak you tramp son-of-a-bitch . . . wet your pants!"

There was still over a hundred and fifty miles to go, so Frankie took his leak. But his fighting instincts had been aroused and though hooded, cuffed and outnumbered four-to-one, he wanted more. Like a bat operating on sonar only, he heard the driver say something to Paul Lehmann who, sat on his right in the back seat, leaned slightly forward. Frankie exploded upwards, smashing his forehead into Lehmann's face, catching him flush on the left cheek and nose.

As he followed in, aiming to bite him, Hutchinson, the only one unmarked, turned round and smashed a lead cosh into Frankie's hooded face. He collapsed back into his seat, blood trickling out from under the hood before dripping off his chin onto his filthy shirt.

Two hours later, five miles south of Vegas, they pulled off the highway.

As the SUV skidded to a halt on the dusty track, Eugene Sanders and Michael McBride were leaning against the parked-up Mercedes.

The four men bundled the hooded Frankie off the back seat and out the open door.

To Eugene and Michael it was a strange yet somehow familiar sight, a kind of throwback to another era.

"Take the bag off his head and cut him loose; now!!" Michael barked, as surprised by how aggressively protective he felt towards Frankie as he was by the adrenaline surging through his veins.

The men did as they were told and removed the hood.

"Hey Corp, you OK?" Eugene said glowering at the four men who all looked uneasy.

"I'm fine," Frankie replied, looking anything but fine. The scar under his bottom lip had re-opened and he had dry blood all over his chin.

But three of the four men were carrying obvious battle wounds and try as he might, Michael couldn't stop himself regressing. His old ways may have been suppressed for two decades and more but seeing his former Corporal carrying the scars of battle saw the fighting instinct rear up from somewhere deep inside him. "Guys, I'm really impressed; only three of you carrying injuries I mean! And it was only four-to-one, with the one cuffed and blindfolded!! Remind me to call you next time we go to war!!"

It wasn't just his words, his body language spoke volumes too. If Frankie's four captors wanted it, they could have it. Everyone knew it. In the macho testosterone-filled world all seven men were from, the sarcasm and challenge cut like a knife. All four *Softly Softly* employees avoided eye contact; it was their way of declining the challenge.

"Pussies!" Eugene said dismissively. "C'mon Corp, let's go get you cleaned up."

Irish and *Kong* had made their point but Frankie wasn't finished. He had a score to settle.

Hutchinson was the only one of the four unmarked. He'd been the driver and the one to hit Frankie with the cosh. As Grimaldi finished untying his hands, Frankie shifted position slightly but not so much anyone would notice. It put him closer to and more alongside Hutchinson. He rubbed his hands and rotated his shoulders as if trying to get his circulation going again. Then, without any warning, he backhanded Hutchinson with a left fist to the throat. He dropped like a stone, clutching at his neck.

"That's four out of four!" Frankie said as he walked off towards his former colleagues.

"Nice one Corp," Kong said the same time he fired off a menacing look aimed at ensuring the men's indignation stayed just a feeling.

"You look great Corp; how you doing?" Irish said, lying. He was genuinely pleased to see Frankie but hated the fact he'd come so close to losing it. But it simply confirmed what he'd always known, that any contact with men who, like him, carried the tag ex-Bleeding Dog, wasn't good for the soul. It was why he'd avoided it for over thirty years and why he'd still be avoiding it if circumstances hadn't forced a reunion.

As the three climbed into their silver Mercedes, Paul Lehmann glanced down at Marty Hutchinson who was on his knees, frantically trying to get sufficient air into his lungs to keep himself alive. Then he looked over to his right, at Beattie, and at the bite-mark on the fleshy part of his cheek and then he turned to Grimaldi to his left and clocked his massively swollen, obviously broken nose. And last but not least, there was him. Still on one eye after being knocked cold nearly three days earlier, he now had a badly damaged nose thrown in for good measure.

Watching the Mercedes pull away had Lehmann posing himself a question he'd asked a hundred times: "Just who the hell *are* these guys?"

CHAPTER THIRTY-NINE:

When they reached the Royal Plaza Hotel, Rudi Kingsbridge was waiting for them.

He'd already met Eugene face-to-face but it was the first time he, Frankie and McBride had set eyes on one another in over thirty years.

"Hey guys, it's good to see you. How are you?"

The men exchanged the briefest of handshakes, grunted at one another, and that was that: pleasantries over.

Kingsbridge had hoped there'd be a sense of team, of celebration even, but he was way off the mark. The four middle-aged fifty-something's were four very different individuals not a super-elite Special Ops team invisibly going about their work for Uncle Sam.

That was then and this was now.

When Kingsbridge greeted Frankie he noticed the freshly opened scar under his bottom lip.

"You get some trouble Corp? You look just like you did that time we were in Sydney. Remember that? We sure gave those Aussies a beating huh?" As he shook Frankie's hand the fake friendliness quickly disappeared. "Awww Corp, you stink. You smell like you ain't taken a bath since we left Vietnam!"

If he meant it to be funny, nobody laughed; it was just like before.

"Let him be!!" McBride growled protectively, his sudden aggression evident to all. He knew the reunion would be difficult but he hadn't expected it to be so tough, Kingsbridge still possessing the uncanny knack of pressing all his buttons. Battling to keep *Irish* firmly locked-up, he added, "Just back off him!" this time a fraction more calmly, more relaxed.

"He's filthy!" Kingsbridge said indignantly. "We can't talk when he's like that. Go take a shower Corp; it's in there," he added, pointing to the bathroom. "And Corp, I'm sure I saw something moving in the crap on your teeth, so give them a treat too and brush 'em!"

"Hey!!" Eugene said sharply through a trademark scowl. "Like Irish said man; back off!!"

"OK, OK, we'll take a break till he's done. I'll see if I can get him some clothes."

Thirty-five minutes later the four men were sat round the suite's conference table, Frankie all scrubbed up wearing grey T-shirt and black slacks.

"OK, let's get going," Kingsbridge said, somehow assuming the right to lead the meeting.

He'd thought sending Eugene and Marlena to Antigua would see things cool down and perhaps even go away altogether. But since seeing the follow-up article in the most recent issue of *American Dream*, he knew they needed to get organised.

"My lawyer says that if they track us down, we should blank 'em and say nothing. He reckons that even if they find us there's less than a fifty-fifty chance it'll get to court and if it does, it would be perfectly reasonable for guys like us, with a covert military background, to refuse to give evidence. We take the Fifth and say nothing."

Michael had received similar advice from Robert O'Meara. But he wanted to stir the water.

"What's wrong with telling the truth?" he said, his words dropping like bombs from a B52.

"How did I know you'd be the awkward one Mick?"

"It's not meant to be awkward; just tell me why telling the truth isn't an option?"

"Well first, there's the almost certain probability that if it goes to trial, we'll go to jail. Secondly there's even a distinct possibility we'll get the death penalty . . ."

"I'm already serving a death sentence?" said Frankie with a shrug of his shoulders.

"That's your choice Corp; nobody makes you live in a cardboard box."

"You . . ." Frankie muttered the same time he slid his chair back ready to take it further.

"Woaah, hang on now guys," said Eugene, trying to calm things down.

"Let him finish Corp," McBride said calmly. "That's two reasons. You got any more?"

"Yeah I got a third reason for you Mick. We all swore an oath of allegiance that we'd never speak a word of what happened, not to one another and not to anyone outside the Dogs."

Though *Irish* was screaming to be let off the leash, Michael kept him tied up, refusing to react. As he wondered how to respond, Frankie beat him to it.

"Listen film star," he snarled, fixing a stare on Kingsbridge. "I may have nothing, but right now, something tells me that puts me at a distinct advantage to you. I go to jail and I get three squares-a-day and a bed to sleep in. You go to jail and what happens? It doesn't take much of an imagination! You seen the movies; handsome son-of-a-bitch like you is gonna be in big demand! You'll be some black buck's bitch, with the sorest crapper in Fort Leavenworth!!"

"Hey, let's not talk about going to jail, huh?" Eugene said unable to stop himself smiling.

"Yeah," said Kingsbridge, "So where you at Mick?"

"I'll tell you where I'm at. While I don't especially want to be locked up, I have to accept we did what we did and it just might be time to pay."

Kingsbridge threw his hands up, muttering in protest but Michael continued.

"As far as the death penalty is concerned, if we have to die we have to die. I've had the same legal advice about taking the Fifth and saying zip but I'm not sure I will or I can. What happened on the riverbank was wrong. I knew it then, I know it now. I should've stopped it. Instead I became part of it. Not one day has passed since, where I haven't regretted what I did. But it happened and I can't change it. But I tell you this I ain't gonna lie about it. If I'm asked a direct question and feel I have to answer, my answer will be a truthful one."

"Hey that's just great man," exclaimed Kingsbridge, coming over all theatrical. "So where does that leave us? And where does that leave the oath of allegiance?"

Like Eugene, Kingsbridge had noticed McBride wasn't swearing or cussing. He suspected that somehow, it was linked to his impending answer.

For Michael McBride, the moment of truth had arrived.

"Look, the way I was couldn't be further from who I am and what I am today."

"Hey man we've all changed," said Eugene.

"No Eugene, this goes further than that. In 1982, I went to a Billy Graham crusade . . ."

Kingsbridge interrupted again. "He's a Jesus freak! The son-of-a-bitch has become a Jesus freak!! I always knew there was something sick about you McBride."

Frankie jerked his chair back a second time. "There's only ever been one sicko in this team sicko, and that's *you*. You were the one who killed us. On that Christmas mission man, where we wasted the General before running for the chopper. I saw you sicko. I saw you with my own two eyes, you sick son-of-a-bitch. Not to mention the incident in the Central Highlands when you was giving it to the old bird. It's *you* that's the sicko!"

"What you talking about Corp? What happened Christmas time?" Michael asked, looking genuinely puzzled.

"Nothing happened," Kingsbridge interrupted.

"Shut your mouth Hollywood!" Eugene said, blasting his way into the conversation. "Let the Corporal speak. What happened Corp?"

"Remember? We popped the General in the ravine and made our getaway with Charlie in pusuit. Me and cherry lips reached the chopper first. You two were running for your lives and we were giving you cover from the chopper as you were running towards us. Then, out the corner my eye, I see sicko here, lower his CAR-15 and . . ."

"And what?"

Frankie hesitated. "And let go twelve, maybe fifteen rounds in . . . in . . . McBride's direction."

"You what?" Michael screamed as he stood up out his seat, raw aggression instantly replacing the calmness and control. No-one knew, least of all him, if he'd reached the point of no return. In a blur of movement the mighty Kong pole-axed Kingsbridge with a heavy back-hander to the forehead sending him reeling backwards, his chair suddenly collapsing under him. It was a bizarre sight; Kingsbridge flat on his back with his legs in the air. His head may have been cushioned by two hundred bucks-a-yard carpet, but it wasn't the sort of position anyone would expect to find one of America's richest men.

"I'd say it's time I went back to my cardboard box. I got nothing against you and you," Frankie said looking at McBride and Sanders in turn. "But you . . ." he added contemptuously, his eyes locked on the egg-shaped bump rising out the middle of Kingsbridge's forehead. "I cannot find words to describe the contempt I feel for you. You think you got it all, but really you got nothing. Ask these two what they really think of you. I've never talked to them 'bout it but I know they think the same as me. Money can't buy you respect sicko."

"Corp, gimme a minute before you go," Michael said, hiding his surprise at the depth of bad feeling his former Corporal had for Kingsbridge. "Let me finish what I was saying before I was so rudi interrupted."

It was a timely quip that helped lighten the tension.

"My life's changed and yeah, I've become Christian," he said matter-of-factly, looking directly at Kingsbridge. "But it's the best thing I ever done. I have a wonderful wife and family that I love in a way I never thought possible. I head a successful family business and love my job. And today's the nearest I come to losing my temper in more than twenty years. I don't ask you to understand it because I still don't understand it all myself. But you all know me. You know how I was. The anger, the frustration, the fighting, they've all gone. But my new life has rules and standards and I won't be lying to save myself or to save you. We did wrong and if we have to pay, so be it. While I can't change history, I can determine what I do in the future and like I said, there'll be no lying. So, regarding the oath of allegiance I swore in '72, let me say that firstly I was out of my mind when I agreed to it, though that's no excuse, and secondly, it's been superseded by the oath of allegiance I swore to God. And I won't be breaking *that* no matter what."

Kingsbridge motioned to interrupt but Michael ignored him.

"So let me repeat something. If I'm asked a direct question and the circumstances are such I feel I have to answer, the answer I give will be the truth, at least the truth as I see it. I'll try to avoid such a scenario if I can. I mean I won't go looking for the opportunity to spout off and I won't be offering information to anyone but if it's unavoidable, only truth is coming out of my lips."

"And there's one other thing you need to know," he added as Kingsbridge feigned a yawn. "I've been to see her, the girl I mean; last week in Florida. I went to apologise."

"You did what?" Kingsbridge hissed. "That's an admission of guilt you stupid Mick. You apologised to the Gook bitch to appease your pathetic conscience. We're in this together you Bible-bashing son-of-a-bitch."

"She ain't no Gook bitch," said Michael aggressively. "And from what I can see, we ain't no team either. And because of you, we never were no team."

"Like I said, it's time I went home," Frankie interjected.

Their reunion hadn't been a happy one.

Celebration was out of the question; they were four men with nothing to celebrate.

CHAPTER FORTY:

The two days following the Vegas meeting were amongst the most miserable of Rudi Kingsbridge's life.

The meeting hadn't gone as he'd hoped. In fact it had been an out-and-out disaster. And when it came to McBride, a thirty year absence hadn't made the heart grow fonder. He still despised him, his revelation he'd become a Jesus freak making him despise him all the more.

For forty-eight hours his mind had been racing.

He hadn't told his wife Kay about the story and as far as he knew, she didn't have a clue about the big problem looming on their horizon. He wondered if the time had come to tell her. He also wondered what he should do about McBride.

Should he have Marcus Monroe deal with it? It would cost him plenty but that wasn't an issue; he was rich enough to be able to afford it whatever the price. The problem was however good or talented the hit-man, nothing in his past would've prepared him for trying to take out someone like McBride. He may have been ex-fighting machine, ex-Bleeding Dog, now born-again Christian, but he was no unsuspecting fat-cat who'd crap his pants at the thought of a telescopic lens being pointed his way.

He knew a hit had the potential to go wrong and that could end up being very hard to explain, especially to the mighty Kong!

As bad as Kingsbridge thought things were, they were about to get worse; the catalyst to his misery, a telephone call from Claudia Kaplan.

* * * * *

As the clock struck four, Claudia breezed confidently into the boardroom.

"Good afternoon team," she said with a smile, her eyes roving the room. "Today is probably the biggest and most significant board meeting in our history. Marcia brought an enlightening report to yesterday's war cabinet meeting. I've asked her to share it with the whole board. Marcia?"

"Thanks Claudia," Marcia said revelling at being centre stage once again. "In a nutshell, our enquiries have revealed the identities of two more Bleeding Dogs. Sanders the black guy, has made several calls to Chicago and two or three to Foxboro, Massachusetts. It turns out both the people he's calling were serving in Vietnam at the time of the incident."

"This is former Marine sharpshooter, Michael McBride," Marcia said, clicking the remote control so his face appeared on the screen behind her. "Yes, he's handsome but he's also a successful businessman, CEO of the family construction business no less. He's happily married to Maddie, his wife of more than twenty years. They have three children, two boys and a girl, who look like all-American kids. The family are committed Christians and I must say, it feels a little strange linking him with the Bleeding Dogs. I wasn't convinced until *Aldrich Matthias & Lyman* sent me a video of him being interviewed on *Today with Abbie Morales*. He talks about his past, his regrets and the fact he made some big mistakes. He stresses how important it is for everyone, young and old, to make good choices. He talks about how a war situation can mess up your thinking and how easy it is to cross a line. He then goes on to talk about becoming a Christian in 1982 at a Billy Graham crusade. And again he refers to choices – he's big on choices this guy – and says that a strong Christian faith anchors you and allows you to operate off a firm foundation."

"This is all very interesting Marcia, heart-warming even," Phil Woodcock said, "But do we have anything that looks even remotely like evidence?"

"Well if you mean do we have a signed confession Phil, the answer's no," Marcia responded, matching his sarcasm. Claudia smiled. She liked Marcia. She liked her feistiness; it reminded her of herself when she'd been at *Newsweek*.

Phil grunted and returned to his doodling.

"Our conclusion is . . . that Michael McBride is *No.4!*" Marcia declared, clicking the remote so the head outline and pen portrait from the original story were on screen.

"And that brings me to *No.1*. Sanders' calls to Chicago have been traced to KBI, the Kingsbridge Bank of Illinois. The first twice he used the main switchboard number, the one available from the phone book. But the last eleven times he's called, he's used a private unlisted number that rings on Barney Mayer's desk. Mr Mayer is PA to the bank's chairman and CEO . . . one Rudi Kingsbridge!"

There was a sharp intake of breath all over the stunned boardroom.

Marcia paused. "Most of you will have heard of Mr Kingsbridge and for those who haven't, you'll almost certainly know his face. He's another handsome son-of-a-bitch!"

Marcia clicked the remote seven or eight times, each click putting a different magazine cover on the screen.

"This is making me go weak at the knees," said Phil Woodcock sarcastically.

"Me too; he's gorgeous!!" chirped sales director Jessica Bell.

"I didn't mean it *that* way," Phil responded indignantly. "I can see . . ."

"Phil," Claudia interrupted. "Let Marcia finish; then we'll talk."

"Thanks Claudia," Marcia said, appreciating her boss' help but also appreciating the fact she was letting her deliver what was perhaps the biggest news in the magazine's short history. "Mr Kingsbridge is something of a paradox. On the surface, he's happily married to Kay, ex-super model Kay Ferrano. They have two kids and live in Lake Forest, thirty miles north of Chicago, in a French Chateau. But despite the picture of domestic bliss, rumours are everywhere he's a serial adulterer, albeit one with a difference. He's very selective and it seems he keeps a kind of personal harem to satisfy his extra-marital needs. His wife doesn't know anything about it so it's a well kept secret, though not too well, 'coz we found out!"

Marcia was beginning to enjoy herself.

"Rudi Kingsbridge served with relative distinction as a paratrooper in the 101st Airborne and interestingly, he flew out of Vietnam just two days after the incident . . . on June 19th 1972."

"What's interesting in that Marcia except that he was in Vietnam on the seventeenth?" asked financial director Maurice "the Poodle" Farrell.

"Good question Maureese; I'm glad you asked. Remember the letter from O'Donnell to his brother Gus?"

she said clicking the remote so the entire letter appeared on screen behind her as if by magic. "While it all makes interesting reading, there's a line I really want you to focus on."

She clicked again and up came a paragraph with one line emboldened and underlined.

<u>One of the two, the psycho with the film star looks, took a hit today – a nasty knife wound to the shoulder – but even that doesn't seem to add up.</u>

"We think Kingsbridge *is the psycho with the film star looks*. Enquiries have revealed he flew out of Vietnam on June 19th 1972, into Rockwood Hospital, Sacramento, where he underwent three ops in seven months, all for injuries sustained while on active service. Actually, it was 'injury' not 'injuries' and the injury . . . was a *knife wound to the shoulder!!* Oh and there's one more thing; you'll recall that one of the key elements of *No.1*'s profile was that he wore black ties around each arm, just above the elbow."

Even before she finished speaking, she'd begun clicking the remote, the clicks getting progressively louder amidst the deathly silence that'd descended all over the boardroom. With each click, a new photo appeared on screen, each one obviously a military shot, every single one, showing Rudi Kingsbridge with black ties encircling his upper arm, just above the elbow.

Marcia looked across at Claudia before clicking the remote one last time. As she sat, her boss stood; their synchronization inch perfect. With an ultra close-up of Rudi Kingsbridge's face filling the screen behind her, Claudia addressed the room.

"Team, situations like this define careers and establishes destiny. Today is decision day. I don't intend to make an impassioned speech or endeavour to persuade any doubters. As you know I personally own seventy-six per cent of this business. You all know what I say goes; it has to. But I want this to be a team thing. Are *you* up for it? But understand, before you answer. The flak will fly and the heat could be unbearable. Already we've had letters from the Secretary of Defense, the U.S. Attorney General, the Vice-President of the National Security Council, and the Vice Chief of Staff of the U.S. Army, as well as from Army Special Operations Command and from Marine Headquarters in Quantico Virginia. Hell, it wouldn't surprise me if the President called my cellphone!! They all deny the existence of Bleeding Dog Company and all want us to back off. Now, I don't know about you but I'm not the type to be intimidated. Team, I say we go for it."

She'd said she wasn't going to make an impassioned speech but that was exactly what she'd done. It was no accident.

All round the room, heads were nodding, Phil Woodcock the only exception.

"Phil: you not in agreement?"

"It's not that I'm not in agreement Claudia; I just don't want us to be unduly hasty. As far as we're aware, none of our competitors are even on the radar so it's not like we're in danger of being scooped or something. I think we should do more checking."

"We go to press in five days Phil, so time's not on our side. These sons of bitches did it. It's time they paid. We're running with it Phil!"

"They'll sue us Claudia."

"Phil, being sued is only a problem if we're wrong, and we are not wrong," she said, her eyes scanning the room. "I had hoped we'd have a degree of unanimity, but while Phil has registered his, shall we say, disenchantment, is there anyone else who wants to raise an objection?"

It was Jessica Bell who broke the silence.

"How you thinking of playing it Claudia?"

"We name everyone. We explain once again that the unit was the brain-child of Lt. Col. William T. O'Donnell. We reveal General Matthew Kedenberg as the Washington based four-star general who authorised the team's formation. Quoting O'Donnell's letter, we divulge what the unit was about, what they got up to. We reveal that their hands-on trainer and chief motivator was Master Sergeant Doug Miller. We paint short bios on everyone we mention – date and place of birth, where they grew up, military record, date of death if they're deceased etc. We get some quotes from people that knew them, or guys they served with. We tell the story that the Bleeding Dogs were so far undercover, the world was led to believe that Miller was already dead when he was very much alive! Then we turn the spotlight on the four. Citing O'Donnell's comments, we tell the story of how *No.1* and *No.4* hated one another and the way the friction undermined the group and sent the leader, *No.3*, round the bend. Then we name them. We also name Eugene Sanders as *No.2*. We run up-to-date bios and we got plenty on each of them. I mean tap Kingsbridge and McBride into Google and there's reams of stuff available. Then, we finish by restating our commitment to bringing the known trio to justice and likewise, to finding the team leader and making sure he joins them on trial."

It was obvious Claudia wasn't thinking off the top of her head. She'd thought the whole process through. Everybody knew it.

"And I'm thinking . . ." she said, pausing, "We run Kingsbridge's face on the Midwest front cover. It'll be sensational. He and Kay Ferrano are right at the top of Chicago's A-list. Then, inside, we run a bar down two of the pages with the low-down on Sanders and McBride."

American Dream magazine though national, published five different regional versions and usually, each regional had its own front cover. Aside from Bill Clinton and Tiger

Woods, the only time the magazine had run the same front cover through all five regions was two months earlier, when Bian's face graced the cover of every one of the record twelve-and-a-half-million sold.

"McBride isn't big enough to get the front page spot in the northeast issue," Claudia said. "If he was a New Yorker maybe, but he isn't. So we'll do an inside feature that reveals him as *No.4* with page bars outing Kingsbridge and Sanders. Similarly, the Southern issue, and perhaps the Central one too, we'll lead with Sanders. So that'll mean only the West Coast issue won't get the story big-time." With all her thoughts of the previous twenty-four hours crystallizing as she spoke, she added, "The big issue now is photos. It's possible we'll have something in our library for Kingsbridge. But the quality must be exceptional. If not, go to the agencies; we'll pay whatever it takes but it better be good."

Her board could see her gearing up for battle.

"OK then; its action stations. Eight hours before we hit the news-stands, we'll make calls to Kingsbridge, McBride and Sanders. Marcia, can you make sure *Aldrich Matthias & Lyman* get me cellphones for all three as well as business and home landlines?"

"Of course Claudia. It'll be interesting to see how they react, especially Kingsbridge!"

"Phil you OK with this now?" Claudia said looking straight at her Legal Affairs Director wondering if she'd have to fire him.

"I'm fine Claudia. I may have reservations about the speed but we'll endeavour to get everything as tight as we can legally speaking."

"Good," said Claudia, looking at each of her board in turn, before adding, "OK team let's give it to these sons of bitches: right between the eyes."

* * * * *

Rudi Kingsbridge's cellphone went straight through to his answering service.

"Good evening Mr Kingsbridge. This is Claudia Kaplan founding editor at *American Dream* magazine. I'd be most grateful if you could return my call when you get this message."

The conference phone was in the middle of the massive boardroom table.

"What an anti-climax!" she said looking around at Phil Woodcock, Marcia Sullivan and BJ.

Claudia wanted her war cabinet to witness the calls and Phil had suggested they record them just in case one or more of the men let something slip or if something needed to be reviewed. Even more basic, the magazine might need to cover its tail.

"I think we'll try his home number."

The phone rang five or six times.

"Rudi Kingsbridge."

The war cabinet looked at one another like startled rabbits.

"Rudi Kingsbridge," he said a second time.

"Mr Kingsbridge, my name's Claudia Kaplan, founding editor of *American Dream* magazine. I wanted to show you a professional courtesy by letting you know that tomorrow morning our latest issue appears with you on the front cover."

"You what . . .?"

"The magazine carries a story that names you as one of four perpetrators of an alleged murder, vicious assault and violent rape on three generations of Laotian women on June 17th 1972."

Claudia was an experienced operator. She knew that after making the accusation, it was time for silence. With Kingsbridge cursing and swearing the other end of the line, the four *American Dream* directors looked at one another pensively. They hoped he'd lose it, give something away, but he pulled himself together before he went too far.

"This is some kind of a sick joke, right?"

"This is no joke Mr Kingsbridge."

"I know you don't I? We ever get it on?" he said smugly, every word pulsing with arrogance. "You ever have the pleasure of getting serviced by me? Nah . . . You're that crazy dyke bitch that worked for Jim Bailey."

Claudia didn't respond.

"Now listen to me bitch, I am innocent," he snarled, every other word a swearword. "In any case, you haven't got a chance of tying me to something that happened over thirty years ago. You run this story and I'll sue your cheap lesbian ass to hell and back."

"Mr Kingsbridge, the magazines are already on their way to the news-stands. When you rise from bed tomorrow, you won't need to look in the mirror to see yourself. Just buy *American Dream!*"

"You bitch! You got any idea who you're playing with here? Mess with me slut and you'll find out fast what it's like to be out'a your league! Understand?"

"It'll be interesting to see what it's like to be out of our league Mr Kingsbridge. But we do understand the publishing business and we also understand that sometimes the things we write get us into trouble and we end up in court. We understand that fine. That's our league, Mr Kingsbridge. So as far as you suing us is concerned, let me encourage you to go ahead. Sue us. We'd welcome it. I'm sure you have a great story to tell."

"You bitch!!"

"See you in court!" she said, clicking the phone dead before he could respond.

"Yessss!!" exclaimed BJ. "I reckon he's just waved goodbye to a good night's sleep!"

"Well done Claudia; you were brilliant," Phil said, calmly.

"Thanks Phil. I'm on a roll; shall we do Mr Sanders next?"

Eugene didn't swear as much as Kingsbridge but in the threat department he left the man he once knew as Hollywood trailing in his slipstream.

"Listen to me lady," he growled slowly and deliberately, "I am gonna kill you. I'm gonna kill your husband. I'm gonna kill your kids. And if you gott'a dog you can watch me eat it in front of you. I am gonna suck the blood straight out'a your veins. It's been a while since the cannibal in me showed his face but for you I can guarantee his return. You back off me lady or I swear, your bitch eyes will be bobbing up and down in my soup."

"Sounds like the sort of boy you'd take home to meet Mom and Dad!" Marcia said, gently patting Claudia to help her stop shaking.

"Makes me kind'a glad I ain't got kids, or a husband or a dog for that matter!" she said shakily.

"Are you up to calling McBride?" Phil asked gently.

Claudia nodded as she typed in Michael McBride's cellphone. When he answered she explained what was about to happen just as she'd done to Kingsbridge and Sanders. But with McBride there was no sense of surprise, no sense of being caught off guard. Instead, he was calm and polite.

"Oh, OK; thanks for calling," he said before hanging up.

As the phone went dead, the war cabinet looked at one another dumbstruck, before cracking-up with nervous laughter.

"That has to be the freakiest twenty minutes of my life! I wonder what Kingsbridge is doing right now?"

"He'll be on the phone to his lawyer I bet," BJ said with a smirk.

He was. But he was screaming not talking!

His face had been on the front cover of lots of magazines over the years. He usually enjoyed the profile it gave him; saw it as just reward for a life of success and achievement. But not this time! *American Dream* was one piece of exposure he'd have gladly done without.

"All in all, I'd say that was a good night's work," Phil said, the others nodding in agreement.

"This is really going to happen isn't it? It'll be awesome," Marcia chirped excitedly.

Claudia nodded. "I think you're right Marcia. It's gonna make OJ look like a minor traffic violation!!"

CHAPTER FORTY-ONE:

It was four more months before Frankie was identified as the missing piece in the Bleeding Dogs jigsaw.

Aldrich Matthias & Lyman discovered that both Sanders and McBride had been in Vegas on the same day, which, by coincidence, happened to be a day when Kingsbridge's movements were unaccounted for. The investigation team knew the four had met but didn't know where, their big break coming when a drunken *Softly Softly* detective started bragging in a bar one night. What the gumshoe didn't know was that the person he was bragging to was with *Aldrich Matthias & Lyman*.

It led to the Royal Plaza in Las Vegas and to the hotel's state-of-the-art closed circuit television system.

Viewing the tapes proved both laborious and expensive, costing almost fifteen thousand dollars in bribes.

But the cost was worth it, every cent value for money.

A series of images taken from the cameras in the foyer produced crystal clear images of Sanders, McBride and a third person walking into the hotel together and though he wasn't pictured with the other three, a further set of images placed Rudi Kingsbridge at the scene later the same day.

It was the start-point for a nationwide manhunt, a manhunt that ended with a hobo who spent his days begging in LA's Obregon Park and his nights in a drunken stupor under the overpass where the 60 crosses the 710.

Identified as *No.3*, the hobo's name was Frankie Fernando.

* * * * *

Just five miles from Obregon Park, Santino's was a world apart from Cardboard City. With one of the most expensive menus in the city only the fat-cats and the well-heeled could eat at Santino's. The chef was reputed to be one of Italy's finest and everything – service, food, décor, furnishings – was luxury all the way.

"Oh Jade: it's been *so* long. We were so close, all the way through our student years at USC."

"It feels like yesterday, doesn't it? You look wonderful Claudia. You haven't changed a bit. You look just like you did at USC."

"And so do you," Claudia responded, reciprocating the compliment as much with her eyes as with her words. It was like they'd never been apart, the two talking about old times while giggling like excited school-girls.

"Jade, you've done so well! Weren't you the youngest ever female to make U.S. Attorney! Before your thirty-fifth birthday wasn't it?"

"A hundred and twelve days to be precise," Jade replied, proudly and exactly. "Mind you, I've since been consigned to second place. Beaten by eight days! Can you believe it?

But I'm still the youngest ever U.S. Attorney on the Ninth Circuit!"

The Federal Court system divides the United States into twelve judicial circuits. The Ninth Circuit, out on the West Coast, is by far the biggest geographically speaking, the great states of Wisconsin, Washington, Montana, Idaho, Oregon, California, Arizona, Alaska and Hawaii all falling inside its jurisdiction.

The twelve Circuits are further sub-divided into ninety-four Judicial Districts including one or more in each state. With five, California has more than any other state. California Central, one of the five, had been Jade LaHoya's patch ever since President George W. Bush signed her commission during his first few months in office.

Ten years before, she'd been the rising star at Rubin Schwartz, one of California's biggest and most respected law firms. After defeating Dale Eisner, the U.S. Attorney at California Eastern, in two high-profile cases, Eisner head-hunted her, promising to help her become America's youngest ever female U.S. Attorney. She could've been the youngest ever partner at Rubin Schwartz at more than twice the salary but the prospect of creating a "first" in all American legal history meant more than a few extra dollars in her bank account.

Jade LaHoya liked being first and it wasn't like she'd starve either way.

Always a quick-witted sharp thinking advocate, her four years as U.S. Attorney built her a formidable reputation as one of the best trial lawyers in the country. One adversary famously said of her, "If her good looks don't kill you, her sharp words will." It was a description that stuck, oft-quoted in press and TV reports. Though she never let on, Jade loved it.

"Talking dreams Claudia; I'm your number one fan! *American Dream* is a must on my coffee table. It's wonderful. Some of the stuff you run is just brilliant. I loved that piece you did on Enron. And that gripping story last year about the girl raped in Vietnam . . ."

Claudia couldn't believe her luck. "Oddly enough, it's that story I want to talk to you about."

"Really?" Jade said raising a glass of water to her lips, noticing Claudia staring at her wedding ring. "Yes, I'm married," she said almost apologetically. "Six years now; I've even got a daughter in second grade. Now, that's enough about me . . ." she said pausing, keen to change the subject. "Tell me about this story Claudia. I'm intrigued. Didn't I read something about you identifying two of the perps, or was it three?"

"We know who all four are now."

"Wow! So what advice can I give you?"

Claudia spent the next fifteen minutes reviewing the entire case. She then neatly lifted a file from her attaché case and nudged it across the table.

Jade flicked through till she came to a photo of Rudi Kingsbridge.

"Good looking son-of-a-bitch," she said matter-of-factly.

"Murdering, raping son-of-a-bitch more like."

"He's one of your guys?"

"Yeah, he's one of them."

"Are you sure?" Jade said slowly, the penny suddenly dropping in a moment of realization. "You asking me to take the case Claudia? Prosecute it I mean?"

"Yes I am Jade."

Claudia was concerned she'd say no but Jade's pulse was racing at twice normal speed. In a fifteen year legal career, she hadn't just built a reputation as a ruthlessly efficient litigator; she'd also established herself as a woman who'd let nothing stand in the way of ambition. The People versus Fernando, Kingsbridge, McBride and Sanders was the stuff of dreams. She could already see herself on the courtroom steps.

Claudia needn't have worried. Jade had already made up her mind. There was no way she was going to say no to getting her face on network TV.

* * * * *

The meeting at Santino's kick-started the legal process into action with Jade emphasizing the need to keep *American Dream's* interest secret.

"Defense lawyers would be rubbing their hands if they knew we'd met," she said. "They'd argue Bian was in it for the money and media exposure so it's important we keep the magazine out the picture and portray our motive as pure: simply that justice must be served."

It meant subsequent meetings were more clandestine affairs but the choice of venue was less of a problem to Claudia than another of the consequences of Jade's advice: getting Bian and Troy to file a formal complaint with the FBI.

Jade explained that without an aggrieved party prepared to lodge a complaint, there could be no case. Claudia told Troy and he broached the matter with his wife. She snapped at him for a day or two but came round after speaking to Father Mesnel on the phone. The Catholic priest may have had a completely different motive to Troy but somehow his starkly contrasting approach managed to get the result he had wanted all along.

A few days later, husband and wife walked into the FBI office on Tampa's West Gray Street.

After telling Claudia about his visit to the FBI three years earlier, she advised Troy to seek out the same officer he'd spoken to first time round. Troy was a meticulous record keeper. In minutes he found the date he'd made the initial report, the query number it had been allocated and the name of the officer who dealt with it. Federal Agent Jerome McWilliam hadn't been interested in an incident that'd taken place years earlier, ten thousand miles from Tarpon Springs. Troy remembered his exact words; they cut him like a knife. "See my desk," he'd said, "Every case current and local. I ain't got time to chase aging shadows in Southeast Asia!"

All he did was issue the case with a report number. He didn't make a single phone call.

Three years later, Troy introduced him to Bian and instantly recognised he'd be more attentive second time round. Agent McWilliam couldn't remember the case and was surprised to see his name on the file. Embarrassed, he smiled what he thought was his most charming smile, firstly at Troy and then a much more lingering one at Bian.

"I think we'd better start from scratch!" he said hoping Troy and Bian would let it go.

"No problem," Troy said magnanimously.

"Right, you got my full attention." They did, or at least, Bian did.

A year later, the FBI's investigation was complete. It involved thousands of man hours, numerous flights back and fore to Laos, the exhumation of Minh Ngoc's body and hours of interviews with Tong Tenh in Laos and Father Mesnel in France. In addition, Kingsbridge, McBride, Sanders and Fernando had been interviewed on three separate occasion, each officially informed he was under investigation concerning, "alleged crimes and misdemeanours committed against three women at Ban Hatsati, Laos, on June 17th 1972."

It was another case of the noose tightening round their necks.

* * * * *

From Florida, the file went to Washington.

Jade had lots of good contacts with the DC Feds and she'd been carefully keeping them sweet for months. When she got the tip-off to say the file had finally reached Washington she immediately declared her interest in the case as U.S. Attorney for California Central. Her e-mail outlined the fact that one of the four alleged suspects was a resident of her constituency. She also confirmed she'd met and interviewed the complainant, Mrs Bian Templeman, and threw in for good measure that if the case was to go to trial then LA was better placed than most, given the city was the gateway into the U.S. for people travelling from Pan-Pacific countries like Laos, Vietnam and the like.

It was a convincing argument.

She received an immediate reply. Under the case number it said, "FBI agents have carried out an extensive investigation and believe there is a prima facie case to answer."

It was their way of saying they'd looked into it, this is what we got and do you want it?

Jade sent a second e-mail confirming that as U.S. Attorney for California Central District, she intended to file the case in Los Angeles, at the Western Division Court Building at 312 North Spring Street.

She hadn't arrived at her decision to choose North Spring by chance. Like everything else in her life, it'd been carefully thought through. Her first reason was pure convenience; her own office was situated at North Spring. And secondly, the building was the most impressive of the three Courts available to her, with a highly photogenic façade, long flight of steps and high colonnades.

It was important everything looked good on TV, especially her.

With the FBI's filing criteria satisfied, the case files were sent west to LA.

When they arrived, they filled a twelve by twelve room. But Jade LaHoya wasn't overly concerned. Her mind was on the next step and there was someone she needed to see.

* * * * *

Joshua L. Burridge, the *L* standing for Lexington, had been a Federal Court Judge for twenty-seven years.

He loved his work. It was the only thing in his life. Thirty-five years earlier, he'd broken a long-run of thirteen-hour working days fancying an extra few hours gardening with his wife. But the half-hour drive from his thriving San Diego law practice home to Carmel Valley led to a life-changing event. His wife wasn't in the garden as he'd expected; she was in the bedroom. But she wasn't alone. Miguel, the muscular Mexican handyman, fifteen years her junior, was showing her how handy he could be.

It was a devastating moment that led to divorce and to his two sons moving to Florida with their mother. More positively, it also led to a move to LA and a more influential circle of contacts.

Burridge was a razor-sharp operator: silver-tongued, quick-witted and politically astute. He could assess situations and people very quickly and without fail, when he identified some*one* or some*thing* that could help further his career, he could appear the nicest man in the world. But his niceness was skin-deep, more about convenience than character.

Formerly a California state Judge, he was the last federal judicial appointment made by the Carter administration, taking his place on the Ninth Circuit roster in the fall of '79. He was forty-five years old. His work gave him status and status gave him a degree of self-esteem; but it was never quite enough to fill the hole his ex-wife had blown in his self-image. He never remarried but it didn't stop him having an eye for the ladies, especially pretty ones. It was what first attracted him to Jade LàHoya in the late-Eighties at USC where she was a student and he was a part-time lecturer in International Criminal Law. With her big hair, voluptuous curves, lovely white teeth and big blue eyes, he thought her stunningly attractive. It also helped that she had a vivacious personality and an infectious, almost naive enthusiasm for the law and for the goodness of what it stood for.

Though instantly attracted to her he never let on, his lack of confidence never allowing him to imagine the age difference was bridgeable. So whenever she sought his opinion, he just did the caring lecturer bit and enjoyed every minute of her company.

Once she graduated and left USC she became no more than a pleasant memory. Then, one day several years later, he was delighted to hear she'd been head-hunted by Dale Eisner. He was pleased for her but even more pleased for himself. Her appointment into his patch meant it was inevitable she'd prosecute cases in his courtroom.

In the decade and more since, the two had become as close as judge and prosecutor relations could appropriately get. The fact Burridge was well into his seventies hadn't diminished the twinkle in his eye one jot. Jade played up to it, shaking her hair like a teenage innocent, flashing her toothy smile or dwelling for a second or two as she bent over his desk or got up out of a chair. If it helped him come down on her side in the courtroom, she saw it as worth it.

Burridge enjoyed mooting topical legal issues with Jade. It reminded him of his student days at Stanford when he used to sit around Cooley Courtyard or Crocker Garden debating pearls of wisdom taught in class. But with Jade, there was an added bonus: her physical appearance as stimulating to his eye as the discussions were to his intellect.

He was looking forward to seeing her again later that day. She'd rung him twenty-four hours earlier asking if she could see him that afternoon. He'd said he'd be delighted and that he had nothing on. He scratched two appointments out of his diary as he did so.

They'd wait; she couldn't.

* * * * *

"Good to see you Judge," she said, flashing one of her trade-mark smiles.

"Always a pleasure Mrs LaHoya; what can I do for you today?"

Though he didn't know it, she'd had been preparing for their meeting for months. Joshua L. Burridge had been selected to try the highest profile case in American legal history, the selection panel just one person: Jade LaHoya.

She'd carefully considered two or three candidates and thought through the various ways she could influence procedure. Timing was everything. All she had to do was file the charges on a day when she knew her preferred judge would be on the bench. If she called it right, once the Judge saw the potential of what she knew was a career-defining case, she was certain he'd stay with it through the arraignment all the way to trial.

In her opinion, Burridge perfectly fitted the profile she was looking for. Though he was a Democrat he believed in the death penalty. Of fourteen people executed in California since the re-enactment of the death penalty in 1977, two had been sentenced by him. Similarly, he was responsible for sixteen of the six-hundred and fifty inmates sat on California's Death Row.

Burridge was a man who didn't suffer fools gladly and Jade didn't know anyone less likely to take a bribe. He hated war, always ran a tight courtroom and was also an outspoken critic of central government overstepping its authority. Most important of all, he'd always been an advocate for cameras in the courtroom, and seven months earlier, had become the first Ninth Circuit Judge to try a federal criminal case in front of TV cameras.

Jade was certain he'd see it the same as her. She was right; he did.

She put forward what she described as a purely hypothetical case, explaining the magnitude of public interest, the need for the American public and, given the case's global dimension, the need for people all over the world to have access to proceedings.

The Judge knew there wasn't anything hypothetical about the scenario she described.

"Given that it's *purely hypothetical* of course, I'm wondering counsellor, what it is you're asking me?"

"Judge, you and I go back a long way. What you think is important to me I guess . . ."

Joshua Burridge knew she never guessed anything. She knew exactly what she was doing.

"What I think about what?" he said, patiently playing the game by her rules.

"Well, if such a case came about, hypothetically speaking of course, would it be a case that you'd wanna try? And would it be a case you'd feel would be in the public interest to admit TV cameras into your courtroom? Obviously, I'm speaking hypothetically of course"

"Of course!" he replied, the faintest trace of a smile crinkling his lips. After a brief period of consideration, he readied himself to answer. "Well, in the hypothetical scenario you've posed: *yes*, I'd want to take the case and *yes*, I'd almost certainly admit the cameras into my courtroom. But of course, my answers are as hypothetical as your questions!"

"Of course!!" Jade replied smiling, happy she'd got what she came for.

* * * * *

Television cameras had been an everyday occurrence in state courts since the early-Nineties and innovations like Court TV had made the real legal system as popular with viewers as the Hollywood razzed-up version. In addition, high-profile trials like the O.J. Simpson case had generated massive public interest as well as record-breaking viewing figures.

Put simply, they made for good TV.

Though the Supreme Court opposed the cameras, the esteemed nine were eventually forced to concede defeat to a determined Senate and overwhelming public opinion. Late in 2005 Senate Judiciary Committee Chairman Arlen Specter declared that TV cameras being allowed into the federal court system was "a question of *when*, not *if*."

He was right. Within months, Congress had passed a bill permitting broadcast access to all three levels of federal courts, leaving the decision to say *yes* or *no* solely at the discretion of the presiding judge.

Joshua L. Burridge was the first Ninth Circuit judge to admit cameras into his courtroom and in doing so he became just the sixth in the whole of the United States.

He wasn't afraid to make history; nor was he intimidated by the spotlight.

In fact, he revelled in both.

CHAPTER FORTY-TWO:

Jade LaHoya and her staff worked overtime most of the summer.

She'd long-since identified the case as *the big one* and she had no intention of messing it up or letting it pass her by.

Investigations can sometimes take years and because the federal court system, unlike the state system, doesn't put limitations on funding, prosecutors are encouraged to do a thorough job. Another bonus over the state system is the ongoing access to international agencies and of particular benefit was the link Jade established with Interpol and with the French Security Service. Given that Laos was a French colony till 1949 and the French influence was still very much in evidence at the time of the incident, the link helped improve her context for the case.

She made three separate visits to Laos that summer, Bian accompanying her on two of the trips. For Jade, it was enlightening if a little traumatic, to see everything first hand: the site at the riverbank, the fields Tong Tenh and Mai-Ly worked together, Minh Ngoc's grave etc. She was even there when the FBI pathologist exhumed Minh's body.

Spending so much time with Bian proved beneficial too, helping Jade understand what made her tick, her gentleness and innate niceness. She marvelled at the lack of bitterness and anger and also saw what Claudia had told her many times, that left to her own devices Bian would have been happy to let sleeping dogs lie. It was Troy, who felt the Dogs should pay.

Jade and Bian got on well and on the long flight back to LA after their second visit to Laos, she took the opportunity to broach something that'd been on her mind for months. "There's something I need to ask you Bian. Do you think Nguyen Thimay would take a paternity test?"

Bian had seen less and less of her son ever since he first went off to Yale in the mid-Nineties. After graduating top of his class, he went on to do research and a masters in viral pathogensis at Oregon State University. He'd been at OSU when he and Bian had first visited Laos in early 2000. It was a time of great soul-searching for Thimay. He'd asked Bian about his father and been devastated to hear he'd been born as a result of a rape. In Laos, his uncle Tong Tenh told him the full story: how his mother had not been brutalized by one man but by four. It was a massive shock which he'd dealt with in much the same way as she had: he locked it away.

He'd planned on returning to Florida after his masters but was horrified when he heard that Troy and Bian were talking to *American Dream* magazine. It was what prompted him to stay in Oregon. He wasn't short of job offers, opting for a role with Katex Microbiology in Portland.

Few places in the U.S. are further from Florida.

He refused to talk about the investigation and each time Troy or Bian mentioned it or even alluded to it, he blanked them, sometimes even leaving the room altogether. His visits to Florida became less frequent and Bian hadn't seen him in over six months. Their only contact was a weekly telephone conversation but it was always Bian who had to make the call.

Mother and son had never had so little to do with one another.

"I don't think he'd go for it Jade," Bian said before posing her own question: "Why do you ask?"

"Paternity would establish that one of the three white guys is the father of a child conceived as a result of the incident. That puts them at the scene. And if one is at the scene, it won't be hard with your brother's testimony, to prove all four were there. It would make things much easier."

"I can see that but Jade, I know how Thimay thinks. Knowing his real father is one of three rapists is hard to take; knowing precisely which one would be even harder. I'm sorry but I can't see him agreeing to a paternity test. It would reveal something he'd rather not know."

"OK, I understand," said Jade, sensing it was time to back-off.

The last thing she wanted was to alienate her star witness.

* * * * *

For months, the case dominated Jade LaHoya's life.

Every angle was covered, except one. She was still unsure of what to charge the men with.

There were three main cases to answer: the assault on Mai-Ly, the rape of Bian, and the murder of Minh Ngoc. Early on, she'd hoped to prosecute all three under a war crimes umbrella, establishing that the acts were committed by U.S. servicemen serving in Southeast Asia at a time when the U.S. was at war with Vietnam. But neither the military nor the Defense Department would play ball and despite every threat she could think of, she couldn't get a single high-ranking individual, or office or department – either governmental or military – to acknowledge there was any case to answer. She thought about naming and shaming but she knew it would only antagonise the likes of Harvey Bettinger in Washington. As U.S. Attorney General, Bettinger was the Federal Government's chief law enforcement officer and that made him her boss, a boss who'd already fired several warning shots across her bows.

Without Bettinger's tacit support, she knew she had zero chance of securing the co-operation of the military and less than zero of prosecuting the men for war crimes.

The conclusion wasn't just disappointing; it had other consequences too.

"Team, we're hitting a brick wall on the war crimes front," she said to the half-dozen key players on her staff. "No-one's talking. The Justice Department jungle drums are all negative and without actually saying so, Harvey Bettinger has done his best to warn us off. Frankly, we're on our own and it's clear we have to fight this one alone."

She sighed and took a deep breath. "We haven't lost a major trial for over three years. We are winners and we'll keep winning so long as we stick with what we know and let's face it, we don't know war crimes. Now, essentially, we got three crimes committed against three individuals, the case complicated by the fact it all happened over thirty years ago and that two of our victims are long-since deceased, one of them, Minh Ngoc, killed as a direct result of the incident. This obviously raises Statute of Limitations issues but there's another complication too, in that the entire incident took place outside the United States so there's some confusion concerning jurisdiction. But thankfully, something called 'extraterritoriality' comes to the rescue and gives us the jurisdiction we need to press charges and try the case. While as a department, we've never tried anything under extraterritoriality we do know a few federal judicial districts that have."

Ami Ricker, Jade's head of research, looked confused. "What's extraterritoriality Jade?"

"Basically, it's the jurisdictional element that allows for the prosecution of citizens for crimes committed outside of one's own country. It's been around a long time but it's been tightened of late to cover cases where say, American paedophiles travel to Third World countries for the purposes of having sex with minors. They go thinking they're safe because they're a long way from home. But extraterritoriality allows us to try them as if the offense was committed in their own street! Ed and I have come up with a half-dozen examples of recent prosecutions where extraterritoriality has been central to the case."

She nodded to Ed Nishi sat opposite her.

"Thanks Jade. Yes, all six cases involve procuring sex with minors but I can't see any problem in extraterritoriality extending its net to cover our guys."

The point was typical Ed Nishi: definitive, strong, confident. It was the main reason he'd be Jade's number two in the People versus Fernando, Kingsbridge, McBride and Sanders. As a thirty-two year old Japanese-American, Jade also felt Ed's oriental features could add value, a kind of symbolism, to the prosecution case.

The rest of her team were administrators rather than lawyers so Jade knew she had to spell out the position carefully and with clarity.

"So," she said, taking the reins once again. "Extra-territoriality allows us to try the case but the unanswered question is, *on what charges?* Under the war crimes banner, there's no time limit, so we could've gone for the whole lot. But because the war crimes route is blocked, the Statute of Limitations really complicates things. In fact, it's a mine-field, and potentially, the defense will create such a sand-storm we'll all be old and wrinkly before we finally get to court."

"I'm already old and wrinkly!" chirped Clark Shaffer, head of public affairs, his quip helping ease the tension.

"Seriously though," Jade said with a smile. "The clock *is* ticking. It's now or never."

"So what are you thinking Jade?" Ed Nishi asked, already knowing the answer. He'd been the only one she'd briefed. The question was his way of opening the door for his boss.

"Well, firstly, the assault looks a no-no to me I'm afraid. Thirty years has probably put too much distance between us and the crime."

That was the easy bit; now came the big one, the bombshell. She took another deep breath.

"I regret to say I've come to the same conclusion on the rape. Even though the victim is still with us and we've got first-hand testimony, the defense lawyers will be rubbing their hands at the Statute of Limitation implications. Thirty-odd years is a long time and they'll pull every stroke they can to delay, delay and delay some more. It's perfectly feasible all four defendants will be dead before a rape case can be brought to trial. Though it hurts me to say, I think we need to leave the rape, like the assault, on the shelf."

"Oh Jade!" Ami Ricker exclaimed, her disappointment echoing what everyone in the room was thinking, everyone except Ed Nishi. He'd expected it, because the strategy was one he'd helped arrive at.

"No, the time's come to focus on what we do best; what we know. And no-one does murder better than us. It's quick, clear and concise with no Statute of Limitation complications, given there's no time limit for murder. We have a victim. We've exhumed her body, admittedly thirty years after the offense was committed, but the FBI pathologist's report clearly indicates the cause of death was a blunt instrument smashed into her forehead with such force it shattered her skull and broke her neck. We got great eye witness testimony, from Bian and her brother. We can call villagers who helped clean up the immediate mess of the incident. And we've got the Catholic priest to give us quality after-the-fact testimony, both personally and through his diaries. Though the army denies it, we can prove that the four guys know each other, that they were working together on active service in Southeast Asia and that they were at the scene on the day the incident took place. We may even be able to prove that one of them is the father of Bian's child, *if* we can get the kid to take a paternity test. But that's a big *if*. But even if we can't prove paternity we have stacks of evidence and testimony, like the black guy's birthmark, that puts the men at the scene. Ed, what was it the skin guy told us?"

Ed Nishi opened his notebook.

"The chances of there being another black man, the same age, same size, with comparable muscularity and same skin tone, with the same star-shaped birthmark, the same shade, situated in the same place, half-way up his right buttock . . . is more than . . . thirty billion to one!!"

"Given there's just six billion people on the planet," Jade declared, "I think we've a pretty good chance of proving Eugene Sanders was at the scene! Ultimately, all we have to do is get him to drop his pants! And if *he's* there, they're *all* there. After all, they were a team: the Bleeding Dogs. Gung-ho crap! They'll be the Bleeding Puppies by the time we finished with 'em!!"

She paused, composed herself ready to deliver the final verdict.

"So there we are guys. We stay with what we know, what we good at. We prosecute a murder trial with everything we got, and we got plenty. We look at conspiracy to commit murder – Ed's still working on that one. We use the assault and the rape especially, as testimony to help prove motive: that their lust justified the removal of anything in the way of them exercising the demands of such lust. Killing, murdering, it was all in a day's work to these guys. But this time they went too far; they landed on our desk!"

Like a coach team-talking her players prior to the big game, Jade looked at each in turn before delivering her parting shot. "OK guys," she said pausing, "Let's do it!"

CHAPTER FORTY-THREE:

Six weeks later Jade LaHoya and Ed Nishi were in court to see Judge Omar Dinkley empanel a new Grand Jury. They'd have preferred to be somewhere else but given that every case they wanted to bring to court over the next eighteen months would need to pass the Grand Jury litmus test of probable cause, they both knew it was a necessary evil.

Behind the rail sat over ninety upstanding citizens of LA and fussing round them, clipboards in hand, was an army of blue badge carrying Jury Service staff.

Of the ninety, most were hoping and praying it would be anyone but them.

Empanelling a Grand Jury was something the fifty-one year old Judge could do standing on his head. "Ladies and gentlemen, it is my pleasure to welcome you to the California Central District Court this fine August morning," he declared in his squeaky high-pitched voice.

After explaining the role of the Grand Jury, how it worked and how important it was to the legal system, he and Jade and her team began questioning the potential jurors and by mid-afternoon the original ninety had been pruned to seventy-three.

"The court clerk will now draw nineteen names from the box," squeaked Judge Dinkley.

Five minutes later, the clerk placed nineteen small cards in front of the Judge.

"OK . . ." he said before beginning the process of calling the names.

On hearing their name, each juror walked towards the front of the courtroom before being shown to a seat either in the jury box itself or on the chairs immediately in front of it.

After the nineteenth had sat down, Judge Dinkley spoke directly to those still sat behind the rail, most of whom were wearing expressions somewhere between relief and outright delight. "I know how disappointed you'll be at not making the cut," he said. "So it brings me true pleasure, outright joy even, to inform you that while you've not been selected for the new Grand Jury, you will be carefully considered for service as a trial juror. I hope that allays your disappointment and sincerely look forward to seeing you in my courtroom sometime soon."

It was as funny as Judge Omar Dinkley got.

Next, he turned his attention to the chosen ones, the nineteen.

"The court clerk will now read the oath."

"Do you solemnly swear that you will faithfully discharge your duties as grand jurors; that you will fairly hear and decide all issues and matters before you, so help you God?"

The nineteen answered with a chorus of "I do's" and sat back down.

"Ladies and gentlemen," the Judge squeaked, his voice in stark contrast to the rich baritone of the court clerk. "You have been duly sworn as grand jurors for the United States District Court and will serve for eighteen months. As a grand juror your duties will not be onerous on your time. You will meet every day this week and thereafter spend one-day-a-month considering cases placed in front of you by the U.S. Attorney and her team."

The Grand Jury's part within the American legal system is set by the Constitution, the Fifth Amendment declaring, "No person shall be held to answer for a capital, or otherwise infamous crime, unless on a presentment or indictment of a Grand Jury . . ."

Judge Dinkley explained that the Grand Jury's primary role is to determine whether a prosecutor has sufficient evidence to take the accused to trial. "As such," he said, "It is the Grand Jury not the government that determines whether a citizen should be charged with a crime."

With defense lawyers unwelcome and proceedings taking place in secret, the prosecution puts the facts to the Grand Jury, arguing that the case should go to trial. If the jurors agree, they return the indictment with the words *True Bill* written across it by the foreman. If it disagrees, the foreman writes *No Bill*.

In eleven years as a federal prosecutor, Jade LaHoya had never seen the words *No Bill* and she didn't expect any of the cases she held in her hands to be the unwanted first. But just in case, she thought it prudent not to put the most important one at the top. So after securing indictments on a grand theft auto case, an incident of serious domestic violence, and the armed robbery of a Shell Service Station, she found herself looking down at the file ticket that said "People versus Fernando, Kingsbridge, McBride and Sanders."

The Bleeding Dogs had risen to the top and were next in line.

Jade was so confident she hadn't even asked Bian to appear. All she'd done was fly Federal Agent Jerome McWilliam and two of his FBI colleagues over from Florida. Twenty minutes of testimony between them was all that was needed. On the basis of what they'd heard, all nineteen members of the Grand Jury were unanimous. The four men, once collectively known as Bleeding Dog Company, were going to trial, charged with murder and with conspiracy to commit murder.

Their victim, a tiny Laotian woman called Minh Ngoc.

Michael Gonzalez, appointed by Judge Omar Dinkley as Grand Jury foreman, scribbled the words *True Bill* across the indictment the same time Jade LaHoya nudged Ed Nishi, scribbling something of her own on the notepad in front of her.

"YES" she wrote, in capital letters, followed by four exclamation marks!!!!

* * * * *

Michael McBride was in the last place he wanted to be, the spotlight, in front of a Judge who'd asked him a very direct question. He was slow to answer and the Judge became angry, his emotion given an outlet by his vigorously swinging his gavel. Each time he did so, it slammed into its wooden block with a sharp crack which, like his muffled words, echoed inside Michael's head.

"Daddy, Daddy, the police are at the door!" said Charlotte McBride, shaking her father stretched out on the sofa. "They've come for you Daddy."

Michael was awake in a trice, frantically trying to clear the dream from his brain.

He knew the time had come. He'd been expecting it for months, years, maybe even decades.

And at the precise same moment the law enforcement officer rapped on his door, federal agents in Fort Worth Texas, Forest Park Chicago and Cardboard City Los Angeles, were arresting Eugene Sanders, Rudi Kingsbridge, and Frankie Fernando.

After each stated their name, the arresting officer said exactly the same thing.

"I hold in my hands a warrant for your arrest. You are charged with the murder of a human being, namely Minh Ngoc of Ban Hatsati, Laos, on 17th June 1972. You are also charged with conspiracy to murder the same person. You have the right to remain silent. Anything you say can be held against you in a court of law. You have the right to legal counsel and if you cannot afford a lawyer, one will be appointed for you. Your lawyer may be present during your interview and interrogation on these charges if you so choose."

Of the four, only Frankie said anything in response, the other three sticking rigidly to the advice they'd received from their lawyer.

The only thing that left their lips was their breath, and all three were breathing a little faster than normal.

CHAPTER FORTY-FOUR:

"We got 'em Jade!" Ed Nishi declared. "Kingsbridge, McBride and Sanders are in the air and Fernando's downstairs."

"That's great news Ed."

"The officer who arrested Fernando said it was the strangest arrest he'd ever made."

"Why?"

"Fernando had a bottle in his hand but wasn't especially drunk. Apparently he said, 'Where you been? I been waiting for you,' before babbling on about jail putting a roof over his head and feeding him. The officer said his words were clear, as if he'd thought it through, reasoned it out."

"All that wine's fried his brains," Jade said. "What time the others in?"

"McBride will be last, and he'll be in by 06:30 tomorrow morning. What time you planning to interview them?"

"I think we'll let them stew a little and start shortly after lunch. But whatever happens they're up before Burridge on Thursday morning. That's one arraignment we don't want to be late for! And don't forget, I want them isolated till the last minute. Understand?"

"I got it Jade," Ed replied, rolling his eyes. It was the twentieth time she'd mentioned it. "You need to go home Jade; rest-up for tomorrow."

"Yeah, I will, but I got a few things to attend to first. But, thanks for caring," she said as she added another item to the to-do list on the pad in front of her.

Two seconds after Ed closed her office door, Jade LaHoya picked up her phone.

"Hey Claudia, how are you? I got some news . . ." she said, already scratching the topmost item off her list.

* * * * *

With his hands cuffed behind his back, Michael McBride was led to the waiting police car.

"It'll be OK honey. Phone Marm; tell her to let Robert O'Meara know what's happened."

"OK Daddy," Charlotte sobbed, the flashing blue light of the police car intermittently picking out the tears streaming down her face. The pretty teenager had thought she was a big girl, equipped for anything. Now she knew she wasn't.

Robert O'Meara arrived at the Boston FBI Office ten minutes before his client. Though a little surprised by its suddenness, he'd always known the moment would eventually arrive.

For the lawyer defending the three other Bleeding Dogs, one Benjamin Charles Akerman, there wasn't even the slightest element of surprise. He was already in the air, sat six rows behind his most important client cursing the fact fully booked "First" and "Business" sections meant he had to suffer the indignity of sitting in the cheap seats.

Earlier the previous day he'd been tipped-off that Rudi Kingsbridge would to be arrested nine that evening and would be on the American Airlines midnight flight to LA. Minutes later, cool as ice, Akerman called his client to break the bad news before having his secretary book him onto the same flight. He also called Sanders in Fort Worth but Frankie was unreachable, mobile phones not exactly a life-essential in Cardboard City.

As Ben Akerman saw it, being ahead of the game was a privilege of intellect and talent. And he wasn't exactly lacking in either.

He pressed the button to tilt his economy class seat backwards, disgusted it only reclined three or four inches. Six rows in front, he could see Rudi Kingsbridge sat between two federal agents.

"Good night!!" he said grumpily before doing what he always did when he felt sorry for himself: he thought about the money, the money he was making at the expense of his richest client. Representing three clients as one, his fee was three thousand bucks an hour. Adept with figures, he quickly calculated that by the time he started work the following day, he'd be the best part of forty grand richer. And for that, he could even suffer life in the cheap seats.

* * * * *

"The sons of bitches haven't said a single word!"

"But Jade, we didn't expect a confession," Ed said as his boss flicked through the pages of a glossy magazine. "What's that you looking at?"

"The new issue of American Dream; it's out today. Here, take a look. What a brilliant front cover huh?"

"It's certainly eye-catching," Ed replied, admiring a full page cartoon depicting four growling Bullmastiff type dogs, all chained up behind bars under a headline that blasted, *GOT YOU!! Bleeding Dogs Arrested!*

"There's some great coverage inside too," Jade said.

"This is one magazine really ahead of the game!" said Ed sounding naïve, but never doubting for a second where the magazine got its information from. Even so, he was blissfully ignorant that the entire time-line for the People versus Fernando, Kingsbridge, McBride and Sanders was being dictated by *American Dream's* production schedule. Ensuring the magazine got the front page it wanted for its October issue was the only reason Jade LaHoya had waited till the last week of September to apply for the men's arrest warrants.

Ed was fishing but Jade had already moved on.

Her mind was on the arraignment scheduled for ten the next morning before the Honourable Judge Joshua L. Burridge.

* * * * *

"Is she asleep?" Jade asked as her husband re-entered the room.

"Yeah, and we're all alone!" he said looking forward to a few hours with the beautiful wife he'd hardly seen over the previous six months.

Even before he'd sat down, the phone rang. He knew it wasn't good news.

"Good evening Mrs LaHoya; Joshua Burridge here. I think we need a meeting before tomorrow's arraignment. I've asked defense counsel to come to chambers nine-thirty this evening. Can you make it?"

There was no way she was going to let Burridge meet defense counsel without her being there.

"Yes Judge, no problem," she answered, miming "I'm sorry" to her husband who was already on his way out the door.

"Excellent; and Mrs LaHoya, use the rear entrance."

By the time she pulled off the Santa Anna Freeway she could see why the Judge suggested she use the back door, the front steps crawling with reporters and a dozen film crews.

"How are you Judge?" she said with a smile before nodding to two men stood six or seven feet in front of Burridge's massive mahogany desk.

"Glad you could make it Mrs LaHoya, let me introduce Robert O'Meara, defense counsel for Mr McBride," he said pausing so Jade could shake his hand. "And this is Ben Akerman, counsel for Messrs. Kingsbridge, Sanders and Fernando."

Again he paused, this time a little longer as he searched through the papers on his desk.

Akerman immediately saw his chance.

"You are gorgeous and we are gonna look so good together on primetime TV!"

He'd caught her off-guard but she hid it well and didn't rise to the bait.

At thirty-five, Ben Akerman was the archetypal slick, sharp-shooting lawyer: quick, articulate and a gifted orator. He also happened to be tall, lean, and very good looking, his thick mop of sandy blonde hair sitting atop his strong, exceedingly handsome features. Jade had put on something smart but simple, certainly nothing so sharp it could be construed as power-dressing. Akerman however, looked film-star perfect: Gucci shoes, fifty thousand dollar Rolex and an exquisitely tailored Versace suit in a blue so dark it was nearly black. It was a combination that made Jade feel decidedly plain, frumpish even. It was all in the mind though; Jade LaHoya would have looked good in a black bin-liner!

"Now we're all acquainted, let's move on," the Judge declared. "As you've seen, we're attracting considerable media attention, so I want us to move quickly. The arraignment is set for ten tomorrow."

"Sounds fine by me Judge," Jade said flashing a smile straight out of a toothpaste commercial.

She'd known about the timing of the arraignment for the best part of a week.

Akerman eyed her suspiciously, wondering if he was missing something.

"What's happening here counsellor?" he whispered, "You giving the Judge something more than advice?"

Once again, she refused to bite anything other than her lip.

"We'll hear the case in court number one," Burridge continued, blissfully unaware of the games being played out by two of the three lawyers in front of him. "It's the only galleried court we have and by far the largest."

It was Jade's turn to spot her chance.

"And court number one is the only one big enough to accommodate you and Mr Kingsbridge's inflated egos!" she snapped, speaking at almost normal conversational pitch. Jade knew Burridge was a touch deaf, especially if he didn't have the benefit of looking straight at the person speaking. As his head was down in his papers, she sensed a chance for some retaliation.

"Nice one Mrs U.S. Attorney," Akerman replied looking at his watch. "It's nine forty-five. Shouldn't a wife and mother like you be at home ironing or washing the dishes or something?"

She snorted in disgust.

"But I have to warn you counsellor," he continued, "Playing happy families as a housewife is no way to prepare for a courtroom encounter with me! I'm gonna eat you alive and I bet you can guess which bit I'll start with?"

"I'm not used to losing counsellor," she retorted as the Judge lifted his head. "I was born to stand on the winner's rostrum."

"Right then," Burridge said, oblivious to the verbal exchange, "Is there anything else we need to consider that won't wait till morning?"

"Yes Judge, I got something."

"Yes Mr Akerman."

"Judge: I'd like to express my dismay at the obvious lack of privacy my clients are being forced to contend with. First of all there's hardly much of a case to answer from what I can see and secondly, I just can't imagine how it's going to be possible to find twelve people who haven't already been prejudiced by the media's obsession with this case?"

"I take it therefore counsellor, you intend filing a motion for change of venue?"

"Yes Sir."

"Well, let me save you some time. Motion denied!"

"But Judge . . ." Akerman whined, looking at O'Meara expecting support.

Michael McBride's lawyer stayed silent.

"I think we'll leave it there for tonight," said Judge Burridge firmly, closing the file in front of him. "We'll see you all in the morning."

"Who's the *we* Judge? You on the same line of scrimmage as the prosecution?"

Burridge wasn't amused, his response curt and heavily peppered with four-letter words.

But Akerman didn't flinch.

"Nice one counsellor," Jade said smugly, as the three lawyers walked down the hall towards the huge circular foyer at the centre of the building. "There's nothing like antagonizing the Judge before a case gets started. You learn that one at law school counsellor?"

"Do me a favour lady! I can see straight through you: flicking your hair, flashing your teeth, and shaking those melons. Don't go thinking that making an old man drool will do you any good come trial time."

"Trust me counsellor, you're seeing things that aren't there and hearing things that aren't said."

"Is that so?" he said thoughtfully, planning a surprise. "So what about dinner?"

"What about it?"

"What about joining me for dinner? I can see you wondering, so why don't you just come straight out with it?"

"Wondering what?" she said, walking into his trap.

"Wondering what it'd be like to get *me* between the sheets."

She smiled, broke left as he turned right, "In your dreams counsellor; in your dreams."

It was a good effort but completely fraudulent; she'd thought about nothing else since shaking his hand thirty-five minutes earlier.

* * * * *

O'Meara and Akerman emerged from between the massive sixty foot pillars at the same time; O'Meara walking away from the cameras while Akerman walked directly towards them, like a moth attracted by the light.

They may have both been defense lawyers but that was where any similarity ended. Robert O'Meara had never felt so far out of his depth in his life. He knew he wasn't in the same league as Jade LaHoya and Ben Akerman and without saying so, the Judge had reinforced as much in chambers when he barely even acknowledged his existence. He couldn't blame him; after all, he was a sixty-two year old general practitioner and they were two of America's sharpest and slickest trial advocates. It was like Little League and World Series!

"What am I doing mixing it with film stars? I should be retiring not figuring in America's highest profile case!!" he said, in danger of hitting an all-time low. He was also worried for his client, his friend Michael McBride. Their two families had been friends for nearly a hundred years and there was a lot at stake. Though she hadn't said so, O'Meara was certain Jade LaHoya would be chasing the death penalty. So, it couldn't be more serious.

And then he wondered what he'd wondered a million times; why ever was he involved?

Like each time before, he had the answer in a split-second; it was all down to Michael McBride.

"You may not be a top criminal lawyer Robert," he'd said, "But I couldn't be hiring myself a better man. There's nobody on this Earth I'd rather have standing by me in the courtroom so do me a big favour, and take the case."

And that was it. Robert O'Meara couldn't say no. How could he? He already thought his friend the finest man he'd ever met. And what may or may not have happened in Southeast Asia over three decades earlier wasn't going to change that one little bit.

* * * * *

"Good evening Charlene," Ben Akerman purred as he spotted *NBC Nightly News* anchor Charlene Bortman.

The cameras, TV, Akerman liked to think of it as his world. Seeing his handsome features on television was a regular thing in Chicago and had also happened several times nationally. But he knew this was different; this time it was the big one. As he flashed his warmest, suavest smile at Charlene Bortman he imagined his face appearing on TV screens all over the planet.

It sent a tingle down his spine.

"Mr Akerman, are you representing Rudi Kingsbridge?" Charlene said thrusting her microphone forward. In less than thirty seconds it was just one of dozens. But the interview was with NBC Nightly News and more importantly with their beautiful reporter and Ben Akerman had eyes and words only for her.

"Yes Charlene, I can confirm that I represent Mr Kingsbridge and I'm pleased to tell you that we'll be vigorously defending every single one of the trumped-up charges laid against my client, in fact, against my clients; I'm also representing Mr Sanders and Mr Fernando."

"How *is* Mr Kingsbridge?" Charlene asked, ignoring two-thirds of his clientele.

It didn't surprise him; downtown America was only interested in his most important client. Akerman understood, sympathised even; he too, was only interested in Rudi Kingsbridge.

"He's in good spirits thank you. But like all of us, he finds it difficult to understand how this fairy story has taken more than thirty years to surface and wonders if the energy behind it is that basest of motives, money. He's also concerned that the vast array of community work he's involved in will suffer if he's unable to return to Chicago."

"Will you be applying for bail and will you be filing for a change of venue?"

"Yes on both counts Charlene. I ask you, just how can my clients get a fair hearing in LA? It's already a media circus and we haven't even gone to trial yet!"

The multitude of microphones surrounding him gave credence to his point.

"As I see it, all four defendants have already been convicted in the media. Now don't take this personal Charlene but you and your media colleagues argue you're on a crusade for the truth but the real truth is you destroy people's lives. For the life of me, I just can't see that this is about justice at all; it's already in danger of becoming a freak show! And it's clear that Mr Kingsbridge has been unfairly prejudiced by articles that have appeared in *American Dream* magazine and in a whole host of other press and TV reports that have since made the decision to follow their lead. Whatever happened to the presumption of innocence Charlene?"

"Do you think your client is innocent Mr Akerman?"

"The only thing my client or perhaps I should say, my clients, are guilty of, is being professional soldiers. These men are war heroes Charlene. America and the American people may still be struggling to understand Vietnam but it can't on the flimsiest of charges raised by a woman whose motives frankly look highly dubious, put four of the finest soldiers ever to serve our country on trial simply for being soldiers."

The sharp news anchor knew he'd avoided answering the question. So she put it to him again.

"Do you think your client is innocent Mr Akerman?"

"Yes Charlene," he replied smiling, "Of course my client is innocent."

Lying wasn't a problem to a man who lied for a living. Constant practice made it easy.

CHAPTER FORTY-FIVE:

By eight forty-five next morning, court number one was packed to the rafters.

Fifteen minutes later, the door to chambers opened, the court clerk blaring, "All rise! Court is now in session, the Honourable Joshua L. Burridge presiding."

"And this is only for the arraignment!" he said to himself, surprised by the sea of people and by the air of excitement. He'd scheduled six arraignments for nine o'clock and another half-dozen for ten. He knew that like himself, the crowd was interested in just one of them. With immaculate timing, the sixth case closed on a continuance just as the big hand on the court's over-sized clock pointed directly upwards. It was ten o'clock. His fingers reached for the file marked People versus Fernando, Kingsbridge, McBride and Sanders. When he called it, the hum of the crowd intensified dramatically and rose still further as court officials ushered the four handcuffed defendants into the courtroom via the side door that led up from the confinement blocks. One after another they filed in before being shown to their seats and having the handcuffs removed.

Even though the four unsmiling men were well into their fifties, they looked formidable.

"They look mean as hell," Ed Nishi said, his words reflecting what the rest of the room was thinking. "What must they have looked like thirty years ago? Imagine trying to sleep knowing they were coming for you?"

As Akerman pulled out Rudi Kingsbridge's seat, he noticed Ed whispering in Jade LaHoya's ear. Making sure she could see him, he did the same, whispering to his client alongside him. At the same time, he nodded his head in Jade's direction so she'd see they were talking about her. Kingsbridge turned to give her the once over, smirked the smarmiest smile she'd ever seen, puckered his lips and sent a kiss flying off in her direction. Still smirking, he turned back to Akerman and the two resumed their smiley, hush-hush conversation.

"Those two are made for each other!" Jade said in disgust, more for her own benefit than Ed's. She hated the fact she'd been attracted to her courtroom rival and felt increasing relief it was wearing off.

The Judge called the court to order before explaining what needed to be done so that both statute and court protocol was complied with. He then explained that because there were four defendants, he'd need to read the indictment over each in turn before asking them to plead.

"I think we'll do this in alphabetical order," he said. "Mr Fernando, would you please stand?"

Frankie pushed his seat back and stood to his feet, as did Akerman.

Judge Joshua L. Burridge cleared his throat. "I am holding a copy of an indictment returned by the Grand Jury of the good people of Los Angeles presenting that you, one Franklyn George Fernando, did murder one Minh Ngoc, a human being, and that you did conspire along with others to murder the aforementioned against the peace and dignity of the United States of America."

Total silence descended over the court as he added, "Do you understand the charges Mr Fernando?"

"Yes."

"How do you plead?"

"Not guilty."

After taking Kingsbridge, McBride and Sanders through the same process and hearing each of them enter similar pleas, the Judge said, "Counsellors, now that we've dispensed with the formalities, please approach the bench."

As the three lawyers left their seats, Jade noticed once again that Kingsbridge's eyes were on her.

"My client likes you; thinks you're a stunner!"

"You two are obviously close."

"We are, he's my mentor and role model!"

"OK counsellors," the Judge said curtly. "We got the charges; we've heard the pleas. Now it's time we got this show on the road. I called you forward because I wanted to privately warn you against any theatrics in my courtroom, especially you Mr Akerman. I saw you on *Channel Four News* this morning and I was not impressed."

"No way Judge; I've had three film offers already!"

"Forgive me if I look a little bored counsellor but like I said, there'll be no games in my courtroom. This case is going to trial so let's fix a date and write it in our diaries shall we?"

"Yes, Judge," the three lawyers chorused before turning to go back to their seats.

"You're a natural aren't you?" Jade said sarcastically, adding, "A natural born jerk-off!"

"You noticed the eyes you and me getting?" he replied, ignoring the putdown and deftly changing the subject. "But then again, we do make a good-looking couple!"

His timing was perfect, the punch-line delivered as they separated ready to resume battle positions.

"Let's set us a date for trial then," Burridge said loudly, his words directed into open court. "What we looking at counsellors? How long you need to prepare your case? Mrs LaHoya?"

"We're ready to go right now Judge and tomorrow's good too!" she said flashing a fake smile at Akerman.

"Mr Akerman? What about you? Where are you with your evidence?"

"Judge I couldn't possibly prepare a defense for my three defendants in less than twelve months," he said, looking at Robert O'Meara hoping for a little support.

O'Meara and Michael McBride were in deep conversation and the deadpan expression on the lawyer's face gave nothing away.

"Twelve months! I could well be with my maker by then!" exclaimed the Judge, much to the amusement of the gallery. "I thought sixty days, and you want twelve months. Well, I suppose I'll have to compromise. Seventy days it is."

"But Judge, don't you think that's unnecessarily hasty?"

"If I did counsellor I wouldn't have suggested it. Whining may be acceptable in a Chicago courtroom but it's not acceptable out here on the West Coast. If you insist on griping Mr Akerman we'll make it six weeks. What's it to be?"

Akerman didn't answer. His eyes were locked on Jade LaHoya grinning from ear-to-ear.

"So where does that take us to Judge?" she asked, enjoying the victory.

"To 3rd December I reckon. Who knows, we may even get done by Christmas. You happy with that? Mrs LaHoya?"

"Fine by by me Judge."

"What about you Mr O'Meara?"

"Yes Judge, we have no issue with the time-line."

"And you Mr Akerman?"

"Your honour, the court may force us to comply to overly onerous deadlines but given this case should never have got to court in the first place, I'll be damned if I'm going to work against the clock once we get to trial!"

"I'll take it you agree then," Burridge chirped, deliberately winding Akerman up even more. "So let me sumarise. We have December three, four and possibly five set aside for jury selection with opening statements after lunch on the fifth or first thing the following morning, the sixth. All pre-trial motions and extenuating matters should be filed by November 19th. Is that it, or is there anything further?"

"The People oppose any request for bail," Jade said loudly, doing her best to get in first.

"Your honour!" Akerman exclaimed indignantly. "The United States Attorney opposes something that hasn't been asked for!"

"I think defense counsel makes a valid point Mrs LaHoya. Perhaps you ought to wait until the words leave his lips before arguing that what he's said is incorrect!"

Jade LaHoya grimaced at the putdown.

"Are we done then?" the Judge added hopefully.

With his eyes fixed on his adversary, Akerman said, "Just a second Judge?" He had his hand in the air and was leaning forward, furtively whispering to Rudi Kingsbridge.

"Yes, what is it Mr Akerman?"

"Your honour . . . we'd like to request bail!" Akerman said through the most mischievous of smirks. "My clients do not constitute a threat to society. Mr Kingsbridge in particular, is very active in the community. He is personally responsible for programs that keep youngsters off drugs, house the homeless, feed hundreds of families forced to subsist below the poverty line and make college education available to Chicago's migrant community. These programs would be adversely affected if he were to be denied his liberty pending trial."

"By the sounds of it, Mr Kingsbridge is an extraordinary man."

"Yes Sir, your honour," chirped Rudi Kingsbridge from his seat. "And you Sir," he added, "Are an extraordinary judge of character!"

It was a quip that brought the house down.

"Order! Order!" Burridge screamed. "It's very unusual to be asked to consider the matter of bail in a capital murder case Mr Akerman, but given the unique nature of the circumstances, I am prepared to consider it. Do you have a precedent?"

"Yes Sir," he declared as all three lawyers rose from their seats.

"Judge, this is ridiculous!" Jade blurted, again, trying to score a point first. "These are desperate men your honour, murderers."

"I think you mean *alleged* murderers counsellor," Akerman snapped. "Whatever happened to the presumption of innocence? Or do you just hang 'em from the nearest tree out here in LA?"

"That's enough counsellors! Mr O'Meara do you have any views you'd like to share with us concerning the issue of bail?"

"My client has no strong feelings on this issue your honour," he replied, Akerman rolling his eyes beside him. "While Mr McBride values his liberty and is not guilty of the charges, he would understand if your honour felt he should be detained in custody till trial."

"Thank you Mr O'Meara, that's most helpful," said the Judge, his eyes speed-reading the papers Akerman had given him. "Well, we have a retired FBI officer, a Mr Lindley DeVecchio, allegedly involved with the mob in New York, charged with murder yet securing release on a one million dollar bail. I'd say that constitutes a precedent wouldn't you?"

His question was met with stony silence, all three lawyers preferring to leave him to it.

"Yeah, OK, I'll run with it," he said after a lengthy pause.

"You can't be serious Judge!" Jade protested, sounding like John McEnroe.

But it was to no avail. Three lawyers returned to their seats, only two smiling.

"Bail is set at one million dollars!"

Kingsbridge patted Akerman on the back before looking at Frankie and Eugene alongside him.

"Don't worry about the money guys. It's on me," he said quietly and smugly.

If he was expecting any thanks it wasn't forthcoming.

"You bet it is movie star," Eugene growled, the sharpness of his words matched only by the ice-cold menace of his stare. "The only reason we're in this courtroom is because of you. We ain't here on no rape charge are we?"

"Shush!" said Akerman, worried the unwanted exchange would reach ears it shouldn't.

But Eugene wasn't finished. "I've a good mind to kill you myself you posing son-of-a-bitch," he added, making sure the round was credited to his account.

It was the Judge, albeit unbeknowingly, who ensured the spat couldn't escalate.

"Anything more we need to discuss counsel? Because I got one if you haven't."

"We'll be filing a motion for change of venue Judge," Ben Akerman said, trying frantically to clear the scary image of Sanders from his thoughts. He knew that if he could get the case tried in Chicago his chances of winning would be greatly enhanced. A jury in LA wasn't going to be easy to influence by fair means or foul and for certain, they weren't going to be impressed by Rudi Kingsbridge's work in the communities of Chicago which had been carefully orchestrated ever since the first article appeared in *American Dream*.

"You can file a motion for change of venue if you wish Mr Akerman, but I can assure you it'll be denied. In my opinion, justice is as likely to prevail here, in front of the good men and women of Los Angeles, as it is any place else. Indeed, with one of your clients residing in LA, I'm surprised you're so keen to wave goodbye to our fair city. I'd also add that our accessibility for prosecution witnesses from Southeast Asia is another reason why we're perfectly positioned to try this case."

Given there was nowhere in the United States further from Los Angeles than Boston and that Massachusetts was one of the few states in the U.S. that didn't have the death penalty, the Judge expected Robert O'Meara to support his co-defense counsel's change of venue motion.

"What about you, Mr O'Meara? You have any thoughts on this?"

"We have no objections to the case being tried in Los Angeles your honour."

Akerman puffed out his cheeks in exasperation.

It was the knock-out blow Burridge needed.

"Motion for change of venue is denied!"

Ed Nishi gave his boss a congratulatory pat on the back. The nightmare scenario had been put to bed; the case would be tried on their patch.

"Anything further?" the Judge added after a pause.

Jade immediately stood to her feet.

"Mrs LaHoya?"

"Judge, we'd like to put on record that we reserve the right to file paternity evidence regarding the natural parentage of one Thimay Templeman, formerly, Nguyen Thimay, son of Mrs Bian Templeman, formerly Bian Nhu Dinh."

"Consider it on the record," the Judge confirmed, noticing his favourite prosecutor was still on her feet. "Is there something else Mrs LaHoya?"

"Yes Judge, we have one more thing. If the court finds the case against one or all the defendants proved, we'd like to formally record that we intend seeking . . . the death penalty!!"

It was pure theatre as bedlam descended all over the courtroom.

Burridge shouted "Order! Order!" and banged his gavel as bailiffs tried to restore calm.

It was two or three minutes before the Judge was able to continue. "Thank you Mrs LaHoya. You may consider your notice served. Now, if there's nothing further, I'd like to say something."

He cleared his throat. It was time for another bombshell.

"It is clear from the massive press and TV presence, that this is a case of huge public interest. In the light of this, I have decided to permit television cameras to cover the trial proceedings starting with opening statements. I realise there will be some objections but since Congress has entrusted me with sole responsibility, I feel certain my decision is both appropriate and correct. Court officials will begin discussions with broadcasters forthwith. We will allow a maximum of three camera positions but additional lighting will not be permitted. Thank you one and all. And counsellors, I look forward to seeing you December 3rd."

With that he rose from his seat, announced to the court clerk he intended taking an hour's recess and watched with a mix of dismay and amusement, chaos descend all over his courtroom. Reporters were rushing for the exits desperate to get to their laptops, while television journalists frantically tried to reunite themselves with waiting film crews.

The news wouldn't wait and big, big news couldn't wait.

Burridge was still shaking his head in disbelief when he reached his chambers. As he settled into his favourite overstuffed chair, his senior clerk had a long glass of orange juice waiting for him.

"Well Roberto, have we given the frenzied media hordes enough to feast on?"

"I think so Judge! For certain, it'll take an earthquake of apocalyptic proportions to keep you off tomorrow's front page!!"

"You know what Roberto? I think you're right!"

Judge Joshua L. Burridge couldn't remember the last time he'd felt so pleased with himself. It had all gone wonderfully well. From the moment Jade LaHoya first put her purely hypothetical case to him early in the summer, he'd known it was going to be the one he'd waited for his entire legal career. The People v. Fernando, Kingsbridge, McBride and Sanders would prove to be his defining moment. Lance Ito had got OJ and Rodney Melville Michael Jackson but he, Joshua Lexington Burridge, was going to try the biggest of them all. He already saw it as *his* case and sharp-shooting, high-dollar lawyers like Akerman could try all they want to prize it away but they didn't have a chance. December was set in stone. It was going to be the pinnacle of his career, his swansong, and not even the President of the United States could take it from him.

As he readied himself for the waiting cameras, Ben Akerman had no idea he was in the Judge's thoughts. As he walked across the foyer towards the front entrance he saw Robert O'Meara talking to someone.

"Thanks for your support with the change of venue motion," he said sarcastically.

O'Meara looked decidedly unimpressed. "Mr Akerman, you must be under some kind of mistaken impression. We may both be representing defendants in this case but please understand me when I say that we are *not* on the same side."

As he walked down the steps, he saw Akerman immediately surrounded by reporters. A split second later, Jade LaHoya appeared from between two of the giant colonnades. A young pretty news reporter got to her first, praying it was the moment she hit the big-time before thrusting her microphone to within inches of the chief prosecutor's lips.

"Mrs LaHoya," she said, "Is it right that you'll seek the death penalty if you win the case?"

"Yes; absolutely!" she answered sounding as if such an outcome would be as beneficial to mankind as discovering a cure for cancer.

Robert O'Meara was happy to leave them to it, glad he *was* from another world.

He was looking forward to going home; December would come soon enough.

CHAPTER FORTY-SIX:

Hushed silence descended across the small army of legal secretaries as Michael McBride walked through O'Meara & Sons general office on his way to meet the firm's senior partner.

Everyone knew who he was and what's more, they all knew why he was there.

"It's good to see you Mike; how you bearing up?"

"I've felt better!"

"I guess it's been tough on you."

"Yeah, but it's all self-inflicted, Robert. It may have been a long time ago but it might just be time to pay."

Robert O'Meara knew his client's thoughts; he'd shared them virtually every meeting they'd had. But this time it sounded as if he was being especially hard on himself.

"But Mike, you're *not* guilty of these charges."

"That's what you lawyers call a technicality if you ask me Robert. I may not be guilty of murdering or conspiring to murder but I am guilty. Instead of stopping what happened or dying in the attempt, I took part. There's no way you could even begin to understand the shame and guilt I've carried all these years."

"But Mike, we have to stay focused. You weren't even at the scene when the woman was killed! The People aren't charging you with rape, they're charging you with offenses you didn't commit. And that Mike, makes you innocent."

"What you say may be true Robert, but I'm still guilty."

Michael had been plagued by thoughts of his daughter Charlotte suffering at the hands of desperate lust-filled men. Would it take him to the place where he could kill again? He couldn't even imagine the heartache, yet he'd played a part in inflicting that self-same pain down on a family of innocents.

"Anyway Mike, the trial begins in three days. Do you have any instructions?"

"No," said Michael unhelpfully.

"What about jury selection Mike? Have you thought about who our ideal juror is?"

"I don't think that's for us Robert."

"But Mike, these people will decide your guilt or innocence on something we both know you're innocent of. And Mike, if this goes wrong, there could be a death sentence waiting for you."

"Don't worry Robert, if it goes that far I can live with it so to speak! Let's leave jury selection to prosecution counsel and that smarmy hot-shot defending the others."

Robert O'Meara had known Michael McBride for decades; he knew that no matter what he said his client wasn't going to change his mind.

"Whatever you say Mike; whatever you say," he replied, the resignation obvious in his tone.

* * * * *

Three days later, it was 3rd December: trial day.

Robert O'Meara picked his way through the melee of excited reporters, news anchors and camera crews all stood on the court steps. It was bedlam, two maybe three times as many as there'd been for the arraignment. He rebuffed the few reporters who recognised him with a stern "no comment" and skipped up the steps trying to look as confident as he could.

It was all an act; he couldn't remember ever feeling more nervous or nauseous.

Half-way up, he passed Jade LaHoya surrounded by a pack of hungry journalists and then, nine or ten steps higher up, he saw Ben Akerman in deep discussion with Charlene Bortman, the *NBC Nightly News* anchor.

Both were where he'd left them more than two months earlier: confidently preening themselves for the TV cameras.

"The beautiful people surrounded by their adoring fans!" he said sarcastically. "Some things never change!!"

* * * * *

"Mr Akerman, are you confident you'll get the jury you want to try the case against your client?"

"Its *clients* Charlene, not *client*," Akerman replied making a point but still managing a smile.

Charlene Bortman restated her question, acquiescently adding the all important *s*.

"It's more apparent than ever Charlene that the unprecedented levels of media attention mean a fair trial for my clients is impossible," he replied in his most charming tone. "The jurors would have to be from Mars not to have been prejudiced by the media's obsession with this case!"

"Does that mean you're planning another motion for change of venue?"

"I think Judge Burridge has made it abundantly clear Charlene, that he and he alone will be trying this case!" Akerman glanced at his watch. "I have to run Charlene but let me leave you with a little something for your viewers."

Charlene giggled, flirtatiously flicking her long blonde hair.

"Knock, knock!" he said.
"Who's there?"
"Rudi"
"Rudi who?"
"Great; you can be on the jury Charlene!"

As he walked away laughing, he saw Jade LaHoya.

She too was bringing an interview to a close, aware the clock was ticking. As she neared the top of the steps, the two courtroom rivals ended up side-by-side, Akerman still smiling after his quip.

"Good morning Mrs LaHoya. You sure are looking good today! It's no secret counsellor, I am really looking forward to seeing *you* in action; and it'll be good to see you do your thing in court as well!!" he said, his tongue creepily wrapping itself round the innuendo.

"Save it for the cameras and your adoring fans," Jade retorted sharply, as the two crossed the circular foyer. "You ready to talk plea bargain yet?"

"Not guilty is not guilty counsellor. That kind of plea doesn't leave a lot of room for negotiation!"

"Change your plea now and we'll save the tax payer a small fortune."

"You're bluffing counsellor. You'd be as heartbroken as me if this case didn't go to trial. You're already salivating at the thought of getting your pretty face in front of the camera night after night! But don't you worry darling, I give my solemn promise that your dream *will* come true."

Jade looked confused as he left his point hanging in mid-air.

"What chance?" she said, putting herself at his mercy.

"Your chance to flash those beautiful melons on prime-time TV!!"

Akerman's timing was perfect, the punch-line leaving his lips just as the two opened the huge doors into court number one.

There was nothing she could do save take it on the chin.

It was round one to Ben Akerman.

* * * * *

The court was jam-packed for the start of what was being described as the biggest trial of all time. Fed by a frenzied media, everyone had a view, an opinion. One poll published in the week leading up to the trial showed that while ninety-four per cent of Americans could identify Rudi Kingsbridge only twenty-eight per cent knew who Vice President Edwin Bradley was.

Even though the trial had yet to start, it was already a global phenomenon.

In a Gallup survey of global media interests, over six thousand reporters were expected to cover proceedings either from afar or in person and one hundred and sixteen newspapers and magazines, many from outside the United States, confirmed they'd be represented throughout the trial. The U.S. networks, CNN, and the major television and satellite companies in the UK, Australia, New Zealand, South Africa, Canada, China, Japan, and throughout Western Europe and the Far East were all covering the trial from start to finish. The setting up of the courtroom television operation involved a dozen outside broadcast wagons with over two hundred miles of cable servicing thirty-eight television stations and nineteen radio stations. In addition, there were more than a hundred video feeds ensuring every last trial detail could snake its way round the globe, eventually reaching into one hundred and sixty-eight countries.

With the likes of Oprah, Larry King, David Letterman and Jay Leno seeming to want to talk about nothing else, the talk-show circuit had been on trial overload for more than two months, the most tenuous link to the case or to its major players somehow guaranteeing a spot on primetime television. Similarly, four hastily produced books on the case had miraculously hit the news-stands in the ten weeks since the arraignment, their authors all getting much more than just their fifteen minutes of fame, TV unable to get enough of their *expert* opinion.

The lawyers too, were on overtime.

Rudi Kingsbridge alone had been personally responsible for filing over twenty cases: eleven against newspapers, one against *American Dream*, six against other magazines, and all four book authors.

But the whole thing had become the equivalent of a media tsunami: an unstoppable force of nature that would have to run its course.

The case of the People versus Fernando, Kingsbridge, McBride and Sanders was already a multi-million dollar industry. Ben Akerman didn't care. He was just happy that lots of the millions were finding their way into *his* bank account.

He couldn't wait for the trial.

In fact, he'd never looked forward to anything so much in all his life.

* * * * *

When Joshua L. Burridge opened his door into court the atmosphere was positively electric.

Unbeknown to the Judge, five minutes earlier, the crowd had gasped as the four handcuffed defendants were shown to their seats. Even though photographs were banned inside the courtroom a half-dozen flashes went off all over the gallery. Magazines need their picture, even if it guaranteed ejection for the photographer.

One such snapper was *American Dream's* Mannie Ortez.

Claudia Kaplan was taking another flyer and after a great deal of deliberation, the reliable Mannie had been selected as her hit-man.

He may have pressed the button just once but frame number seven of a super-fast sixteen frame series was exactly what his boss was looking for: four desperate looking fifty-something's, hands cuffed behind their backs, walking to their fate in front of a watching nation, watching world.

With the headline *You're Going Down!* it was a front page worthy of the magazine's special Christmas issue. Like Bian's ultra close-up that got the ball rolling and the dynamic cartoon that appeared on the cover of the October issue, Mannie's front-page photo graced all five regional issues of *American Dream*.

And inside was the latest instalment in the magazine's crusade for the truth, the story quoting *Jonah the Whale*, an inside source not dissimilar to *Deep Throat* in the Watergate revelations.

By any criteria, it made for gripping reading.

Claudia Kaplan and Mannie Ortez were well pleased, Jade LaHoya less so. She loved the front cover, loved the picture. But being referred to as a whale was something she needed time to get used to.

* * * * *

"All rise! Court is now in session, the Honourable Joshua L. Burridge presiding."

Burridge wasn't in a hurry; he was centre stage and intended enjoying himself. It was the moment he'd waited for his entire career. As he slowly paced the ten steps to his seat, he looked out towards open court. It was way beyond standing room only, every space taken; a thousand people crammed into court number one. He'd never seen anything like it.

The seats immediately behind the bar were occupied by the one hundred and nine people who'd been called as potential jurors. Counsel for the defense had asked for a larger number of jurors to be served than normal because of the huge profile the case had generated. Burridge agreed and one hundred and forty summonses had been sworn two days earlier. Because the names were taken from the voters register and it was always out of date, thirty-one potential jurors had either died or moved, or simply preferred to watch on television rather than take their chance of a ring-side seat.

Like the leading players, the freshly painted court looked picture-perfect, refurbishment budgets frozen for years suddenly released with the stroke of a pen in the two months before the trial.

The Judge sat perfectly central on the freshly varnished raised front bench. It gave him the best view in the house. In front of him, slightly to his left, was the stenographer who sat sideways on, facing the witness stand and jury box. As he pressed the enter key on his laptop, Burridge could see he was safely networked to the stenographer's laptop just twelve feet away. As he saw it, being able to review the evidential transcript at the press of a button was one of the few advantages modern technology had brought to the courtroom.

Burridge thought he detected a slightly nervous air to the prosecution table to his right. Tucked in behind their laptops, Jade LaHoya and Ed Nishi looked tense, while their runner and gopher, intern Kathy Arnott, looked positively nauseous. All three were sipping water from Styrofoam cups, desperately trying to free their tongue from the roof of their mouth.

Twenty-five feet to his left was the defense table. The four defendants were front on: McBride to the far left, Sanders the black man to his left, then the haggard looking Fernando, with Kingsbridge, perhaps one of the most recognizable faces in the world at that precise moment, on the quartet's extreme right. McBride's lawyer Robert O'Meara sat sideways on, to the left of the table, directly opposite co-defense counsel Ben Akerman, lawyer to the other three defendants. They all looked sombre, stern even, except the smiling Akerman who looked positively buoyant.

Beyond the prosecution and defense tables was the bar, the railing, with two swing gates centred directly opposite the Judge. Once the jury had been sworn in, the areas beyond the bar would be occupied by small armies of advisors, assistants, researchers, runners, gophers and legal interns who although allowed to pass papers and the like over the bar, would not be allowed to cross it. That privilege was limited only to those nominated as parties to the case.

Next, Burridge turned his eye to two more areas requiring his authorization and approval: the security and the cameras. It was after all, his courtroom, and it was he who called the shots.

Security was both ever-present and extensive, each of the two ways into court guarded by officers of the LAPD. The main entrance had two men inside and two outside while the door to the confinement blocks also had two guards. All six were armed.

The remote control camera fitted at ceiling level, high above Judge Burridge's seat was switched off and the three fixed camera positions, one central high-up in the gallery and one either side of the court at ground level were all unmanned. Burridge had barred the cameras from jury selection, ruling that live broadcasting wasn't to begin until prosecution and defense counsel were ready to make their opening statements.

The Honourable Judge Joshua L. Burridge took one last lingering look before bellowing, "Order! Order!" the same time he slammed his gavel into its wooden block.

It was the official start of the highest profile case in legal history.

CHAPTER FORTY-SEVEN:

Ben Akerman knew exactly who his ideal juror was.

His preference was for younger women but unlike his lifestyle preference, he wasn't looking for women who were either beautiful or as he would say, stacked, or both. He wanted women who were late twenties to early forties, dowdy looking, perhaps a little overweight but not too fat.

He believed such women found themselves helpless in his presence. "They go ga-ga," was the way he modestly explained it to his vast army of researchers. "They love me; they can't help themselves. If I asked them to put their hands in fire they would, so harbouring a reasonable doubt where the client is concerned is always a piece of cake by comparison!"

While he suspected Jade LaHoya and her staff would've been scouring the list of jurors both sides had been given just thirty-six hours earlier, he doubted she'd have given it the attention he had. Akerman & Co. had a "juror's department" totally dedicated to getting the inside track on potential jurors and given that Rudi Kingsbridge was bankrolling the case, Akerman also had access to both the sophisticated and the less sophisticated skills of *Softly Softly*.

His approach had been developed over many years. As a defense lawyer he wasn't interested in proving anything beyond a reasonable doubt; that was for the prosecution. Ben Akerman's goal was simple, get at least one juror to harbour a doubt. He didn't care if it was a big doubt, little doubt, or whether it was reasonable or unreasonable, imagined or illusory. It just needed to exist. If it did, his clients walked. If not, they'd get a one-way ticket to Death Row. Worse still, his reputation would be in tatters.

"Find me Thomas! Who's my Thomas?" he'd demand of his aides and researchers.

The disciple Thomas, known as *doubting Thomas*, was about as far as Akerman's biblical knowledge stretched. As a devout atheist, he wasn't interested in the Bible. Nor was he interested in morals, or even in right or wrong. The only thing he cared about was winning and for that he needed a Thomas.

His ABCD system saw jurors analyzed and grouped according to sex, race, age, profession, any known history etc. The A's were the preferred jurors; the D's to be avoided at all costs. Women rated higher than men, whites higher than blacks or Hispanics. Younger women were preferred to older women with the dowdy type scoring higher than the lookers. Liberal was better than conservative and educated preferred to non-educated. The reasoning was always the same. "Who can I most easily manipulate?" he'd scream at his aides before demanding, "Find me Thomas!"

Akerman knew what he was looking for. He wanted a woman; a woman who'd never had a good looking man in her life. He wanted her to drool over him, and given that Rudi Kingsbridge was also considered outrageously handsome, to drool over his client too. He wanted her desire, however obvious or however latent or secret, to plant the seed that someone so drop dead gorgeous couldn't possibly say anything but the truth.

But he had another reason to go for the dowdies; they were bound to have a negative reaction to Bian's stunning and ageless good looks. "They'll be jealous as hell," he said, "And envying the prosecution's star witness could fuel doubt and see them lean our way."

In his thought processes, all men were automatically D's. "Any guy with a flicker of life in him will go with whatever *Melons* says and when Bian Templeman takes the stand, they'll be drooling so much they'll be cleaning their shoes with their tongue!"

But he did have an exception. "The only male who'll score higher than D will have to be a bona fide, triple AAA faggot. He won't be able to resist me and given that Mr Kingsbridge is an icon within the gay community it might even give us a sort of each-way bet; a kind of safety net!"

But the homosexual vote was a just-in-case one. Years of history told him that white women found him more attractive than black and that his oratory skills and impressive intellect appealed to the better educated; the ill-educated were often intimidated and therefore, less likely to go with his arguments and rationale. Liberals were usually found amongst the better-educated and were preferred to conservatives for two reasons. First, liberals had a way of finding reasonable doubt in the most cut and dried cases involving the death penalty and second, if the unimaginable happened and he lost the case, the liberals could be the difference between an out-and-out death sentence and a long stretch at San Quentin.

Ben Akerman was in top form throughout the long two days it took to prune one hundred and nine down to a round dozen, the chosen ones: twelve, faithful and true. In the end they turned out to be a straight six/six split, men to women.

Two men and one woman were black and one man a Latino. One of the three white men, a thirty-five year old, was obviously homosexual. Of the five white women, four were what Akerman and his people would've described as *straight A's*, the fifth's attractive good looks rendering her a relatively unhelpful *C*.

His quartet of straight A's exactly fitted the profile, with the homosexual his outside bet and number one target if the time came for blackmail or to get heavy. But that always had the potential to get messy. His hope was that he'd find the girl of his dreams amongst the four.

As he watched the Judge swear in the jury, he snidely said to himself, "You four may look like the ugly sisters but which one of you fancies being called *Tom* for short?"

CHAPTER FORTY-EIGHT:

Robert O'Meara's surprising decision to sit out jury selection helped speed matters up, day two of the trial ending with the chosen twelve in place.

"Court is adjourned till nine-thirty tomorrow morning, at which point we'll hear counsel's opening statements," Joshua Burridge declared.

December 5th was LA's coldest day for ten years.

"Wow, its sharp counsellor!" Ben Akerman said to Jade LaHoya as the pair found themselves walking up the steps to the court, twelve feet apart.

"I thought it was this cold in gangster-land in high summer!" Jade snorted all feisty-like. She'd worked out of North Spring Street for seven years and, ten minutes earlier, she'd parked out front for the very first time. She wanted to make a grand entrance for the waiting cameras so the convenience of the rear car lot lost out to the public car park across the road on North Broadway. It was an unfortunate coincidence that as she arrived at the foot of the steps, Akerman jumped out of his chauffeur driven, jet black Mercedes.

"Us arriving like this, together I mean, will have the press pack talking," he said with a grin.

"You are dreaming counsellor!"

"But don't worry for a second," he said still smirking, "I'll tell them you were magnificent; everything I expected and more!"

"You can tell them any lies you want. But me, I'll tell them the truth."

"And what's that?" he said, walking into her trap.

"That you went all limp on me!"

"Wow, it's icy out here!"

"That's just frosty counsellor. The ice comes later!"

"Charlene!!" Akerman crooned at his favourite news anchor waving twelve maybe fourteen steps higher up, amidst the melee.

"Now don't you forget now," he said turning back towards Jade, a hint of tease in his voice.

"Forget what?" she said, immediately repeating a previous mistake.

"Don't forget to leave that jacket on. Take it off and we'll all know where to hang our coats!" He feigned a shudder at the cold, "Oooh, it's freezing!" he added, still smirking.

Once again, the delivery and timing was perfect. It left Jade helpless. The best she could offer was a gesture of defiance. She lifted her right hand, the middle finger of which was extended, aimed it at her adversary then made as if to scratch her ear just in case it was caught on camera.

It may have looked good but it didn't help her feel any better.

They both knew it was another round to Benjamin Charles Akerman.

* * * * *

"All rise! Court is now is session, the Honourable Joshua L. Burridge presiding."

"Good morning citizens of Los Angeles." he said, looking spruce in a new neatly trimmed haircut. As he spoke he looked out over the packed courtroom. There wasn't a single space, sitting or standing. He hesitated, shuffled some papers and did his best to look busy. It was a sham. He knew the cameras were on him. They wanted drama; he'd give them drama. Slowly, he lifted his head, looked at all three cameras in turn, then looked sharply right towards the jury who, like everyone else in the vast courtroom, were all staring straight back at him.

"Please be seated," he shouted sternly. For the twelve, it took their eye-line lower, making him even more elevated, loftier, supreme. "Citizens of the jury, I trust the hotel was comfortable and the inconvenience of being away from your families not too onerous."

He wasn't looking for an answer. Truth be told, he didn't care if the hotel the jury had been sequestered to was a fleapit or a palace, and he didn't care if they hated the inconvenience. Theirs was a public duty and like all duties, it needed to be carried out not enjoyed.

"Every morning throughout this trial, I'll need to ask you some questions which you must answer as one or as a group. Now, last night, did anyone try to contact you, talk to you, or influence you in any way?"

They all shook their heads.

"Excellent; did you discuss this trial among yourselves?"

Again, they shook their heads. This time, all twelve were lying.

"Very well, I think we can get underway then. Mrs La-Hoya? Are you ready to present your opening statement?"

"I am your honour."

Like the Judge, Jade LaHoya knew every eye was on her. She took her time, deliberately walking the ten or twelve steps that would bring her eyeball-to-eyeball with the jury.

"It's been four years since I became the youngest ever United States Attorney in American legal history. In that time the responsibility of representing the people of California Central and the government of the United States has weighed heavily upon me, the responsibility seeming to increase year-on-year. I don't know if that's because I'm getting older or because the bad guys are getting badder!"

She waited for the last of the jurors, the homosexual, to stop giggling.

"Truth is, I love my job," she said, cleverly changing the pitch of her voice. "There's Mr Akerman and Mr O'Meara over there representing individuals. Me? I represent hundreds, thousands, millions! Why? Well, because I see myself as *your* lawyer, the people's lawyer, and I see us as working in partnership, helping defend our society against the bad guys. Perhaps this is why I feel the pressure. I know sometimes it's a big worry for me. Like this morning for instance. I woke up and you know the first thought I had? Fear; fear that I wouldn't do a good enough job for you the people of the jury who represent the people of Los Angeles. Yes, mine's a job that comes with pressure. I've always seen my role as a link in the great chain of justice that is our country's legal system. You, the jury, are a key link in that chain. Others are the police, the jails, the courts, this court, our trial system, our great judges – like Judge Burridge – and as I said, *you*, the jury."

Joshua Burridge puffed his chest out, redoubling his efforts to focus on his favourite prosecutor.

"We're all part of a team and we've all got a part to play," she continued, again slightly readjusting her voice pitch. "Ours is a justice system that makes it hard to convict criminals. The burden of proof is an onerous one – *beyond a reasonable doubt* – because we must be sure they're guilty."

She paused, turned slightly, and fixed her gaze towards the defense table.

Almost hypnotically, the eyes of the twelve jurors followed her lead.

"Proving these four defendants committed heinous crimes more than thirty years ago, in a place over seven thousand miles from this great courthouse . . . is going to be difficult! But if we play as a team, with all of us playing our part, we *will* get the result we all desire . . . justice!! I know that *you*, the good people of Los Angeles, of America, are ready to play *your* part"

It was a masterful introduction, Jade LaHoya somehow managing to portray herself as team player, vulnerable, fearful, patriotic, caring, responsible and sincere, *all* at the same time. It was her and the jury taking on the bad guys; the underdogs working together in partnership to make America a safer place.

Ben Akerman thought about objecting but he knew Burridge would go ballistic. The research proved it; the last half-dozen defense attorneys foolish enough to interrupt an opening statement all ending up losing their case. It kept him firmly in his seat, though he did occasionally shift position with a loud huff and sigh hoping it would put his adversary off her stride.

But Jade LaHoya didn't even notice; she was busy establishing relationship with her jury. That was the way she saw it; they were *her* jury, in a sense, working for her. And after warming them up, she was ready to give them something to chew on.

"The case we'll put before you will prove beyond a reasonable doubt that over three decades ago in Southeast Asia, in the tiny nation of Laos, a heinous crime, nay, an *atrocity* was committed. An old woman was viciously assaulted, a beautiful young girl not even sixteen, gang raped, and a woman about my age, coldly murdered without mercy. And let me confirm that the reason we are not prosecuting the aggravated assault and rape here today has nothing to do with guilt or innocence; it is purely down to Statute of Limitation complications.

As she spoke she looked over in the direction of the four defendants and once again, like a shepherd leading sheep, the jurors did likewise. They all had the same look, a look Ben Akerman had seen many times. It said *guilty as charged* and confirmed the U.S. Attorney was at the top of her game.

"It was no coincidence that the environment the men found themselves in had *no* police, *no* courts, *no* judges, *no* trials, *no* juries and *no* jails. In short, there was *no* deterrent. There was *no* lawmaking body and *no* law enforcement agency to police the parameters of acceptable behaviour. The result? Four men crossed a line and ending up playing God!" she said raising her voice, catching everyone by surprise, especially the jury.

The twelve gasped in unison, harmonizing a sharp intake of breath.

"We will prove that all four defendants were in Southeast Asia at the time of the incident and we will prove that they were working together in an elite four-man Special Operations unit called Bleeding Dog Company. They were undercover; in fact, they were so far undercover they were invisible. This was standard operating procedure for what is referred to as 'Black Ops' and make no mistakes, Bleeding Dog Company was the *blackest* of black ops! It was a world of non-stop espionage and it is nothing less than shameful that their existence has been denied by both the military authorities and by the Department of Defense. But despite these denials, we will prove absolutely that they did exist, that they operated behind enemy lines, and that the four men who made up Bleeding Dog Company are sat here in this courtroom today."

Once again, she looked over at the defense table and lifted her hand.

"We will prove that the day of the incident, June 17th 1972, the day coincidentally of the Watergate break-in, another tragedy that shocked our nation." She dropped her head, as if to signify how tragic before restarting. "Yes, we will prove that June 17th not only marked the date of this abhorrent atrocity in Southeast Asia, it also marked the end of Bleeding Dog Company. That very same day, the three-link chain of command above the Bleeding Dogs decided enough was enough and the unit was de-commissioned and broken up. We will prove that the men of Bleeding Dog Company were at the scene and we will prove that they perpetrated heinous crimes on three defenceless women. They were soldiers on the edge, full of battle stress no doubt, but they were also full of something else."

She paused. "No, I'll come back to that one," she said with a hint of tease.

"My esteemed colleagues for the defense will argue it didn't happen; that it wasn't them, that really these men, their clients, are soft, kind, considerate family men who wouldn't hurt a fly. It will be nothing more than a smoke-screen. But when you, the jury, peel away the layers, the matter is an easy one. I'm sure you will come to see it as I see it, as simply a question of choice and responsibility. These men exercised a choice, a wrong choice, which placed them in violation of every single code of moral conduct known to mankind and this includes all military codes and the acceptable conduct of warfare. They made a choice to cross a line and now they must take responsibility for what they did. The fact it happened more than thirty years ago and that it all took place on the other side of the world is completely irrelevant and cannot be allowed to dilute the horror of what they did."

"Members of the jury, the case for the prosecution will prove beyond a reasonable doubt that these men killed and that they *conspired* to kill. We will prove motive. Unfortunately, it's a motive that's been around since time began. It's a four-letter word. It's not a swearword but perhaps it should be, especially when it leads to cold-hearted murder!" She paused again before raising her voice, "The word, ladies and gentlemen, is lust . . . L-U-S-T!!"

Spelling out the letters was like personally hand-delivering a jolt of electricity to every single person inside the courtroom and to six hundred million watching on TV. Somehow Jade LaHoya had managed to make it personal and it was obvious from their expressions that the jury had bought it lock, stock and barrel.

But she wasn't finished; she'd left the best to last.

"These four desperate men, the defendants sat before you today, killed a helpless, defenceless, frail woman whose only crime was that she wanted to protect her daughter. The penalty she paid was irreversible and fatal. It was instant death, execution without trial. That is why if you agree with me that these men *did* commit this crime, we shall ask you to enforce . . . the death penalty! The Bible says an eye for an eye," she said, shifting her gaze to the defense table. "These men dealt in the currency of death and now it's time they paid . . . with their own death!"

She took two or three breaths that were almost audible, the courtroom heavy with enthralled silence.

"Ladies and gentlemen of the jury, as this trial progresses your hearts will bleed. It is a story that defies the normal parameters of pain. It will sicken you. It will hurt you. When you feel these emotions I want you to remember what I've said to you this morning and I want you to remember one thing particularly. Never let this be far from your thoughts. It is the very essence of this case."

She turned to embrace the whole court and especially the three cameras strategically positioned round the courtroom.

Speaking slowly and deliberately, she said, "I want you to remember that these four men, for their fleeting ten minutes of pleasure were prepared to kill. Their lust immersed them in a sea of selfishness that was willing to cruelly exploit without a moment's thought for those it was exploiting."

She shook her head.

"Their desire to relieve themselves . . ."

She hesitated as she seemed to struggle, possibly rethinking the terminology she was using. It was another act, albeit one that further heightened the drama. Jade LaHoya knew exactly what words she intended using.

She tried again.

"Their desire to relieve themselves . . . no, let's be open and frank here, after all we're all adults. Their desire to . . . ejaculate . . . overpowered them! It overpowered them!!" she repeated, her delivery and pitch synergizing perfectly in what was an immaculately timed crescendo.

"For a few minutes of fleeting pleasure, the four defendants sat before you today were prepared to commit acts that would cause pain that could reach far into the future. In fact, the pain is so powerful it has transcended three decades with effortless ease!"

With her back to the defense table, Jade LaHoya missed Michael McBride shut his eyes and drop his chin to his chest.

"That is what's on trial here. Whatever defense counsel might say, that's the nub of this case, the reason we're here. It was callous. It was calculated. It was *murder* and it was *conspiracy to commit murder!* I know I can rely on you, the jury, to do the right thing and find *for* the People against

Franklyn Fernando, Rudolf Kingsbridge, Michael McBride, and Eugene Sanders. Thank you and God bless you all."

Looking round the room, she walked slowly back to her seat careful not to miss out any of the three cameras. It was only twelve paces but she had lots to do. She shot her first look over to the four defendants; McBride was bent forward over his knees, Fernando and Sanders staring aimlessly ahead. Only Kingsbridge looked straight at her. She thought she detected a slight smile or perhaps it was her imagination. Either way, she moved on, to the other things on her to do list. Robert O'Meara was rifling through the pilot case by his side, while Ben Akerman had his back to her. She looked beyond the bar, to Claudia Kaplan sat alongside Gabriel Tyner four rows back. She nodded before shifting her gaze two rows forward to Bian, Troy, Tong Tenh and Father Mesnel. She smiled. It wasn't a jubilant or victorious smile. It was more a respectful one, one that said "I care."

She'd practiced it in front of the mirror every night for two weeks.

As she paced the twenty-five feet or so back to her seat, the room let out a massive corporate gasp, as if everyone had held their breath for over an hour. Once the gasp was out it was replaced by an explosion of excited chatter as the buzz engulfed the room. The people in court number one were saying the self-same thing as millions round the world: "What a start!"

Jade LaHoya had done more than hold her audience. She'd wowed them.

It was brilliant, breathtakingly brilliant.

* * * * *

"Order! Order!" the Judge shouted as he slammed his gavel into its wooden block.

"Thank you Mrs LaHoya," he said impressed but trying not to show it. "Court is in recess for fifteen minutes," he said loudly, looking at the huge clock above the door to the confinement blocks.

Thirty seconds later he was in his chambers, smiling gently to himself. He could imagine the television director sat in the car park, cursing the unexpected break in service as he coordinated the operation for scores of television companies round the world.

"Perhaps he now knows that I'm the only director of this show!"

Roberto, his senior clerk, looked confused. He hadn't a clue what his boss was talking about so he said what he knew he wanted to hear.

"Great start your honour, great start!"

* * * * *

"Hey Mick, Jesus freak, get your chin off your chest. You making us look guilty."

Rudi Kingsbridge's words flew passed Frankie and Eugene to the other side of the table.

Michael McBride slowly raised his head. "You make me sick you miserable son-of-a-bitch," he snarled. "Yeah, we're all guilty, but you're the only one guilty of these charges faggot."

His look, his tone, and his choice of last word had them all hurtling back to the jungles of Southeast Asia. It was like Kingsbridge had thrown the overload switch, tipping him backwards into the dark side of his past, an era when deathly menace enveloped him like a second skin.

Robert O'Meara shifted uncomfortably on his seat; it was the first time he'd felt scared in his friend and client's company.

"Let it be man. Let it go," Eugene said calmly but firmly.

"No, I won't let it go Eugene; it's because of him we're here. You know it; I know it. And I've a good mind to let the Judge and Jury know it too."

"And what about the fact we gave our word to one another?" Kingsbridge said. Although delighted to have provoked his rival, he was concerned with the threat to tell Judge and Jury and with the fact he sounded as if he meant it. But he tried to not let it show.

"Listen pal and listen good," Michael growled, "In my world, a word of honour is not a lifetime's oath of silence."

Kingsbridge knew he had to let it go so after muttering a two-word response, he turned to look round the court.

Michael hated the fact that maintaining self-control had suddenly become like the hardest thing in the world. He knew he'd been taken to the edge but silently gave thanks for the words that ended the confrontation. It meant his regression into his past, his reversion to type, was halted and that he'd not taken his irritation with Kingsbridge to the next level, where it had to become physical. It meant he could make his retreat and return to his guilt and to the shame that went with it.

"Did you mean it Mike? About telling the Judge I mean?" Robert O'Meara whispered nervously.

"I dunno Robert. There's such a battle going on in my head. I wanna do the right thing but deep down I want to smash him to a pulp and watch him bleed. I might feel guilty after I've done it but I know there's part of me that'll feel so much better too."

"Come on Mike, you know that's not the answer."

"Yeah, I know. He really gets to me though, like no-one else I ever met. But really, I'm angry at myself. Things like this contaminate your life. And worse, I went and lied about it, kept it quiet for years. It's like Fergus used to say: lies are malignant. In the end, they infect everything."

But Robert O'Meara wasn't listening; he'd put his legal head back on.

"Will you though?" he said. "Tell the Judge I mean?"

"Nah, sorry Robert; Michael McBride may be many things he shouldn't be but he's no grass."

It was another conversation stopper.

* * * * *

"Jade, that was incredible!" Ed Nishi said to his boss as she returned to her seat.

Ben Akerman thought so too but he thought he'd best keep it to himself. The minute the Judge called a recess, he was off to the men's room, unsure if he needed to take a leak or throw up.

The court was still buzzing ten minutes later when he returned to his seat.

As he pushed open the swing doors, he immediately sensed the dark tense atmosphere over the defense table.

"What's up?" he said, squatting down between Sanders and Fernando, avoiding Kingsbridge who looked darkest of all in the process.

"McBride and Hollywood just had another spat," Eugene said calmly. "Irish wanted to smash his face in, break his nose again, reckoned it'd look good on primetime TV!"

"You serious?"

"Yeah he's serious," chirped Frankie suddenly entering the conversation. "It's a good job McBride's a reformed man or you'd be picking bits of your boss off the walls. I should'a let him kill the son-of-a-bitch in 'Nam."

The conversation got Akerman nowhere, so he found himself forced to turn to Kingsbridge.

"What happened?" he queried sheepishly.

"I'll tell you what's happened Slick! You had better get your act together son or we going down." Turning to his left, Kingsbridge beckoned over towards Jade LaHoya. "Old sex-on-legs got your number Slick. It's time you started to earn all those dollars I been throwing your way or perhaps it's time to get *Softly Softly* nail our faggot juror's cat to his front door? You make the choice Slick but understand this: I am not going down for no Gook bitch."

"I got you," Akerman said, feeling that this time he really was going to throw up.

* * * * *

Jade LaHoya lingered in her chair, soaking up the plaudits Ed Nishi was sending her way. She hadn't expected the Judge to call a recess but now that he had, she thought she could make it work for her.

"Troy, Bian, can I have a word?"

"That was great work Jade," Troy said with genuine admiration.

"Thanks Troy," she replied, appreciating the compliment from a fellow lawyer but keen to move matters on. "Look, we've only got a few minutes and I wanted to have a word just to say don't be dismayed if defense counsel pours scorn on your motives. He's got no hard evidence, no alibi; no nothing from what I can see. So all he's going to do is attack us, try to rubbish what we say. Don't take anything he says personally. He'll just be trying to rile you and if he sees you're upset or angry, it'll just feed him and he'll come after you all the more. The best approach is say nothing while he's speaking and don't let what you're thinking show on your face. Aim to be expressionless. Got it?"

"Yeah, we got it," Troy said speaking for his wife. He knew she'd be shaking too much to talk.

* * * * *

As the court usher announced the Judge's return to the courtroom, Ben Akerman was frantically trying to compose himself ready for his first appearance on the global stage.

He played with his lapel pin for the twentieth time, making sure it was square, and put on his rimless glasses which, given the lenses were plain glass, didn't improve his eyesight one bit.

It didn't need improving; Ben Akerman already had perfect vision.

What no-one knew was the lapel pin was a miniature camera and microphone while the arms of his glasses hid two tiny speakers. Both items were connected to the *Juror's Department* at Akerman & Co. But Mario Burns and Angie Nedal, his two most trusted members of staff, weren't sat eighteen hundred miles east in Chicago. They were just sixty yards away as the crow flies, sat outside the court building in what looked like just another TV van in a car park full of TV vans.

The camera in the lapel pin was wide-angled. Akerman planned on standing with his hands on the jury box handrail so his advisors could have a close-up of his five favourite jurors: numbers three, six, seven, nine, and eleven. They were his four straight A's and the homosexual, juror number nine. His spotters would be studying their faces and body language before advising their boss which of the five he should engage at any given point. He was convinced one of them would be his Thomas and he planned on delivering his opening statement as if the five were the only ones on the panel, in fact, the only people on the planet.

"You ready to present the opening statement for the defense Mr Akerman? Mr O'Meara?" asked Judge Burridge, before adding a second question. "Which of you is going first?"

Akerman shot a glance at Robert O'Meara who looked non-committal.

"I'll go first, Judge," he said, rising confidently to his feet.

He looked immaculate, film star immaculate. He walked slowly towards the twelve and put his hands on the rail, his eyes watching their eyes. He knew the nearer he got the better-looking he became to all six women, even the black woman, and to the homosexual who swooned so much he looked as if he'd faint.

Mario Burns picked it up immediately.

"Ben, the faggot; look at the faggot!!"

Akerman obediently locked his gaze on the homosexual.

"Ladies and gentlemen, what a privilege it is to address you this sharp winter's day."

"Juror seven Ben: and smile!" Angie Nedal said sharply.

Akerman switched his gaze to juror number seven. "I thought it only got this cold in Chicago!" he said, smiling a big warm open smile that was immediately reciprocated.

"We got her!" yelled Angie, excited she'd called it right.

Seconds later, Ben Akerman eased effortlessly into his flow. Like Jade LaHoya, he didn't use notes, didn't need them. He'd written his opening statement a month earlier and ate, slept and drunk it ever since. He knew it backwards. And Mario and Angie in the van knew it too because it scrolled across the huge screen that was linked up to the lapel pin camera. Together with the mainstream TV coverage on three other screens in the van, it helped them guide their boss and gave him the edge he was after, the edge that rolled him towards his goal: extreme manipulation.

"I remember when I was a boy sitting with my father watching a TV documentary commemorating the ten-year anniversary of the end of the Vietnam War. Even though I was young, what I saw troubled me greatly, and I could tell from my father's reaction, it bothered him too. And here we are another twenty-five years down the line and nothing's changed; so many unanswered questions, so much pain still to be dealt with."

Akerman noticed Jade turn her head towards Ed Nishi. He could guess what she was saying. "Here's the first smokescreen Ed. Bet it's not the last!"

"Watching that program, I remember the frantic evacuation of Saigon marking as it did the final betrayal of those who'd believed in us, those who worked for us. You could see the fear in their eyes as they realised we really were going to leave them behind. To get everyone out we needed military intervention but none was forthcoming. This was despite the fact that the North Vietnamese assault on Saigon was a blatant violation of the *Peace with Honour* deal so proudly championed by Nixon and Kissinger. But the truth was, there was *no* peace and there was *no* honour. Congress refused to support our friends. In the end, Watergate would bring down a President and his entire administration; but it also sealed South Vietnam's fate. Fifty-eight thousand Americans died in Vietnam and in those last days we wouldn't even give our allies air support! It is to our eternal shame that we fled Southeast Asia leaving over two thousand men as prisoners-of-war or missing-in-action. Thirty years on, virtually all are still unaccounted for. Put simply, we ran away, our leaders and policy makers prepared to abandon anyone perceived as a political liability. Now, even with the luxury of three decades hindsight, we are still uncertain as to how the Vietnam War began. We're uncertain of its military or political correctness or the effect it's had on American life, the American dream or the American people. The war continues to be a topic of conversation in high school classrooms, on university campuses, in bars and saloons and on TV talk-shows. The underlying motive is always to regain our nationalistic sense of pride and to put to bed the guilt and the inexplicable loss."

After a short pause, he started up again, speaking more purposefully than previous.

"The Vietnam War started slowly, without fanfare. It ended quickly, with no more than a whimper. Unlike previous generations, the men who fought so bravely didn't come home to victory rallies and tickertape parades. Instead, they returned to an indifferent nation that seemed to want to blame them for the loss. It was a sorry end to a sorry war, a war the American people are still struggling to understand."

It was Jade's turn to wonder if she should object.

"The reason I share this is that like it or not, the Vietnam War provides the context to this case. On trial today are four defendants who fought with great distinction in a war that's etched itself into the American psyche. Unlike everyone else it seems, these brave warriors refused to run. But interestingly, those currently in charge of our armed forces all agree on one thing: these men *never* served any other unit other than those into which they enlisted, namely, for my three clients, the Marine Corps in respect of Mr Fernando, the Green Berets in respect of Mr Sanders and the 101st Airborne in respect of Mr Kingsbridge. The Pentagon, the Chief of Staff and a long list of the highest ranking military personnel you could imagine all deny that any of these men served, as prosecution counsel alleges, in that *other* unit, the Special Operations group. Now what was it called? Ah yes . . . that's right . . . Bleeding Dog Company! In fact the Chief of Staff and the rest go even further; they say there *never was* a unit called Bleeding Dog Company!!"

"Ladies and gentlemen of the jury, it will be down to you to decide if you believe the prosecution or some of the greatest military and political leaders of our generation. They say Bleeding Dog Company never existed so that must make it a figment of the imagination of a demented military charlatan or . . ." Meaning Lieutenant Colonel William T. O'Donnell, he paused in mid sentence. With every eye on him, Ben Akerman turned from the jury and looked directly at Claudia Kaplan sat at the end of the fourth row on the prosecution side of the aisle. After eyeballing her for two or three seconds, he added, "... *or* an equally demented magazine journalist desperate to see circulation figures improve!"

He paused again.

"However you choose to look at this case, it is clear these men should not be on trial. If anything, it should be the political and military system that's on trial because it caused the Vietnam War. Soldiers like these should be feted, congratulated, thanked. It's clear they are nothing less than heroes, war heroes! Yet perversely, here they are on trial for their lives!"

He took a deep breath, fixed his gaze on juror number nine at Angie Nedal's instruction and sighed a tired sigh. Not only did it make the frumpy juror want to mother him, it also won him the giggly homosexual's sympathy vote!

"They are most definitely not criminals. Indeed, it's a travesty of justice that they're on trial in the first place. But there you are; that's the way the cookie crumbles when a conspiracy of mammoth proportions is at work I guess. Somebody has to be the patsy; ask Lee Harvey Oswald!"

Again, Jade thought about objecting.

"It saddens me that these fine men, war heroes who fought for their country, who were prepared to die for their country, find themselves here at all. But now that they are, it is both my job and my distinct privilege to defend three of these four great men. We will show by way of the case for the defense that the complete military denial proves that Bleeding Dog Company did not exist, except that is, in the imagination of a Lieutenant Colonel obviously suffering from delusions of grandeur. We have volumes of letters to say as much, all with the seals of some of the greatest military and non-military offices of government that serve our great nation. Put simply there is no record of any covert,

Special Forces group known as the Bleeding Dogs. The Special Operations Group, SOG for short, was totally autonomous. They, like the rest of the military authorities, say that it was *impossible* for the four defendants to have been in Laos on June 17th 1972 as there were *no* ground troops in Laos or Cambodia on or around that date."

"Confused? Me too!" he said sending a beaming smile in the direction of juror number eleven.

"The prosecution talks in definites, certainties. Yet the truth suggests there are only shades of grey. And that equates to doubt and any doubt, big or small, means you will have to acquit my clients. Firstly you have to believe that this alleged act of murder and conspiracy to commit murder really occurred. You must then reach the place where you are convinced, I mean absolutely convinced, that if it did happen that these four men were in Southern Laos when our government, the State Department and the like all say they weren't. However, if you believe that somehow, irrespective of how impossible that may be, there *were* four maverick U.S. soldiers in the area on the day in question, you have to be sure that the four defendants were the maverick four! Preposterous I know, but there's more. Just suppose for a second that you get to the place where incredibly, you are sure of all these things, you have to then be totally convinced that they committed the crimes alleged by the prosecution! Mrs LaHoya and her team will do their best to convince you that they have bucketfuls of hard evidence but the truth is all you'll see is flimsy bits and bobs that will require you to be at your most imaginative to spot the alleged link to my clients. I cannot imagine for one second that the burden of proof, *beyond* a reasonable doubt, could be satisfied by such evidence. The prosecution will paint a black and white case. Indeed, Mrs LaHoya has already begun this process with her eloquent opening statement. She speaks as if it's already a done deal but there are *so many* unanswered questions."

"Now we all know the details of this case. We can all read after all! Our newspapers, magazines and television screens have been filled with nothing else for months. We all know that the prosecution's key witness will be Bian Templeman. We know her story. It's been told over and over. The advantage for me as counsel for the defense is that I can refer to her evidence, her story, *now* in my opening statement rather than having to wait for her to give evidence on the stand. Let me add at this juncture that this is probably the *only* advantage of having this case tried in the media before we get to court!"

He looked around the courtroom before continuing, letting his biting sarcasm sink in.

"A whole host of questions have to be asked and answered when it comes to Mrs Templeman and her evidence. The first is the most obvious. Why on earth would she wait more than a quarter of a century to tell the world of this alleged horror? Could it be that this stunningly attractive woman now passed her prime has a desire to be restored to the limelight?"

He turned to look straight at Bian, her face as expressionless as his.

As he turned back to the jury, Mario Burns in the van screamed, "Ben, number six! She doesn't like Bian. She's one jealous bitch!!"

Akerman's eyes fixed on juror number six.

"Let me rephrase that slightly. Perhaps Mrs Templeman's being in the limelight in this trial, seeing her face beamed into hundreds of millions of homes all over the world, is just a swansong for a fading beauty?"

"And here's another thought. What if she's experiencing financial problems or money worries? I would wager she's been inundated by media offers, every one keen to give her a platform to tell her story, all no doubt prepared to pay handsomely for the privilege. And suppose for a second that her marriage – a marriage she's admitted has had its problems – is experiencing renewed difficulties. Perhaps she's worried that her son, an adopted child, will be written out of her husband's will, disinherited at the stroke of a pen. Perhaps this entire case and the allegations it makes is an effort to ensure that she and her son can be independently financially secure for the rest of their lives. How *can* we know? How can *you* know? The answer is we can't. But does it cause a doubt? Does it bring her motives into question? I think so. And let me remind you that *any* doubt is a *reasonable* doubt and that if you should reach this point of doubting, you *must* acquit the defendants."

"But then there's another scenario. You will be told over and over that Mrs Templeman was raped, gang raped. You will be told that it was in the act of trying to prevent the rape that Mrs Templeman's mother was killed. Well, let's ignore her mother's death for a second; after all, we'll never really know how that occurred will we? For all we know, she died from heat exhaustion one hot summer's night!"

Though his words *were* out of order it was his sarcasm that tipped Jade LaHoya over the edge.

"Objection!" she screeched, in her most indignant voice. Her hand was raised and she was holding the report from the FBI pathologist who'd examined Minh Ngoc's remains. "As far as I'm aware your honour, heat exhaustion has never caved anyone's skull in!!"

It was her turn to be sarcastic.

"That's enough counsellors!" said the Judge. "The objection is sustained. Approach the bench please . . . *Both* of you!!"

"Mr Akerman, you're an experienced counsel or so I've been led to believe. You'll know therefore that an opening statement is an opportunity to acquaint yourself with the jury and to outline your case. It is *not* the time to try the case! That's what the examination and cross-examination of witnesses is supposed to be about!"

"Hey Judge, sorry if I strayed. I just got excited; cameras and all that!"

"OK, but don't let it happen again or I might be less inclined to give you the leeway you seem to take as if by right."

"You're doing good counsellor, real impressive," Jade chirped as they turned towards the court. "But I hope your clients remembered their gas masks!" she added, just before Akerman broke right towards the jury.

It was her round but Akerman wasn't interested; his job was only half-done.

"As I was saying before counsel so rudely, I mean, before counsel interrupted me," he said, moving quickly into his flow. "Let's suppose for a moment that this, shall we say, sexual incident, did happen. How do we know it was rape and not consensual sex? Sound ridiculous? Well, maybe. But think of it in these terms. This was a village girl who may've seen hundreds of young girls throw themselves at American GI's. It is perfectly feasible that she could have arrived at the conclusion that getting pregnant was her ticket out of her circumstances, her passport to America. After all, isn't that exactly what happened? As we've heard on TV and read in the magazines, having a Caucasian baby got Bian Templeman into the American Embassy when thousands were being denied entry. Her baby put her on the helicopter and her baby gave her access to the United States, the Promised Land."

Pausing once again to get his instructions, he fixed his gaze on juror number three.

"Who is to say she didn't plan it all? Who is to say, that the opportunity to have sex with four American servicemen was a chance too good to let pass her by?"

"Your honour!!" shrieked Jade LaHoya the same time Troy squeezed Bian's hand so hard she thought he'd crush her fingers.

"Mr Akerman, I suggest you bring this to a conclusion as soon as possible," barked Judge Burridge, clearly not amused.

"Yes your honour, I'm nearly done," he answered, as he turned back to the jury.

"Whatever your standpoint, you have to admit that all these scenarios could be true. If that puts a doubt in your mind, let me repeat, you must acquit the defendants. While I cannot speak for my colleague, Mr Robert O'Meara who represents Mr McBride, I can say unequivocally that in defense of my three clients – Mr Fernando, Mr Kingsbridge and Mr Sanders – we will show absolutely that there is *more* than a reasonable doubt that one, an incident took place by the riverbank in Laos at all, and that two, if it did take place, that these three defendants were the perpetrators of that offense whatever that offense may have been!"

He smiled, turning slowly as if to walk away. After glancing at Bian he paused, appearing to suddenly remember something. In actual fact, he was listening to the instruction from his advisors sat outside in the van. For over an hour they'd been considering which juror should be the recipient of the final epitaph, the climactic killer line.

Both Mario Burns and Angie Nedal were in agreement. It had to be juror number three.

"Its number three Ben; she's fallen for you, head over heels," Angie blurted into the microphone.

Ben Akerman turned slowly back towards the jury. He smiled again, his eyes fixing a deep lingering look at juror number three. He knew everything about the tired, frumpy-looking thirty-eight year old. He knew she was divorced and he knew she was the mother of two wayward teenage sons who gave her nothing but trouble. He also knew she couldn't help herself. As their eyes met, she melted. He could sense her reasonable doubt increase as she fantasised that he could be hers.

"Just for the record, I believe this is not a case about justice or murder at all," he said sternly, his voice getting louder and firmer as each word exited his lips. "It's about Bian Templeman's desire to put her beautiful face in the public spotlight and perhaps even more importantly, to get her hands on cold, hard cash; as much of it as she can carry! It's about money! Money!! Money!!! Money!!!!"

By the end he was shouting at the top of his voice, the thousand plus people crammed into court number one screeching and yelling as pent-up emotions were given a release by the feverish climactic frenzy.

The Judge slammed his gavel shouting, "Order! Order!" But no-one was listening.

Jade LaHoya too, was on her feet. "Judge, counsel is out of order!" she blasted three or four times, the exasperation she felt magnified by the big smirk she'd spotted on Rudi Kingsbridge's face.

"I agree Mrs LaHoya," Burridge snapped angrily, once the buzz around the courtroom had died away sufficiently for him to be heard. "Counsellor, neither the jury nor this court is interested in your opinions or innuendo. If there is any repeat I will hold you in contempt! You got it counsellor? Button it!!"

"No problem, your honour. I'm finished," he said, raising his hands defensively as Jade sat down. There was nothing she could do save glare at him, daggers drawn.

As he passed her on his way back to his seat, Akerman winked at her. It was like pouring gasoline on a raging camp fire and it was another round to Ben Akerman.

Jade LaHoya knew she was too late; the words were out and once out, they always land.

* * * * *

Once Burridge was sure everything had settled back down, he turned to Robert O'Meara.

"Mr O'Meara, are you ready to make *your* opening statement?"

"Thank you, your honour," O'Meara answered as he stood to his feet.

But before he could take his first step, his client grabbed his arm forcing him to bend forward from the waist so the two could converse in whispers.

"Mr O'Meara? We're waiting!"

"Just a second Judge; could you give me a moment please?" O'Meara said, his tone indicating his surprise at the unexpected interruption.

"Take your time; take your time!" Burridge said sarcastically, rolling his eyes for the cameras.

"Your honour, we would respectfully like to decline your kind opportunity to make an opening statement."

"You mean you don't want to say anything?"

"Yes, your honour, I mean no your honour. We do not wish to say anything," O'Meara stuttered.

"Nothing at all?!!"

"No Sir."

"Well I've never heard of that before! No matter. Court is adjourned till one-thirty this afternoon, at which point Mrs LaHoya you may call your first witness."

It was game on.

* * * * *

"Michael, you're paying me five hundred an hour. The least you could do is let me do my job!"

"Robert, I pay you five hundred bucks an hour because you're my friend not my lawyer. I'm sorry if what I did hurt you but after that rubbish from Akerman I didn't think it appropriate for us to say anything by way of opening statement. And Robert, the way I'm feeling, I don't think we should say anything as far as cross-examination is concerned either. So unless we think there's something specific that needs to be asked or unless you see a point of law that needs clarification or something, I think we'll stay shtumm!"

"What a waste of money!!"

"I told you Robert, it's not about the money," Michael said, standing up to allow the court guard to handcuff his hands behind his back. "It's about friendship and trust."

"Straight up Mike, if we didn't have that friendship I'd have walked long ago."

"I know Robert. I know," he said before being ushered out towards the confinement block.

It was time for lunch; lunch in his cell, all alone.

* * * * *

As she motioned to leave the courtroom, Jade LaHoya couldn't resist it.

"Great stuff Mr Eloquent Attorney! You're the only man I know who can talk all day and say nothing! One long stream of endless crap!!"

Her words weren't throwaways. They had a target: Ben Akerman.

As she'd neared the swing gates ready to exit the courtroom, she'd noticed him standing a few feet back from the prosecution table. Though he wasn't speaking to anyone in particular, he had a smug, I'm-so-pleased-with-myself look on his face.

It was like a red rag to a bull.

Jade might have hoped to catch him off guard but Akerman was ready and waiting, still pumped up from his opening statement.

"Careful counsellor," he replied sharply, gently removing his rimless glasses and putting them back into their case, "Or I might think you were jealous because I was outstandingly brilliant and looked better on camera than you."

"What a joke! You were on your feet for over an hour and said zip, dick, absolutely nothing!!"

"Yeah but ask yourself whether any of my jurors took a reasonable doubt into their lunch break with them"

"When did they become *your* jurors?"

"The split-second they experienced their first lingering doubt. If they have *no* doubt, they're yours. But the tiniest doubt, they're *mine*. That's the rules of the game, counsellor!" Akerman replied with a smirk. "You know your trouble counsellor? You take things too seriously. You need to relax. A good looking girl like you deserves the best. Me!! Let's face it honey, it's glaringly obvious the man in your life isn't satisfying you. You get that pretty butt of yours over to the Four Seasons tonight and I guarantee you'll be relaxed by the time I'm through. I know *all* the right buttons to press."

"You arrogant son-of-a-bitch! Your schmoozy charm might work on your brainless bimbos but trust me counsellor, it makes make my flesh crawl."

"Ouch, you can be so vicious! That tongue of yours is sharper than a cut-throat razor!"

"I'd like to cut your throat!"

"I love a hint of aggression in my women!"

"I'll show you aggression mister. Wait till I put my witnesses on the stand. All you'll be good for is catching flies you'll be so lost for words."

"Now who's dreaming?" Akerman quipped, obviously thinking he was funny. "Look why don't you do yourself a favour sweetheart? Drop the case now and save yourself some embarrassment. Going head-to-head with me is not for the faint-hearted lady."

"As I think I may have mentioned previously counsellor, you and your boys are going down. All they'll need where they going, is a gas mask!"

* * * * *

Nine days later, Ben Akerman was a worried man.

Two of his straight A's had defected. No longer did he have either their ear or their eye. The sheer weight of evidence presented by prosecution counsel convincing them of two things; one, Akerman wasn't worth it, and two, the four defendants were guilty.

That left him with jurors three and seven who were no more than hanging by their fingernails, and juror nine, the homosexual, still the outside bet and still just managing to keep his cat from being nailed to his front door.

The situation was as hopeless as Akerman had ever experienced.

It wasn't just the overwhelming power of the prosecution case, it was the fact that his defense strategy had been built around smudging, fudging and discrediting both the evidence and the prosecution witnesses themselves. As it stood, the defense didn't have a single witness. He had three defendants to defend, all of whom were almost certainly guilty. He had nothing to offer bar some character references, no-one to specifically say his clients weren't there, or that they didn't do it.

But for Ben Akerman, the eternal optimist, something would turn up.

And if it didn't there was always the faggot's cat.

* * * * *

When Jade LaHoya declared, "Prosecution rests," she couldn't have felt more pleased with herself.

Her key witnesses had come across as very solid people who were unlikely to be lying. Father Francoise Mesnel, the first witness she called, established an excellent platform for her to build on. Three of his diaries from the mid-Seventies were admitted as evidence and though he needed a French translator and it slowed proceedings down to a crawl, the jury clearly hung on every highly believable word that came out his mouth.

The other witnesses – Bian, Gus O'Donnell, the FBI investigating officers, the FBI pathologist, three villagers from Ban Hatsati and finally Tong Tenh – just built one upon another, the case solidly constructed from the bottom up.

The only time anything looked to be going wrong was the Sunday before Bian was due to give evidence on the Monday morning. She looked as if she was falling apart until Nguyen Thimay called her at the LA Hilton to say he and his girlfriend would be in court the following day. Thimay had reacted badly to news that Bian and Troy were speaking to *American Dream* magazine. With mother and son barely talking, they hadn't seen each other face-to-face in over a year. The news that her son was travelling down from Portland to support her lifted Bian's spirits and helped give her the strength to face the four men who'd had such devastating effect on her life.

She started nervously but after a day-and-a-half in the witness box being gently eased along by Jade and Ed Nishi, she warmed to the task. But Akerman's two-day cross-examination was brutal, forcing her to examine virtually every point she'd made to the prosecutors in minute detail. While she creaked a few times and was frequently close to tears, she managed to hold it together. By the end, she was exhausted and missed the first day-and-a-half of her brother's evidence. She may have been tired but the world-wide TV audience was enraptured, TV ratings for her first day on the stand exceeding even the figures for the Super Bowl and the 2006 soccer World Cup Final.

Tong Tenh was the final and key witness, Jade LaHoya leaving best to last. Despite the fact that Tong also required an interpreter, his testimony was so gripping he had the jury, the court and the watching TV audience all spellbound as he described what he'd seen more than thirty years earlier. His revelation about the star-shaped birthmark created a media sub-plot so globally massive it made the "Who shot JR?" mystery from 1980's soap *Dallas* look positively trifling.

The pathology report and Tong's testimony were in complete agreement; Minh Ngoc, his mother, was killed by a direct blow to the head with a rifle butt.

As the prosecution called their witnesses, Akerman hounded each of them mercilessly, picking holes in their testimony wherever he could. In stark contrast, Robert O'Meara, asked by Judge Burridge if he'd like to cross-examine, would stand to his feet and say, "Thank you Judge, but we have no questions for this witness at this time."

The comparison with Akerman's belligerence had Jade LaHoya convinced that McBride had something up his sleeve, something like a very solid alibi.

She was wrong; she just didn't know Michael McBride.

It was three twenty-five on Friday afternoon when she finally brought the case for the prosecution to a close, the Judge chirping, "Thank you Mrs LaHoya. Court is adjourned till nine-thirty Monday morning, when counsel can present the case for the defense."

All through the trial, Ben Akerman had been the darling of the television millions. He'd consistently scored higher in the opinion polls than his opponent, much to her disgust, but he knew that as abundantly blessed as he was in the looks, charisma and talent departments, it wasn't going to be enough to see him through.

This time he needed help and he needed it quick.

It was to come from the most unexpected source.

CHAPTER FORTY-NINE:

It was one-and-a-half-hours into the meeting when Frankie Fernando spoke for the first time.

His five-word sentence exploded like a stun grenade: "I wanna take the stand," he declared.

Rudi Kingsbridge was first to react. "It'd be suicide to let you take the stand!"

Frankie directed just two words at Kingsbridge before turning to Akerman. "If you won't put me on the stand you're fired," he said his eyes firm, cold, but slightly crazy looking.

"Easy Corp, it's OK man," Eugene said gently, trying to soothe the situation.

Akerman shot a glance at his paymaster looking for direction.

"Why you wanna take the stand Corp?" Kingsbridge asked in as non-confrontational a way as he could.

"First up, it's none of your business," Frankie growled, "But paying due respect to Eugene here, who could well be asking the same question, I'll answer it anyway. I was the leader; I may not have been much of a leader but I was still the leader. I want to make it clear that whatever the jury decides happened out there, as team leader, I bear ultimate responsibility. And secondly, I got a story to tell and I want the chance to say my piece."

As he was speaking he drifted from the lucid and the intelligent even, to the slightly crazed and all the way back again.

While Frankie was a loose cannon, Akerman suspected he could score some sympathy from the jury, especially since he was living in LA even if his address was *no fixed abode*. A war hero hung out to dry by an ungrateful nation to the point where he'd become a hobo was bound to press a few buttons. It also couldn't harm his case. After all, lost is lost.

Rudi Kingsbridge had been directly fingered in Tong's testimony and the case for the defense had reached the place where there was nothing to lose. Akerman had started the trial hoping to deny the existence of Bleeding Dog Company. But the evidence indicated the Bleeding Dogs had existed and even more importantly, the jury was of the opinion that it was the four defendants who formed its personnel roster. It all left Akerman clutching at straws; so Frankie taking responsibility for *his* team, even if he shot off a few loose ones, had to be viewed as a bonus for his number one client and paymaster.

At precisely nine-thirty Monday morning, Joshua L. Burridge called the court to order.

"Judge, may I approach the bench?" Akerman asked.

With Jade stood by his side, he explained his predicament.

"We have a situation Judge. One of my clients wants to take the stand. It's possible his testimony could be antagonistic to the other defendants I represent. Therefore your honour I'd like permission to confer with my clients with a view to possibly filing a motion to sever."

If Burridge granted the motion it would see at least Frankie and possibly Eugene get their own lawyer.

"How long you need Mr Akerman?"

"It's only just been sprung on me; now in the last fifteen minutes," he replied, lying through his teeth.

"I think we'll all take the day off?" the Judge said sympathetically. "Court is in recess till 9:30 tomorrow morning!"

Akerman smiled, first to the Judge, then to his adversary shaking her head in disbelief.

As she returned to her seat, he caught her eye and winked. All she could in return was mime curses.

Unlike the packed courtroom and the millions watching on TV who all felt as if the carpet had been pulled from under their feet, Ben Akerman was delighted to have the extra day to gather his thoughts and meet with his clients. He spent several hours coaching Frankie who was probably his most unresponsive client ever. He had a group meeting with all three and then a one-on-one with Kingsbridge. All day, all weekend, he'd been trying to identify the best advice he could give his most important client before allowing him to make the call. After all, he paid the bills. Following some animated discussion, the decision was made to let Frankie take the stand and for Akerman to continue to represent all three.

When Burridge stepped into the courtroom the following morning, he was pleased to see Ben Akerman still representing three clients; halfway through a trial was no place to introduce new lawyers to what was a very complex case.

"Mr Akerman, I see you've been retained by all three of your three clients. Are you ready to put the case for the defense?"

"I am Judge."

"Would you like to call your first witness?"

"The defense calls Franklyn Fernando," he said confidently, immediately sending an excited buzz round the courtroom.

His confidence was an act. He had no idea what either he or the court could expect from his witness. Putting a defendant he suspected was guilty on the stand was something he'd steered clear of his entire career. The way he saw it, it was tantamount to legal suicide. It was always safer to have the client sit the trial out, the enforced presumption of innocence preventing both prosecution and jury from inferring anything from any reluctance to testify.

"Putting this lunatic on the stand is like playing Russian roulette in the courtroom," he whispered to Kingsbridge as they watched Frankie walk towards the witness box.

In Akerman's opinion and in the opinions of Mario Burns and Kathy Nedal, nine of the jury had already decided all four defendants were guilty. Frankie was a wild card but he'd either confirm their guilt or perhaps, just perhaps, he'd create the key element of doubt in either of the two remaining straight A's or the homosexual, all of whom appeared to be hanging by a thread.

"Would you tell the court your full name please?"

"Franklyn George Fernando."

"Date of birth?"

"August 16th 1945."

"Address?"

"Central City East, Los Angeles: under the intersection where the 60 crosses the 710."

"You live under the highway?!!"

"Yes, we call it Cardboard City."

Frankie hadn't said it to be funny but the courtroom still erupted into laughter.

Burridge barked "Order! Order!" and threw in two sharp raps of his gavel for good measure.

Frankie wasn't smiling, his features icy-cold.

"Mr Fernando, were you in the military and did you serve in Vietnam?"

"Yes Sir."

"Is it true that you're a war hero who while on active service was awarded the Silver Star and Medal of Honor for bravery, sound judgment, outstanding resolve and courageous action?'" Akerman asked, reading from the papers he held in his hand.

"I was awarded the medals but I ain't no hero. I just did my duty."

"Thank you Mr Fernando. Your modesty is duly noted. Do you remember the dates of your arrival in Vietnam and your departure?"

"I arrived March 8th 1965 and left late summer '72. I'm not sure the exact date."

The latter part of his answer brought Jade LaHoya to the edge of her seat coughing to attract attention. She scribbled vigorously into her notepad, hoping the jury didn't miss the fact that Frankie's window of service, covered June 17th, the date of the incident.

"Wasn't March 8th 1965 a significant date in the history of the war?" Akerman asked, already knowing the answer.

"Yes Sir, it was the date the first ground troops arrived in Vietnam."

"So you were one of the very first soldiers to go to Vietnam?"

"Yes Sir."

"And you served till when?"

"August '72. But like I said, I can't remember the exact date."

"You were in Vietnam for pretty much the entire war then?"

"I guess."

"Did you have opportunities to come home Mr Fernando?"

"Yes; but I had nothing to come home for."

Akerman paused. "What's your most lasting memory of the war Mr Fernando?"

"Coming home!"

"Coming home? Could you elaborate?"

"Just after I got back I remember going into the local store. I was waiting at the checkout when I saw someone I knew. 'Look, Frankie's back from 'Nam' he said to a friend before greeting me. Before he said anything, I'd been chatting to the cashier and she was warm and friendly. After he'd said what he said, she couldn't look at me. I felt embarrassed, angry; I never told anyone again I'd served my country in Vietnam. Do you think that's fair?"

"No, that doesn't sound fair to me Mr Fernando . . ."

But before he could continue, Jade LaHoya interrupted.

"Objection Judge! Is this relevant?" she said with a sigh, feigning boredom.

"Counsel, where is this going?" the Judge asked Akerman, looking as if he might agree.

"I'm just acquainting the witness with the jury your honour," Akerman said before shifting his gaze towards Jade. "This witness is one of the most highly decorated war heroes to have served this country; a Medal of Honor winner no less! Perhaps prosecution counsel could show a little more respect. I'm sure my client's earned it!"

"I agree counsellor," Burridge declared before sending a scowl out towards the prosecution table. "Mr Fernando's war record and status as a Vietnam veteran must be respected and I'm prepared to grant you a little leeway. Objection over-ruled!"

After nodding a "thank you" to the Judge and smirking at his courtroom rival, Akerman posed his next question.

"Let me take you back Mr Fernando, to March '65. What were you thinking as you landed at Da Nang?"

"I was thinking how young and excited we all looked. Most of us expected Charlie to be scared stupid. Three weeks later he bombed the Embassy in Saigon! It was his way of telling us he wasn't impressed! I don't know what kind of emotions Charlie felt but getting intimidated wasn't one of them. You don't intimidate Charlie."

"Who is this Charlie?" asked Akerman, wanting to make sure all the jurors understood what or who Frankie was referring to.

"Who's Charlie?" Frankie said, obviously amazed anyone could pose such a question. "Charlie's the stuff of your worst nightmares, the ultimate enemy. It never paid to underestimate Charlie but everywhere I looked everyone seemed to be doing just that: soldiers, officers, our government, our nation. We'd be given orders to locate and destroy the enemy but you don't sneak up on Charlie; in his backyard he always knows where you are. Some of them were farmers by day, fighters by night. We'd walk into villages and they'd stare at us as if we were from Mars. The problem was, friend or foe, they all looked the same! It was a crazy scene."

His eyes glazed over but he wasn't finished.

"Wrinkled old crones or beautiful young women, it didn't make any difference; each of them potentially, was an assassin ready to drop a grenade into your lap or watch you drink a soda with ground-up glass in it. Have you any idea what living with that kind of danger can do to a man?"

Frankie dropped his head, suddenly appearing tired and old.

"You OK Mr Fernando?" the Judge asked with obvious concern.

Frankie nodded as Akerman smiled slightly. The Judge was on-side but he wondered if the jury was buying it.

"Mr Fernando, were you happy with the way that those in charge ran the war?"

"Objection!" piped Jade LaHoya for the second time, "Just where is this going your honour? We aren't interested in Mr Fernando's opinions."

"Excuse me Judge but I think we are," Akerman retorted sharply, fixing a glare on his adversary. "Mr Fernando is an expert witness. He served longer on the front-line in Vietnam than almost anyone else. He was a leader of men and a decorated war hero. In my book that makes him an expert witness and that means we *are* interested in his opinions! Judge, this man is due our respect and our gratitude. He served our nation with distinction."

"Once again counsellor, I agree. Objection over-ruled!"

"Thanks your honour," Akerman said, turning away from the Judge so he could smirk directly at Jade LaHoya the same time his hand signal left her in no doubt the score was "two-nil" to him.

"Arrogant son-of-a-bitch!" she mimed, more angry at her own impatience than anything else. Twice she'd called it wrong and the Judge wasn't happy. She'd get her chance to have a crack at Fernando soon enough; all she had to do was bide her time.

"Mr Fernando, let me repeat the question. Is it true that you feel let down by those in charge of the war and by the reaction to the war at home?"

"Both those things were a disgrace!" said Frankie, seeming to spit the words out. "The government thought it was all about firepower but without will power, firepower can only win you a fight, it won't win a war. The TV coverage made sure it was a war the public didn't have the stomach for and a war the government wouldn't empower its soldiers to win. War is a fight to the death. If you haven't got the stomach for it, it's best not to go to war. It wasn't a game of checkers played between consenting adults or the LA Rams one end and the Dallas Cowboys the other! It was bloody and brutal! And everywhere we went we had *CBS News* cameras stuck up our butts!"

Frankie looked exasperated as he took a deep breath before continuing.

"A half-a-world away, the American people seemed to think it was just another life situation to be played by the rules. Well, Charlie didn't play by middle class America's rules! He'd do *anything* to win."

Aside from nodding gently every thirty seconds or so, Akerman said nothing. This was Frankie's moment and the court and millions around the world were hanging on his every word.

"Charlie only had two ways home, death or victory. He'd either win or he'd die trying. You couldn't beat Charlie without killing him. And what did we do? We sent college kids to fight him. What a load'a crap!" he said shaking his head in disbelief. "Knowing people were demonstrating against us turned my stomach. They were supporting the people we were fighting. Charlie took great strength from the fact that a chunk of America supported him and not us. Me? I still resent it. It killed us! I cannot and will not forget. The way our government ran the war was a disgrace. The anti-war demonstrators were a disgrace. It undermined us. When men died, there was no sense they'd died to advance the cause because there wasn't one."

With every eye on him, Frankie's head dropped into his hands as he battled to keep back the tears. Elsewhere in the courtroom, some people were openly sobbing.

"You OK?" Akerman asked, not really caring. All he cared about was that his three key jurors, his last hope for a Thomas, like the Judge and like everyone else, were enthralled. He wanted more of the same.

"Is it true Mr Fernando that in your opinion American soldiers were unprepared for the complexities of Vietnam?" he asked, the question intentionally vague.

Jade considered objecting but thought the better of it. As she looked round the courtroom at the television cameras she turned and whispered, "This is great TV Ed, but it's not scratching the surface of the real issue is it?"

Ed didn't answer. Like the watching millions, he was focused on Frankie who looked bemused, scrambled, as if he didn't understand his lawyer's question.

Akerman picked up on it immediately and repeated himself. "Mr Fernando, in your expert opinion, do you think our soldiers were unprepared for the complexities of Vietnam?"

Frankie's face cleared slightly as he readied to speak. Surprisingly, his words came out articulate and lucid, belying his vacant and confused expression.

"The fighting was intense; and everyone looked the same! We couldn't differentiate friend from enemy. The stress was unbearable. Ordinary kids were plunged into a totally alien environment. Most of them came from a world that was easy, comfortable, where they had access to everything they needed, including entertainment. Charlie's world was so far removed from that it wasn't true. His idea of R & R was a cup of cold rice and some rat meat! When the two worlds collided there was chaos. We couldn't compete. How could we?"

With his tone inconsistent, his mood swung like an emotional pendulum.

"This was an unseen war; war in the mind but with death everywhere. Nobody died of natural causes in Vietnam! Day or night, we were always on patrol, trying to anticipate where the enemy would be. When we'd go into a village everyone looked the same. Can you imagine how hard that makes things? They didn't wear signs saying *I'm the bad guy!*" he said raising his voice in exasperation. "As a result, everyone had to be seen as the enemy. This was a world, a culture, where the enemy could just as easily be a child with a grenade or an eighty year old woman carrying an AK47. But what could people like you know about combat or combat conditions? How could you possibly know? The answer is you can't and you don't. I dunno what's the most stupid, me wasting my time telling you these things or you expecting men who operate in the most extreme abnormal conditions to behave normally. The whole world's crazy if you ask me."

The last sentence saw Frankie swear for the first time.

The Judge wasn't amused. "Mr Fernando!!"

It was obvious to the Judge, and to everyone else too, that Frankie was on the edge.

But Akerman continued regardless.

"Did you see any atrocities during your time in Vietnam?" he asked before quickly adding, "Did you ever see anything that could qualify in your eyes say, as a war crime?"

Tempted to object once again, Jade forced her backside down into her seat.

As he paused to deliberate his answer, Frankie took a sip of water. When he spoke, he was fighting back the tears. "Atrocities? War crimes? Can't you see it's all relative? The Vietnam War was fought in a place where there were no rules. I saw things you wouldn't see in Montana or Michigan for sure but for Vietnam the abnormal often became normal. That was the way it was. It *was* a hellhole! And into that hellhole we sent kids who were ill-equipped, mentally, physically and emotionally. I was a professional soldier who had the privilege most of the time, espccially during my latter years, to work with other professional soldiers. Some of them are in this room today. Most of the time, it was my privilege to serve my country alongside them. Like everyone else out there, we made mistakes. Of course we did. But war is war; it's not like going to the office! You can't ask me to justify what happened!"

And then he came to the part Akerman had been trying to tease out of him for over an hour.

"But whatever you decide happened out there, I want you to know that I take full responsibility for it, for the tragedy. Whatever the hell that was!!"

It was the closest Frankie came to addressing the issues of the case. He'd said more in seventy-five minutes on the stand, than he had in the previous three decades. Brought to the point of emotional breakdown, he'd visibly aged, easily looking like a man approaching senior citizenship. But he still hadn't finished.

"You just can't understand what I'm talking about can you? I may as well be talking French!" he snapped, suddenly finding a surge of energy from somewhere. "Like their shadows, these men knew death followed them everywhere. It doesn't make for normal relationships because it wasn't normal. There was a kind of brotherhood at work. The country didn't support us. Our disgraced government was distracted to the point of apathy. The men had no choice but to fight for each other because our buddies were the only ones who cared. Now it's over, you people can forget it to the point where it never happened. I don't have that luxury. The war may be over but the dying isn't. I've died a million deaths since and not one has been glorious. The battles don't stop just because the shooting stops; it's just that the battleground moves from the jungles and the mountains into your head."

By the time he got to the end, Frankie collapsed, his head falling into his hands.

"Are you OK Mr Fernando?" the Judge asked. Frankie peered up at him, his eyes looking straight through him. The Judge's voice sounded all muffled, like as if it was coming in from somewhere else, somewhere distant. Emotionally, Frankie'd been to the edge and beyond. His eyes were watery and wild, spaced-out, crazy looking. His demons were back big-time and they were out to fry his brains. It was abundantly clear he was anything but OK.

"May I have a few minutes with my client your honour?" Ben Akerman asked.

Judge Joshua Burridge looked at the large courtroom clock. In one-and-a-half-hours of testimony neither the defendant nor his counsel had come anywhere near addressing the real issues of the case but he couldn't help but have sympathy for Corporal Franklyn Fernando.

"Yes, I think we'll take an early lunch. Court will reconvene at one-fifteen."

CHAPTER FIFTY:

The extended lunch break saw lots happening behind-the-scenes.

The television producers were rubbing their hands. Frankie's session had been beamed live into a hundred and sixty-eight countries, the most yet, and the immediate feedback from around the globe indicated the final viewing figures were almost certain to exceed one billion.

Ben Akerman was delighted with Frankie's testimony but less pleased with two impromptu meetings that took place during the recess.

He was summoned to Judge's chambers where Joshua L. Burridge told him that in nearly forty years as a judge he'd given Frankie more leeway than any witness he could ever remember.

"Whatever you got planned for the rest of your defense strategy counsel, you make sure you don't abuse the privilege I offer."

"Yes Sir, I really appreciate it Sir," Akerman replied, underlining it for good measure with, "No problem Sir."

Ben Akerman didn't usually do servile but he wanted to keep the Judge on-side, the case for the defense needing all the help it could get.

And then, in the men's room, he bumped into Robert O'Meara.

"Ah, Mr Akerman, I've been looking for you."

"You have?"

"Yes. I felt I should inform you that like Mr Fernando, my client plans on taking the stand."

It took Akerman completely by surprise but his efforts to extract any explanation as to why Michael McBride wanted to testify were politely but firmly rebuffed by co-defense counsel.

"It is my client's decision," O'Meara said impassively, turning to leave the bathroom. "He has declined any advice on the matter and I'm informing you simply as a professional courtesy."

If Frankie was a loose cannon then McBride had to be a loose atomic bomb!!

The stunned Akerman stood there for a few seconds before tidying himself up. When he looked down, he noticed he'd urinated all over his shiny black shoes, his two thousand dollar shiny black shoes.

"Damn it!" he said out loud, shaking his foot.

When he got back to the courtroom, people were excitedly milling around taking advantage of their last chance to speak unchecked.

The four defendants were already in their places, though only Frankie was sitting. He was absent-mindedly playing with a pen, staring into space, lost in his thoughts.

To Frankie's right stood a worried looking Eugene Sanders.

On Eugene's right stood Michael McBride who was engaged in conversation with his lawyer, O'Meara relating news of his brief conversation with Akerman in the men's room.

On Frankie's left was Rudi Kingsbridge who was just about to take his seat when Akerman tapped him on the shoulder.

"McBride's decided he wants to take the stand," he whispered.

"You what . . ." shrieked Kingsbridge loud enough for everyone within thirty feet, including Jade LaHoya, to turn and look. "You Bible-bashing Mick son-of-a-bitch!" he said, his contempt for McBride as visible as it was audible. As they glared at each other across the big table, McBride looked calm, implacable, Kingsbridge the opposite, angry, bristling aggression, his words peppered with expletives. "You gonna sell us down the Swanee ain't you Mick? But understand now, if you do, you'll be dead before the end of the day!"

He looked more than capable of carrying out his threat but the court bailiff interrupted, bellowing, "All rise! Court is now in session, the Honourable Judge Joshua L. Burridge presiding."

At precisely the same moment, the television director sat in the giant outside-broadcast vehicle in the car park, shouted "Go!!" and six green lights came on all over the vehicle's massive interior, confirming the broadcast was going out live to hundreds of millions of people all over the world.

"Camera One, stay with the Judge; in close," he said, his microphone linking him to the cameramen's headphones. "Camera two, pan back. I want all four defendants in shot. Remote camera, in as close as you get with all four in frame: we need a good front-on close-up."

Rudi Kingsbridge was still on his feet. The director had picked up on his glowering scowls across the table, and the fact his lips were moving as if he was muttering to himself. He was. But it was strictly adults only.

"Keep the remote camera and camera two on Kingsbridge," the director instructed. "He looks angry as hell 'bout something!"

Kingsbridge was the last person in the room to sit, his observation of court protocol coming a distant second to the irresistible urge to curse the man he hated most in all the world.

"Miserable Mick son-of-a-bitch!" he muttered as his backside came into contact with the chair, his head turning slightly to the right so his words could be directed at their target.

His curses were to be his last words on Earth.

It wasn't Michael McBride who wouldn't see the end of the day; it was Rudi Kingsbridge.

Alongside him was Frankie Fernando, once his Corporal, the former leader of Bleeding Dog Company. He'd sat in the chair for fifteen minutes waiting for the moment he'd dreamt about on-and-off for more than thirty years. He hadn't said a word. He'd decided it was time for action.

He was holding a biro which he'd been toying with while he waited. In his big right hand it made the quantum leap from writing implement to instrument of death.

In a flash, he extended his arm out and around, reaching to the far side of where Kingsbridge was sat before stabbing its pointed end deep into the left side of his neck. With a sharp pull upwards the puncture in Rudi Kingsbridge's carotid artery suddenly became a wide-open inch-long gash.

Kingsbridge clutched at his neck instinctively knowing his life was over, death on its way. There was blood everywhere, cascading out under pressure, squirting to his left and right, ricocheting off his hands all over the panic-stricken people closest him.

It was total pandemonium, everyone dumbstruck or screaming at the horror.

Caught unawares at first, Judge Joshua L. Burridge saw the movement and panic and screamed, "What the . . ." before shrieking "Bailiff . . . bailiff!! Court is in recess!!" the same time he repeatedly smashed his gavel down into its wooden block.

But it was all to no avail; no-one was listening, least of all Rudi Kingsbridge. He had blood on his hands, only this time, the blood was his.

Born into the genetic line of Jacob Schmidt as the last in a long line of bastards, Rudi never had a chance.

He had no way of knowing that when the four had met up in Las Vegas, Frankie made the decision he had to die. He'd thought about it every day since. But before he could action his decision, the former leader of Bleeding Dog Company first wanted to say his piece.

The world needed to know what 'Nam was like; what it was really like.

And then Kingsbridge must die.

With the cameras rolling, their lenses turned to ultra close-up, Rudi Kingsbridge breathed his last breath as millions round the world held theirs.

A minute or two later, surrounded by a pool of his own blood, the lights went out on the man the select few once knew as "Hollywood."

He was gone; gone to meet his maker, leaving the others to face the music.

THE EPILOGUE

SIXTEEN MONTHS LATER

With the sun on her back, sand between her toes and a long cool drink in her hand, Claudia Kaplan was feeling more relaxed than ever. The post-trial, January issue of *American Dream* magazine outsold even *Newsweek* and in so doing, put a tick against the only outstanding item on her wish-list. Worth more than one hundred million dollars, Claudia had long-since passed the only other entry, exceeding forty million by her fortieth birthday.

Two weeks after beating *Newsweek* into second place she told her board she was resigning her position, selling her shareholding and retiring to Grand Bahama. The trial had been amazing: a once-in-a-lifetime experience that couldn't be followed. That was why she'd called it a day. There were no regrets save maybe one; she'd never summoned the courage to ask Bian if she fancied jumping the fence.

* * * * *

After the trial's premature end Jade LaHoya found herself numbered with Hollywood's biggest names on LA's celebrity circuit. Constantly in the limelight, in huge demand for interviews and fronting *Sixty Minutes with Jade LaHoya* on Court TV, she loved every minute.

While she felt Rudi Kingsbridge had gotten what he deserved, she also felt robbed of the opportunity of seeing him convicted. The evidence however meant there'd be no retrial; it was obvious there'd been no conspiracy to commit a murder that Kingsbridge had been singularly responsible for. She knew it even before the trial had finished but with Frankie Fernando locked-up, she let Sanders and McBride stew for another six months before officially dropping the case.

She'd been in conflict with her boss, U.S. Attorney General Harvey Bettinger ever since first filing the case. Unperturbed by the trial's sensational ending, she continued to lobby him hard but still he refused to support any prosecution for war crimes and for the rape on Bian in particular. Four months after the trial had finished the conflict suddenly became highly public: Jade using an appearance on *Oprah* to directly accuse the Attorney General of obstructing the course of justice. It caused a sensation, not only marking the official end of the case against the Bleeding Dogs but also underlining Jade's need for a new job.

But as with everything else in her life, Jade LaHoya left nothing to chance; she knew exactly what she was doing. Two days earlier she'd begun secret negotiations to go back to Rubin Schwartz and so keen were her former employers to re-sign her they'd opened their bidding with an eight figure offer.

Less than twelve months after the biggest trial in history, she crossed the courtroom. She wasn't especially excited at the prospect of defending defendants who were mostly guilty but she *was* looking forward to spending her twenty-two million dollars-a-year paycheck. She also liked the idea of being the best paid lawyer on the entire West Coast.

Jade LaHoya hadn't changed; she still liked being first.

* * * * *

Ben Akerman was another with mixed emotions in the aftermath of his moment in the global spotlight. He'd enjoyed almost every minute of it but most of all he'd enjoyed Frankie's assassination of his number one client, Rudi Kingsbridge.

It saved him the indignity of losing.

Sixteen months later he was just an hour away from receiving a delegation of millionaire Democrats. He knew what their agenda was; they wanted him to run for the U.S. Senate. While he intended making it look like he was more than satisfied to stay being a lawyer he was already dreaming about being President of the United States.

He looked a million dollars, literally. Dressed in a brand new light grey Armani suit, he smirked as he checked himself one last time in the mirror.

"I'll be the best looking American President in history and what a gift I'll be to the TV industry!"

* * * * *

Forty-eight hours after Rudi Kingsbridge had been killed on live television, Judge Joshua L. Burridge made the decision to retire. He knew nothing could ever compare, so like a sports star at the top of his game, he felt it was time to quit while he was ahead. But like icing on the cake, he knew he needed a swansong. He'd been working on it for over a year and in just three weeks he'd have his legacy; the seventeenth of the following month marking HarperCollins release date for *It Happened in My Courtroom*. It was Joshua Burridge's literary debut and given his unique insight into the highest profile case in legal history, a guaranteed bestseller.

* * * * *

For Michael McBride the aftermath of the trial was a soul-searching time.

Seeing his arch enemy killed as the world looked on kicked-off a maelstrom of emotion but the overwhelming one was relief: relief it wasn't him who'd done the deed. He knew it could so easily have been different because being around Rudi Kingsbridge had been a challenge infinitely more difficult than he could ever have imagined.

After a few days off and while still on a one-million-dollar-bail, he quickly immersed himself in some of Cork Construction's biggest projects. As expected, he'd been universally welcomed home by family, friends and work colleagues; all agreeing their lives had been much the poorer for his absence.

A month after the trial Michael flew Eugene and Marlena up from Fort Worth for a visit. On the Sunday morning, Eugene surprised him by saying he and Marlena wanted to accompany the McBride's to church. Eugene enjoyed it and especially enjoyed listening to Pastor Bill Pickard and later, to meeting him.

That afternoon when he and Michael were out strolling round Sunset Lake, Eugene said, "Mike, when we started to talk again after being apart for so long, I knew there was something different about you. The change from before was massive. If it'd been anyone else man, I might've laughed it off. But I couldn't, because it was *you*. We were like best friends for nearly four years. I knew what you were like and I could see the change was real. It really affected me after Vegas and all through the trial too. Mike, I need to know more about this Christianity thing; tell me the whole story."

Later that same evening, Eugene Sanders committed his heart to Jesus.

A month later he and Marlena made the move to Foxboro, Eugene finding it difficult to grasp that becoming a Christian could have such huge effect on his life, particularly on the peace he felt and the deep contentment he'd always thought beyond him.

Instead of fixing helicopters for a living, he serviced the vans, trucks, diggers and cranes of Cork Construction's plant fleet. In the year since making the move from Texas, Eugene and Michael had become inseparable. The two trained together; running, lifting weights, both somehow looking as if time had stood still over their lives. Eugene was more massive than ever and still dreaming the dream that one day he'd win the Senior Universe title while

Michael, was just content to be back in the kind of condition he'd enjoyed in his twenties.

It was one of life's great paradoxes that two men who'd once killed people together now found themselves praying together.

One of their prayers was answered six months to the day Rudi Kingsbridge was publicly executed. While sipping an orange juice after a session at the gym they were surprised to see Jade LaHoya on TV, stood on the courtroom steps.

"Our investigations have revealed that Michael McBride, Eugene Sanders and Franklyn Fernando are not guilty of murdering Minh Ngoc and not guilty of conspiring to murder her. All charges pertaining to this matter have now been dropped. Mr Fernando is still in custody of course, pending investigation in the matter of the murder of Mr Rudi Kingsbridge."

As every person in the bar cheered at the news, Michael had the thought that even though they were guilty, the waiting and the wondering was over.

Finally, they were in the clear.

* * * * *

Just like their husbands, Maddie and Marlena, who'd become a Christian herself, had become best friends. They had much in common. They both gave thanks they weren't deprived of their men longer than they were. They both loved shopping and loved it even more when they shopped together. They loved being Christians, attended the same church and working in the kid's ministry together. And most important of all, they were both married to rapists. It meant they each had someone who could understand their pain.

* * * * *

Michael and Eugene returned to LA a half-dozen times, once to meet with Jade LaHoya, the other five to visit their former Corporal who was locked up at the Anaheim Mental Health Facility pending tests and evaluations. Frankie Fernando was looking at a first degree murder charge and given there were 1.26 billion witnesses who saw him do it, he couldn't really argue they were all mistaken. Michael fired Ben Akerman, got Frankie a new lawyer and paid his legal bills. The advice was unequivocal, insanity the only option that would keep him off Death Row. Frankie didn't mind, he'd been to the Looney Bin before.

* * * * *

In the sixteen months since the trial, nothing much had changed down Farmville way. Bobby Joe Rose and his two friends Mo and Ernie were still making their daily pilgrimage to Jumpin' Jack's, supping their Wild Turkey and telling and re-telling their stories. The trial had been a welcome piece of excitement for Bobby-Joe but like so much of his past it already felt a very long time ago. It also did little to appease the feeling of loneliness that followed him everywhere. How he missed his beloved wife Suzie and how he missed Doug Miller, his very best friend.

* * * * *

Ever since returning from Los Angeles Father Mesnel had been in poor health with a chest-bug he couldn't shake off. Nine months after the trial he died quietly in his sleep clutching a bestseller he'd been avidly reading over the previous four or five weeks. *Serving God in Southeast Asia* was the story of his life's work, his legacy to the human race. Though he greatly enjoyed living the book and writing it, few things gave him more pleasure than seeing it in print. Bian had helped him publish it and seeing the book ride high in the bestseller lists meant his dream had been both achieved and exceeded.

On his bedside table were two letters, one from Tong Tenh, the other from Bian.

Brother and sister were the great success stories of his life of service and he was thrilled to read about Tong's latest business venture and delighted Bian had followed through on her idea to provide top class medical treatment for the people of Ban Hatsati and the surrounding villages. Only seconds before he died, the photographs of the Mesnel Health Clinic made him go goose-pimply all over.

Father Francoise Mesnel died a happy man.

* * * * *

Tong Tenh enjoyed the trial, his time on the stand finally separating him from his demons.

In the sixteen months since, his sister had visited Ban Hatsati on more than a half-dozen occasions. She'd made the Mesnel Health Clinic a reality and invested over a half-million dollars into her brother's rice business. The investment had bought Tong more fields, more workers and even more crucially, given him access to top class marketing and distribution know-how. Within three months it paid dividends, clinching him a supply agreement with *Thai-Joe*, Southeast Asia's booming fast-food restaurant chain.

Tong was on his way to becoming one of Southern Laos' first indigenous millionaires.

* * * * *

Bian fainted after witnessing the brutal end to the trial.

Though it took her a week to get over the shock, she'd felt different ever since. It was like she'd finally cut herself free from a big heavy anchor weighing her down. It showed through in her ageless beauty which even though she was nearer fifty than forty, showed no signs of waning.

A month after the trial, Troy quit his job. After breaking the news to his two partners, he agreed to sell them his share of the thriving law firm. He wanted a clean break and wasn't interested in negotiating a consultancy agreement that could've proved lucrative. Instead, he pocketed a ten million dollar check, closed the door and walked away.

Bian threw herself into her projects in Southeast Asia and took special delight in planning, constructing and staffing the Mesnel Health Clinic situated on the Saisettha side of Ban Hatsati.

The global profile of the case meant she was a woman in demand. Despite this, she turned all requests for interviews down flat, save those with *American Dream* magazine. She could've earned herself millions of dollars but she was quite content with the $4.2 million she received from the *American Dream* trust fund. At nearly twice Claudia Kaplan's best-guess estimate, it easily paid for the Health Clinic, for an investment in her brother's rice business and for the twenty-five thousand copies of Father Mesnel's book that helped ensure it rode high in the bestseller lists.

One offer she did accept was the Presidency of the American Southeast Asia Foundation which specialised in helping Vietnamese, Cambodian and Laotian youngsters living in the U.S. to dream their dreams, gain an education and fulfil their potential. She fitted the job profile and its profile fitted her desire to help others wherever she could. It was a perfect match.

Troy filled his time by playing golf and helping his wife bring her projects to fruition. She loved the fact they were spending more time together and she loved how close they'd become. But she had no idea he was also working on a project of his own, a secret project. Even though his lust for vengeance had just about been satisfied, he felt as if the whole episode needed some kind of historic underlining, a kind of final word. That was why whenever he could, he'd sneak off to his den. He was already one hundred and fifty pages into what he anticipated would be a five hundred page book. He expected *Pursuing the Dogs* to be a global bestseller. He wasn't sure if Bian would approve; that was why he hadn't told her. The time to tell her would come soon enough and when it did, he'd be ready; just like before.

* * * * *

When he arrived at court to see Bian give evidence, it was the first time Nguyen Thimay had seen his mother in over a year. Though he'd objected to her and Troy talking to *American Dream*, he'd avidly followed the case on television and in the press. He experienced so many different emotions seeing her on the stand facing the men who'd abused her, facing Kingsbridge, McBride and Fernando, one of whom was his father.

In the sixteen months since the trial, "Which one?" was a question he'd asked himself a hundred times-a-day.

He'd married his girlfriend of three years shortly after the trial and though he'd never voiced the question to her, she'd picked up on his fascination with the case. When he'd told her the whole story, she'd blurted he was too handsome to have Frankie for a Dad. That meant the choice narrowed to two. But what if it was Kingsbridge? That would be the worst outcome of all, given it was he who'd killed his grandmother and abused his mother the most malevolently.

McBride had come out of the trial best of all, his remorseful expressions and lawyer's stance proving the point. Thimay hoped that Michael McBride was his father, the possibility he wasn't making him resolve to never take a paternity test.

Thimay Kingsbridge was a nightmare he knew he couldn't handle.

* * * * *

Four months after the trial Gabriel Tyner learned the hard way that sixty-something's are not anatomically designed to bound down stairs. After one typical three-stairs-at-a-time effort in the *Tampa Bay Today* building, he lost his footing, fell headlong and smashed his head into an iron balustrade. He died instantly, his plan to write a conspiracy theory blockbuster dying with him.

* * * * *

Ever since their first cruise, Gus and Darlene O'Donnell loved to travel. But in the end it was travel that killed them. In June, six months after the trial, their plane landed at Barcelona, the start point for a leisurely six-week drive across the south of France to Italy and down to Rome. Though their journey took in Monaco, Monte Carlo, Cannes and St. Tropez they didn't get any further than the Central French Alps. Having driven up Alp d'Huez in good weather, they descended in thick fog. Out of control, their hired Peugeot 407 left the road on one of the treacherous mountain's twenty-one hairpin bends. Gus had two last thoughts as his car flew through the air towards certain death: he wondered if there was a hereafter and he wondered if his beloved brother William would be waiting for him if there was.

* * * * *

The day Rudi Kingsbridge died his wife Kay, formerly Kay Ferrano supermodel, was sat in the same place she'd been throughout the trial, the end seat three rows behind the bar on the defense side of the main aisle. It wasn't till she'd seen the replay on TV that she understood the full extent of the raw violence that killed him. She was devastated. But her sense of devastation paled to insignificance when the media vultures began picking over the bones of her dead husband; revelations he'd been a serial adulterer who kept a dozen women on active service at any one time taking her to the point of emotional breakdown. She may have become a dollar billionaire and her children Andy and Becky may have attained similar status under the terms of the will but she'd been instantly persuaded she was better off without him.

As fate would have it she'd been a widow for almost ten months when she bumped into Jacob P. Remford at a gala dinner event. Shortly after the trial, the furniture billionaire wasn't amused to see his wife Margot named in American Dream magazine as one of Rudi's original *lucky dozen*. The lightening quick divorce cost him a two billion dollar out-of-court settlement but a net worth of nearly ten billion meant he still had plenty left over. Sixteen years her senior, his opening line was "Miss Ferrano, it seems both you and I were cheated on; can I take you to dinner?" Kay said yes to dinner and yes to his subsequent marriage proposal. The newly weds moved into Remford's one hundred million dollar estate in Kenilworth, north of the city, while an even more expensive home was being constructed in Palm Beach Florida. Though Kay's daughter Becky lived with them Andy chose not to, preferring instead to split his time between Harvard Business School and Chateau Chantalle, the terms of her dead husband's will ensuring the Harvard tradition continued and the family home stayed in the family.

* * * * *

Andy Kingsbridge wasn't sure if he missed his father.

His eighteenth birthday clashed with prom night at Warman's School. The best looking guy by far, his date for the evening was the golden-haired school beauty queen, Alisha Fitzroy. Andy's seductive charm had got him a result in the car park even before the couple got out his silver Mercedes convertible. It was a special day; not just because he was eighteen or because he'd bedded the Prom Queen. It was also the day he became a billionaire and inherited a mansion overlooking Lake Michigan.

Earlier the same day he'd been going through his father's stuff in his study, reading his letters and diaries and looking at photographs. He was especially gripped by his time in Vietnam and realised how much like his father he was.

Six or seven hours later, just as his lust with Alisha Fitzroy was breaking, he found himself thinking just like his Dad; he was thinking of vengeance and wondering how he could hate someone he'd never even met.

Yes, Andy Kingsbridge was just like his father, a chip off the old block. Rich, outrageously handsome, insufferable and a womaniser, they also had something else in common; they both hated Michael McBride.

Young Andy hadn't just inherited a ton of money and Chateau Chantalle. He'd also inherited his father's title: the last in a long line of bastards.

* * * * *

As his son played Lord of the Manor with the Prom Queen, Rudi Kingsbridge was just fourteen miles away as the crow flies. His decomposing body lay in a box at Lake Forest Cemetery, only its lead lining preventing him from being eaten by the worms.

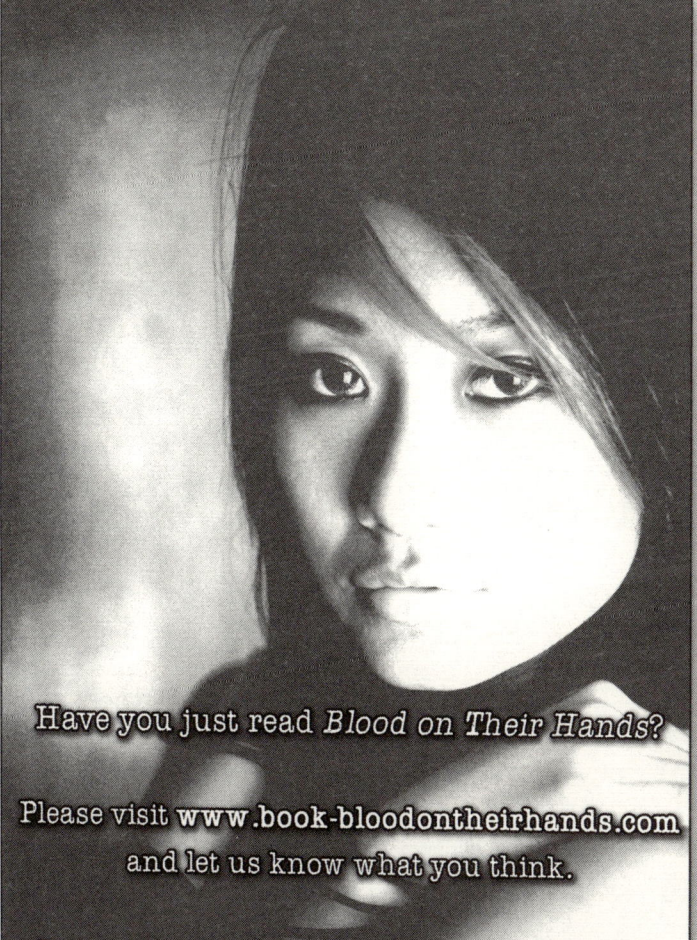

Have you just read *Blood on Their Hands*?

Please visit **www.book-bloodontheirhands.com**
and let us know what you think.

Tell us who your favourite character is, which scene you enjoyed the most, or write a full book review. Just click the "feedback" button.

You can also download your free
Blood on Their Hands desktop wallpaper.

Calling all authors and potential authors

Your book needs a MEDIA TRAILER

Improve your chances of success by giving your book project a head-start over the competition

- Make landing an agent so much easier
- Give your agent every chance of finding a publisher
- Help drive sales cost-effectively

And if you intend going down the self-published route

- Give your marketing campaign it's all important beginning point
- Synergise the relationship book/trailer/website
- Blitz the internet's social media sites with focussed viral marketing

For Further info please visit:

www.21twentyone.net

21:Twenty-one
MEDIA TRAILERS

Coming soon from 21 Twenty-one publishing

Available Sept 2009

666 ...Mark of the Beast

Phil Davies & John Bullock

An epic journey into the end times; the place where prophecy becomes reality as history, the present and the future converge!

www.book-666markofthebeast.com